Marriage by Design

Four couples.

Four marriages . . . of convenience.

Each bride has her own reason; each groom has his.

But a marriage by design can become a marriage of desire. A marriage of convenience can become a marriage for love. . . .

Watch it happen in these four delightful new stories!

ABOUT THE AUTHORS:

CATHY GILLEN THACKER believes that love and laughter go hand in hand. Not surprisingly, her warm family stories and fast-paced romantic comedies are very popular with readers. She's written thirty-seven novels and numerous nonfiction articles, and her books frequently appear on the Waldenbooks bestseller list. Cathy's originally from the Midwest but now lives in Texas with her husband and three children.

JASMINE CRESSWELL is a multitalented, multipublished writer who's received several awards for her books. She's written contemporary and historical romances, Regencies, mysteries and mainstream fiction. Jasmine's background is international: she was born in Wales and educated in England, then joined the British Foreign Office. While working at the British Embassy in Rio de Janeiro, she met and married her husband, Malcolm. The family—they have four children—has lived in a number of exotic locations, including Australia and Italy. Jasmine and Malcolm, who recently moved to Florida, have just celebrated thirty years of marriage and the birth of their second grandchild. In 1995, watch for Jasmine's exciting new novel, *Desires and Deceptions*.

GLENDA SANDERS began her writing career as a journalist and became a much-published romance novelist. She won the prestigious Rita Award in 1992 for her book *The Human Touch* (a Harlequin Temptation title). Glenda writes a range of stories—from intense, emotional dramas to warm, witty comedies. She lives in Florida— where many of her books are set—with her husband and son; her newly married daughter, Kathy, has just moved to Minnesota. In fact, while Glenda was working on "Don't Tell Grandfather," she and Kathy were also working on preparations for a wedding very different from the one in the story!

MARGARET CHITTENDEN is originally from England and now lives with her husband, Jim, in the state of Washington, "around the corner from the Pacific Ocean." (Their two grown children also live on the West Coast.) Margaret has published more than a hundred short stories and articles in magazines such as *Good Housekeeping* and *Ladies' Home Journal*. She has also written three children's books and twenty-three novels, including mysteries, romantic suspense, mainstream and romance fiction. She's particularly well-known for her stories featuring "paranormal" elements.

MARRIAGE by DESIGN

CATHY GILLEN THACKER

JASMINE CRESSWELL

GLENDA SANDERS

MARGARET CHITTENDEN

Harlequin Books

TORONTO • NEW YORK • LONDON
AMSTERDAM • PARIS • SYDNEY • HAMBURG
STOCKHOLM • ATHENS • TOKYO • MILAN
MADRID • WARSAW • BUDAPEST • AUCKLAND

MARRIAGE BY DESIGN

Copyright © 1994 by Harlequin Enterprises B.V.

ISBN 0-373-83295-8

MARRIAGE BY DESIGN first printing April 1994

The publisher acknowledges the copyright holders of the individual works as follows:
DEAR FAIRY GODMOTHER
Copyright © 1994 by Cathy Gillen Thacker
MARRIAGE ON THE RUN
Copyright © 1994 by Jasmine Cresswell
DON'T TELL GRANDFATHER
Copyright © 1994 by Glenda Sanders Kachelmeier
THE ENCHANTED BRIDE
Copyright © 1994 by Margaret Chittenden

This edition published by arrangement with Harlequin Enterprises B. V.,

® and TM are trademarks of Harlequin Enterprises B.V., used under license. Trademarks indicated with ® are registered in the United States Patent and Trademark Office, the Canadian Trade Marks Office and in other countries.

Printed in U.S.A.

CONTENTS

DEAR FAIRY GODMOTHER   9
Cathy Gillen Thacker

MARRIAGE ON THE RUN   89
Jasmine Cresswell

DON'T TELL GRANDFATHER   195
Glenda Sanders

THE ENCHANTED BRIDE   295
Margaret Chittenden

DEAR FAIRY GODMOTHER
Cathy Gillen Thacker

Prologue

"SPECIAL DELIVERY letter for you, Meg."

No sooner had the mailman left, than Meg Winthrop tore into the envelope from her hometown of Tanglewood, Texas. The script was childish, the message urgent.

Dear Fairy Godmother,
Save us from the evil witch. Daddy might marry her. We want you for our mother.

—Billy and the twins, who are waiting to be rescued. And Jason and Lily, who want to be rescued, too.

Meg put down the letter and frowned. Darn that Dusty MacKauley. What was he up to now?

Chapter One

"OKAY, I WANT an explanation and I want one now," Dusty MacKauley demanded irascibly as he paced the suddenly immaculate living room of his century-old ranch house. He regarded his children sternly. "What in blue blazes is going on here?"

"What makes you think there's something going on, Daddy?" twelve-year-old Lily asked, as she pushed her glasses higher on the bridge of her nose.

"Maybe the fact that all five of my children are lined up like ducks in a row, dressed in their Sunday best. On a Monday afternoon. And the house is cleaned up."

"We're just trying to help," sixteen-year-old Jason said, giving Dusty a look of choirboy innocence, as he took a comb out of his back pocket and smoothed his straight dark brown hair. "You know, now that we're on summer vacation and everything."

"Uh-huh." Dusty looked at his kids suspiciously. "You guys think I was born yesterday? Is that it?"

"No, sir," they said in unison.

"We know how old you are," five-year-old Billy piped up. "You were thirty-eight on your last birthday!"

"Shh! You know you're not supposed to mention that!" eight-year-old Susie scolded.

"Yeah," Sallie chimed in, taking her twin's side immediately. "Stop that or you're going to make Daddy feel old!"

The truth was, Dusty already felt old. And barely able to cope. Which was why he'd been thinking about getting married again. It was becoming increasingly clear that his kids needed a mother. No one could replace Lizzie in their affections, of course. But he couldn't help but think it would be nice to have a woman in the house again, helping him ride herd on the kids.

"The twins are right. Daddy is in good shape," Lily continued, looking at Dusty as if he needed some complimenting.

"For someone his age, anyway," Jason added seriously.

"Thanks a lot," Dusty said dryly.

"Come on, Daddy. You know what we mean," Lily protested with a blush.

Yeah, Dusty did. Hard physical labor kept all six feet three inches of him fit and trim. As usual, it had been too long between haircuts, but his dark brown hair was scrupulously clean beneath his black felt Stetson, and his square jaw was clean-shaven and dabbed lightly with after-shave.

"But maybe you might want to get dressed up, too," Sallie added slyly.

"Why?" Dusty's blue eyes swept his scuffed boots, faded jeans and pale blue Western shirt. "What's wrong with the way I'm dressed?" he asked, incensed.

Guilty looks were exchanged, but no one spoke.

The sound of a car door slamming made the kids all perk up expectantly. Dusty strode to the window. Finally an explanation. Only it wasn't a car he recognized; in fact, it was a rental. And the person driving it had already gotten out.

Frowning, Dusty strode to the front door and yanked it open before the bell had even rung. He stopped dead in his tracks as he stared at the vision of loveliness in front of him. It had been—what?—nearly eighteen years since he had come face-to-face with Meg Winthrop, and yet, in that time, so little had changed. At thirty-eight, she was still one of the most beautiful women he had ever seen. Tall, slender, with an angel's face and a body that curved in all the right places. But the years spent working in California had added a sophistication he wasn't prepared for. She looked as if she had just stepped out of one of those fancy Rodeo Drive beauty salons. Her hair, which had always been sexy as hell, fell in thick golden waves to her shoulders and had that rumpled just-out-of-bed look. Maybe it was the light, the deft touch of makeup she wore, but her cheekbones seemed more pronounced, her lips fuller, more sensual. Her eyes were the same long-lashed fiery green.

Dusty was aware of the kids giggling behind him. They knew better than anyone how rare it was for him to be at a loss for words. He found his voice and kept his tone cool. "Meg." He touched two fingers to his Stetson by way of greeting. This was, undoubtedly, why all the kids were dressed up, he thought. They were excited about seeing their fairy godmother for the first time. Prior to this, their contact with Meg had always been through fax, photos, letters and gifts.

"Glad to see you remember me, Dusty," Meg said, her tone equally cool.

The normally shy Billy dropped his teddy bear and dashed forward. He tackled Meg around the waist and gave her a fierce hug. Within seconds, Jason, Lily and the twins had surrounded Meg, too. She hugged each child in turn. All had tears glimmering in their eyes as they drew apart. "You came to rescue us!" Billy said in a choked voice. "I told the other kids you would!"

"Rescue you from what?" Dusty asked, beginning to get more than a little furious as he realized he had been the only one in the room not in on whatever was going on.

"Uh...Auntie Meg can explain," Jason said. "Come on, kids. We better leave Meg and Dad alone. I think they have a lot to talk about." Jason herded his brother and sisters up to the second floor.

When he was sure they couldn't be overheard, Dusty turned back to Meg. "I suppose you were in on this, too."

Meg dug around in her purse and pulled out a crumpled envelope. "Just read this before you go shooting off your mouth, Dusty. Then we'll talk."

"'Dear Fairy Godmother,'" Dusty began. By the time he had finished his children's letter to Meg, he was swearing.

Meg smiled at him. She sauntered across the room, sank down gracefully onto the U-shaped sofa and crossed her legs delicately at the knee. "So who's the evil witch?"

Suddenly it all began to make sense to Dusty. Obviously the kids were upset because he'd had the same woman to dinner with the family twice in the past two weeks. "Donna Gardener," Dusty said, "and she's not an evil witch."

"The kids think she is."

"That's because she suggested to me that I make them eat all their vegetables, do daily chores and wear clothes that are neatly ironed, as well as washed."

Dusty wasn't about to admit it to Meg, but after that disastrous dinner, he had just about crossed Donna off his list of potential mates. She'd make a good drill sergeant and a presentable wife, but he didn't think he'd be able to bear having her around twenty-four hours a day any more than the kids would've. Of course, Dusty reasoned further, had anyone asked him how he felt, he could have explained that to the kids. Instead, they'd taken matters into their own hands and had Meg fly out from California on some sort of emergency mission.

"Look, Meg—" Dusty paced back and forth restlessly "—you did not have to come all this way. You could have just sent me the letter."

"I owe Lizzie more than that," Meg said. "She entrusted those children's welfare to me—"

"Yeah, and she did it over my vehement protests," Dusty cut in.

"—and as their fairy godmother, I plan to see they are well taken care of."

"As you just saw," Dusty repeated, gritting his teeth, "they're all fine."

Meg stood. "How about bringing my suitcases in, Dusty?"

Dusty scowled. He didn't know what Meg was up to, but she damn well wasn't going to get away with it. "You can't stay here!"

Meg arched a golden brow in feminine challenge. "Why not?"

Dusty released an exasperated breath. "Because Tanglewood is still a small town, it's not proper, and I have an example to set," he said.

"It's perfectly proper, Dusty," Meg disagreed. She drifted closer and tipped her face up to his. "I'm an old friend of the family, lest you forget," she finished softly.

Dusty tried his hardest not to let her nearness get to him. "People will talk," he repeated.

"Why?" Meg kept her eyes defiantly on his. "Because you and I were engaged before you married Lizzie? That was eighteen years ago, Dusty."

As if he could've forgotten! He might have been married to another woman and had five children with her, but he still recalled with disturbing clarity what it had been like to kiss Meg Winthrop and hold her in his arms. He still recalled what it had been like to want to make love to her so badly that he couldn't think about anything else. "Shh. The kids will hear."

"Dusty, this is a small town, and our breakup was fodder for the town gossip mill for years. I am sure the kids already know that you and I have a past."

Dusty glared at her. He resented Meg's showing up now after she had managed to avoid seeing him directly for years. "I do not want to get into this with you," he warned stiffly.

"Oh, I'm sure you don't."

"So say goodbye to the kids," Dusty continued, "and take yourself off back to California and those television shows you produce."

Meg favored him with a tight smile. "All three of my shows are on hiatus for the summer. All I'm doing now is reviewing and approving scripts for the upcoming seasons."

"Well, I'm not on hiatus, Meg."

They stared at one another. "Look, Dusty, I know it hasn't been easy on you the past two years since Lizzie died," Meg said gently. Her eyes were filled with compassion as she touched his arm. "We all miss her terribly, especially the kids."

The mention of his kids' feelings kicked his paternal instincts into overdrive. "How do you know this?" Dusty demanded.

"Because some of the letters they've sent me would break your heart," Meg said, her eyes unexpectedly filling with tears. She blinked furiously and turned away. "Anyway, I've tried to do what I could to ease their loneliness—"

"Which brings us to the next point. Those extravagant presents you keep sending the kids have got to stop."

Meg whirled to face him. She gave him a pointed accusing look. "Lizzie never minded."

"Well, I do."

Meg waved off his complaint as if it didn't even warrant discussion. "Anyway, back to what I was saying," she said firmly. "I loved Lizzie and I love those kids of yours."

But not me, Dusty thought, his heart aching for what he and Meg had briefly had so long ago and then lost. Never me. At least not enough. . . .

"They're the children I never had," Meg continued.

Dusty began to see where all this was leading. He wasn't going to let her stake any claims here. "It is not my fault you chose never to get married," he said.

Meg's green eyes widened in silent censure. "Did I say it was?"

"No."

"But you're right. My relationship with you soured me on the idea of marriage—to anyone. I wasn't ready to give up my identity."

Dusty swore vehemently beneath his breath and rolled his eyes. "Here we go again. . . ."

"But now I'm at a different point in my life," Meg continued in that stubborn tone he knew so well. "I realize I've missed out by not marrying and having a family of my own."

"Uh-oh," Dusty said, and braced himself for the worst.

Meg strode closer in a drift of warm feminine perfume. Her green eyes took on a determined glow. Her soft full lips curved into a Madonna-like smile. "Knowing now that it might never happen for me, I've decided to take what I've been given and run with it."

Alarm bells went off inside Dusty's head. He tensed. "What the hell are you talking about?" He jammed his hands on his hips and towered over her.

"I'm going to stay the summer and be the mother the kids have needed. And if that works out, I'm going to relocate here permanently and help you finish raising them. They need a mother's love, Dusty. I know I wasn't here for the funeral—"

"That couldn't be helped," Dusty interrupted. "You were backpacking in the Sierras. By the time we were finally able to get a message to you two weeks later, everything had already been done."

"I know, and I tried to help just the way I always had, by talking to the kids about their problems on the phone and by writing to them."

"So go on doing that," Dusty advised flatly.

"It's not enough, Dusty. Not anymore. Not when they all miss their mom so much." Her eyes met his. "I let them down after the funeral by not returning to help them through their grief." Meg's voice dropped to a guilty whisper. "I can't let them down again."

DUSTY APPEARED TO TENSE from head to toe. He hooked his thumbs in the front pockets of his jeans. His square masculine jaw took on an aggressive, slightly dangerous and thoroughly contemplative tilt that made Meg feel as if she'd just walked into a tiger's lair. Finally he frowned and spoke.

"This is not some television show, Meg, where you can approve the scripts and direct the characters. Or walk out at the end of the season. This is real life, on a central-Texas ranch that's just barely breaking even."

Meg had figured Dusty would fight her on her plans. She had been prepared to do battle with him. What she hadn't been prepared for was her own reaction at seeing him again. Just being around him made her heart race, her knees weaken and her palms perspire. Just being around him made her feel all of twenty again—as if everything was still on between them, still up in the air, waiting to be worked out.

"What's your point?" Meg asked impatiently. Dusty had always been handsome to a fault and he was still that, she admitted reluctantly. But he was also damnably single-minded, and that annoyed the heck out of her.

"My point is you'd never be happy here," Dusty said, his thin masculine lips curving into a disdainful frown. "Not even for a couple of months. That's why you left Tangle-wood, in case you've forgotten, because it was too small and too boring."

Meg noticed that the silky hair spilling out from beneath the edges of his black cowboy hat was still the same rich brown it had always been, without a hint of gray. His body was similarly youthful, taut and trim all over. He even dressed pretty much the same, in worn snug jeans, a pale blue Western shirt and scuffed boots. "I left because I wanted to have a career," Meg corrected archly.

"Well, now you've got one," Dusty replied. He sauntered nearer until Meg was so close to him she couldn't help but notice the sinewy outline of his chest beneath his shirt. His dark blue eyes narrowed on her in silent warning. "So I suggest you go back to it."

"As usual, you're not listening to me, Dusty," Meg retorted stubbornly. "I told you. I'm not leaving. I'm staying to help raise the kids."

"You're the one who's not listening, Meg. No woman lives here unless she's my wife." He backed her up against the wall until their bodies were aligned front to front, softness to hardness, and tilted her head back. "So unless you're prepared to head down the aisle with me," he whispered with a taunting grin, "I suggest you forget all about being a mother to those kids of mine."

Meg's heart pounded. "You're bluffing."

Dusty tipped his hat back with the tip of his index finger. His lips curved into a Texas bad-boy smile. "No, babe, I'm not."

Meg knew when Dusty was bluffing. Maybe he'd forgotten she could bluff, too. "Fine," she said with an insouciant shrug. "Then I'll marry you. But it'll be a marriage in name only."

"Don't count on it, sweetheart," Dusty drawled. He sidestepped and blocked her path. She backed up. He went with her, pushing his lower body against hers. Holding her pinned against the wall, he lowered his mouth to hers and delivered a breath-stealing kiss. Meg told herself she wouldn't respond. But it was like trying not to enjoy chocolate-chip ice cream. Her taste buds were in heaven and so were her lips and her tongue. Kissing Dusty was like being on a magic-carpet ride. Everything was swept away. The world took on a dizzying tilt. Desire swept through her in mesmerizing waves.

All this time she thought she had magnified her memories of the electricity they'd made. All this time she'd been wrong.

Meg was trembling when he let her go.

"Now, shall I show you to your car?" he asked in a silky voice edged with warning.

It was the laughter in his eyes that sent her over the edge into dangerous territory. Meg arched a brow. "There's no way I'm letting you get the upper hand with me, Dusty," she replied in the same don't-mess-with-me tone.

Dusty regarded her smugly. "I already have it."

Not so, Meg thought, not so at all. Two could play this game. He had called her bluff. She would call his. "We'll see about that," she retorted smoothly, then favored him with a confident smile. "The day after tomorrow okay with you?" Now we'll see who runs, she thought.

Dusty's dark brows drew together. He tipped his hat back a little farther. "For what?"

"Our wedding, of course." Meg stepped away from the wall, lest he get any more ideas about kissing her, and stalked to her purse. She opened it and took out a pocket-size leather-bound calendar. She thumbed through the pages. "I think an afternoon service would be most appropriate."

Dusty sauntered closer. The look he gave her was one of pure male victory. "Sure you're up to the humiliation?" he needled.

Meg felt a flicker of unease. Defiantly she pushed it away. She was not going to let Dusty beat her with a counter bluff. "You're saying you'd leave me standing at the altar?" she asked sweetly.

"Nope." Dusty's knowing smile broadened into a wicked grin. "I'm saying I'd meet you there."

He really thought he had her running scared, Meg thought in disgust. Well, she'd show him how wrong he was. "I can handle it," she said breezily. She might have run from Dusty and his incredibly outdated demands once, but she sure wasn't going to do it again. If she did leave again, and she didn't think she would, it would only be in victory.

To Meg's disappointment, if Dusty was suffering any misgivings, he sure wasn't showing them. "Well, so can I," Dusty said smugly.

"You're leaving already?" Billy asked when Meg went up to say goodbye to the children.

"Just for a day or two," she said. Until Dusty calmed down and came to his senses. It wouldn't take long before he realized that the whole idea of their being married to each other was ridiculous and he'd call it off. "Then I'll be back to stay." Hopefully, without a wedding ring on her finger. However, if Dusty insisted on going through with this, as his last bluff had implied, then Meg had a few surprises of her own up her sleeve. Dusty might force her into marriage, but he wouldn't have the last word—not now, not ever.

"Thank heaven. I thought I'd die if we had to put up with that Donna Gardener," Lily said.

Meg's heartbeat picked up at the mention of this other woman in Dusty's life. "Donna's really that bad?"

"And then some," Jason confirmed. He met her eyes, looking very much the young adult he was. "I don't think she likes kids at all, Meg."

"Surely your father wouldn't marry someone who didn't like kids," Meg began.

"He doesn't know she doesn't like us. When he's around, she's always real sweet to us. You know, real motherly. It's only when he's not here that she lets us know how she really feels."

"And how is that?" Meg asked gently.

"Like we're in the way," Lily said.

"Like she doesn't want us here at all," the twins added glumly.

"Daddy doesn't know we heard, but she's been trying to get him to elope," Lily continued. "Telling him she'll take care of the house and us and everything. He was almost ready to do it, too."

"Which is why we wrote," Billy said.

"You'll stop him, won't you?" Susie asked.

Sallie nodded her head vigorously. "You'll tell him you'll be our mother?"

Meg smiled. "I already have." She just didn't want to be Dusty's wife. "Now, is everybody feeling better?"

They all nodded except little Billy. "I got a question."

"Okay, shoot," Meg said.

"If you're our fairy godmother for real, how come you're not wearing a sparkly white dress? And where's your magic wand?"

Chapter Two

DUSTY KNEW he was in trouble the moment he turned onto Maple Street and saw all the cars parked in the Community Church parking lot. He edged his pickup close to the curb, hoping against hope he had gotten the time or the place wrong. No such luck.

"Dad." Jason bolted up to the pickup. "Where've you been?" he admonished impatiently. "Everyone's waiting!"

Dusty stepped out of the truck and stared at his son in disbelief. "You're wearing a tux."

"Yeah, I know." Jason frowned at him. "You're supposed to be wearing one, too."

Dusty's mouth tightened with displeasure. He fell into step beside Jason and headed for the side entrance, near the Sunday-school classrooms. "No one told me the wedding was formal."

"Meg said you'd probably fight her on it. That's why she went ahead and ordered your tux. It's inside."

Great. Dusty sighed. "How many people are in there?"

"Let's put it this way," Jason retorted dryly. "The church is packed."

Dusty swore silently. Leave it to Meg to pick up right where the two of them had left off, as if nothing had ever happened. As if she hadn't walked out two days before their marriage was to take place, leaving him to suffer the humiliation and pick up the pieces alone.

He was about to tell Jason the bluffing was over, the whole wedding was off—his choice this time—when he walked into the church and saw the rest of his children gathered in the choir room. The girls were in pretty pink-and-white dresses that made them look like fairy princesses and that must have cost a mint. Little Billy was in a child-size tux identical to Jason's. And all their faces were shining with a happy anticipation he hadn't seen since before their mother's death. Dusty was immediately filled with guilt. He had done his best, overseeing the ranch and being both father and mother to the kids. Obviously it hadn't been enough. Otherwise, they wouldn't be this thrilled to see him marrying Meg. They wouldn't be welcoming Meg into their home with open hearts and open arms. They'd tell him they didn't need a replacement mom.

"Daddy, come on, you're going to be late," Lily said sternly.

Beside her, the twins jumped up and down, nearly losing their flowered headpieces. "I get to be a flower girl, Daddy!" Susie said.

"So do I!" echoed Sallie.

"I'm the maid of honor," Lily added, looking more grown-up than Dusty could ever recall seeing her.

"I'm the best man," Jason said.

"And I'm the ring bearer," Billy said.

Dusty rubbed his jaw. When Meg hadn't called the wedding off, he had figured it would be a simple ceremony with just him, Meg and the kids. He'd figured she'd want to play house until she tired of it and then hightail it back to California. A wedding this size indicated she planned to stay for more than the month or two she had initially committed to. Dusty felt his gut tighten. Two months with Meg in the same house. There was no way he was going to get out of this without ending up in bed with her. No way. He swore silently. He did not want to be this involved with anyone. All he'd been looking for was a mother for his kids. But Meg would never be content with just that. No, she'd want to direct him and direct the kids until she had everything exactly the way she wanted it. Then she'd walk out on him. Again. Damn it all to hell.

"Come on, Dad. Stop scowling. You can wash up and change in the men's room," Jason said, taking charge as if he were the father and Dusty, the teenage son. "I brought your shaving kit."

"Good thinking." Dusty wouldn't mind embarrassing Meg, but he didn't want to embarrass the kids. Like him, they would be here for a long time to come. So, like it or not, it looked as if he'd have to go through with it.

Several minutes later, Dusty stepped out of the men's room, his son by his side. He stepped into the chapel and took his place at the altar to the minister's left. The organist smiled and began playing "The Wedding March." The twins came up the aisle looking like angels as they sprinkled rose petals over the white satin carpet that had been rolled out. Billy followed, looking very important as he carefully carried two gold rings on a velvet pillow. He was followed by Lily, who looked impossibly grown-up. Behind her came Meg on her daddy's arm.

And she, too, was a vision. She wore a white satin gown with a high neck and a full skirt. Her mane of glorious golden curls had been swept away from her face. Her white veil was attached to a pearl-and-lace tiara. Looking at her soft pink lips and her misty green eyes, memories of happier times came back in a relentless flood. Dusty recalled dating Meg all through high school and spending summers with her while they were in college. He recalled their first kiss, and their last....

"Now she looks like a fairy godmother," Dusty heard Sallie whisper in satisfaction.

"Yeah," little Billy said, "and look, Susie! She's even carrying a wand!"

Darned if it wasn't true, Dusty thought, as he saw the fairy-princess-style magic wand hidden in the bridal bouquet. Meg's eyes met his as he joined her at the altar. The rest of the ceremony passed in a blur. Dusty wasn't quite sure why his feelings were in turmoil. Maybe it was just seeing Meg in that beautiful gown, looking so delicate and pretty, that brought back all the feelings he'd had for her when he was a randy teenager besotted by love. But suddenly he felt years younger, ready to take on the world—and Meg.

Not that he should allow himself to care for her, he warned himself severely. Not after the way she had walked out on him years ago. Hell, she'd probably do it again, as soon as she tired of this charade.

Dusty frowned as the minister pronounced them husband and wife. There was a hushed silence as he looked down at his new bride. He saw the expectant color flow into her cheeks and knew she wanted him to stay cool and not get carried away. Well, wasn't that just too damn bad, he thought, as his starched collar itched him unbearably. Here was his chance to pay her back, and he was damned if he wasn't going to be reckless enough to take it.

"You may kiss the bride," the minister said as Meg's cheeks turned even pinker.

"Don't mind if I do," Dusty drawled, then bent his head. And gave it all he had. Meg's lips softened immediately under his, even if her hands were against his chest pushing him away. She kept her lips pressed tightly together, too. Dusty was tempted to see if he couldn't part them, just a little bit . . . but then he heard Sallie and Susie giggle, and he remembered that it wasn't just a church full of people watching, but his children, also!

Reluctantly he cut short the kiss.

Nevertheless Meg was blushing fiercely when he finally came up for air.

From the pews beyond someone whispered, "And you said they weren't in love anymore! Ha! Guess he just proved you wrong!"

The guests broke into spontaneous laughter. The organ started up again. Dusty tucked Meg's arm in his and started back down the aisle. For the next few minutes, they accepted the best wishes of family and friends. Then they dashed through the shower of confetti to the limo waiting at the curb.

Meg was breathless as she settled into her seat. Dusty had the urge to kiss her fiercely again, but forced himself to curtail it. There would be time for that later when he had his emotions under control.

"You went to a lot of trouble here," Dusty remarked as soon as they were en route to the local veterans hall, where the reception was to be held.

Meg looked out the window at the tree-lined street. "Don't go making this out to be more than it is, Dusty," she advised him with a world-weary tone that left him momentarily stunned. "I'm just giving my parents the chance to follow through on all those wedding preparations they made for us years ago."

For the first time Dusty allowed that their breakup might have hurt Meg, too, even if her cursed stubbornness and limitless ambition was the cause of it. He studied her, trying not to notice how ethereal she looked all in white. "That the dress you bought?" he asked casually.

"Yes."

It's pretty, Dusty thought. And you're pretty in it. But he wasn't going to say it. Not after what she'd just put him through. As he thought about the way she'd surprised him at the church, his temper flared once again.

"We need to get something straight," he said curtly. "I'm not some actor you can write lines for and tell where to stand and push around."

Meg touched her tiara, as if making sure it was securely pinned. "I can see you haven't mellowed with age."

Neither have you, Dusty thought. She was still the same highly volatile woman he'd fallen in love with. The same highly volatile woman who'd broken his heart so badly he'd thought it would never mend. He leaned back in his corner of the limo. "No matter what you do, you'll never get the upper hand in our relationship," Dusty continued in a tone he knew would irritate the heck out of her. "I'm the husband now," he informed her imperiously. "I'm calling the shots."

He expected his chauvinistic speech to make her mad. All it did was make her laugh. "So you think," she said.

Dusty was about to reply when he noticed the limo had stopped and the driver was getting out to open their door. They'd continue this discussion, but they'd do it later, when he could show her firsthand what he meant.

He got out of the car first. Her skirts clasped in one hand, she put her other hand in his and held tight as he helped her out. It was a peculiar feeling, having her hand in his. Dusty tried not to think how right it seemed, how soft her skin felt. It had just been too long since he'd been with a woman, he thought. Way too long.

They didn't speak again until all the guests had arrived and the band had started to play. Dusty glanced at the empty dance floor.

"They're waiting for us to dance," Meg said.

"Well, we wouldn't want to disappoint them, would we?" Dusty drawled. He took her in his arms and swept her out onto the center of the floor. Clasping her tightly about the waist, he pulled her close.

"You're holding me too tight." Meg pushed the words through her teeth.

"Glad you like it," Dusty said with a smirk, and felt her tremble in his arms, the same way she had trembled when he kissed her. They danced some more.

"You laugh now, but you're going to pay for that kiss back at the church," Meg said sweetly.

Dusty grinned down at her. How could he have forgotten how much he enjoyed Meg's fire? She might not be good wife material, no matter what she thought, but she was a helluva challenge. And Dusty loved challenges, always had. He wondered what it would take to make her melt in his arms again.

He tightened his arm around her slender waist. He leaned closer so he could whisper in her ear, "Darlin', the pleasure was all mine. Besides, I figured it was what you wanted—" Dusty pressed his lips to her temple defiantly "—since you're the one who arranged this circus."

"If you must know, Dusty, the big church wedding was all my mother's idea. She never gave up on the two of us getting back together one day, even after you married Lizzie." Meg sighed. "You know how stubborn she is when she gets something in her head."

"As stubborn as her darling daughter?"

"Then, when I found out she'd saved everything—the dress, the invitations, even the decorations for the church— well I had to let her use them!"

"Of course," Dusty agreed mockingly. He sized Meg up, noting the way her breasts were heaving beneath the satin and lace of her tightly fitted dress. "Why don't you just admit you've always wanted a big church wedding?"

Meg glared at him without blinking. "I'll do no such thing," she muttered. "I went through with all the pomp and circumstance of a big church wedding for one reason and one reason only. I didn't want to break my mother's heart."

Dusty whirled Meg around and around until they were in a deserted corner of the dance floor, instead of the very middle of it. "What about mine?" He pressed his lips close to the delicate shell of her ear and felt her quiver in response. "You didn't mind breaking it eighteen years ago!"

Meg jerked her head back, her green eyes bright with passion. "You were the stubborn one, as I recall," she said stiffly.

Dusty shook his head. "I would've married you—"

"Had I given up my career," Meg recited.

Dusty frowned. Dancing suddenly stopped being so thoroughly enjoyable. "You knew I had to stay here to run the family ranch."

"And you knew I wanted to write for television," Meg replied.

"Well, you've certainly done that." Dusty scowled down at her.

"Yes, I have. And you saved your dad's ranch from ruin." Meg released a quavering breath. "Now all we have to do is finish rearing your kids."

At the mention of his children, something inside Dusty gentled. "Not many women would want to take on bringing up another woman's kids," he said softly. Meg had given up a lot to be here, even if she was only likely to stay for the summer.

"Lizzie was my best friend. The fact that she married you one year after we broke up never changed that."

They danced some more in silence, both of them thinking hard. Dusty knew Meg missed Lizzie. Hell, they all did. But he also knew Lizzie would have wanted him to go on. She wouldn't have wanted their kids growing up without a mother, and Meg and Lizzie had been so close all through their girlhood and into adulthood that they were practically two halves of a whole.

Lizzie had vicariously enjoyed Meg's career, while Meg had vicariously enjoyed motherhood through Lizzie. There wasn't a part of their souls the two women hadn't shared over the years. In fact, there were times Dusty could have sworn the two had been telepathic when it came to knowing what the other thought and felt. So it made perfect sense to Dusty that his kids would want to be close to Meg. She was the nearest thing to a mother they had. The question was, could she be a wife? And why was he even thinking like this?

"Stop frowning," Meg whispered. "People are looking at us and wondering what's going on!"

Dusty rolled his eyes. "Gosh, what a surprise that is," he drawled. "You charge back into town, visit the ranch for thirty minutes, and marry me two days later. Why, whatever could they possibly find unusual in that?"

Meg gave him a withering stare. "Would you be serious, please?"

"I thought I was," Dusty quipped.

Meg stepped on his foot—deliberately, he was sure.

Dusty had another thought, and he broke into a grin. "Now what are you thinking?" Meg demanded nervously.

He tightened his hand on her waist and pulled her as close as the dress and starchy petticoats would allow. "That I could use a wedding night," he whispered wickedly in her ear.

Meg turned pale. There was no doubt in Dusty's mind she knew exactly what he meant.

She leaned back and glared up at him. "Well, you're not getting one," she said, and her cheeks turned a deep attractive pink.

Dusty grinned at her, glad there was still one way to unnerve this woman. There was nothing he liked better than having the upper hand with Meg. "Wanna bet?" he needled.

"You loathsome scoundrel," she whispered.

"You bet," Dusty agreed with a salacious wink.

"Dusty! Meg!" Meg's mother passed in a whirl of excited activity. "Time to cut the cake!"

Dusty stopped dancing and took Meg by the elbow. "Duty calls," he said cheerfully.

"Duty," Meg replied haughtily, as she picked up her skirts and brushed past him, "only extends so far."

Chapter Three

"NOW I DON'T WANT any argument," Meg's mother said. "You and Dusty need time alone."

If only her mother knew, Meg thought. "Mom, really—"

"Go on back to the ranch. Your father and I will take great care of the kids."

"Yeah, Dad," Jason said with a sly smile. "Go for it."

Dusty glared at his son. His son grinned back mischievously.

"Look, I don't know what you're up to now..." Dusty began as he drove the pickup back to the ranch.

"This was not my idea."

"Sure it wasn't."

Meg crossed her arms. "Mother just didn't understand why we didn't want a honeymoon."

Devilry glinted in Dusty's eyes as he slanted her a look. "She thinks our marriage is going to be a real one, hmm?"

"In every respect. Fortunately," Meg informed Dusty archly, "she's wrong."

They didn't speak again until Dusty pulled up in front of the ranch. Meg bolted from the truck and headed for the house. She'd been counting on having the kids underfoot tonight to keep things sane between Dusty and her. But they would be back tomorrow, she reassured herself firmly.

She walked inside. She wasn't sure when or how it had been done, but the house was filled with flowers. A bucket sat on a linen-covered table, a magnum of champagne poking out of the ice.

Dusty headed straight for it.

"I'm not drinking tonight," Meg said.

"Can't risk loosening up those inhibitions even a little bit, huh?" Dusty said with a needling grin. "Well, don't worry. It'd take more than a bottle of champagne to make me want to sleep with you."

"You would have to bring that up," Meg said stiffly.

"What? That we never had a wedding night?"

"It was the one smart move we made while we were engaged."

"I'll drink to that." Dusty sighed and poured champagne into a glass.

"So will I." Willing to do anything to stop the tidal wave of longing and memories swiftly flooding back to her, Meg grabbed a glass and held it out to him. He poured her a generous amount, set the bottle down with utmost care, then lifted his eyes, and his glass, to hers. "To a match made in ... Texas," he said, as their glasses clinked.

Meg's cheeks flamed as she took a sip.

"Thought I was going to say something else, didn't you?" he teased.

"It wouldn't have surprised me."

"But I didn't."

"Score one for you."

"And you," Dusty said generously, as he kicked off his shoes and sank down on the U-shaped sofa. "I certainly didn't expect a church full of people."

Meg's feet were killing her, too. She kicked off her heels and settled onto the sofa. "I admit I was getting a little nervous." She smoothed the full rustling skirt of her wedding gown. "I wasn't sure you'd show up."

"Had to," Dusty said with a grimace. "The kids need a mother. That's become increasingly clear."

Meg told herself not to be disappointed by his unromantic attitude; it was, after all, exactly what she wanted. Her eyes lifted to his. "Is that the only reason you married me today?"

Dusty pinned her with an uncompromising look. "What other reason could there be?"

I don't know, Meg thought wistfully. Maybe love. But unable to say that to him, she merely shrugged and said lightly, "Texas is a community-property state."

"What's mine is yours and vice versa. Now that's a thought," Dusty drawled.

Meg looked around. While the house was scrupulously clean, most of the furniture and all the window coverings had seen better days. Meg longed to make it nicer for Dusty and the kids. "Dusty, what would you think if I had some of my furniture from California moved in here? You know, just to spruce things up a bit."

Dusty's jaw set. "No. I like things just the way they are."

"Change is good sometimes."

He rolled to his feet. "Change is dangerous." He stalked out onto the back porch. The sun was setting.

Meg followed.

"You shouldn't have married me," he said without turning around. "It's never going to work, not in a million years."

"I know," Meg said. She stared at the horizon, where the sun was setting in a blaze of scarlet and gold.

The next thing she knew, Dusty firmly set down his glass, took hers from her and set it down, too. Wordlessly he pulled her into his arms. Maybe it was the champagne. Maybe it was the mood, but Meg couldn't seem to summon the willpower to resist what she knew was coming next.

Her eyes closed as Dusty's mouth drifted down to hers. And suddenly it was as if they had stepped back in time. It was as if the years apart had never happened. Dusty had always held the keys to her heart—and he still did.

"We shouldn't—" she protested as he picked her up and headed for the stairs.

He didn't slow until he'd reached the master bedroom, dropped her onto the bed and stretched out beside her. "We're married." He nuzzled the sensitive area just beneath her ear.

"But—" You don't love me, she thought. You just kiss as if you do.

"Stop talking, Meg," Dusty growled. "Stop talking and just feel."

"But, Dusty..."

His hands were already on the back of her dress, undoing the row of tiny pearl buttons. His mouth drifted lower to her chin, her throat. "The kids said you looked like a fairy godmother today, and you know what? They were right," Dusty said. "When I saw you coming down that aisle, my heart damned near stopped. And the rest of me—"

"Dusty!"

"I want you, Meg," he whispered as he drew the dress from her shoulders, down over her breasts. "I always have."

The next thing Meg knew, his mouth was on hers again. He kissed her fiercely, caressed her gently. He'd never been one to hurry, and he didn't hurry then. Every inch of her was treated to the same tender loving care.

Meg kept telling herself to fight it, fight him, but the more he kissed her, the more he caressed her, the less willpower she had. By the time they were completely undressed several minutes later, she had no resistance left at all.

Dusty followed her down onto the bed and covered her with his weight. Meg knew it was wrong—they hadn't taken their wedding vows the way they should—but it felt right, anyway, being alone here with him. It felt like a wedding night, one that had been far too long in coming.

"Dusty?" she whispered, already trembling as he parted her thighs with his knee and then followed that with long, loving strokes.

"I know, darlin'." He kissed her again, deeply.

She moaned and arched up into his loving touch. "This doesn't mean—" She gasped as the first undulating waves of completion hit her.

"I know..." Dusty said huskily.

And then he was a part of her, and she was a part of him. And nothing else mattered. Nothing at all.

MEG LAY in Dusty's arms. The champagne was wearing off and so was the intoxication of being with him once again. She sat up, aware that she had never been more confused.

He caught her arm. "Where are you going?"

As if he didn't know. "I can't believe we just did that," Meg moaned, clutching the sheet to her breasts.

"Yes. You can." Dusty's blue eyes darkened with understanding. "The passion was always there for us, Meg, even at the end. That never changed."

"But your love did, Dusty."

He quirked a dark dissenting brow. "You left me, remember, darlin'?"

"Only because you wouldn't come with me," Meg whispered.

He sighed, let go of her arm and swept a hand through his dark tousled hair. "I'm not going over all this again," he said grimly.

"You're right. It's time we buried the past and moved on to the future."

He crooked a finger and waggled his eyebrows at her. "Come back here, then."

"No." Meg held up both hands to ward him off. "No more sex just because we're married."

His gaze darkened sensually. "I wasn't expecting this," he said seriously. But now that it had happened, Meg thought, he wasn't fighting it, either.

"And I was?" She stormed about, gathering her clothes. "You must really think I'm a fool. Do you honestly think I don't know why you did what you just did?"

He looked confused. "Since you're so on top of things, suppose you tell me why I just made love to you, then, if it wasn't because I think you're the sexiest woman on earth."

Meg whirled so fast she almost lost her sheet. "To get even with me."

"For what?" Grinning, he watched her re-drape herself with linen.

"Leaving you. And then coming back, uninvited, to help raise your kids. You must feel like I backed you into a corner, particularly after I countered your less-than-gracious marriage proposal with the wedding that was originally planned for us years ago."

"Hey." Dusty sat up. He was beginning to look annoyed again. "No one forces me to do anything."

Meg frowned. "Would you have married me if there hadn't been a church full of people today?"

He hesitated, then evaded. "I don't see what difference it makes."

Meg glared at him. She knew she never should have let him make love to her. "I do."

"We got married for the kids," Dusty said as he pulled on his pants and zipped up. "So they'd have a mother again, a normal home."

And love had nothing to do with it, Meg thought. She was still wildly in love with him and always had been, but he didn't give a hoot about her. She hurled his shirt at him. He caught it against his chest.

"Then it's a good thing you satisfied your sexual curiosity tonight, cowboy, because this is never, ever, going to happen again!"

Chapter Four

"I DIDN'T THINK fairy godmothers made you wash dishes," Billy complained.

"Everyone has to take a turn doing dishes." Meg bent to give him a hug.

"How come we have to do chores every day now, anyway?" Jason scowled at Meg from the doorway.

"Yeah," Lily agreed. "Daddy never made us. Neither did Mama."

Which explained, perhaps, why the house had been in such utter chaos and Dusty so anxious to find a wife. "It's not fair for one person to have to do everything," Meg explained. "Besides, we all live here, so we should all pitch in to keep the house tidy and the meals on time. Self-sufficiency is a good thing."

"Not from my vantage point," Jason complained even more vigorously.

"Well, it is from mine," Dusty announced, strolling into the room. "I want you kids to do whatever Meg asks you now, and no complaints."

Lily glared at Dusty and then Meg. "I don't like this," she said flatly.

"Yeah," Jason put in. "No one told me this was going to turn into a boot camp for kids when the two of you got married." Lily and Jason exchanged aggrieved looks and then stomped out of the room together.

Billy finished drying the last dish. "Can I go now, please?" he said.

"*May* I go now, please," Meg said with a smile and a hug. "And yes, you may."

Billy darted out. Silence fell.

Dusty watched Meg wipe the counters. He wondered what it would have been like if he and Meg had married long ago, or just married for real now. He wondered what it would be like if she was sharing his bed every night, sleeping in his arms, instead of on the other side of a rolled-up blanket. Then he pushed the thought away.

He was getting in too deep, beginning to depend on Meg. He knew this wasn't going to last, that when she tired of the game they were playing, she would probably leave. And even if she didn't leave right away, she was only here for the kids. She had made that plain enough.

So why was he standing here, daydreaming about making their relationship a real one, when he knew it wasn't going to be? Dusty scowled. It was past time he got realistic again. This time, he told himself sternly, when Meg left he was not going to be left feeling as if he'd gotten kicked in the gut by a mule. He would enjoy the free baby-sitting and maid service while it lasted, however long it lasted, and he wouldn't be sorry when it was gone.

"The kids missed you at supper," Meg reprimanded quietly, turning to him.

The kids, Dusty thought, not her. He stuck his thumbs into the front pockets of his jeans. "Yeah, well, that's what I came in to tell you," he said tersely, making up a fictitious reason for staying out all night as he went along. "I, uh, won't be here tonight, either. A coyote's been stalking cattle down near the river. I've got to go back out. I won't be home until morning."

"COYOTE, MY FOOT!" Meg mumbled the next evening, as Dusty came in for a shower.

"Now what are you grumbling about?" He was stiff and sore from a night spent sleeping scrunched up in the cab of his pickup and a day working on the range. He wanted a hot meal and an even hotter shower.

Meg jammed her hands on her waist. "I know you made up the story about the coyote."

"How?" Because we don't have any coyotes around here anymore and haven't had them for years? Dusty thought.

"Because you didn't take your rifle!" Meg strode toward him, her hips moving fluidly beneath the short denim skirt.

"Hey." Dusty raised his hands in surrender and tried not to think about how good those hips had felt beneath him. "I never said I was going to shoot him."

Meg made a disrespectful sound. "Mmm-hmm. And what were you planning to do? Play gin rummy with him?"

Dusty turned his glance from the gentle curves of her breasts beneath the snug, white, long-sleeved cotton shirt. He looked into her green eyes and drawled in a way he knew would provoke her, "It might've been a her, and what does it matter to you what I do with any coyote?"

"An apt description," Meg muttered, her face suffusing with sudden angry color. She looked at him jealously and folded her arms in front of her. "Almost as apt as the evil witch."

Dusty blinked in confusion. She'd lost him, but good. "What are you talking about now?" he demanded irascibly, wanting more than ever to take Meg to bed and make mad passionate love to her all over again.

"Donna Gardener! You were with her again last night, weren't you? That's why you were out all night. You were trying to cover up your philandering!"

"You're jealous!" he whispered, liking the thought of that a lot, because it meant she cared at least a little.

Meg's eyes flashed. "Don't flatter yourself!"

Dusty grinned and stepped closer. He was about to take her in his arms and put that declaration to the test when racing footsteps sounded in the hall. A second later, the twins bounded into the master bedroom. Dusty stared at them in amazement. Sallie had short curly hair. Susie had long straight hair. "Hi, Daddy!" they said in unison. "How do you like our new look?"

Dusty turned to Meg slowly. As long as he could recall, the twins had delighted in dressing exactly alike. Now, if you didn't look closely, on first glance you'd never even know they were twins! "Was this your idea, too?" Dusty asked with a smile of approval he couldn't begin to feel.

"No, it wasn't, but I did think it was way past time they emphasized their individuality," Meg responded in all seriousness.

Sallie and Susie bobbed their heads in agreement. "We wanted to look different for a long time, Daddy, but we just didn't know how to tell you that."

Had the twins only told him they wanted their own style, he would've been glad to outfit them differently. But he hadn't known, because they hadn't felt they could come to him with even such a simple request. Knowing he had failed his children again filled him with pain. "You girls look very nice," Dusty said with a smile. He bent and gave each child a kiss and a hug. "Now if you ladies will excuse me, I've got to chuck these filthy clothes and have a shower."

DUSTY EMERGED from the shower to see Meg standing by the vanity. "We need to talk," she said.

"Can't it wait?" Dusty didn't like being around her. Being around her when he was damn near naked was almost too much to bear. It made him remember their wedding night. And all the times before, in the years before, when he had kissed and caressed her, in anticipation of the day they were married and could take the passion they felt for each other to the limit.

But that wasn't happening. Not with anywhere near the frequency he wanted. Making love to Meg once wasn't nearly enough for Dusty, and he didn't see how it could be for Meg, either.

Ignoring the fact that he was clad only in a towel, she strode nearer. "No, it can't. I owe you an apology about the twins. I guess I should have asked you if it would be okay to let them change their hair."

Dusty shrugged. He picked up a comb from the vanity and ran it through his wet hair. "I trust your judgment."

"But you're angry with me, Dusty," Meg said, watching as he slapped on deodorant and after-shave. "I can feel it."

The towel slid another inch lower. Dusty caught it before it slid to the floor completely and resecured it. "Maybe that's because you're everyone's fairy godmother around here except mine," he said, wishing again that Meg would get the hell out of here and let him dress in peace. He was going to be hard for hours as it was.

"What's that supposed to mean?" Meg demanded.

Dusty looked at Meg's soft lips, tousled golden hair and soft skin, and decided he wasn't the only one who should be throbbing. He took her by the shoulders and backed her up against the vanity, then moved forward until her thighs were cradled in the warmth of his. The towel was thick, but not thick enough to hide what he was feeling. "It means maybe I could get more out of this setup, too," he said, wanting her to know what she was doing to him, so she'd quit.

Unfortunately, being so close to her had the opposite effect on him. Being that close to her only made him want her all the more. Suddenly her softness, her proximity, her inherent desirability and the chemistry flowing between them were all too potent to resist.

She'd been jealous and suspicious.

If she cared enough to imagine he was having an affair with Donna Gardener, it could only mean one thing.

She still felt she had a claim on him.

Maybe it was time he explored that claim.

He lowered his mouth to hers.

Meg gave a strangled gasp of dismay, even as her lips parted to receive his kiss. "Dusty, no . . ." she said, sounding a little panicked.

Dusty sighed and drew back, his lips still aching for her kiss. He met her eyes, his displeasure with this game they were playing unmistakable. "No?" he echoed disbelievingly.

Meg swallowed and pushed ineffectually at his chest. "No," she repeated. Her chin thrust out stubbornly.

Dusty swore and stepped back, his emotions and his body under tight control. He didn't know how much more of this he could take. He glared at her and delivered his next words in a low gruff voice designed to let Meg know just how close to the edge she was pushing him. He had control of his emotions and his passion now. He couldn't guarantee how long it would last. "Then don't come in here when I'm half-dressed, or you're liable to get more than you bargained for, babe."

DUSTY HAD DINNER with Meg and the kids, then retreated to his study to do work on the ranch books. It was almost midnight when he headed for the second floor. The kids were asleep, but the light in the master bedroom was burning bright.

Dusty shut the bedroom door behind him and glared at Meg. What in blue blazes was she up to now? "What the heck is this?" he demanded. Instead of the rolled-up blanket he and Meg had been using as a divider in the middle of their bed, he saw a sleeping bag rolled out on the floor.

Meg pointed. "There's your bed, cowboy. Use it."

Dusty glared at her. He knew what she wanted. She wanted him to try to claim his marital rights so she could turn him on and then turn him down again. Barring that, she wanted him to be so ticked off by the new arrangement that he'd storm out and sleep in the pickup again.

Dusty looked at the sleeping bag, then at Meg, the bed, then at the sleeping bag again. Slowly he began stripping off his clothes. They fell, one by one, in a heap on the floor until he stood naked before her.

Meg swallowed, but to Dusty's amusement, didn't turn away, even though she obviously wanted to. "That's nothing I haven't seen before, cowboy," she drawled. She climbed into bed, a vision of loveliness in her own chaste white nightgown. She reached over and turned out the light. "Good night."

Dusty thought briefly about trying to claim his marital rights, anyway. He had a feeling it wouldn't take much at all to seduce her. But he wasn't about to force himself on Meg, and right now he doubted even an ice-cold shower would cool the fire burning in his loins. So he picked up the sleeping bag, placed it on his half of the bed and then climbed into it.

Meg gasped softly as the bed shifted beneath his weight. She eyed his bare chest, then the sleeping bag he'd drawn up nearly to his waist. "See that you stay in that thing, cowboy."

"Don't worry," Dusty said, meaning it. His temper was burning as badly as the fire in his loins. "This one night your virtue is safe with me."

Chapter Five

"WHAT ARE THESE?" Dusty asked the following night. He held up a plastic-wrapped package for Meg's inspection.

"Pajamas. If we're going to be sharing a bedroom, then you're going to wear them. No more sleeping in your jockey shorts. No more sleeping without them."

Dusty quirked a brow. "Is that an order?"

"You can call it anything you like, just so long as you do it."

Dusty pulled the pajamas out of the package. They were light blue. The shirt, he was not going to wear. The pants seemed like a good idea. He had ached with desire the whole night through when he'd slept naked in the same bed as Meg. So maybe it wouldn't be such a bad idea to keep some clothes on.

"Where's my sleeping bag?"

"In the closet where it belongs," Meg said. "You can have half the bed. Just be sure to stay on your side."

"I'll try not to trespass." Dusty grinned. She was warming up to him again whether she wanted to admit it or not. But what that meant, exactly, was not something he wanted to think about. It was enough just getting through each day.

He climbed into bed. Meg climbed in, too. She had a script with her and her reading glasses.

Dusty folded his hands behind his head. "I didn't know you wore reading glasses," he said, wondering what else he didn't know about her.

Meg rolled her eyes. "Only for the past twenty-five years."

"I never saw you in them before."

Meg pushed a lock of golden blond hair behind her ear. "That's because I was too vain to wear them before," she murmured absently, then turned to him with a frown. "Is the light going to bother you?" She paused, her red-ink pen poised above the script.

Dusty realized it was the first time he'd seen her work on anything but the usual household stuff since they'd been married. He tried not to think how nervous that made him. He didn't want her leaving again, not when things were just starting to smooth out between them.

But not about to let her know that, Dusty shot her a crooked grin. "Would it make you turn out the light—" and, he thought, crawl on over here to my side of the bed "—if I said yes?"

"No." She gave him a stern look and went back to writing in the margins of the script.

Just as he'd thought. Stifling a frustrated sigh, he turned on his side away from her and closed his eyes. When he woke again, the room was dark and her side of the bed was empty. Dusty glanced at the clock. Three in the morning. Where the heck could she be?

He lay there a few more minutes, waiting. No Meg. Deciding this bore investigating, he got up and walked through the upstairs hall. He noticed little Billy's bed was also empty, saw the lights on downstairs and followed the signs to the kitchen.

Little Billy sat on Meg's lap, his head against her shoulder. Meg had her arms around him and was holding him close as she stroked his hair. "Everyone has bad dreams, honey."

"I know," Billy said rather tearfully as he rubbed his eyes, "but when I have them I can't go back to sleep, Auntie Meg."

"You know what always helped me?" she said softly. "A glass of milk and a cookie. Would you like to try that?"

Billy sniffed loudly and nodded.

"I'll get it," Dusty said, deciding it was time to make his presence known. He padded into the kitchen.

"Did I wake you?" Meg asked in concern.

Dusty shook his head and tried not to think how lovely she looked sitting there in her nightgown and robe, his five-year-old son cuddled in her lap. "No. Thanks for getting up with Billy."

"She's my fairy godmother. That's what she's s'posed to do," Billy said, yawning. He accepted the cookie Dusty handed him with a muted thanks.

Dusty had to admit Meg looked like an angel in her white cotton gown. It was demure and high-necked, and it covered her from wrist to ankle in sweeping voluminous folds. With her golden hair tumbling over her shoulders, she looked incredibly soft and womanly. Without her makeup, she seemed even younger and more vulnerable. Like there was a part of her that had been missing, too, only she just hadn't known....

Now who was being hopelessly romantic, Dusty thought, irked with himself. He knew better than to entertain any sappy fantasies where Meg was concerned. He was disappointed every time.

Billy finished his milk and ate the rest of his cookie.

"Better?" Meg asked softly as she rubbed his back with gentle motherly strokes.

Billy nodded and released a tremulous sigh. "I think I'm ready to go back to bed now," he said bravely.

"How about I tuck you in and maybe read you a story?" Meg suggested.

"Okay. But I need to leave the light on," Billy said. He stood and took Meg's hand.

"That sounds like a good idea," Meg said.

Wishing his presence were needed a little more but knowing it wasn't, Dusty helped tuck Billy in and then went back to bed. Meg came in half an hour later. "He's asleep again," she said as she stifled a yawn and climbed beneath the covers.

"You're really good with him," Dusty said admiringly. "I think he's missed a mother's loving touch."

Meg turned on her side, so they were stretched out face-to-face. "Is he the only one?"

The urge to reach out and touch her golden hair was so strong it was almost painful. "What do you mean?" Dusty asked hoarsely.

Meg's green eyes glimmered with longing and something else—a mixture of vulnerability, hope, wariness. "I mean, did you make love to me on our wedding night because you missed having a woman around?" she said.

Dusty saw the hurt shimmering in her eyes and knew he'd wounded her. "I loved Lizzie with all my heart and soul," he said. "You know that, since you were her best friend from the time the two of you were toddlers."

"And we stayed best friends even after she married you," Meg added.

Dusty nodded. "But I also know she's gone, Meg. No amount of wishing is going to change that. We have to move on. You, me, the kids . . ."

"But did you make love to me because you missed her?" Meg persisted.

"I made love to you because I missed *you*," Dusty said, looking into Meg's angelic face. He saw the longing in her eyes grow stronger. Feeling the same sensual pull, he drew her gently into his arms, then rolled so that she was beneath him and continued his confession. "All those years... I was married and I was happy, and because I was happy I didn't give our ruined relationship a second thought. But when Lizzie was gone, the emptiness returned. I didn't think it would ever be filled again. Until you showed up."

Knowing it was what Meg wanted, too, Dusty kissed her deeply. Meg melted against him. As the moments drew out, she kissed him more and more passionately. Dusty lost all sense of time and place. There was only the feel of her beneath him, so soft and womanly. Only the touch of her hands on his back, going lower to anchor his hips against her and draw him closer still. Only the restless shifting of her body, the parting of her thighs.

Dusty unbuttoned her gown and buried his face in the softness of her breasts. He traced the curves of her body with his fingertips, then his lips. She urged him closer still. "Make love to me, Dusty," she whispered. "Make love to me all the way..."

Dusty paused, every inch of him throbbing. He looked into her eyes. "No regrets this time?"

Meg shook her head. "No regrets," she whispered.

Her permission was all the encouragement he needed. Dusty divested himself of his pajama bottoms. Meg slipped off her gown, then moved so she was astride him. The breath left Dusty's lungs as she lowered herself onto him and they became one. Dusty didn't want to rush. His body was clamoring for release, but he wanted to savor every second, every touch, every kiss. This had been a long time coming, and he was going to take a long time enjoying it. He rocked against her, pushing her toward the edge, then withdrew and lifted her over and onto her back. He covered her with his weight and kissed her long and lovingly before sliding lower and kissing her again. She arched against him, gasping and trembling as she reached the pinnacle. Dusty waited until her shudders subsided, then moved upward and began the slow erotic process of possessing her once again. And this time, when he loved her, she held nothing back, nothing at all. This time their loving was complete. This time when it ended she didn't pull away.

Slowly their breathing returned to normal. Dusty continued to hold Meg close, even though his feelings were in chaos. He couldn't believe how intense his feelings for Meg were. It was almost as if she had never left him. As if the eighteen years they'd been apart had never happened. And yet . . . he was confused, too. Was it love or desire he was feeling for Meg, and could he risk either, knowing how she had left him once, and how she might leave him again?

As much as he didn't want to think about it, he couldn't forget the way she'd been working on that script earlier. . . .

AN HOUR LATER, Meg was still wide awake. She frowned as she listened to the sound of Dusty's deep even breathing. She turned away from Dusty, but try as she might, she couldn't seem to go back to sleep. She knew Dusty thought everything was settled just because they'd made love, but for her, all their lovemaking had done was complicate matters even further.

She closed her eyes against the moonlight still streaming in the window. From the time she had left Texas for a career in Hollywood, she had always been so sure she knew what she was doing. But lately, everything was topsy-turvy.

First, there was the very real need of the kids. They needed a mother. As for Dusty and her—well, they'd always felt the need to throw down the gauntlet to one another—that was what had made their relationship so exciting and so stormy. But the last few days, the edges of reality and romantic fantasy had become blurred. Was she staying here with Dusty and the kids for the same reason she had really agreed to marry him—just to prove that she could? Or was she doing it because she was still in love with him, always had been and always would be?

And what about Dusty? Was he merely reaching back into the past just to fill up the emptiness of the present? If that was the case, surely his feelings for her wouldn't last. And if they didn't, what would she do then?

Go back to California?

Stay here and resign herself to becoming an in-name-only wife once again?

She sighed. That idea was unattractive. So unattractive, in fact, that she couldn't help but wish they hadn't made love. Again. She didn't want to go back to California. She didn't want to stay unless Dusty loved her heart and soul, exactly the way he should, and not just for now, but forever.

She wanted it all.

The question was, did Dusty?

Chapter Six

"IT'S AN INTERESTING IDEA...yes...I'll think about it. 'Bye."

Dusty watched as Meg hung up the phone. The excited color in her face made her look even prettier than usual. "What's going on?" he said, aware she'd been on the phone for the past thirty minutes.

"That was the network. They want me to produce another drama."

"Are you going to do it?" Dusty asked casually.

"I don't know. I told myself I was taking the next few months off. But if I did it, I'd have to get started now and work all summer to develop the story line and characters so we could film a pilot by next spring."

"But you want to do it, don't you?" Dusty prodded.

Meg shrugged and went back to icing the cinnamon rolls she'd just made for the kids. "It's no secret I've always liked writing best. And this series would be set in Texas. It'd be kind of like rediscovering my roots."

"What else?" Dusty prodded, sensing there was more.

Meg grinned. "The money is fabulous and they've promised me a debut slot between two other hit shows on the Monday-night lineup if they like the pilot."

It sounded like a dream come true for her. Dusty crossed his arms on his chest and wished she didn't look so pretty standing in the morning sunlight that streamed through the kitchen windows. "So what's stopping you from taking it?"

he asked, aware he already felt a little threatened. As if she was going to leave again.

Meg gave him a level look. "I promised to help you raise the kids."

At least she felt in conflict about her choice this time, Dusty thought. The last time she hadn't. Then, it had been business first, last and always. He moved past her to help himself to a cup of coffee. "You couldn't exactly do that if you went back to Hollywood, now could you?"

"No. I couldn't." Meg frowned and turned away from him.

Dusty told himself it didn't matter to him one way or another what Meg did, but inwardly he was shaken. Last night they had made love as if they'd never been apart. This morning, Meg was on the verge of leaving him again, whether she admitted it to herself or not.

Meg set the platter of rolls on the table and poured herself a cup of coffee. "What do you think I should do?" she asked.

He'd always figured he'd want to get married again someday, if only so his kids would have a mother, but he had never figured he would really want to have a wife again. And yet here he was, wanting someone to share his hopes and his dreams, wanting someone to love and hold close at night. He would never learn.

"Don't you have any opinion at all?" Meg persisted, her green eyes glimmering with hurt.

Dusty gulped his coffee, then pinned her with a laser-edged look. "Even if I were a real husband to you, darlin', which I'm not, I'd be hard-pressed to answer that one. If I said yes, you'd no doubt interpret it to mean I didn't care enough about you to protest your absence in my life, and if I said no, I didn't want you to take the job, then you'd accuse me of being unsupportive of your career."

Meg shook the golden hair from her face. "You already were that," she said in a steady voice.

"So you let me know," Dusty replied dryly.

Silence fell between them. Dusty didn't know what Meg was thinking, but he knew what he was thinking. He was thinking about the way she had looked in her nightgown in the middle of the night. He was thinking about how soft and giving she'd felt when they'd made love, and the way she'd kissed him back—like she really meant it.

But as always, he had put too much store in her passion and not enough in the lifelong ambition that had driven her away from him.

"If I turned this job offer down—" Meg began.

"You won't," Dusty interrupted, irritated to have just made a fool of himself over Meg—again.

"But suppose I did," Meg persisted quietly, stepping closer. "Would it make a difference to you?"

Dusty shook his head. He was tired of playing these games. "Don't lead me on, Meg, into thinking you can change." He put his coffee mug on the counter with a decisive thunk. "Because we both know you can't."

MEG WATCHED through the kitchen window as Dusty strode toward his pickup.

She knew it was stupid, but she couldn't help but be hurt by Dusty's indifferent reaction to her job offer. Years before, when they'd been engaged and she'd had the chance to go to California and make something of herself, he'd been anything but indifferent. He had begged and pleaded and finally absolutely forbade her to leave Texas. Did his lack of reaction now mean he'd grown up, or was it that he no longer cared where she lived or what she did?

The phone rang. Depressed and confused, Meg went to answer it. This time it wasn't for her. She flicked on the intercom. "Lily, phone," she said.

Lily came into the kitchen. "Thanks."

Meg went back to watching Dusty out the kitchen window. He was loading veterinary supplies into the back of his pickup. She supposed he was headed out to take care of the herd.

To her left, Lily picked up the receiver and held it to her ear. "Gee, well, thanks for inviting me, but . . . I think I'm needed at home tonight. Yeah, I'll call if things change. 'Bye."

"What was that about?" Meg asked as her twelve-year-old stepdaughter hung up the phone.

"Oh, nothing. Just a slumber party."

"Don't you want to go?"

Lily poured herself a glass of juice and wouldn't meet Meg's gaze. "Slumber parties are childish," she mumbled.

"You've been to too many of them, hmm?" Meg sympathized.

"She hasn't been to any!" the twins said, charging out of the adjacent pantry, their favorite cereal in hand. "She's always invited but she never goes." They sat down at the table.

"Is this true, Lily?" Meg asked.

Lily shrugged. She helped herself to a cinnamon roll and some fruit, then seemed unable to eat either. "Well, I really couldn't when Mama was sick because she needed me to help with the kids, and then after, well, Daddy still needed me to help with the kids. Besides, it just doesn't sound like a lot of fun going over to someone else's house to sleep."

Meg's heart went out to Lily. She had been robbed of so much. "Maybe you should give it a try, anyway," Meg encouraged gently. Lily hadn't been able to be a kid in a long while. It was past time she went back to having fun and acting her age.

"Maybe she should just do what she feels is right for her," Dusty interrupted, striding into the kitchen again.

"Meg, I need to talk to you for a minute." Dusty took Meg by the hand and guided her outside. He didn't stop until they were standing by an old iron water pump, well out of earshot of the house. The morning was balmy and sunny. Meg could tell the day was going to be a scorcher, just as she could tell Dusty was royally ticked off at her.

He dropped her hand and glared at her. "Don't push Lily into doing something she doesn't want to do," he advised curtly.

Meg glared back. "You have to be one of the densest men I have ever met." And one of the handsomest. No one wore jeans and denim shirts like Dusty.

He tipped back his hat. "You're an authority on child-rearing, I suppose?"

Meg crossed her arms over her breasts. Being alone with Dusty like this was a little too intimate for comfort. Maybe because she feared—or was it hoped?—that he would choose to settle this argument of theirs with another bone-melting kiss. "Can't you see there's a problem?" she asked.

Dusty shook his head and frowned at her. "The only problems here are the ones you're making!"

Meg could see she was not going to change his mind. She rolled her eyes. "Maybe I've watched *The Wizard of Oz* video with Billy a few times too many, but I feel like I'm dealing with the scarecrow here."

He relaxed one knee and leaned toward her, over her. "And how is that?" he said.

Meg tilted back her head, but didn't move away from him. "If you only had a brain—"

Lily came out of the house and stood on the back porch. "Meg, whose turn is it to do the breakfast dishes today?"

"Susie and Sallie's." Meg gestured Lily closer. Ignoring Dusty, she continued, "About the slumber party. I think you should go, honey. If you're not having a good time you can call me and I'll drive over and get you."

Lily bit her lip. She looked as if she wanted to go but was still a little apprehensive about doing something she'd never done. "What if it's the middle of the night?"

Meg smiled at Lily and wrapped an affectionate arm about her shoulders. "It could be four in the morning, honey. It won't make the slightest difference to me, I promise."

Lily released a long sigh. Happiness sparkled in her blue eyes. "Okay, I'll go, but if I'm not having a good time, I'm coming home," Lily said.

"I understand completely," Meg agreed.

Dusty and Meg watched Lily run back into the house.

"You're making a mistake," Dusty predicted as soon as they were alone again.

Meg glared at him. How had she forgotten how narrow-minded he could be? It seemed the only mistake she had made recently was marrying him. "We'll see," she said.

THE PHONE RANG at midnight. Meg and Dusty both jumped for it, but Meg got it first. So Dusty left the master bedroom and headed for the extension in the upstairs hall. "How's the party, honey?" Meg asked.

"I'm having a great time," Lily said, above the din of pop music in the background. "Thanks for telling me to go. I don't know what I was so nervous about!"

"I'll see you in the morning, then?" Meg said, smiling.

"Yes. But don't come too early," Lily cautioned. "I want to stay and have breakfast with my friends."

Meg put down the phone. Dusty put down the extension. He came back in the bedroom and shut the door behind him.

"See? Everything is fine," Meg said, picking up the legal pad she'd been scribbling on. She'd been making notes on the new series all day. It had helped keep her mind off Dusty and the fight they'd had that morning—and the passionate way they'd made love the night before.

Unfortunately Dusty didn't look anywhere near as relieved as Meg expected him to at the good news from Lily. "What if it hadn't been?" He stretched out on the bed and folded his hands behind his head. "What if Lily'd gone and had a miserable time?"

"But she didn't!"

His eyes cut to her sharply. "That's not the point!"

"Then what is?"

Dusty scowled at the ceiling. "You're making too many changes here, too fast."

"Look, I know I've changed everyone's routine, but that was the entire point of our marrying," Meg said in exasperation.

His gaze narrowed contemplatively. "Sure it wasn't something else?" he asked silkily.

"Like what?"

"I don't know. Research for your new TV show. It is going to be a family drama set in Texas, isn't it?"

Her temper snapped. Mindful that the children were all asleep, she turned her face to his and whispered harshly, "That's a low blow, Dusty." She emphasized her point by poking an index finger at his chest. "I would never use your children for gain in my career."

He caught her hand and held it. "Then maybe you just wanted to show me what a better parent you could be."

Meg's pulse skittered and jumped beneath his touch. She jerked her hand from his and sat back against the pillows on her side of the bed. "You're right. I want your children to be happy. It seems you need some help on that score."

Dusty sat bolt upright. He turned toward her and sat cross-legged on the bed. "What's that supposed to mean?" His jaw thrust out pugnaciously.

Meg swallowed and tried not to think about how appealing he looked clad in just the light blue pajama bottoms. She stared down at the yellow pad in front of her. "It means you're about as good a parent these days as you are a husband."

Her accusation struck a nerve. Dusty picked up a pillow and plumped it between his hands. "I've given up a lot more than you have, darlin'," he growled.

Meg watched as he tossed the pillow back against the headboard. "Such as what?" she prodded.

His hands flat on the mattress, Dusty leaned closer. "My house, my name and my bed."

Meg leaned back, away from the tantalizing smell of soap and after-shave that clung to his rangy frame. "I think you've had your fair share of rewards," she said stiffly.

Dusty quirked a brow, looking anything but sexually satisfied. "Like what?" he said, goading her deliberately.

Meg vaulted from the bed and stalked to the vanity. She picked up a brush and began running it through her golden curls with vigorous strokes. "Like free maid service, Mothering for your children. Not to mention sex with me!" The words were out before Meg could prevent them. Sorry she'd said them, for she knew how Dusty would take them—like a bull took a red cape waved in front of his nose—Meg fell silent.

Dusty vaulted from the bed. He crossed the room in three long strides. He leaned over Meg, putting a hand on either side of the vanity behind her. "For your information, dar-lin', I haven't had nearly enough sex," he said angrily, his eyes hotly raking her slender form, lingering on her breasts, before returning to her face. "And if you think I have," he warned, as his eyes darkened and his voice dropped an-other husky notch, "then you've got a thing or two to learn."

"Damn it, Dusty..." Meg groaned as he cupped her face with one hand and lowered his mouth slowly, provoca-tively, to hers.

At the very last second, he pulled back.

Meg was flooded with disappointment.

"You're right." Dusty moved away from Meg abruptly. There was no hiding the rigid proof of his arousal. "We shouldn't do this," he growled.

"At last, a wise decision," Meg said glibly, needling him. She stood and went to the closet for her robe, hoping to hide the crowning imprint of her nipples against the front of her satin pajama top.

Dusty followed her to the closet. His eyes raked her breasts, letting her know he was already aware of what she was trying to hide. Meg grabbed for her robe, anyway, and struggled into it.

"Because if I kiss you," Dusty continued softly, lifting a hand to her face and touching her gently, "you're going to kiss me back, darlin'. And if you kiss me back, then I'm go-ing to touch you," he whispered sensually. "And then you're going to touch me." He leaned closer, his lips touch-ing her temple. "And the next thing you know, we'll be making hot, wild love again," he said lazily, tangling his fingers in her hair.

Meg tossed her head. With her hand on the solid warm wall of his chest, she pushed him aside and strode past. "You're incorrigible!" she snapped.

"Don't forget frustrated as hell." Hands on hips, he watched her pick up her legal pad and pen. "But don't worry. That's not going to last, either." His smile was grim. "Not any longer than this marriage of ours is."

Meg swallowed. As much as she hated to admit it, she was afraid he was right. This marriage of theirs just couldn't work. Even on a purely platonic level.

Chapter Seven

"DADDY, WHERE ARE YOU going with those flowers?" Billy asked.

Dusty paused beside the sandbox where Billy was playing with his dump truck. "These are for Meg."

"How come?" Billy asked.

Because I behaved like a caveman with a hormone problem last night, Dusty thought. And then I made the problem worse by sleeping on the sofa.

Maybe the flowers would take the edge off her anger. At least Dusty hoped they would. He hated fighting with her. The world always seemed brighter when they got along. And it couldn't be good for the children to see the tension between them. "I just figured she might need a little cheering up, that's all." Particularly if she feels as bad about our fight last night as I do, Dusty thought.

His heartbeat quickening and his spirit lifting with the anticipation of seeing her, he headed on inside. To his delight, the house was filled with the aroma of roasting brisket and freshly baked brownies, promising an excellent dinner that evening. Laughter emanated from the kitchen.

The only thing amiss was the formal dining room. It hadn't been used since Christmas. But today, a lacy linen tablecloth covered the large table, which had been set with the china, silver and crystal Dusty and Meg had received as wedding gifts. An elaborate arrangement of flowers, flanked on either side by candles in silver holders, decorated the center of the table.

Meg must've been working on that all morning, Dusty thought with an appreciative smile, which probably meant she was as anxious to make up with him as she was with her.

He heard Meg's low musical laughter and headed toward the sound, the apology he'd spent the past half hour preparing running through his head. He was about to turn the corner when he began to make out what was being said.

"Of course you can do it." Meg's voice floated toward him like a welcoming caress, and Dusty hastened his pace.

"No, I can't, Meg," Jason argued passionately. "When it comes to girls, I always say or do the wrong thing and end up making a complete fool of myself."

Not wanting to interrupt what was obviously a private conversation between Meg and his son, Dusty paused just beyond the portal. The bouquet of roses held loosely in his hand, he watched Meg give his son a sympathetic smile and an encouraging pat on the shoulder. "You want to know a secret, Jason? Those girls you're dating are just as nervous as you are," she said gently.

"No, they're not," Jason protested.

"Yes, they are. They're just a little better at hiding it, that's all. But there are a few tips that'll make getting to know your date a little easier."

A few tips, Dusty thought. This sounded like another of Meg's manipulations.

"I can use any advice you've got," Jason said.

"Okay. First, you have to be a good listener," Meg said enthusiastically. "When your date talks to you, look into her eyes and really listen to what she's saying."

Watching Meg with his son, Dusty was reminded of a clip he'd seen of Meg not too long ago on "Entertainment Tonight," talking to an actor on one of her shows.

"Second," Meg continued, "make her think you care about her, Jason, show you've got heart."

"Is this how you do it on TV?" Jason asked.

You've just hit it right on the head, son, Dusty thought. Meg might've left California, but she hadn't left her work behind. Not really.

"And in real life," Meg replied. "What goes on in television dramas is essentially the same as what goes on in real life. At least that's what we're striving for. . . ."

Great, Dusty thought. Meg was now producing what went on in his household as if it were a damn television show, not real life. How long before she lost interest in that, too, and wanted to move on to greener pastures?

He entered the kitchen, threw the roses down on the table and stalked back out.

"Dusty?" Meg dashed after him.

When he didn't stop, she ran to catch up. "What are you doing home in the middle of the day?"

Dusty used the first excuse that came to mind. "I came in to get my leather work gloves."

"I thought you kept your gloves out in the tack room," Jason said, coming up to join them.

Thanks, Dusty thought sarcastically. "I didn't see 'em." But not wanting his son to know how upset he was with Meg, Dusty shot his son a grateful glance. "I'll go back and have another look," he said. "Might be I just missed 'em."

Jason nodded, accepting Dusty's explanation without question. "Is it okay if I go into town? I want to stop by the Sonic Drive-in and uh...try out my new...uh...well, I've just got someone I want to see."

Great, Dusty thought. Now Meg's teaching my son how to act interested and interesting to girls. Was that what she was doing with him, too? Acting like a mother and devoted wife?

Oblivious to Dusty's thoughts, Meg laughed softly and encouraged his son with a pretty smile. "Sure, Jason, go ahead. Just remember to be back by five. My parents will be here for dinner at six, and I want everyone in their Sunday best."

Her parents. So all the preparations were for them and not for him, Dusty thought grimly. He should have figured as much. He was a fool to keep hoping against hope that things would ever work out with Meg and him.

Jason darted out. Dusty started to go, too, but was stopped by Meg, who clamped a hand on his forearm. "Not too cool, cowboy, sleeping on the sofa last night," she said in an I-couldn't-care-less-if-you-don't-sleep-in-our-bed tone.

Dusty narrowed his eyes at Meg, wishing she didn't look so damned pretty in an apron and jeans. He quirked a brow and gave her an unmistakably rapacious look. "Missed me?"

"In your dreams, cowboy." She paused, her temper finally getting the better of her. "But it was still a juvenile way to behave."

Dusty thought he'd been very adult, keeping his ardor in check. He gave her a heavy-lidded glance. "Don't tell me you lost sleep over me," he drawled. He'd lost sleep over her.

"Don't flatter yourself," Meg replied stubbornly. "I just don't want the kids upset because they think we're not getting along."

"For the record—" Dusty sighed heavily "—none of them know where I slept. I hit the couch long after they were asleep, and I was out working long before any of them were up. But if it worries you so much, I'll be sure to let *you* have the sleeping bag on the bedroom floor, instead of the living-room sofa the next time we have a fight. Will that satisfy you?"

"You insist on being difficult, don't you?"

"Yeah, I guess I do." Dusty was afraid if he hung around much longer he'd end up kissing her again, despite himself. He tipped back his hat. "Now if that's all . . ."

"It's not," Meg said flatly.

"Well?" Dusty quirked a brow when she didn't go on immediately.

She rubbed her arms nervously and looked up at him. "You'll be here for dinner tonight, too, won't you?" she said.

So now they were down to brass tacks. She didn't want to be embarrassed in front of her family. "And what part do I play in this family drama?" Dusty asked with exaggerated politeness.

"The loving husband and father, of course," Meg said stiffly, but there was a hint of vulnerability in her eyes that hadn't been there before.

Dusty almost fell for it and took her in his arms, until he recalled what she had just said to his son. *Look into her eyes . . . make her think you care about her . . .*

Yeah, right. Here she was doing the same damned snow job on him!

Obviously feeling the tension that gripped him, Meg swallowed. Another second passed. She dropped her hand and stepped back. "Dusty, is everything all right?" she asked softly.

His heart aching for something that could never be, Dusty muttered, "I only wish."

"But—" Meg protested.

"Later, Meg." Dusty dismissed her curtly. "I've got fence to repair."

"I KNEW you shouldn't have rushed into marriage with him," Meg's mother said, when six and then seven came and went with no sign of Dusty.

"I'm sure he just lost track of the time," Meg said, trying not to let on to her folks how hurt and humiliated she felt. "You know how it is when you're repairing fence."

"You're awfully understanding," Meg's father said with a relaxed grin. "Your mother would've skinned my hide if I'd done something like that to her."

And I just might do the same to Dusty, Meg thought furiously. Not wanting her parents to see how upset she was with her new excessively stubborn and temperamental husband, Meg merely smiled. "I think I better take the car and go out and look for him. You don't mind serving dinner to the children, do you, Mother?"

"Well . . . if you're sure Dusty wouldn't mind."

"I'm positive." Meg looked into the living room where the children were gathered around a board game, all dressed in their Sunday best. This night should have been so special. "Besides, the kids are hungry," Meg continued, repressing her disappointment determinedly. She took off the ruffled white apron that covered her black dinner dress. "I'll be back as soon as I can."

Her mother continued to look a little worried. "All right, sweetheart," she said.

"'Bye, Meg!" Little Billy waved. Meg waved back. "You all be good now," she said.

Not bothering to take the time to change, Meg grabbed her keys and rushed out to the car. When I find you, Dusty MacKauley, she fumed, her temper working overtime, you had damn well better have a good excuse for standing me up this way!

He was working on the fence on the lower twenty. When he saw her, he glanced up, then glanced immediately back down and resumed his work.

Slamming out of the car, Meg marched over to him. "Do you have any idea what time it is?" she demanded, her high heels sinking in the thick buffalo grass.

"Let me guess." Dusty looked up again. Sweat dripped off his brow. His clothes were filthy. He needed a shave. And a shower. "I missed dinner."

Meg held on to her temper with effort. "The question is why?" she prodded coolly.

Dusty stretched a line of barbed wire from one metal post to the next. "As I recall, I never said I'd be there."

Meg stomped closer. "But you knew I was expecting you."

He lifted his shoulders in a disinterested shrug. "Someone ought to have told you we don't always get what we expect around here."

"Put down those pliers and listen to me! You humiliated me in front of my parents, Dusty."

Dusty tipped back his hat and regarded her steadily. "I guess that makes us about even, then."

"Even!" Meg lifted her arms in silent fury. "What did I ever do to you?"

Dusty's frown deepened as he finished securing the barbed wire to the post. "You cast me in the part of the father in this little family drama you've been directing all week."

"I have not been directing your family."

"Oh, no?" He tossed the pliers into the box at his side with a loud clank and yanked off his work gloves. He rounded the area where the fence was still down and towered over her. "Then what do you call changing the way the twins look, forcing Lily to socialize and teaching Jason how to impress the girls he's dating with his courteousness and sensitivity?"

Meg lifted her chin pugnaciously. "I call that being their mother."

Dusty stalked over to his pickup. He picked up a thermos from the front seat, unscrewed it and drank deeply of the ice water. Finished, he pulled a red bandanna out of his pocket and wiped his face. "And what about teaching Billy to depend on you, to come to you when he has a nightmare, instead of me?" Dusty stuffed the bandanna back into his pocket.

Meg crossed her arms in front of her and leaned against the side of the pickup. "I also call that being his mother," she retorted, aware the sun-warmed metal at her back was nothing compared to the sizzling heat emanating from Dusty.

He glared at her, his powerful chest lifting with every deep angry breath he took. He stepped closer. "You're going to break all their hearts when you leave. You know that, don't you?"

Meg's heart pounded at his closeness. She wished there was an easy way out, but there wasn't. "I never said I was leaving."

"Not yet," Dusty agreed confidently. He cupped her chin in his hand and gave her a level look. "You will."

Meg released a wavering breath. She ached all over. Because she wanted him to hold her. Make love to her again. Make this terrible tension between them end, not just momentarily, but for good. Her whole body relaxing, she sidled past him and walked in the direction of the setting sun.

"This is about that offer I got yesterday, isn't it?" she said with a sigh, feeling suddenly unbearably weary. She rounded on him accusingly. "That's why you're so irascible, because you still have a problem with my success in my career." And always would.

Dusty's jaw set. He quirked a dissenting brow. "It's not your career that bothers me so much as your propensity for putting it, and yourself, first."

"You're one to talk!" Her emotions in high gear, Meg advanced on him. "You criticize me for trying to help your kids, but what have you done for them lately, buster?"

"I've kept this place going!" Dusty shouted.

"Well, it isn't enough!" Meg shouted back, feeling thoroughly exasperated, as well as hurt that his regard for her was so low. "You can't just provide them with a roof over their heads or clothes to wear. You've got to be there for them, Dusty." She waved a lecturing finger beneath his nose. "You've got to notice when they're unhappy and do something to help make things better!"

He caught her hand and held it against his chest. "Meddle, you mean."

She jerked her hand free, or tried to, he refused to let her go. "No, Dusty," she corrected in the most even tone she could manage, "I mean parent."

His grip loosened slightly. There was still no way in hell she could wrest free. "I love my kids," he said in a much quieter tone. His blue eyes were suddenly as confused and contrite as hers.

Meg swallowed. Her throat ached with the effort it took to hold back the tears of frustration welling up in her eyes. "No one's ever said you don't," she returned, "but I'm tired of your absentee-parent routine, Dusty, the way you head out every time the going gets the least bit rough."

Dusty scowled and released her so quickly she stumbled backward. "There happens to be work to be done around here!" he said, even as he caught her and kept her from falling flat on her backside.

Meg held herself very still. She was determined to make her point. "You're hiding."

Dusty gripped both arms and walked her backward, until he had her backed up against the side of the pickup again. "Well, you're hiding, too," he said, very low.

Meg tried not to think about the way his lower half felt pressed against her. "What are you talking about?" she demanded.

Dusty anchored his hands on her shoulders. "I'm talking about your absentee-wife routine!" he said. "You're all loving one moment, cold as a block of ice the next!"

They stared at one another stormily.

"I should have known this marriage of ours would never work!" he said hotly.

"We both should have," she agreed, just as hotly. "But we didn't, and now we're stuck."

At the word "stuck," Dusty seemed to freeze.

"No, Meg, we're not," he said. "We walked away from each other once. We can do it again."

That sounded like the preface to a goodbye. Fighting the panic welling up inside her, Meg crossed her arms and tried to slow her pounding heart. "Are you coming back to the house with me?" She was desperate to get back there, desperate to get back to "normal."

Dusty's jaw clenched. "Nope."

"What am I going to tell my parents?"

He shrugged. "Tell them anything you like. Hell," he taunted, "live dangerously and tell them the truth."

"And that is?"

His eyes glittering, he gave her a knowing look. "That we can't continue to play these games with each other."

Games! Meg stared at him in shock, her feelings in turmoil. "This is all a game to you?" she asked hoarsely.

His jaw clenched so tightly a muscle twitched, Dusty countered impatiently, "You're telling me it isn't a game to you? That you don't enjoy tossing down the gauntlet and then calling my bluff just to see what I'll do next?''

Meg couldn't deny that she loved the sparks they generated when they were together. Dusty made her feel challenged and alive in a way no other man ever had or ever would. But she also knew that although Dusty would always desire her, and she him, he would never allow himself to really love or trust her again. Not after the way she had walked out on him the last time. And she couldn't live there any longer, pretending to all the world to be his wife, knowing he didn't love her the way he used to love her. She had to accept that she was just the convenience he'd promised her she would be when they agreed to this marriage. She'd ruined things between them when she'd chosen her career over their relationship years before, and he was never going to trust her or really love her again. He would always desire her, but desire just wasn't enough for her, not anymore. She needed to be loved, heart and soul, forever and ever.

"All right, Dusty." Meg sighed sadly. "You've won."

"Won what?" Dusty countered sarcastically. He looked at her and his eyes darkened. "This round?"

"You've won the whole match," Meg said firmly. She looked Dusty straight in the eye. "There isn't going to be another round. There aren't going to be any more games. You want your freedom, cowboy. Well, you've got it."

Chapter Eight

"BUT WHO'LL BE our fairy godmother if you leave?" Billy asked as Meg packed her bags.

"Yeah," the twins said in unison. "We need you to be our mom and help us do stuff, Auntie Meg."

Meg paused to give them a group hug. "Listen, kids, I was there for you before I married your dad, and I'll still be there for you. I just won't live in the same house anymore."

"Does this mean you're going back to California?" Jason asked sadly.

"No, honey, I'm not." Meg had made up her mind about that much. "I'm going to stay right here in Texas with you guys."

"But where will you live?" Lily asked.

"With my folks for now. But I'll probably get a house in town as soon as possible, something with office space for me, and lots of bedrooms and baths so that you guys can visit whenever you want. Maybe even spend the night."

"It won't be the same," Jason predicted sadly.

"I know," Meg agreed. She swallowed around the lump in her throat. She had started out marrying Dusty because he had challenged her to, and ended up wanting to be married to him for real. Unfortunately it hadn't worked out. Meg didn't like that. But there wasn't anything she could do to change things, either. "But it's the way it has to be. I can't be your dad's wife anymore."

"Why not?" Lily asked.

Because he doesn't love me, Meg thought, not anymore. "Because it just hasn't worked out," she said. She shut her suitcase.

One by one, she kissed the kids goodbye, then picked up her suitcase and headed for her car.

DUSTY RETURNED HOME long after midnight. The television and stereo were both on loud. Jason was on the phone. Lily had her nose in a book. The twins were playing tea party. Billy was lying in front of the TV watching *The Wizard of Oz*.

"What's going on here?" Dusty asked, nearly tripping on one of the toys scattered across the front hall. The house looked like a disaster area. "Where's Meg?" he asked with a frown. "And what are you all still doing up at this time of night?"

"Meg left hours ago, right after her mom and dad," Lily said without looking up.

The news hit Dusty like a blow to the stomach. "Where'd she go?"

"To her parents' house," Susie said.

"For the night?"

"For good," Sallie corrected sadly.

"Yep, Dad," Jason covered the phone and glared at Dusty. "You blew it. She's never coming back."

Dusty didn't want to believe that, but recalling the way they'd fought earlier, he knew it was true.

"I miss Meg," Billy said from his place on the floor.

"So do we," the twins said. They glared at their father, too.

Dusty sat down on the sofa. He suddenly felt very old and very tired.

"You don't seem too surprised," Lily noted after a moment.

"I'm not, I guess," Dusty confided slowly to his kids. He rested his hat on his knee and creased the brim with his fingertips. "I guess, if I'm to be honest, I expected this from her all along."

"How come?" Jason got off the phone and ambled over to sit beside his dad.

Dusty sighed and wondered how to explain the loss of a dream. "Because Meg always put her career first," Dusty said. "She never really liked it here, even when she was growing up. She couldn't wait to get out of Texas even then." Dusty sighed and sat back on the sofa. "I guess she just got tired of it again."

Lily closed her book and moved to sit on Dusty's other side. "Meg didn't leave town, Daddy," she said. "She's still here."

Dusty felt a flicker of hope. He quickly smashed it down. "Maybe she's leaving in the morning, then."

"Nope. She's not leaving at all," Billy said from his place on the floor.

"Yeah," Susie agreed. "She's not leaving us, Daddy. She's staying for us until we've all grown up and don't need her anymore."

Sallie glared at Dusty. "She's only leaving you 'cause you don't love her enough."

"Don't love her enough!" Dusty echoed. He sat forward, incensed. "What the . . . what's she talking about? I married her, didn't I?"

Lily rolled her eyes. "I think she wants more than that," Lily said.

Jason nodded. "I'm sure she does. Meg's a romantic, Dad. I thought you would've figured that out."

Maybe he should have, Dusty thought. He looked at his kids, a plan already forming in his mind. Slowly he began to smile. "How'd the five of you get so smart?" he teased.

"Easy," the kids said in unison. "Meg!"

"SHE DOESN'T WANT to see you, Dusty," Meg's mother said from the doorway.

Dusty knew it was nearly two in the morning, but some things couldn't wait. He didn't want Meg thinking this was the way life was going to stay. "Tell her it's important," he said.

"It's not going to make any difference," Meg's father insisted. He looked down his nose at Dusty. "You damn near broke her heart, son. Not just once, but twice now."

Dusty nodded contritely. "I know, sir, and I'm sorry, but I can't very well fix things unless I talk to Meg, now can I?"

Meg appeared at the top of the stairs. Her parents were in their nightclothes, but she was still in her sexy black dress.

Her glance surveyed him from head to toe. If she noticed he'd taken the time to shave, shower and slap on some after-shave and clean, ironed clothes before coming over, she didn't show it. "Go away, Dusty," she said. "You and I have said all there is to say!" She turned on her heel, marched back down the hall and slammed her bedroom door.

Her parents and Dusty all sighed in unison. "She always was one for door slamming," her mother said after a moment.

Her dad gave Dusty another once-over. Finally he said, "I guess it wouldn't hurt to give Dusty one more chance to do right by her. They are married, after all."

Dusty sent Meg's folks a grateful grin. "And we're going to stay married if I have anything to do with it," Dusty said firmly.

"Well, in that case, do your best. Mercy knows it's high time the two of you got together and stayed together," Meg's mother said fervently.

"My feelings exactly," Dusty said.

He took the steps two and three at a time and headed straight for her bedroom. "Meg, let me in."

"Go away!" Meg shouted through the closed door.

Dusty could hear her pacing. "We have to talk, Meg."

"When hell freezes over!"

Dusty leaned a shoulder against the frame and crossed one foot over the other. "I'm not leaving until we talk," he said.

"We have nothing to talk about," Meg replied.

Dusty sighed. This really wasn't at all how he'd imagined it. He leaned closer. "How about the fact that I love you?" he said through the door. "Doesn't that make any difference?"

There was a short silence. Meg opened the door and looked at him suspiciously. "What did you say?" she asked.

"That I love you," Dusty repeated softly. He took in the way she looked, with her golden hair all tousled, her cheeks flushed pink, her eyes glowing with both love and suspicion. "I always have and I always will," he said softly.

Meg's lower lip thrust out delectably. "Loving isn't enough," Meg grumbled, and started to shut the door.

Dusty caught it with his hand. "Do your parents still have that wooden swing out in the backyard?" he asked. He gave her a coaxing grin. "You know, the one that hangs from the maple tree?"

"Yes, why?"

"Because it's about time we sat in it again," Dusty said, and scooped her up into his arms.

"Dusty, it's the middle of the night!" Meg said.

"So?" He grinned at her and whispered wickedly, "I won't tell the neighbors if you won't." He carried Meg down the stairs past her folks. "We'll just be out back in the swing," he said.

"We won't interrupt," Meg's father promised.

Meg clung to Dusty's neck. He could feel her trembling. "Mother, do something!" she said.

"Work it out with her, Dusty," Meg's mother advised. "And just so you know, Dusty, if you're ever late for a dinner with us again, I'll skin you alive personally."

"Yes, ma'am, I'll take that under advisement," Dusty said.

"I wish you wouldn't make promises you have no intention of keeping," Meg grumbled as Dusty sat in the center of the wide wooden swing and pulled Meg down across his lap.

"What makes you think I can't turn over a new leaf?" he asked. He nuzzled her neck contentedly. "You have."

"Oh, Dusty." Meg sighed and softened against him a little more.

"Oh, Dusty, what?" he prodded gently.

Meg buried her head in his shoulder and played with the pearl snaps on his shirt. "It's never been a question of our loving each other." She paused and bit her lip. "That was the case from the beginning, wasn't it?"

Dusty tangled his hands in the fragrant softness of her hair. "I think so, even when we were too stubborn to admit it."

"But I want a real marriage," Meg continued to insist.

Dusty cupped her chin and lifted her face to his. "What makes you think I don't?"

She trembled and gave him a look.

Dusty knew he deserved her distrust. "Okay, so maybe I've been saying I didn't. And as it happens, I really didn't want a real marriage at first, mainly because I didn't trust you to stay." Dusty paused and wiped a stray tear from the corner of her eye. "Your dad said I broke your heart. Well, you broke mine, too."

Meg vaulted off his lap. She marched past the swing to the oak trees bordering the backyard. "All the more reason we shouldn't be together." She folded her arms stubbornly.

Dusty followed her to the trees. He placed his hands on her shoulders and turned her to face him. "Look, Meg, I know you're good at your work. I know you can't walk away from it. So if you want to do this new show—" Dusty paused and took what he knew was a giant leap for him "—then I'm all for it."

Meg's eyes narrowed. Tense seconds ticked by. "You wouldn't mind me traveling back and forth to California all the time?"

"I'd miss you, but I'd understand. And I'd cherish the time we had together all that much more."

"Are you just saying this because you still need a wife to run your house and a baby-sitter to ride herd on your kids?"

"No." Dusty took her into his arms and held her against him. "I'm saying it because I can't live without you and don't want to live without you." He drew a deep breath and held her even closer. "You're a part of me, Meg. I don't think I ever realized how much until you came back into my life." He buried his face in her golden hair. "I don't think I could bear to lose you again."

Meg clung to him. "I don't want to lose you, either, Dusty," she whispered.

"So whatever it takes to make this work, I'll do." Dusty said. He paused and took another giant leap, one he'd been too stubborn and self-centered to consider eighteen years ago. "If you want me to sell the ranch and move to California—"

"No." Meg put up a hand to stop him. "I'm tired of California," she said passionately. "That's why I came back. Because I needed to live here again. I needed to come home, Dusty."

He understood that. But he also knew how much she loved her work. "Can you produce that new show from here?" he asked.

Meg shook her head. She looked surprisingly happy for someone who was about to give up the opportunity of a lifetime, Dusty thought.

"No, it'll have to be filmed in California, because that's where all the soundstages and equipment and actors are, but I've been thinking a lot. What I enjoy most about television is the process of developing a show and getting the scripts off the ground. I can be a story editor and oversee script development from right here."

Dusty frowned. He didn't want her taking a demotion because of him. And this sounded like a demotion to him. "How would the network feel about that?"

"Probably pretty good. They've been wanting me to devote myself exclusively to developing new series for some time. Living here, I'll have the time to do that. And, the best part is, I'll be able to make my own schedule, so I'll be able to devote as much time as I want to you and the kids."

Dusty's heart sped up to triple time. "What about your other shows?"

"I've already handed the producing chores over to some very talented people who trained under me. I'm not worried about that. I'm sure they'll do an excellent job. It's the future I want to concern myself with." Meg wreathed her arms around Dusty's neck and gave him a sexy smile.

Hope welled up in him, but he cautioned himself not to take anything for granted. He had done that before to calamitous result. "Future with your job, or future with me?"

"My future with you and the kids. I'm warning you, though, if I come back with you, it has to be for keeps this time." She held up a lecturing finger. "No more walking out when the going gets rough. No more spending the night on the range or the living-room sofa."

"I promise from now on that our bed is where I'm going to be, with you cuddled in my arms. And as long as we're talking about new projects..." Dusty scooped her up in his arms and walked back to the swing. He sat down with her in his lap.

"Yes?"

He traced the sensual curve of her lip with his finger. "How about we work on one of our own?"

Meg sucked in a tremulous breath. She touched her lips to his. "I've always wanted your baby, Dusty."

He ducked his head to hers. "Good." He smiled, then gave her a long, deep, yearning kiss. "Then that's settled, too."

They swung back and forth, quietly savoring the moments. "Girl or boy?" Meg asked at last.

"Doesn't matter," Dusty said contentedly. "The only thing that counts is that we're together." After eighteen years apart, it was about time.

"I like the sound of that." She stood and held out her hand. He took it and rolled to his feet. "Come on." She smiled happily. "Let's go tell the kids their fairy godmother is home to stay."

A Note from Cathy Gillen Thacker

A marriage of convenience—between two people who once loved each other deeply—makes perfect sense to me. But then, I've never put much stock in the way things ought to be.

You see, I have one of those marriages that wasn't *supposed* to work, at least according to the statistics. Charlie and I married while we were still in college. We had no money, no jobs, and were both struggling to get our educations and decide which career paths to take. But amid all the uncertainty we were very sure of one thing: we loved each other and wanted to be together. Not in a few years, when everything was settled, but right then, while we were making the decisions that would determine the rest of our lives. We knew we were a team, and teams do best when they're together.

The wedding was small, with just our immediate families in attendance, our honeymoon an overnight stay in a state park lodge. A day later, we were living in our efficiency apartment on the Miami University campus and back in class. I'd like to tell you our first apartment was a decorator's dream, and that everything went smoothly from the start. But of course it didn't. I discovered in the first three days that Charlie only believed in taking out the trash when he could no longer see the wastebasket amid the debris. He discovered that I didn't put the cap back on the toothpaste—ever. *My* idea of cooking was following a recipe and frantically calling my mother long distance every five minutes to see if I was doing it right. *His* idea of cooking was opening something packaged or canned and heating it *almost* all the way through. And that was just the beginning of discovering our faults and flaws! Before the first week was over, we both wondered what we had done. Where was that perfect person we had fallen in love with?

The truth was, of course, that the "perfect" people didn't exist. We were both human, smart as whips, stubborn as mules and opinionated to a fault. And...we realized we still loved each other very much—even though we knew we had a *lot* to work out.

These days, Charlie has learned to live with my not putting the cap back on the toothpaste, and I take the garbage out whenever I see fit. I do most of the cooking. He looks after repairs on the cars. We both mow the lawn and do laundry and can handle any emergency, domestic or familial, that comes up. We have three wonderful children, two of whom are now in college; the youngest is in middle school. We've moved cross-country several times. Endured the ups and downs of both our careers. Guided our children in the search for theirs. And he can still make me laugh like no one else. We share our fears and secrets, hopes and dreams, on a daily basis. And after nearly a quarter of a century of togetherness, he remains not just my lover and life partner, but my best and dearest friend.

From my experience I've learned two things. First, marriage is worth every ounce of hard work and sacrifice you put into it. And second, forget the statistics. You don't need money or career success or the perfect place to live to make a go of marriage. You don't even need to be a certain age. You do need love—lots of it—and patience in abundance. Tolerance and understanding will naturally follow, as will the dividends from loving well and being loved well in return.

I wish you all happy marriages of your own.

And I hope you enjoyed reading Meg and Dusty's love story in "Dear Fairy Godmother" as much as I enjoyed writing it.

MARRIAGE ON THE RUN
Jasmine Cresswell

Chapter One

OTHER PEOPLE had eccentric great-aunts who kept too many cats, or wore funny hats, or always ate TV dinners. Great-Aunt Bette blew up garages. She didn't mean to, of course, but her chemical experiments had a disastrous tendency to go explosively wrong. Consequently, when Laura checked her answering machine and heard Great-Aunt Bette proclaiming an emergency and asking her to come to Columbus at once, Laura called the airline and booked the first available flight. She considered the chances no better than fifty-fifty that her aunt's newest garage would still be standing by the time the plane landed in Ohio.

But for once it seemed she'd been too pessimistic, Laura thought, paying off the cab that had driven her from Columbus airport to the quiet, tree-lined suburb of Arlington, Ohio. Aunt Bette's house and garage were both still standing, and the latest roof looked unscathed. No smoke belched with chemical fury from any of the windows. Most astonishing of all, the grass in the small front yard was neatly mowed, a concession to suburban order that Aunt Bette usually ignored as beneath the dignity of a scientific genius such as herself.

Laura jumped nervously when a feminine voice sounded behind her, calling her name. She spun around and saw one of Aunt Bette's neighbors waving across the garden fence.

"Hello, Renée." Laura spoke cautiously, preparing herself to hear the worst, despite the neighbor's cheery smile.

"Laura, how nice to see you, and looking so calm, too!"

Her stomach clenched. "Should I be looking, um, worried?"

Renée chuckled. "I guess not, with Stefano waiting for you. Bette wasn't sure when you'd arrive! All set for the big day?"

What big day? And who was Stefano? Laura started to sweat, but long experience had taught her it was much better to confront Aunt Bette directly, not get garbled versions of the current calamity from friends and neighbors. Somehow, she managed to return Renée's beaming smile.

"We're all set," she said, just as if she knew exactly what she was talking about. "Isn't it a lovely evening?"

Renée rolled her eyes. "Well, the humidity has been driving me crazy, but I can understand how you feel, I was just the same— Oops, there's my phone. See you tomorrow, my dear."

Glad to escape, Laura waved goodbye and continued up the path to the front door. Renée and Aunt Bette had always been good friends, so if Renée was cheerful, perhaps the situation wasn't too serious. Ringing the doorbell, Laura allowed herself a faint glimmer of hope. Maybe Aunt Bette simply wanted Laura to write a rude letter to the United States government. Aunt Bette conducted running battles with various government departments, including the IRS and the FBI. Her animosity toward the IRS rose and fell according to the season and the status of her tax return, but her dislike of the FBI had been unwavering ever since the occasion, some twenty years earlier, when the bureau had chosen to investigate one of her exploding garages. Bette had despised the FBI special agents assigned to the case.

"They were even more dim-witted and boring than Walter Willis," she would say in recounting the story. "Good grief, they thought that the mere existence of some absurd local ordinance was a valid reason to stop the march of scientific progress." Walter Willis was Aunt Bette's ex-husband, the man she had dropped out of college to marry. To accuse someone of being more boring than Walter was Bette's greatest insult.

Laura knew better than to get embroiled in a discussion about Walter Willis. Instead, she concentrated her efforts on writing placating letters to government officials and doing her best to keep Bette out of jail. She loved Aunt Bette and was anxious to keep her a free woman, if at all possible.

But where was Aunt Bette? Shifting uneasily, Laura peered in through the leaded-glass panel set into the door. All she could see was a stretch of empty hallway. The house remained ominously silent. Why hadn't her aunt answered the door? Laura's brief moment of optimism vanished, gobbled up by dread. Visualizing her aunt either pacing the concrete floor of a prison cell or stretched out unconscious over a rack of poisonous test tubes, she rang the doorbell again, longer this time, and banged the old-fashioned door knocker for good measure.

To her relief, the response this time was immediate. She heard the sound of footsteps coming from inside the house, and after another ten seconds or so, the door was finally opened, although not by Aunt Bette. A tall dark handsome man, with a pair of spectacular smoldering brown eyes, stood framed in the doorway. As soon as he saw Laura, his mouth quirked into a devastatingly sexy smile that displayed perfect white teeth and an entrancing mischievous dimple in his right cheek.

Laura took one look at the man, and her heart plummeted right to the soles of her sensible summer sandals. Aunt Bette, she decided grimly, was in even worse trouble than she'd feared.

"Hello, you must be Laura. Your aunt has been so anxious for your arrival." The man took her hand in a firm warm handshake. "I am most sorry to keep you waiting, but Bette and I were in the basement."

Every one of Laura's alarm systems jangled in immediate red alert. "In the basement?" she said, in a voice slightly cooler than an Arctic ice floe. "Doing what?"

"We were ... experimenting." If she hadn't known better, she'd have sworn the man was being deliberately provocative. He held her gaze, his eyes twinkling with what many women would no doubt have considered lethal charm.

"I am Stefano Corelli," he said. "I am your aunt's friend and also her colleague. Please do come in. Bette has been waiting for your arrival with much eagerness."

This must be the Stefano Aunt Bette's neighbor had mentioned. He not only looked like a cross between Rudolph Valentino and a young Marlon Brando, but he also spoke with a beguiling hint of an Italian accent. The hairs on the back of Laura's neck prickled, and her palms started to sweat. This man meant serious trouble, she knew it beyond any possibility of doubt. Aunt Bette's foibles weren't limited to blowing up garages and writing rude letters to the lawfully appointed agencies of the government. She also suffered from a disastrous tendency to pick unsuitable friends who turned out to be charlatans at best, or outright criminals at worst. This man was too darned handsome and too darned sure of himself to be honest. What could a six-foot hunk of sexy Italian manhood find interesting about seventy-two-year-old Aunt Bette?

Laura had well-honed instincts for sniffing out fakes. Having grown up in Manhattan, with parents almost as eccentric as her great-aunt, she prided herself on possessing all the practical worldly wisdom the rest of her family lacked. She knew from experience that men with melting eyes, sensual smiles and cute dimples were *always* too good to be true. When you got to know such men a little better, you discovered that they were frauds who wore tinted contact lenses and spent hours practicing their smiles in front of the bathroom mirror. Nine times out of ten, they even had their dimples surgically implanted.

The man—Stefano—smiled at her again, and Laura's stomach gave an odd little jump. Of warning, no doubt. When she realized he was still holding her hand, she pulled away from his clasp, her movements jerky and uncoordinated.

"Stefano Corelli? My aunt has never mentioned your name. You must be a new acquaintance." She spoke with the cool courteous formality she had found most effective in dealing with Aunt Bette's retinue of no-hopers and entered the familiar hallway of her aunt's home without waiting for him to issue a invitation.

Stefano stepped aside, gesturing with European flair to indicate that she should precede him. "Yes, that is true. I am a very new friend of your aunt, but I hope also a good one."

Laura looked up at him, meeting his gaze but refusing to respond to the friendly welcome she saw in his eyes. Charm, for most of the con men Aunt Bette collected, was an even more necessary quality than good looks, and Laura dismissed his overtures for what they were worth—precisely nothing.

"How did the two of you meet?" she asked, putting down her overnight bag and leading the way into the comfortable cluttered living room. She looked around anxiously for subtle signs of whatever her aunt's current problem might be. On the surface everything seemed to be normal—at least for Aunt Bette—but Laura's stomach was already performing a jig of anxiety. Her instincts were infallible where her aunt was concerned, and she was beginning to suspect that she had walked into the midst of a major problem.

"How did your aunt and I meet? We found each other at a university cocktail party." Stefano gave another of his devastating smiles. "As a newcomer to the department of chemical engineering, I was feeling most alone. Your aunt was kind enough to tuck me under her wing, and we have spent much time together ever since."

That figured. Stefano had obviously spotted a gullible victim and latched on like a leech. Poor Aunt Bette hadn't stood a chance. "My aunt is an exceptionally generous woman," Laura said.

"She is indeed." Stefano showed not a hint of guilt. "It was a privilege to meet her. She is a woman of...astonishing intellect."

Laura heard the tiny hesitation before he spoke the last couple of words, and she smothered a quick flare of defensive anger. It was all right for her to question Aunt Bette's achievements, but she resented this outsider's obvious sarcasm.

"Are you sure you're qualified to judge my aunt's intelligence?" she snapped.

He looked taken aback, but any response he might have made was lost in a flurry of air and the bounce of sneaker-clad footsteps. Aunt Bette erupted from the basement, perennially innocent blue eyes sparkling and hair spiking around her head in a silver halo of excitement.

"Laura, dearest, you've come!" Her aunt enveloped her in a bear hug that smelled of equal parts Giorgio perfume and something sulfurous. After giving her niece a kiss, she pushed her away and examined her critically. "You're looking better than usual. Your clothes are still hopeless, but you've changed your hair. Being blond suits you."

Laura blushed. Trust Aunt Bette to notice the change in her hair color and to comment on it with Stefano listening. Laura's hair was thick and wavy, but it's natural color was a boring nondescript brown. A couple of months ago she'd been seized by a burst of spring fever. On the spur of the moment, she had walked into her local salon and asked the hairdresser to highlight the mousy strands with streaks of bright apricot gold. Laura was self-conscious about the dramatic result, which she realized was totally unsuited to her life-style. As a senior accountant working in the tax department of Peabody Foreman, a giant New York law firm, she needed to dress soberly.

But somehow, despite her doubts about the new hair color and the outspoken disapproval of Brett Hotchkiss, her boyfriend, she had gone back to the salon three weeks ago to have the golden streaks renewed. Laura was alarmed at what this desire for flamboyance indicated about her character. It seemed as if some secret part of her bore a disturbing resemblance to Aunt Bette. The truth was that she felt a tiny kick of pleasure each morning as she stepped out of the shower and blow-dried her hair into a dazzling cloud.

Bette gave her another hug. "You must be thirsty after your plane journey. We must all have a drink," she said, a declaration that could produce anything from carrot juice to coffee to vintage burgundy. "No, no, Laura, you've had a long flight. Sit down and get acquainted with Stefano while I make the tea. I know you two are going to like each other a lot. I'm just sure of it." With a beaming smile at both of them, Bette disappeared into the kitchen.

Stefano sat down, leaning back against the sofa cushions and looking thoroughly at home. "I have noticed a funny thing," he said, giving Laura a smile that was considerably less warm than the one he'd greeted her with. "Whenever a friend of mine introduces me to someone and tells me I'm going to like that person, it never seems to work out."

"In Aunt Bette's case that isn't surprising," Laura said. "Her judgment about people is terrible."

Stefano's smile tightened still further. "Do you find it so?" he inquired blandly. "For myself, until I met you, I would have said her judgment was excellent."

Until I met you . . . During the course of her work, Laura often found herself trading barbs with corporate financial sharks who used words as a form of unarmed combat. Under the circumstances, it was strange that Stefano's mild gibe hurt. Quelling an impulse to apologize, she sat down in a snug old armchair and sent him a stern assessing look. "You were about to tell me some more about the circumstances under which you and my aunt met, Mr. Corelli."

"No, I wasn't," he said softly. "You were conducting an inquisition on that subject. I had expressed no intentions at all. But now I will do so. The prickles of dislike coming from you are making me uncomfortable, so I believe I will go into the kitchen and help my good friend, Bette. I can rely on her to provide company that is always most enjoyable. Excuse me, if you please."

He rose to his feet, shoved his hands into the pockets of his slacks—a piece of clothing that accomplished the amazing feat of being both fashionably baggy and yet skintight across his hips—and strolled with casual nonchalance toward the kitchen.

Ill-mannered lout! Laura fumed silently for a couple of minutes, but by the time Bette returned, she'd mellowed enough to realize she was being ridiculous. Stefano's only crime so far was to exude an aura of blatant sexuality that left Laura feeling uneasy. Which, when you got right down to it, was her problem, not his. She watched almost enviously as Bette and Stefano sauntered into the living room, chuckling over some private joke. Stefano was carrying a large tray laden with a teapot, cups, saucers and a plate of warm muffins wafting delicious smells of apple and cinnamon. He set the tray on the table and bowed over Bette's hand.

"All ready for you to do the honors, signora."

Laura's stomach muscles clenched in suspicion. Why the heck was Stefano being so nice to Bette? What did he stand to gain? Then she told herself to stop being ridiculous and give Stefano the benefit of the doubt. Maybe he was just exceptionally gallant and bowed over old ladies' hands all the time. She forced herself to smile at him as she went to the table, sniffing appreciatively. "Those muffins look wonderful, don't they, Stefano? I didn't know you'd taken up baking, Aunt Bette."

"I haven't. Stefano made them." Bette beamed at her new protégé with maternal pride. "Wait until you taste his zabaglione. He's a great cook."

"How...unexpected," Laura murmured, her suspicions returning with the speed of light.

"Not at all," Stefano said, offering Bette the plate of muffins and grinning at her affectionately. "These days, every smart bachelor realizes that the way to a woman's heart is through his kitchen."

"True," Bette said. "Your cooking would have won my heart a hundred times over, even if you'd been a dud as a scientist. These muffins are scrumptious." She sat down and sighed contentedly. "Now, Laura, you must tell me how everything is at home. And at work, of course." Bette turned to Stefano. "Have I told you that Laura is likely to be the youngest woman her firm has made partner? And the first partner ever who isn't a lawyer."

Stefano squeezed Bette's hand and grinned affectionately. "I think you may have mentioned it once or twice, *cara*. In between telling me how beautiful she is and how sweet-tempered."

Bette flicked away a crumb. "Well, was I right?"

Stefano looked up, his gaze locking with Laura's. "Your niece is most exceptionally beautiful," he said.

Laura felt heat flare deep inside and rush upward into her cheeks. She glanced down and found herself staring at Stefano's strong brown fingers curled over Aunt Bette's tiny blue-veined hand. She blinked and hurriedly focused her thoughts on her aunt's original question.

"Everyone is fine at home," she said briskly. "Dad likes the new director of the orchestra, and he's been teaching a master class at the Juilliard, which gives him a lot of satisfaction. And Mother is working on a new story line for her soap, which she thinks will be a surefire ratings winner. She's combined a missing heir, a baby who needs a lifesaving transplant and a love triangle involving a woman, a man and a person who could be either."

"Either of what?" Bette asked, looking puzzled.

"Either a man or a woman. Mother plans to decide later in the season when she has a few more plot twists laid down."

For once Aunt Bette seemed at a loss for words. "It sounds spectacular," Stefano said. "Your mother needs only to make her man/woman into an Elvis reincarnation, and I'd say she was on to a ratings blockbuster."

Laura laughed. "Good point. I'll suggest that to her."

"I'm not going to ask you to explain what you're talking about," Bette said. "Let's change the subject to something I can understand. How is Brett? Still working hard?"

"Very hard, and he's fine, thank you. Hoping for a promotion next month."

"That's good, dear. He seems such a nice solid young man."

"He's very reliable," Laura agreed, giving her aunt a grateful smile. Bette was always willing to accept other people's life-style choices, which was one of the reasons Laura loved her so much. Unlike Laura's parents, who had taken a totally unreasonable dislike to Brett, Aunt Bette never said he was a stick-in-the-mud or attempted to persuade Laura to end the relationship.

"Brett is Laura's boyfriend, as well as her boss," Bette explained to Stefano. "He's just finished writing a book. What's the book about, Laura, dear?"

"The tax implications of profit repatriation for American corporations."

"How . . . fascinating." Stefano reached for another muffin.

Bette smiled brightly. "Brett is an exceptionally well-informed young man, and he's always anxious to share everything he knows with anyone willing to listen. Have you two gotten any further in settling on a wedding date?" she asked Laura, pouring more tea all around.

"Er, no. Actually we aren't even officially engaged," Laura mumbled, taking her cup back from Bette.

Now why had she felt compelled to produce that piece of information? Laura wondered. Brett had asked her to marry him more than two months ago. And last month he'd produced a tasteful diamond solitaire ring, which he politely asked to slip on her finger. She had stuttered and hesitated and finally refused, although she was quite sure that one day soon—very soon—she would accept his proposal. In fact, the more she thought about it, the more difficult it was to understand why she hadn't agreed to marry Brett the moment he asked. He was everything she wanted in a man: calm, organized, thoughtful, conservative. And a crashing bore. She quickly pushed the disloyal thought away. It was surely a mark of her erratic upbringing, and her own lingering immaturity, that she couldn't distinguish between a well-ordered life and a boring one. Brett was a man who had the details of his life under firm control. That didn't make him dull or tedious or any of the other adjectives her parents constantly used to describe him.

"Brett and I are both so busy at work," she said. "Sometimes our personal lives just have to take a back seat."

"To corporate taxes," Aunt Bette said, with suspicious blandness. "Well, you know I've never quite been able to understand your mutual devotion to IRS form 1040."

Laura had long since given up trying to convince her aunt that counseling corporations on their tax liabilities involved more complex and far more interesting decisions than how to fill in the blanks on a standard tax-return form. She decided it was time, past time, to get the subject away from her relationship with Brett and back to basics. Such as why Aunt Bette had summoned her from New York with a frantic telephone message.

"Well, boring forms or not, I'm terribly busy at work, Aunt Bette, so maybe we should get right down to business. What exactly is the problem you need me to help you with? Why did you ask me to fly out here to visit you?"

For the first time, Aunt Bette began to look a little nervous. "It's just a small favor," she said. "Nothing that would inconvenience you in a major way."

Laura sighed. "Out with it, Auntie. The more you protest like that, the more nervous I get. What is this 'small' favor you want me to do?"

"Absolutely nothing to get excited about."

"Then tell me."

Aunt Bette drew a deep breath. "I need you to marry Stefano," she said. "Tomorrow morning, if you wouldn't mind."

Chapter Two

LAURA STARED at her aunt in shocked silence. Then she laughed. "All right, Aunt Bette, now please tell me the real reason you sent me that frantic message."

"But that *is* the reason," Bette said. "I need you to marry Stefano as soon as possible."

"B-but why? Wh-what for?"

"I'm not suggesting a real marriage, of course. Just the sort of union they used to call a 'marriage of convenience' in my mother's day." Bette seemed to think this explanation made her proposal entirely reasonable. She smiled brightly. "I can quite see that you wouldn't want to enter into a real marriage with a man you didn't know. Besides, I daresay Brett wouldn't be at all happy with the idea of your marrying Stefano. Not if it was going to be permanent."

Laura recovered the use of her voice. "He certainly wouldn't! What's more, *I'm* not at all happy with the idea. In fact, I couldn't possibly consider it. It's crazy!"

Bette leaned forward and took her niece's hand. "You have to understand the problem, dear, before you can leap to conclusions about whether my solution is crazy. The point is that if Stefano doesn't get married soon, he's going to be arrested and thrown into jail. You wouldn't want that, would you?"

"Don't bet on it," Laura muttered. All her doubts about Stefano rushed back in a tidal wave of disapproval. She had no difficulty believing he was in trouble with the law, but how matrimony would help his plight, she couldn't imagine. Whatever the details, he was clearly using Aunt Bette for his own ends. Any desire to laugh or treat her aunt's suggestion as a joke vanished. "Aunt Bette, if Stefano's committed a crime, marrying me isn't going to keep him out of trouble."

"Actually I have not committed a crime," Stefano said. "Not even a very small one."

Laura swung around, her expression severe. "The police don't usually waste their time and energy pursuing innocent people."

"They are overworked and understaffed. They are also human." He shrugged. "Sometimes they make mistakes."

"And in your case, they've made a mistake?"

Stefano didn't seem to hear her sarcasm. He smiled cheerfully. "But of course. In my case they have made a most terrible mistake. Besides, it is not precisely the police who are chasing me. It is the enforcement officers of the Immigration and Naturalization Service. They wish to deport me as an illegal alien. They have threatened to fly me out of the country on the next available plane." Stefano looked hurt at the mere thought that anyone, least of all the INS, might want to get rid of him.

"Precisely how have these INS agents made a mistake?" Laura asked. "If you're not an illegal immigrant, why do they think you are?"

"Well, it is just possible that—technically speaking—I may be an illegal resident. Under a strict interpretation of the rules, you understand." Stefano gave another charming self-deprecating shrug. "But it is all one big mix-up, you know? Unfortunately I cannot convince the Immigration and Naturalization Service to stop chasing me long enough to listen while I make my explanations. They say that I have entered the country without legal papers, and now they wish to make an example of me by deporting me. It seems there have been too many foreigners entering the United States on student visas and then disappearing into the criminal underground when it is time for them to go home."

"And that's what you've done?" Laura asked.

"How can you ask that when I am here with Bette? Of course I am not disappearing into the criminal underground." Stefano sounded wounded that she could even suggest such a thing. "Nor did I enter America on a student visa. At least, I did not do so intentionally. I came here under a quota that grants special residence status for experts and scholars."

Laura knew better than to judge people purely by their outward appearance, but it was very difficult to imagine Stefano, with his athletic body, melting brown eyes and sexy dimple, fitting into the category of "expert and scholar."

"And what, precisely, are you an expert on?" she asked, barely bothering to conceal her sarcasm. *Women* was the answer that flashed into Laura's mind.

For the first time Stefano looked embarrassed. "I would not claim that I am an expert on anything."

"Nonsense," Aunt Bette interrupted. "He's a professor at the University of Bologna, in Italy, and he's also this year's visiting professor in chemical engineering at Ohio State, a position that entitles him—"

Laura blinked at Stefano in amazement. "You're a *professor* of chemical engineering?" The question tumbled out with an embarrassing lack of tact.

"Why, yes." Stefano appeared amused. "Is there some reason I should not be a professor?"

She swallowed hard. "No. No, of course not. It's just that you look so, um, young...." That wasn't quite what she'd intended to say, but it was better than telling him he looked too damn sexy to be a chemist.

"I am thirty-five," he said. "Nearly thirty-six. Even in Italy, that is quite old enough to have accumulated several college degrees. And once you have enough fancy letters after your name, there is always some university that feels obliged to hire you."

Laura didn't think it was quite as simple as he made it sound to attain a full professorship by the age of thirty-five, but she didn't allow herself to be sidetracked. After years of dealing with Aunt Bette, she had learned how important it was to stick to the main subject. "But if you're a member of the faculty at Ohio State, I don't understand the problem. Why hasn't the university's legal department taken care of your visa mix-up?"

His shrug was eloquent. "They have tried, but it is one of those horrific bureaucratic muddles that are everyone's fault—and nobody's. Alas, the clerk who processed my paperwork seems not to have filled out the correct forms, but she no longer works for the university, so nobody knows why she failed to complete the proper paperwork. And nobody, of course, has any explanation as to why the error was not spotted until now, when it is too late to make the necessary applications for a correction."

The knowledge that Stefano was simply the victim of a paperwork snafu filled Laura with relief. The man's ethical standards were no business of hers, except as they affected Aunt Bette; but oddly enough she was rather glad he hadn't committed a real crime. For some reason she wasn't at all anxious to see him clapped in jail. She risked giving him a cautious smile.

"Look, Stefano, I think you're worrying too much about your visa situation. Bette has a jaundiced view of the government, and she's probably scared you more than she should. I deal with the Internal Revenue Service every day, and the folks over there make the INS look like Sunday school teachers." She leaned forward, stressing her point. "Reason will get you much further than emotion, Stefano. Just tell the INS they've made a mistake. Be polite, but firm—"

Stefano sighed. "I wish it were so simple! But, alas, the INS doesn't wish to be reasonable and accept a correct revised application. The university lawyers are working on my behalf, but naturally they cannot permit me to remain in the employ of the Chemical Engineering Department when my status is not legal. Their hands are tied. My lawyers are, however, confident that when my case comes up for official review, I will certainly be given permission to remain and teach my courses."

"Then I don't see why you have a problem."

Stefano smiled wryly. "Unfortunately the INS insists that I must return to Italy to await the outcome of the court hearing they plan to hold."

"That must be frustrating for you and for everyone," Laura said. "But it seems quite fair and reasonable, given the problems this country has with illegal immigrants."

Aunt Bette snorted. "Fair, you say? *Reasonable?* I suppose it might be, except that the INS estimates it will take five years for Stefano's case to come to trial."

"Five years!" Laura was appalled. "But that's outrageous!"

"It could be even longer than five years," Stefano said gloomily. "Or a few months less, of course, although even the INS does not hold out such a hope." He spread his hands wide in a helpless gesture. "For the university it is frustrating that I cannot fulfill my contract and deliver a series of lectures during the fall semester, but they have given up hope of—how do you say?—fighting city hall. But for your aunt, and now for me, it is vital that I stay in the country. Our work together has reached a critical point—"

"An extremely critical point," Aunt Bette asserted. "I can't possibly go on without him."

"Actually, *cara*, I'm not at all sure that is true. You learn so fast.... Anyway, suffice to say that Bette has become my champion against the raiders of the INS. A most fierce and noble champion, I should add. She was very excited when she came up with this plan for a marriage with you as a way to salvage my right to live and work in the United States. I told her we could not hope that you would say yes, but Bette . . ." Stefano glanced at Bette, his gaze almost tender. "Your aunt—she is most persuasive."

"I believe you. Aunt Bette's a scrappy fighter." Laura sighed. Her aunt's heart was as wide and generous as the Mississippi, but she had no grasp on practicalities. Laura didn't doubt for a moment that it was Aunt Bette who'd come up with the crazy idea of marrying her off to Stefano. The scheme was vintage Aunt Bette. Realizing there was no way to convince the woman that the idea was unreasonable, Laura turned to Stefano again in the hope he would have a better understanding of reality.

"Stefano, I'm sorry. I can see this is a rotten situation for you. I've read some of the stories in the newspapers about the activities of the INS, and I realize the whole agency is overworked and backed up in their paperwork to a point that's a national scandal. But you can surely understand that I can't marry you just because you're having visa problems." She shook her head. "I'm sorry, but the whole idea is crazy! Not to mention illegal. The truth is, we could both end up in jail if anyone found out what we'd done."

She should have known better than to add those final sentences. Aunt Bette took up the charge at once. "Illegal!" she exclaimed, jumping to her feet. "Hah! In this country it will soon be illegal to blow your nose without asking for permission from the government! We citizens have got to stand up for our rights—"

"But that's the whole point." Laura cut off her aunt before Bette could launch into one of her impassioned lectures on America's vanishing liberties. "Stefano *isn't* a citizen of the United States. He is an illegal alien."

Her aunt was not to be bested. "But if you marry him, he won't be illegal anymore, and certainly not an alien. Ridiculous phrase, 'illegal alien.' It sounds as though the INS expects him to jump aboard his spaceship the moment their backs are turned." Bette wriggled on her chair cushion, smiling triumphantly. "So you see, Laura, you must marry him right away—it solves all our problems."

Long experience warned Laura that direct arguments would be useless. "Why are you so anxious to have Stefano remain in the United States?" She turned to Stefano. "For that matter, why are you so anxious to stay?"

Stefano hesitated, exchanging a secretive glance with Bette. "There are several reasons," Bette said vaguely. Laura had the strangest impression that her aunt looked momentarily scared.

"Aunt Bette?" she said. "Has something happened to frighten you?"

"Good heavens, no." Bette's smile returned at once. "I was worried about Stefano of course, but nothing else. I really need him here, Laura."

"Why?"

Stefano gave Laura another of his suspiciously sexy smiles. "As you've probably gathered, your aunt and I are nearing completion of a very important project," he said. "Bette has achieved a major breakthrough in the technology of fabric manufacture. She has provided the scientific insights and most of the hard work, but I have been able to offer her some good advice on how to take commercial advantage of her discoveries and also how to streamline the process of production."

"We've patented everything," Bette said smugly. "Three major companies are negotiating with us to buy our formula."

"It is amazing to me what extraordinary success your aunt has achieved with such limited laboratory equipment," Stefano said, glancing at Bette with every appearance of genuine admiration. "Frankly, it reminds me once again that in the field of science it is ideas and brainpower that count, not the splendor of the work setting."

Stefano wasn't telling her more than half the truth, Laura was sure of it. Her suspicions about him returned in full force. Too many of her aunt's previous partners had rhapsodized about Bette's amazing achievements, usually only days before they took off with the contents of her bank account. Bette had no formal scientific training, and years of exploding garage "laboratories" had left Laura unable to believe that her aunt really hovered on the verge of a major scientific discovery. Walter Willis, Bette's ex-husband, had a lot to answer for, Laura thought wryly. He had been a chemical engineer, and he was the person who had set Bette off on her lifetime hobby of scientific experimentation. And as far as Stefano was concerned, if he was truly a trained scientist, a professor as he claimed, he would be in an excellent position to know that although Bette was a wonderful kind bright person, she was a rank amateur in the field of experimental chemistry.

"Explain to me some more," Laura said, unable to keep a renewed chill from entering her voice. "I don't understand exactly what it is you've discovered, Aunt Bette."

"In layman's terms, it's hard to say more than that we've developed a process for manufacturing a completely new sort of fabric," she said promptly. "We're very excited about the potential, aren't we, Stefano?"

"Very excited," he agreed, giving her another fond smile.

"What's different this time, Aunt Bette?" Laura asked with more than a touch of weariness. "You've been working on this project for years. I distinctly remember that new-fabric development was the cause of exploding garages numbers two and three."

"And now all my years of work have finally paid off," Bette said. "At long last we'll be able to recoup the cost of all those exploding garages you keep on about, Laura. Maybe we can even charge them off as a development expense on my next income tax return."

"Wouldn't that be great?" Stefano grinned at Bette before turning to face Laura. "Your aunt has taken a giant step forward in technology," he said. "We are working on the last few minor kinks in a process that will enable us to manufacture a fiber that is made of natural cellulose, like rayon, but with the strength and durability of fibers made from artificial polymers, like nylon. The combination produces a yarn that's soft and pliable, but nearly indestructible."

"Think of it, Laura!" Bette's baby blue eyes shone with enthusiasm. "Once my new fabrics are in production, companies will be able to manufacture a cloth that drapes and breathes like a natural fiber but washes and wears like polyester."

"It sounds wonderful," Laura said. "Almost too good to be true, in fact."

"But your aunt has made the impossible dream a reality," Stefano said.

Bette leaned forward in her chair. "There's so little work left to be done," she said. "And Stefano has all the training and the expertise I lack. Alone, we both have good skills. But together, we create a synergy. With his skills and mine, we can reach an answer to these last few problems in a matter of weeks—maybe even days—I know we can. By myself, it would take me another year at least. In fact, I might never resolve the final problems. I've reached the point where my lack of formal training in chemistry is really a handicap."

"You're too modest, *cara*." Stefano patted Bette on the hand. "You are a genius. You would succeed sooner than you believe."

Laura's temper snapped. She couldn't bear the idea of Bette being taken advantage of yet again. "For heaven's sake!" she burst out, directing her anger toward Stefano. "The pair of you don't seriously expect me to believe that you've cooked up a product in my aunt's garage that's going to revolutionize cloth manufacturing in this country!"

"Not in the garage," Bette explained patiently, "in the basement. I have my laboratory in the basement nowadays. So much more room, and we avoid the problem of all those gasoline fumes."

Laura gritted her teeth. "That's not the point, Aunt Bette. How could you and Stefano achieve a breakthrough that's eluded everyone else, including giant chemical corporations like Dow and Monsanto? They've spent millions of dollars on research and development, and you're claiming that the two of you beat them to the punch—with test-tube experiments in your basement, no less!"

Stefano looked at her coolly. "You misunderstand the situation," he said. "*The two of us* haven't discovered anything. It is your aunt who has made the breakthrough. Your aunt alone. And she has achieved this amazing feat because she has one of the most creative and brilliant scientific minds I have ever encountered."

Bette blushed. "You were a big help, Stefano. You know you were."

"Yes, sure," he said, giving her another friendly grin. "I was great at washing test tubes and keying your experimental data into the computer, while you produced the ideas."

Aunt Bette waved her hands in a dismissive gesture. "Stefano, you're much too modest, but we don't have time to argue right now. We have to get you married so that we can see this project through to the end."

His mouth twisted ruefully. "A most excellent idea, *cara*, but it seems that I lack a bride."

"Nonsense. Laura takes a while to shake loose from her inhibitions, but she always sees the point in the end, don't you, dear?"

Laura was struck speechless by this novel view of her behavior patterns. Aunt Bette took advantage of the silence. "You see? She's not protesting anymore. She's beginning to see reason."

Laura stuttered, but Aunt Bette gave her no chance to become coherent. "Well, then, dear, now that you understand the situation, I take it that everything's settled, at least in principle? Laura, I don't want you to think that this marriage to Stefano is going to be a major imposition or anything like that—"

"Heaven's no! What's a wedding or two between friends? Do you want us to have the ceremony before lunch or afterward?"

She should never have risked being sarcastic. Aunt Bette beamed her approval. "Oh, definitely before lunch. The sooner the better. I'm sure that weasely little INS agent is going to track Stefano down any minute now."

"Which INS agent is this?" Laura asked.

Bette, of course, totally ignored the question. "I'd better go and call Judge Waterman right away to confirm our appointment for tomorrow morning." Jumping to her feet with an agility that would have done a woman of thirty proud, Bette enveloped Stefano in a bear hug. "You see, Stefano? I told you she always behaves sensibly in the end."

"Sensibly!" Laura finally recovered her voice. "Look, Aunt Bette, I wasn't serious—"

"Dearest, your problem is that you're always much too serious. But I admit we do need to discuss a few practical details. However, everything can wait until I have Judge Waterman all lined up and ready. Now, where did I put his phone number?" Aunt Bette peered around, pulled out a notepad from under the teapot and glanced at the chicken scratches that passed for her handwriting. "Ah! Here it is! I knew I'd written it down somewhere." She waved the pad with a triumphant flourish and bounded from the room.

An ominous silence followed her departure. Stefano cleared his throat. "I have a most strong feeling that the wedding Bette is arranging will not take place."

His quiet statement pierced the bubble of Laura's anger. Ridiculous, but she almost felt guilty for not agreeing to get married at twelve hours' notice to a man she'd just met. A man she didn't trust and suspected of lying. At the moment, however, Stefano didn't look like a con man. He looked like a handsome intelligent man, struggling to find a way out of a difficult situation. She tried to stop reacting emotionally to the situation and point out to him calmly why Bette's scheme was so impossible.

"Look, I'm sorry, Stefano. I truly wish I could help you out of this tricky visa situation, but getting married is out of the question. The concept of marriage means something special to me...."

"I quite understand," he said quickly. "In fact, I blame myself for allowing Bette to summon you here. Selfishly I did not try very hard to dissuade her from her grand idea. I thought only of Bette's work and how a stupid legalistic tangle will prevent me from helping her to achieve something that will benefit people everywhere.''

"I don't understand what you mean."

"An easy-care fabric that is strong and yet attractive would make life easier for many people. Mothers who must wash their children's clothes, organizations that must provide uniforms, furniture manufacturers that would like hard-wearing attractive upholstery fabric at low prices. The list goes on and on."

The guilt feelings were growing. Laura clung to the threads of her common sense. "Stefano, even if Aunt Bette's project is as terrific as you say—''

"Why do you doubt it?" he asked. "Is that not insulting to your aunt? To doubt her ability to produce a great work?''

"Of course not," she said, horrified by his accusation. "For heaven's sake, I love Aunt Bette—''

"Love her—and patronize her," he said. "The quaint old lady in tennis shoes, who can never quite remember where she left her umbrella. Naturally she could not have developed anything genuinely important."

"No. Good God, no!" The denial was heartfelt, but Laura flushed, appalled to recognize a smidgen of truth in Stefano's accusation. But only a smidgen. She might have doubts about Bette's chemical experiments—and heaven knew, she had some justification for her doubts in view of the many past failures—but she loved her aunt without reservation. Laura not only recognized Bette's insightful original perspective on the world, she genuinely valued it. Ever since she'd been a toddler, Bette had wrapped Laura in a blanket of warm affection and unstinting praise, closing the emotional gap left by her parents' absorption in their own marriage and careers. The truth was that she owed Aunt Bette. Big time.

She got up and paced the living room. "Aunt Bette is very important to me," she said. "I would do almost anything to help her."

"Except sign your name next to mine on a marriage certificate."

"Unfortunately I can't just sign my name and walk away. Once we go through the ceremony, we'll be married. Husband and wife. Joined at the hip and so on and so on."

"We would be married only in strictly legal terms. You would surely agree that a true marriage consists of something more than two names on a government form." Stefano caught and held her gaze. "In fact," he said softly, "even in legal terms, a marriage requires more than two signatures on a piece of paper to be considered complete. There is the little matter of consummation, the physical union of the husband and wife."

Laura was beset by a vivid image of Stefano and herself in bed together, her hair floating in a golden cloud across the tanned skin of his chest, while his legs twined intimately around hers. The picture set her pulses racing and her skin burning with sudden heat. She forced the intrusive picture away, struggling to speak coolly. "Naturally even Aunt Bette isn't suggesting we should go that far to save you from the INS." She was rather proud of the sophisticated way she managed to toss off that comment.

"Naturally not," Stefano agreed pleasantly. "I am sure that she knows you feel as I do about having sex. I never do it, not since I was eighteen or nineteen."

"Never?" Laura squeaked, shocked into indiscretion. "In fifteen years!"

Stefano grinned, brown eyes darkening with hidden laughter. "Ah," he said, "I am pleased that at last I have caught your full attention. No, in fifteen years I believe I have never *had sex*. Personally I prefer to make love with a woman, not simply to perform sexually. And to make love, it is necessary for both partners to feel at least some measure of liking and affection, not to mention a certain amount of mutual trust. And in our case that does not seem to be possible, no?"

"No." Laura cleared her throat. "Definitely not," she said more firmly. "So our marriage would certainly remain unconsummated in every way."

"However, when we apply for the divorce, we should say only that we have irreconcilable differences," Stefano suggested. "The legal process might become more complex if we point out that the marriage has never been consummated, and we certainly don't want to arouse any gossip if we can help it."

"No, we sure don't." Laura gulped. How in the world had they progressed to the point of discussing the terms of their divorce? she wondered. A couple of minutes ago, they'd both been agreeing that the whole idea of a marriage was unreasonable.

Aunt Bette chose this inopportune moment to pop back into the living room. "Everything has been settled with Judge Waterman," she said cheerily. "He'll be here at ten sharp. You know, I'm beginning to feel positively excited. Have you got something pretty to wear, Laura?"

"I have a pale peach cotton dress." She replied automatically, then sat bolt upright in her chair, horrified at how her adamant refusal even to consider the idea of marriage had somehow transformed itself into a discussion of whether or not the union was to be sexually consummated and what she ought to wear for the ceremony. "Wait! I haven't even agreed to go through with this marriage yet. I mean, it's absurd. I'm expected back at work after the weekend."

"That's no problem," Bette said. "You must call Brett right away and explain to him that you need to take a couple of weeks' vacation."

"Two weeks! Aunt Bette, that's impossible! Besides, what am I supposed to say? By the way, Brett, I'm getting married?"

"Are you getting married?" Stefano asked quietly.

"No, of course not!" Her denial was loud with anxiety.

Bette's forehead crumpled in thought. "I'll explain everything to Brett," she said. "But you must agree to stay with Stefano for a couple of weeks at least—no signing the marriage certificate and taking off for New York on the next flight. You know what government officials are like, always suspecting innocent citizens of committing a crime—"

"You're forgetting something," Laura said dryly.

"What's that, dear?"

"We *are* planning to commit a crime. We're aiding and abetting Stefano's attempt to remain illegally in this country."

"Oh, that!" Bette sniffed. "That's not a crime, dear. That's just taking care of straightening out one of the government's more illogical spasms."

For once Stefano seemed to be paying no attention to Bette. He looked across at Laura, his gaze hypnotically intent. "Have I understood you correctly?" he asked. "Have you decided, after all, that you are willing to marry me?"

Laura's stomach dived into a roller-coaster loop-the-loop. She swallowed hard. "Yes," she said, wondering at what point during the afternoon she'd taken total leave of her senses. "Yes, I guess I've agreed to marry you."

Chapter Three

IN THE CAUSE of getting Laura married to Stefano, Aunt Bette transformed herself into a model of swift-moving efficiency. Like a conjurer pulling successively larger rabbits out of a hat, the same lady who had never yet balanced her bank account or been able to find the claim stub for her dry cleaning overcame each and every hurdle with airy aplomb.

Laura's efficiency seemed to decline in direct proportion to her aunt's amazing accomplishments. She stumbled and bumbled through a phone call to Brett, quickly discovering there was no good way to explain to someone you'd been dating for a year that you planned to marry another man. She was weak with cowardly relief when he finally lost his temper and slammed down the phone.

Fortunately she was spared the horror of explaining the impossible to her parents, since they weren't home when she called. Bette seemed crestfallen, as she hung up after leaving a message on their answering machine. "I'm so sorry, Laura. I was hoping they might catch a late plane out here tonight and attend the ceremony tomorrow."

Laura's mouth fell open, either from shock or horror, she wasn't sure which. Before she could recover her voice, Bette—a tornado in sneakers—had moved on to the next item on her list.

By ten o'clock the following morning, when Judge Waterman arrived to perform the ceremony, Laura was worn to a frazzle. Even Stefano, resplendent in a navy blue Italian silk suit, appeared a touch frayed around his magnificent

edges. Bette, however, looked fresh as a daisy in her green
linen dress and perky high-heeled sandals. Indefatigable in
the cause of giving this marriage a gloss of romance, she sent
Stefano into the dining room to entertain the judge with
champagne and orange-juice cocktails, while she took
charge of putting the finishing touches to Laura's bridal
outfit.

"Try to smile, dear." Aunt Bette pushed Laura onto the
stool in front of her dressing table. "You look as if the IRS
has just turned down your claim for a tax rebate."

Laura grimaced. "In the grand scheme of things, that's
beginning to seem like a minor problem."

"You're right, dear. We should always try to keep life's
problems in perspective. Who cares about the IRS? Or the
INS for that matter?" Humming to herself, Bette took out
all the pins with which Laura had fastened her hair into a
neat French knot and brushed vigorously. When her niece's
hair was billowing around her face in a cloud of soft waves,
she beamed with delight. "There, now, that's more like it."

"Like what?" Laura asked, although she couldn't help
sneaking a sideways look in the triple mirror. Her great-
aunt's unexpected talents included considerable skill as a
hairdresser.

"Like a bride. We have to keep up appearances, don't we?
Now, sit still for another minute. I have to find you a neck-
lace." Bette trotted across to her closet.

Laura picked up the silver-framed photo that had sat on
Bette's dressing table ever since she could remember. The
picture showed a young, plump and sweetly pretty Bette
gazing adoringly from beneath the brim of a white straw hat
into the eyes of a handsome man with bright blue eyes and
sandy hair. "This is Walter Willis, isn't it?" Laura said,
when her aunt returned carrying a black leather box. "Your
ex-husband."

"Yes." Bette didn't even glance at the picture. "That was taken on our wedding day."

"Why have you kept it on your dressing table all these years?" Laura asked, suddenly curious. She'd seen the picture a hundred times and never questioned its presence. Today, for the first time, it occurred to her that not many women would choose to display a constant reminder of a marriage that had failed almost forty years earlier.

"Walter Willis took my dreams and trampled on them so completely that it was ten years after the divorce before I could believe in myself again." Bette sounded matter-of-fact rather than bitter. "When I could look at that photo without feeling ugly and stupid, I knew I was cured. I keep it there to remind me that an intelligent woman can easily fall in love with a destructive mean-spirited man. But that's enough about Walter. He's really not worth discussing." She flicked open the lid of the jewelry box and drew out a strand of lustrous pink-tinged pearls. "These were my sister's," she said. "Your grandmother's. She looked a lot like you, you know, tall and fine-boned, not short and squidgy like me." Bette fastened the glowing pearls around Laura's neck and smiled with evident satisfaction. "Mmm...they're perfect. You must have them as a wedding gift." She hummed a few bars of a melody. Wagner's "Wedding March," Laura realized, feeling cold with sudden fright.

"Aunt Bette, come down out of the clouds!" she said. "Listen to me. This setup is a fraud, an illusion. I am not really getting married, and Stefano isn't my genuine husband-to-be. He's an illegal immigrant, and I'm marrying him to keep him out of jail, no other reason."

"Shh!" Bette glanced nervously toward the door. "Sol Waterman may be seventy years old, but he has ears like a hunting hound. Stop worrying so much. Remember you're doing this for a good cause."

Laura's stomach performed its hundredth somersault of the morning. "That's what all the mad dictators say. However immoral the action, they always claim it's for a good cause."

Bette picked up the posy of pink roses lying on the dresser, but she hesitated, not handing the flowers to Laura. "If you have genuine moral objections, you can call this off, you know. Stefano might be jailed for a few hours, even a day or two, but the university lawyers will soon get him released. After all, he's considered one of Italy's most outstanding scientists. Some high-paid lawyer should be willing to hit the INS over the head hard enough to make them sit up and notice that they've made a mistake."

Aunt Bette spoke briskly, but behind her bravado Laura heard the disturbing throb of something that sounded almost like fear. She remembered the furtive exchange of glances she'd noticed earlier between Stefano and her great-aunt. Was Bette scared, Laura wondered, and if so, what could be scaring her? Come to that, why did she need to finish this research project so quickly when she'd been working on developing a miracle fiber for years?

The answer flashed into her mind as soon as she formulated the question, and her hands turned icy. "Aunt Bette, you're not sick, are you?"

"Sick?" Bette seemed genuinely amazed at the question. "Laura dear, I'm healthy as a horse. Can't you see that?"

"Promise me? You wouldn't lie?"

"I promise I'm not lying," Bette said. Her eyes twinkled. "All those years of munching on raw vegetables because I was too lazy to cook seems to have paid off. According to the doctor, my heart's thumping away with more oomph than a teenager's."

"You certainly look kind of sprightly," Laura said, her entire body flooding with relief. She reached out and squeezed Bette's hand, taking the little bouquet of garden roses and burying her face in their delicate pink blossoms. "Well, what are we waiting for?" she said. "I'm all gussied up, so isn't it time for us to get this wedding over with?"

Bette remained silent for another long moment, then she leaned forward and gave Laura a quick kiss. "Thank you, sweetheart. I'm sure you won't regret this."

The doorbell rang and Bette straightened, shrugging off her momentary seriousness. "That will be the Hortons. You remember Nick and Renée, don't you? My neighbors from across the way? They're coming over to act as witnesses for you and Stefano."

"You have this wedding amazingly well organized, Auntie. Anyone would think you'd been planning it for weeks!" Laura spoke teasingly, wanting to lighten the slight tension that lingered between them. She was surprised when her aunt's cheek flushed with guilty color.

"I haven't been planning anything," Aunt Bette said, trotting toward the door. "You just underestimate how efficient I can be when I set my mind to it. Now come along, dear. You don't want to keep Stefano and the judge waiting."

"That," Laura said dryly, "is debatable."

STEFANO WAS WAITING for her by the window in the living room, framed by the dramatic crimson of Aunt Bette's favorite velvet draperies. Oddly enough, he looked almost as nervous as Laura felt. Their eyes met as she walked toward him, and she sensed a momentary bonding, a twinge of empathy that must have had its roots in the fraud they were jointly perpetrating. Laura looked away, burying her nose in her bouquet of roses, trying to think of something—anything—other than the fact that her stomach clenched tight with desire every time he looked at her.

Stefano stepped forward and took her hand. He carried it to his lips, brushing a graceful kiss across her knuckles. Infuriatingly, she felt her heart speed up, so she scowled at the top of his head and told herself that by the time he was middle-aged, he would undoubtedly develop a paunch and grow a bald spot.

He bent his head low over her hand, pulling her toward him, speaking only to her. "You are so beautiful that I have no breath," he said.

Laura's knees buckled, and he steadied her with an arm around her waist. She reminded herself that he was Italian, and his national honor required him to make American women weak-kneed as a matter of principle. The reminder didn't help. She stared at her shoes, because she was afraid of what he might read in her eyes if she risked looking up at him.

The judge, thank goodness, chose that moment to speak. "Hello, Laura. It's nice to see you again, and on such a happy occasion, too."

She managed to find her voice. "H-hello, Judge Waterman."

The judge beamed with paternal reassurance. He was of the old school and obviously approved of brides who blushed and lowered their gaze. He wouldn't be so benevolent if he suspected the truth, Laura knew, and the thought of the deception she and Stefano were perpetrating was enough to stiffen her backbone. She gave her groom another scowl. Trust Stefano to carry his portrayal of the lovesick swain to excess! *She* at least had the decency to keep their pretense of affection within reasonable bounds.

"This is a very happy occasion," the judge declared again, in a tone of voice that permitted no dissent. "Now, my dear, are you ready for me to marry you to this fine young man?"

"Yes." She stared straight ahead, fuming. *Fine young man, indeed. Huh!*

"Stefano, do you wish to marry Laura? To take her as your wife until death separates you?"

Stefano had the audacity to take both her hands and hold them against his cheek before replying. She couldn't make up her mind if she was impressed or infuriated that he managed this feat without crushing her bouquet. He smiled at her with every appearance of exquisite tenderness. "Yes, it is very much my wish that Laura should become my wife."

At least that was true, she reflected, clinging to the remnants of her common sense. Stefano managed to sound so sincere because he was desperate to marry her, even if it was for all the wrong reasons. She thought wistfully that if Brett had shown half Stefano's eagerness, she'd have accepted his proposal long ago. It wasn't that she'd wanted Brett to sweep her off her feet and carry her to his bed while showering her with kisses, but in an entire year of dating, he'd shown no real passion at all. She at least wanted to feel that her husband looked forward to taking her to bed, and Brett simply hadn't seemed to care. She was sure Stefano would never leave his bride wondering whether or not he desired her. When Stefano chose his *real* wife, she would know he loved and wanted her more than any other woman on earth. Laura sighed, admitting to just the faintest tinge of envy.

"Who has the wedding rings?" the judge asked.

"I have them." Aunt Bette stepped forward, holding out a neat little velvet tray with two rings nestled within its folds. After the past several hours, Laura accepted her aunt's efficiency as a matter of course. Stefano took the smaller of the two rings, a thin gold band that gleamed with the patina of age. "It was my mother's," he said to the judge, and Laura had a horrible conviction that, for once, he was telling the truth.

"Do you promise to be faithful to Laura and to support her through the difficult times, as well as the good?" the judge asked.

"I do." Stefano took the ring and, without waiting for the judge to prompt him, reached for Laura's hand. "I give you this ring as a token of my love and a pledge of my commitment to you." He spoke softly, as if he and Laura were the only people in the room. She felt her eyes prick with tears, and she fought them back. This was ridiculous! If she got carried away like this at a fake wedding, she'd need a mop and bucket to soak up the moisture if she got married to a man she really loved.

Stefano gave her hand a reassuring squeeze, almost as if he knew what she was feeling. "You can count on me, Laura. I will always honor you and I promise to cherish you in good times and bad. Whatever happens, I will always be there for you."

He sounded so sincere she almost believed him. He slipped the ring on her finger. It fit perfectly, but she'd reached a point of unreality where she almost expected that.

"Laura, now it's your turn," the judge said.

She took the ring from the tray held out by Aunt Bette. "I give you this ring as a token of my love." The words were no more than trite formula, and she tried not to think of their meaning. Suddenly she looked up and found herself staring straight into Stefano's eyes. From some source hidden deep inside her, a new spate of words welled up. "I promise you that I will always stand by you, Stefano, and that I will always be your friend, no matter what."

He smiled. "A wonderful promise, *cara*. I thank you."

The judge harrumphed. "Very nice. Now, by the authority vested in me by the state of Ohio, I declare you husband and wife...."

She had no idea if the judge added anything else to his ritual patter, because at that moment Stefano stepped forward and took her into his arms. "At last," he murmured, "I may kiss my bride."

Italian men must take lessons in kissing, Laura thought dazedly, and Stefano had undoubtedly earned an A-plus in all his courses. It was her last semicoherent thought for several minutes. Stefano's mouth moved over hers with masterful possession, leaving her clinging to him, tingling with excitement and craving for more. Absurdly, instead of feeling grateful that he didn't take advantage of the situation to deepen their kiss, she kept wondering how it would feel if he teased apart her lips and thrust his tongue deep into her mouth. Her breasts grew heavy and she felt her lips part, and her body instinctively molded itself to Stefano's.

At that very moment, he ended their kiss with chilling abruptness. Blinking, Laura lifted her head and became aware of a smiling applauding audience. Aunt Bette hugged her. "Congratulations, dear, I know you've done the right thing."

Nick Horton thumped Stefano's shoulder and congratulated him on his pretty bride, and Renée laughingly informed Laura that Italian men made wonderful fathers. Judge Waterman handed them a piece of paper that certified they were legally married, and the entire wedding party headed for their cars and the celebratory luncheon that Aunt Bette had organized in a downtown restaurant.

Laura sat in the back seat of the judge's Lincoln Town Car, taking care not to allow even an inch of her skin to touch Stefano's long muscular legs. In view of that post-wedding kiss, she'd decided it was safer if she and her supposed husband didn't come into physical contact with each other ever again.

After a couple of minutes, it became obvious that her resolution was unnecessary. Her new husband was in no rush to exercise any of his conjugal rights. Stefano, in fact, seemed barely aware of her existence. He leaned forward in his seat, staring out of the car's side window with hypnotic intensity. Laura began to feel somewhat frustrated. She had been looking forward to delivering one of the sharp witty putdowns she had lain in bed last night inventing. It was annoying not to need any of them.

The judge and Aunt Bette kept up an animated conversation as the car inched through heavy lunchtime traffic toward the restaurant. By the time they'd been driving for ten minutes, Stefano's lack of interest in his new wife was becoming so blatant Laura began to develop an entirely fresh set of worries. Dammit, didn't Stefano realize he had responsibilities? He was supposed to be crazy in love with her! In order to justify their hurried marriage, he needed to maintain the illusion of a man swept off his feet by passion. Unfortunately, with his back turned to her face, they didn't look much like a pair of torridly loving newlyweds. Distant cousins who'd just renewed a bitter family feud was more like it.

Laura cleared her throat, but Stefano continued to stare out the window. She cleared her throat again. He didn't twitch a muscle. This is the final absurdity, she thought wryly. Somehow, she had to get his attention. Should she kick him or kiss him?

"Stefano." She tried to sound wifely and devoted, but ended up sounding irritated. She laid her hand on his arm. "Stefano, honey." The endearment nearly choked her. "Honey, what in the world is so fascinating out there?"

He stiffened and turned around at once. *"Carissima*—my darling—forgive me. I...um...er...thought I had seen an old friend from Italy."

"And had you?" she asked sweetly. "He must be a very good friend to keep you staring so long."

"Yes, indeed he was. He is. But I am not sure if it was really my, um, friend. I believe so."

"What a shame you couldn't speak to him. I don't suppose you'll be able to find out where he's staying."

"I believe there is no problem in finding him again," Stefano said wryly. "I am fairly sure that he will follow me."

Laura looked up and Stefano gave a slight almost imperceptible shake of his head. What had he meant? she wondered. Was he being followed by a government agent, and did it matter even if he was? After all, that was the whole point of their marriage. Stefano now had a legal right to claim residence in the United States, so he no longer needed to hide from overzealous INS agents.

Judge Waterman looked at them through his rearview mirror, his gaze more than a little puzzled. Stefano must have sensed the judge's attention and realized at once how out of character his behavior appeared for a new groom.

"Mia cara sposa." He twisted on the seat so that his back blocked Laura from the judge's view. Then he leaned forward, murmuring passionate endearments, mostly Italian, and appearing to burrow his face into her neck. With surprising tact, not to mention skill, he managed to keep at least three or four inches of space between their bodies.

He smelled wonderful, Laura reflected, a mixture of soap, woodsy after-shave and sheer man. He felt pretty good, too, with an impressive set of biceps bulging in his arms as he braced himself against the rear seat cushions, straining to create the appearance of holding her close while actually maintaining a polite distance.

Because of her position vis-à-vis the judge, it was impossible for Laura to play her part in the illusory embrace without truly hugging Stefano. Reluctantly she curved her arms around his shoulders. She felt him tense, and her stomach tightened in an answering knot. Of anticipation, she realized, not of repugnance.

Stefano shifted on the seat. He gave an inarticulate grunt, perhaps of apology. The gap between the two of them narrowed to less than an inch, then closed completely when the car bumped over a pothole. Laura's skin instantly erupted in goose bumps, but she didn't move away.

Telling herself she despised physical passion that had no roots in emotional harmony, she sought to get a grip on her runaway hormones. Now was the time to whisper a stinging one-liner into Stefano's ear, reminding him that he'd better keep his distance. Unfortunately her mind seemed to be empty of witty one-liners. Her mind, in fact, was fast emptying of all coherent thought. Her fingers, by contrast, seemed to have acquired a will of their own. They were running up and down Stefano's arms with undeniable eagerness and were soon linked behind his head. At the same time, Stefano was rubbing his cheek against hers, while his lips brushed softly against the corner of her mouth.

A coherent thought finally formed in Laura's addled brain. She wanted him to kiss her. She *badly* wanted him to kiss her.

"Stefano . . ." she whispered.

"Laura . . ." His mouth hovered over hers for a tantalizing few seconds, then moved on. She heard him draw a shuddering breath. "You are a great actress," he murmured. "Thank you, Laura. You have saved the day. I was careless and the judge was becoming suspicious of my indifference."

"You're welcome." The words came out in a husky murmur. Her fingers, she discovered, had finally unlinked
themselves from their clasp around Stefano's neck and were
now twined in his hair. Twined *tightly* in his hair, pulling his
mouth down toward hers. Several seconds elapsed before
she registered that his arms were no longer braced against
the back of the seat. Instead, they were wrapped around her
waist, and his rib cage was crushed against hers. Her breasts
began to ache and her nipples tingled.

Lack of oxygen, she decided. Stefano was much too close
and his weight was becoming oppressive. But for some reason, she made not the slightest effort to cure her problems
by moving away from him and drawing a refreshing breath
of air.

"Laura..." There was a new and urgent note to the way
he muttered her name.

"Stefano..." She sounded like a frog croaking on a lily
pad. Or a woman whispering to her lover.

"Here we are!" Aunt Bette exclaimed. "The restaurant
at last!"

Judge Waterman chuckled. "I think we've arrived just
in time. Our newlyweds nearly ignited a three-alarm fire
back there."

At the sound of the judge's voice, Laura and Stefano
sprang apart. Stefano reknotted his tie—heaven knew when
or how it had come undone—and she patted her hair and
tugged at the skirt of her dress. She didn't achieve much,
since her dress was irretrievably crumpled, and her hair was
happily twisting itself into a riot of unkempt curls as the heat
and summer humidity intensified. Giving up on her appearance, Laura walked into the restaurant looking neither
to the left nor to the right. At that precise moment, there
wasn't a single person's gaze she was willing to meet.

The Hortons were already waiting at a corner table, situated with a pleasant view of the tree-lined walled garden that surrounded the restaurant. A magnum of champagne stood frosting in a bucket of ice, and a waiter hovered in readiness.

"Welcome to the happy couple." The waiter bowed and smiled, easing the cork out of the champagne bottle with professional slickness. "We hope you will enjoy your first lunch as a married couple. The champagne is a gift from our manager."

"Thank you." Stefano had completely recovered his poise. He took the glass offered by the waiter and raised it high. "I salute Laura, my beautiful new wife. Thank you, *carissima*, for all you have given me this day. Because of you, I have the chance to fulfill my most heartfelt dreams for happiness."

He was too darn clever with words, Laura thought, admiring the subtlety of his double meaning. He was too darn clever in lots of ways. "You're, um, more than welcome." That sounded so trite as to be almost embarrassing. She raised her glass. "I hope all your dreams will come true, Stefano."

"Our dreams," he corrected. He smiled at her warmly, touching his glass to hers.

"Our dreams," she agreed, her gaze meeting his. She quickly looked away and swallowed several generous gulps of champagne. His eyes looked so full of desire it was unsettling, even though she knew he was simply playing a part.

She hadn't eaten any breakfast, and the champagne bubbles fizzed straight to her head, leaving her instantly tipsy. At least, she told herself, she must be tipsy. She didn't want to think of any other reason why Stefano's melting brown eyes suddenly inspired her with an insane longing to be alone with him in a darkened room, furnished with a king-size bed.

The meal of poached baby salmon was light but delicious. One bottle of champagne quickly became three. Laura drank her share, although she remained sober enough to notice that Stefano drank almost nothing. The meal ended with espresso coffee and a wedding cake, another of Aunt Bette's organizational miracles. The waiter looked positively benevolent as he stepped out of the kitchen carrying a small white-frosted cake, topped with a plastic bride and groom and set on a fancy silver doily.

The waiter handed Laura a silver cake knife. "Would you and your husband like to cut the first slice, Mrs. Corelli?"

The name made her jump. She blinked. "Oh, yes. Yes, of course." She got up and moved around the table to the serving cart, where the waiter had placed the cake. Stefano joined her, resting his hand over hers as she cut the first slice and slipped it onto the waiting plate.

A movement in the bushes outside the window distracted her attention just as Stefano raised his fork to offer her the traditional first bite. When she instinctively turned to look out of the window, Stefano barely managed to prevent the cake from falling off the fork. She ended up with cream smudged all over the side of her mouth.

"Oh, Lord, I'm sorry."

"Don't apologize. You give me the perfect excuse." He glanced at the judge and winked. "I love your American customs," he said, pulling her into his arms. He cupped her face in his hands and licked the cream from her cheek with elaborate care. "Mmm, you taste simply wonderful."

She felt herself sliding into the hazy dreamlike state that seemed to be her permanent condition whenever Stefano touched her. On the verge of closing her eyes and letting the delicious feelings consume her, she remembered she had something to tell him.

With considerable effort, she focused her thoughts and leaned closer so that she could whisper the words right into his ear. "There's a man hiding in the bushes. He's watching us."

Stefano released her with a deft twirl that left him facing the garden and Laura looking into the restaurant. After a second or two, he looped his arm casually around her shoulders and smiled at their wedding guests as if he didn't have a care in the world.

"You know, Laura and I have suddenly discovered the most urgent need to return to my apartment. I wonder if you would be so kind as to excuse us from finishing dessert?"

Renée Horton laughed. "I'm surprised the two of you lasted this long." She held out a set of car keys. "Here, these are yours. We parked your car in the corner under a tree, so it should have stayed cool. We'll drive home with the judge, like we planned."

Nick Horton winked at Bette. "Good thinking on our part, eh? Looks like the pair of them could use some cooling off."

"On the contrary," Stefano said, with an answering grin. "We are just beginning to enjoy the heat, isn't that right, *cara?*"

The man outside the window was still there, staring at them from between two bushes, his face framed by half-dead lilac blossoms. Laura found herself smothering an acute desire to giggle. He looked like one of the Fruit of the Loom men about to burst into a commercial jingle.

"What? Oh, yes, sure we are." Laura slipped her hand into Stefano's. "Come on," she said, suddenly eager to confront the INS agent with the fact of Stefano's marriage. The guy had a mean-looking face and shifty dishonest eyes.

"We must hurry," she said. "We don't want to lose ... I mean, we need to get home."

Even the judge smiled at that. Laura was too impatient to feel embarrassed. She covered her edginess as best she could, but it seemed to take them forever to exchange good-byes and get out of the restaurant.

"Did you recognize him?" she asked Stefano the moment they were outside. "Is that the INS agent who's been harassing you?"

"No," Stefano said.

She stopped in her tracks and swung around to stare at him. "What do you mean, *no?* Do you think they've put a new agent on the case?"

"I do not believe so." Stefano strode toward the garden. "He will be gone by now, but I suppose we must look, just to be sure."

She followed him along a narrow stone path, slippery with moss. The restaurant garden was apparently designed to be viewed from afar, not strolled through. They arrived at the section visible from the table where they'd been seated. As Stefano had predicted, it was empty.

Laura looked around the sunny flower-filled garden. The lilac bushes no longer aroused in her even the faintest desire to laugh. "Stefano, what's going on here? Why has he gone? Doesn't he want to arrest you?"

"I do not think the man who was watching us is from the INS."

Laura rubbed her arms, which were suddenly chilled. "If he wasn't a government agent, then who was he? And why was he spying on us?"

Stefano put his hand beneath her elbow and directed her back toward the parking lot. He hesitated a moment before replying, "I do not know his name, but I have seen him before. I think that he is the burglar who attempted to break into your aunt's basement a couple of weeks ago. Fortunately I happened to spot him as I drove up to pay a visit to Bette. He was caught in the headlights of my car, and I saw him clearly. Unfortunately I was not able to catch him. He ran into a neighbor's backyard as I was getting out of the car, and somehow I lost him."

Laura couldn't believe she had heard right. "And nobody thought it was worth calling to let me know that Aunt Bette had been the victim of an attempted robbery?"

Stefano unlocked the doors of a gray Buick parked beneath the shade of a leafy oak tree. "Your aunt did not wish to worry you."

"Have the police been notified?"

"Yes, but they have taken no action."

"Why not?" Laura demanded.

"If I were a cynic, I might say that they are too busy chasing down illegal aliens. A kinder explanation is that there is no action for them to take. The burglar smashed a basement window, that's all. He was scared off before he could steal anything." Stefano grabbed her arm. "Where are you going?"

"To talk to Aunt Bette, of course. You know she doesn't even remember to lock her back door half the time. I have to get a security system installed right away—"

"It has been done," Stefano said quietly. "You probably didn't notice, but there are now electronic keypads by each door."

"Aunt Bette will never remember to set them."

"She can't avoid setting them. They buzz at her until she does." Stefano broke off almost in midword and ran toward his side of the car. "Get in!" he shouted. "Hurry! We must get out of here! Now, Laura. Now!"

Chapter Four

LAURA BANGED her head getting into the car and spent the first couple of minutes of their getaway seeing stars. Even so, she was aware of a nagging sense of having overlooked something important in the rush to escape. Something about the man she had seen lurking in the lilac bushes was triggering a memory, but she couldn't bring the picture into focus. After a while, she gave up and turned to Stefano. "What was that all about?" she demanded. "Another sighting of Aunt Bette's burglar?"

"That was an INS agent," Stefano said tersely. "Officer Raymond Dennis. I have christened him Dennis the Menace, because he always seems to turn up when I least desire his company. But I think we managed to lose him. I don't see his car, do you?"

"I never saw his car in the first place." Laura rubbed her forehead, which was still throbbing. Maybe it was the blow to her head that was making her so slow-witted. "I don't understand the problem," she said. "Why do we have to run like criminals at the mere sight of an INS agent? We're married. You now have the right to stand firm in the face of invading INS inspectors."

"You are right," Stefano said, "in theory. However, none of my conversations with the INS so far has convinced me that they are anxious to listen to reason. I am afraid that Dennis the Menace would prefer to jail me first, deport me second and apologize later. Much later."

Laura leaned back in her seat and shaded her eyes from the sun. "I wish Aunt Bette would take up rescuing stray dogs or knitting afghans for senior citizens," she muttered.

"What is that supposed to mean?" Stefano asked, sounding amused.

"Let's face it, I'm a wimp. Major-league, big-time wimp. My palms get sweaty if I drive three miles over the speed limit. I'm not cut out to be chasing mysterious prowlers one minute and fleeing from lawfully appointed government officials the next."

Stefano gave her a considering glance. "Bette doesn't call you a wimp. She says you're her first line of defense whenever she has a problem."

Laura's face softened into a smile. "Well, you know Bette. Once she takes you under her wing, you can do no wrong. She always manages to see the world from her own special perspective."

"She told me that you are the most creative and intelligent of all her friends and relatives. According to her, your major problem is that you are afraid to let your tremendous gift of creativity fly free."

Laura laughed, a touch wistfully. "You just proved my point, Stefano. Bette sees in people what she wants to see, not what's really there. I'm a tax accountant, for heaven's sake, and I *enjoy* my work. The horrible truth is that if I ever met the INS agent who's chasing you—"

"Dennis the Menace?"

"Yes. If we ever met, we'd probably discover we're soul mates."

"I am sure you would not." Stefano glanced away from the road and smiled at her. "I agree with your aunt—you deceive yourself, *cara*. You are not quite the fusty old stick-in-the-mud you would like to pretend. In the first place you agreed to marry me, virtually sight unseen. And in the second place..." His smile deepened. "Well, remember, I have kissed you several times, which was a most enlightening experience. Not to mention . . . stimulating."

Laura felt her cheeks flame. She really disliked the husky intimate way he called her *cara*. She especially disliked the hot restless feelings he could summon up, seemingly out of nowhere, just by looking at her in a certain quizzical way. She turned and stared out the window. "You're right, we seem to have lost Dennis," she said. "There isn't a sign of anyone following us."

"Great!" Stefano accepted the change of conversation with every appearance of equanimity. "Now we can double back down this street here, make a left at Burger King—you see that I have learned how to give American directions—and go to my apartment."

"Do you have any special plans for how we should spend the rest of the day?" Laura asked, pleased she managed to make the question sound businesslike.

He replied with equal crispness, "Obviously it is better if we remain indoors. We do not want to do anything out of character, and we are newlyweds. On their wedding night, I think most couples prefer to celebrate privately, no?"

"Er, yes, I'm sure they do."

He smiled cheerfully. "So, we shall remain inside my apartment and organize our own wedding-night celebration. We shall do nothing to attract the attention of Dennis the Menace." Stefano turned the car onto a pleasant street of restored older homes, close to the university campus. "Here is where I have my apartment," he said, squeezing the car into a narrow parking alley. "The second floor of this house is all mine, and there is a separate outside staircase leading to my front door. Welcome to my home, Mrs. Corelli."

Mrs. Corelli. The name had an oddly attractive ring to it. Of course when she *really* got married, Laura had every intention of keeping her own name and drawing up a prenuptial agreement that would be very specific about mutual expectations and prospective financial arrangements. She realized she was twisting her wedding band around her finger and she quickly stopped. Her mood today had been downright peculiar, and she resolved to behave more rationally from now on.

"Thank you," she said, unlatching the gate into the tiny but well-tended front yard. "It, um, looks like you have a nice place here. We're in German Village, aren't we?"

"Yes, I like this neighborhood a lot. Great restaurants right around the corner, not too far from campus. In Italy, near a major university, we usually cannot find so much space." He grinned. "Not to mention such terrific modern plumbing—and a garden, too."

She looked at the rosebushes clustered in the corner and the neat borders of impatiens and geraniums. "Did you design this garden?" she asked.

He shrugged. "I like to work outside," he said. "Pulling up weeds and mowing grass is good thinking time."

An image of Bette's amazingly neat garden, with its grass properly mowed for the first time in years, flashed into her mind. "You've been taking care of my aunt's yard, as well as this one," she said.

"You sound so accusing that I must plead guilty." He took her hand. "Come on, we need to get inside before Dennis the Menace comes cruising by and spots us."

"Thank you for helping with Bette's yard," she said, following him up the metal staircase. "You've obviously been a good friend to my aunt."

"As she has been to me." Stefano found his keys and opened the door to his apartment with a flourish. "Come inside, Mrs. Corelli." He grinned companionably. "It will be my pleasure to cook us dinner, and afterward, when we have eaten...well, we can choose our entertainment for the evening. If you like to read, I have many recent bestsellers, which I bought to improve my English. I have movies, too, and CDs, if you prefer to listen to music."

"Where will I sleep?" She blurted out the question and immediately regretted it. Good grief, she sounded gauche! And for no good reason. Stefano was behaving like a perfect gentleman.

"I have two bedrooms," he said. "You shall choose one. I will take the other." For a second, Stefano laid his hand lightly on her arm. "Laura, it is my nature to joke and sometimes to tease, but about this I give you my word. You have done me a great favor by marrying me. I shall certainly not repay your kindness by taking advantage of the situation in which we find ourselves. I understand very well that you do not wish this marriage to be given any physical reality, and of course I respect your wishes."

That was great, and she said so as she followed him into the well-lit, newly refurbished kitchen. Except the problem wasn't so much what *Stefano* might get up to, Laura reflected gloomily. The problem was what *she* might find herself tempted to do during the long dark hours of the night ahead. In laying the ground rules for this marriage of convenience, neither Bette nor Stefano seemed to have considered the possibility that Laura might find herself overwhelmingly attracted to the man who was now her lawfully wedded husband.

Laura, unfortunately, had been considering little else ever since she'd first laid eyes on Stefano.

STEFANO POSSESSED an upbeat nature, and he'd always believed he enjoyed an amicable relationship with God.

Watching Laura as she explored his apartment, he realized he'd been horribly mistaken. It was clear that God had decided to punish him for a lifetime of sin. Stefano could think of no other explanation for the horrible twist of fate that had united him with a wife who was both off-limits and everything he'd ever wanted in a woman. Talk about a no-win situation, Stefano thought gloomily. He could indulge his desire and break his solemn promises to Laura. Or he could keep his promises and spend the next several nights sleeping in chaste separation from the most desirable woman he'd ever been privileged to meet.

There was really no choice, and he knew it. So he set out to make himself agreeable, trying to pretend he wasn't constantly holding his breath in case she brushed against him, or fantasizing about how she would look lying naked in his bed, or remembering how she had felt when he kissed her.

Fortunately Laura seemed eager to help him cook dinner, and he breathed a sigh of relief when they fell into an easy camaraderie as they prepared a feast of homemade pasta, with marinara sauce and mushroom caps stuffed with spicy ground beef. Stefano enjoyed good food, and he'd spent some memorable evenings cooking elaborate meals with beautiful women, but he'd never before appreciated how much fun it could be to share a sunny kitchen with a smiling woman, whose eyes sparkled like the Mediterranean on a summer day.

Laura accepted his offer of a glass of Chianti, and they bickered amicably over the exact ingredients for the sauce as they diced pepper, chopped onions, and sautéed ground beef. They managed to combine their two favorite recipes just fine until they got to the point of adding garlic—and that proved to be the end of harmony.

"Two tiny cloves?" Stefano demanded, raising his eyebrows in feigned horror. "How can we make a marinara sauce with only two cloves of garlic?"

"Very easily." Laura clapped the lid on the saucepan. "Everyone knows that garlic should never be more than a subtle undertone."

"I know nothing of the sort," Stefano said. "And I am Italian."

"What's that got to do with anything?" Laura demanded. "Are Italian babies born with cells carrying the recipe for spaghetti sauce encoded in their DNA?"

She tossed her head triumphantly, obviously convinced she'd managed a pretty good comeback. Unwilling to remove her hands from the saucepan lid, she blew at a stray wisp of hair that had fallen over her forehead. Stefano decided she looked adorable.

"Most certainly we Italians are born with special genes," he said, partly to tease her and partly because he had to say something or he would simply sweep her into his arms and kiss her until neither of them gave a damn about the garlic. "And my DNA is telling me that this pathetic excuse for a spaghetti sauce needs at least three more cloves of garlic."

"Hah!" Laura abandoned logic and resorted to brute force. She armed herself with a wooden spoon and barricaded the stove with her body. "Your DNA is obviously scrambled. No more garlic," she said fiercely. "Only the ignorant think marinara sauce has to be loaded with herbs and spices until you can't even taste the tomato."

"Only the ignorant, hey?" Stefano directed her a mock scowl. "Them's fightin' words, lady." He tried hard for a Western drawl, but ended up sounding like Desi Arnez giving a bad imitation of the Lone Ranger.

Laura collapsed in giggles, and Stefano took advantage of her laughter to sneak behind her back and toss the crushed cloves of garlic into the pan.

"Hey!" Laura straightened, pretending outrage. "That's not playing fair!"

"Why? Because I made you laugh?" Before he stopped to consider the wisdom of his actions, Stefano put his arm around her waist and gave a friendly squeeze. "Life is not entirely a grim struggle to do one's duty," he said, smiling down at her and hoping like hell she wouldn't notice he was holding on to his self-control by the merest thread. "Maybe you need to give yourself permission to laugh more often."

He was wrong, Laura thought. If he continued to smile at her like that, what she would need was permission to breathe. His smile faded and his eyes darkened, his gaze fixing on her mouth with fierce intensity. "Do not look at me so," he murmured. "Laura, I beg. You must not."

Her lungs labored to produce enough oxygen. Without success, apparently, because she was beginning to feel hopelessly dizzy. She swayed toward Stefano, and he obligingly removed the wooden spoon from her limp fingers, wrapping his arms more tightly around her waist and drawing her close. Laura's dizziness stopped, but another sensation began—one that flooded her veins with heat and touched her skin with chills at the same time.

"Your aunt told me many times that you are very beautiful," Stefano murmured. "She did not exaggerate."

"Th-thank you."

"You are welcome. But for my sake, I almost wish that Bette had stretched the truth a little bit."

"Wh-why?"

He smiled wryly. "How can you need to ask? It is a most frustrating experience for a red-blooded Italian male to find himself married to so beautiful a woman and know that he must not touch her."

"But you are...touching...me," Laura pointed out, clinging to a vestige of logic in a world swirling with unreasonable emotions. "Y-your arm is around my waist."

Stefano smiled softly. "That is not touching," he said. He drew his hand slowly down the side of her cheek, tracing the outline of her mouth with his forefinger. "*This* is touching," he said huskily. "And...this." He bent his head, seeking out the hollow of her throat and pressing his mouth against the pulse that throbbed there.

The feather-light stroke of his lips against her skin was far more erotic than a kiss. Laura jammed her palms flat against the counter and resisted the crazy urge to grab Stefano's head and pull his mouth to hers. After a moment or two, his intoxicating caress stopped, but she could feel the frantic race of her pulses even when he straightened and moved away slightly. He still held her loosely in the circle of his arms, looking down at her in a silence fraught with unspoken questions. Her nipples peaked, swelling against the light cotton bodice of her dress—her *wedding dress*, she thought wryly—and her stomach tightened with awareness of her own desire. She recognized that she and Stefano were fast approaching a precipice, but she didn't turn away, and she didn't step back out of the danger zone.

Stefano's cheeks darkened with a trace of color. "I believe we have encountered an unexpected problem," he said thickly.

"What's that?" Her voice emerged half an octave lower than normal.

"You know my problem. I am sure you can feel it." He pulled her against him for a split second, making her aware of his hardness, then let her go. "I want to make love to you, Laura, but I have promised that I will not do so." His mouth twisted in rueful self-mockery. "An honorable man does not break his promises."

She stared at the buttons on his shirt. Anywhere so she could avoid his eyes. "You could always say to hell with honor." She wondered if she had gone terminally crazy. Laura the practical, Laura the cautious, was surely not encouraging a man she barely knew to make love to her!

Stefano held her a little away from him. "No," he said regretfully. "I could not say that because I made the promise to you. But *you* could."

His words vibrated in the constricted space between the two of them. Small noises sounded loud in the sudden silence of the kitchen: the bubble of simmering sauce, the hum of the refrigerator, the pounding of her heart. Laura looked up, finally discovering the courage to meet his eyes. In one clear sharp instant of self-knowledge, she recognized that she had been attracted to him from the moment he opened Bette's door. Her insistence on a marriage with no physical consummation had been precipitated by a need to shore up her own defenses, not by any need to protect herself from Stefano's unwanted advances.

She swallowed hard. "To hell with honor," she whispered.

Startled, Stefano looked down at her. "Laura? I am not sure that I have heard you correctly."

She cleared her throat. "To hell with honor," she repeated.

His breath expelled on a thick tense sigh. "What a great suggestion." He bent his head and captured her lips in a long searching kiss. When they finally broke apart, Stefano framed her face between his hands and tilted her face upward.

"I would not want you to feel pressured," he murmured, "but I would like to point out that my bedroom is behind the first door on your left."

Laura blinked and stared in the direction he had indicated, but she didn't move, chiefly because her legs seemed to be incapable of motion. Stefano gazed at her with fierce intensity, all trace of laughter wiped clean by desire. Suddenly he bent down, put his hand behind her knees and swept her up into his arms. He strode along the corridor, nudged open the bedroom door with his knee and deposited her triumphantly in the center of his queen-size bed. Her hair spilled over the pillows in a wild tangle, making her feel both wanton and aroused. He slipped off her shoes and tossed them into a corner of the room, then tugged at the buttons of his shirt, stripping it off and dropping it on the floor.

She reached instinctively toward him. A moment later, he was lying beside her, his arms strong and possessive, his body hard and lean—an infinitely desirable contrast to the down-filled softness of the pillows and comforter on which she lay.

He spoke quietly, his voice a husky promise. "We shall make this a wedding night to remember, my heart. You have my word on it." He smiled then, just a little. "And remember, I am a man of honor. I never break my promises."

Not this one at least, Laura thought dazedly. For sure he wasn't breaking this one. He stroked her with caresses as subtle as they were knowing, as arousing as they were tender. Sensations, dazzling as a rainbow in sunlight, tantalized her body and warmed her soul. The searing heat of his mouth burned into her skin until it seemed that every nerve ending shivered with awareness of his touch. She was alive as she had never before been alive, acutely aware of each separate part of her body and yet aware, too, that she would never feel complete until she was joined to Stefano. When his hands moved between her legs, searching and enticing, she cried out, and he swallowed the tiny sounds of her pleasure into his kiss, returning them to her with his own harsh groans of need. And when they climaxed together, she felt a moment of joy so intense she knew she would remember it forever.

Several long minutes later, when they had both stopped panting, Stefano cradled her head on his shoulder. His hand traced slow lazy patterns over her back. "It has never been like that for me before," he said quietly.

"For me, either."

"It was amazing. Do you think it could ever be that good again?"

"I don't know." She stretched drowsily, already half-asleep.

She felt, rather than saw, his smile. "Let's find out, shall we?"

That made her eyes fly wide open. "Stefano, we can't make love again! I'm exhausted."

"I will revive you," he said.

She yawned, eyelids drooping again. "Mission impossible, I'm afraid."

"Never offer an Italian husband such a delightful challenge," he murmured, kissing her.

Against everything she would have believed possible, Laura felt the faint stirring of response, the sudden acceleration of her heartbeat, the tingle of her skin. He kissed her again, then cupped her breast and rasped his tongue gently across her nipple. She shivered, her hands clutching at him involuntarily, and he laughed softly. "You see, *cara?* Signs of life already."

Signs of life that quickly translated into full-blown desire and culminated with astonishing speed in a climax more shattering than the one that had gone before.

What was happening to her? Laura wondered as Stefano finally drew away. She found no answer to her question, but in the silent afterglow of their tumultuous lovemaking, she had plenty of time to realize that her marriage of convenience had just become ominously less than convenient.

THE PHONE RANG the next morning almost before the sun had broken over the horizon. *Aunt Bette,* Laura thought, stretching drowsily. Her great-aunt could never be persuaded that the rest of the world didn't share her delight in having coffee perking by 6 a.m. at the latest.

Stefano groaned and pulled a pillow over his head. "Answering machine," he mumbled. "Let it ring."

The machine picked up after five rings. "This is Stefano Corelli. Please leave a message after the beep."

A rough uneducated voice spoke. "I'm gonna call back in two minutes. If you're there, Dr. Corelli, you'd be real smart to pick up the phone."

Laura and Stefano both sat bolt upright in the bed, and Stefano lunged for the phone. "I am here now," he said. "Who are you, and what do you want?"

"A real simple request, Dr. Corelli." The answering machine was still on, and Laura could hear the conversation quite clearly. "I want the formula for the fiber you and Bette Prendergast have developed, and I want it soon."

"Who are you?" Stefano repeated. "How do you know about this fiber?"

"Word is out all over town that Bette and her fancy new partner have invented themselves a real hot product."

"Then you should know that we are already negotiating with three major companies for the sale of the formula. Do you wish to be included in the list of negotiators?"

The caller laughed. "Yeah, I guess you could say that. And here's my deal. You bring me the info on your new product, and I'll give you a real good price for it."

"You understand that the other interested parties have already made offers of many millions of dollars—"

"My deal's better, Dr. Corelli, and here it is. You give me the formula, and I'll give you Bette Prendergast. I guess that cute new wife of yours would be real sad if she thought her auntie was missing, soon-to-be presumed dead."

"Bette!" Laura exclaimed. "What does he mean? What's he talking ab—"

Stefano gestured for silence. "I do not understand you," he said curtly.

"Having problems understanding simple English, Dr. Corelli?" The caller spoke with sneering contempt. "Then I'll speak real slow and real clear. Don't go to the police or any other law-enforcement agency if you want to see dear old Bette alive again. Got that?"

"I understand your demands, yes. But how do I know that you really have Bette?"

"Call her house. You'll find a message on her answering machine. But before you place that call, I have some instructions for you, Doctor. So listen up, because I'm only saying this one time. You come to the Café International parking lot on the university campus at eight o'clock this morning. Bring with you the six computer disks that contain your research data. In exchange, I'll bring you Bette Prendergast, alive and unharmed."

"How do I know—" Stefano stopped in midsentence.

"What is it?" Laura clutched his arm. "I can't hear him anymore. What's he saying?"

"Nothing," Stefano replied, his voice harsh. "He has hung up."

"Oh, my God!" Laura felt panic swell inside her. "Oh, my God, poor Aunt Bette! What are we going to do?"

Stefano was already dialing a phone number. "No!" she said, grabbing for his hand. "Don't call the police! You heard what he said!"

"I am calling your aunt's house," Stefano said quietly. "He claimed there is a message on Bette's answering machine. We should check it out. It is possible, you know, that the call was a hoax."

"Oh, of course, I'm sorry." Laura felt her panic subside slightly in the face of Stefano's calm. She swallowed over a rush of nausea as the answering machine clicked in after four rings.

"Laura, Stefano, this is Bette. Please do as you have been instructed. Stefano, take the disks to the university. Otherwise, I don't know what will—" The machine cut off abruptly. The buzz of the disconnected call echoed frighteningly through the room, and Stefano gently replaced the receiver.

"It isn't a hoax, is it?" Laura tried hard to keep her voice from shaking.

"Probably not," Stefano said. He glanced at the bedside clock as he strode toward the shower. "Six-forty-five. We will work on the assumption that Bette has been kidnapped. There is no time to chase across town to check out the house in person, and the voice on the answering machine was almost certainly hers. Fortunately we have time to plan a little and still make the eight-o'clock deadline. This early on a Saturday morning, there will be almost no traffic on the roads."

"You're going to give him—the kidnapper—the formula?" Laura asked, still trying to absorb the incredible

idea that her aunt had invented something valuable and important enough to attract the interest of a kidnapper.

"I shall give him the six disks he asked for," Stefano said,
turning on the shower. "Most certainly. Let us hope that is
sufficient to secure the release of your aunt." He took Laura
by the shoulders and pushed her gently in the direction of
the door. "The second bathroom is down the hall," he said.
"Hurry up and get dressed and we'll talk in the car."

Sick and shaking with anxiety, Laura headed toward the
shower.

Chapter Five

LAURA, WHO HAD ALWAYS taken pride in her common sense and cool efficiency in the face of a crisis, found her competence crumbling. The thought of Aunt Bette in captivity left her paralyzed with worry. However sprightly Bette appeared, she was seventy-two years old, and her reserves of strength weren't great enough to cope with the horrors of being kidnapped. Laura fought back tears as she showered at record-breaking speed. Pulling on jeans and a T-shirt, she shoved her feet into a pair of sneakers at the same time as she swished mouthwash around her teeth. Her fingers were shaking so badly she gave up on her hair and simply shoved it into a haphazard ponytail.

Stefano heard her leave the bathroom and called to her. "I am in the kitchen," he said, poking his head around the door and thrusting a mug of coffee into her hands. "This will help the morning blues."

She swallowed a couple of scalding sips, then set the mug on the counter, glancing nervously at her watch. "We don't have time for this, Stefano. It's past seven . . ."

He picked up the mug and wrapped her hands around it. "You need something to drink," he said softly. "Finish this, *cara*. You have time, I promise."

"But Aunt Bette—"

"Laura, we are ten minutes away from the campus, fifteen at the absolute most. We will achieve nothing by sitting in a empty parking lot waiting for the kidnappers to arrive. Let's take five minutes to drink coffee and make our plans."

"Okay," she agreed reluctantly. She took another sip of coffee and the roiling sickness in her stomach calmed a little. Pacing, unable to stand still, her eye caught sight of a flat plastic box lying on the counter with Stefano's car keys sitting on top.

"Are those the disks the kidnapper wants?" she asked.

"Yes, all six of them."

Laura shook her head. "I don't understand. Bette's the one who set up the experiments, so why doesn't she have a record of her own experimental data? Why doesn't she have a set of disks?"

"She does."

"Then why in blazes didn't she just give the damn disks to the kidnappers?" Laura's voice snapped with tension. "My God, she's risking her life for the sake of a stupid formula! What good will that do her if she's dead?"

"The formula is very important to your aunt," Stefano said.

"More important than staying alive?" Laura slammed her coffee mug down on the counter. "I don't understand what's gotten into her. Bette's never cared about money, and anyway, her income is enough to live on comfortably for the next forty years."

"You misread your aunt's character," Stefano said quietly. "She cares nothing for the money. She wishes only to show you—to show all those who have doubted her—that she has both the determination and the genius to make a great contribution to society."

Laura closed her eyes. "She doesn't have to kill herself in the effort to prove she's important. The whole family adores her. She's like a second mother to me. Good grief, *everyone* loves her."

"And admires her?" Stefano asked.

"Of course," Laura said, but her split second of hesitation betrayed her.

Stefano made no comment. He didn't need to. "You must not imagine the worst," he said, putting his arm around her shoulders. "You are picturing your aunt being tortured or threatened, but that probably has not happened. She also has an excellent reason to conceal the existence of her copies of these disks—"

The sharp ring of the doorbell interrupted Stefano's attempt at reassurance. "It's too early for regular visitors," Laura whispered. "Who can it be?"

"Whoever it is, we must get rid of them quickly."

The ring of the doorbell changed to a thunderous knocking. "Immigration and Naturalization. Open up. This is Agent Dennis speaking."

Agent *Dennis?* Laura smothered a gurgle of nervous laughter. She turned to Stefano. "Oh, my God! Dennis the Menace. What are we going to do now?"

Stefano glanced toward the window. "It is too high to jump," he said regretfully. "And Dennis is blocking the stairs, so I'm afraid we shall have to open the door and let him in."

"My God, Stefano, it's seven-fifteen. We don't have time for chitchat with some overzealous despot from the INS!"

"Then we will get rid of him as soon as possible," Stefano said, walking to the front door. He pulled it open. "Good morning, sir. How may I help you?"

Without waiting for an invitation, the INS agent stepped into the tiny entrance hall.

"Please do come in," Stefano said affably.

The agent glared at him. Then his gaze swiveled around, lighting on Laura with blatant disapproval. He didn't speak to her, however. He directed his attention to Stefano, wav-

ing a sheaf of multicolored forms and puffing up his chest.
"Mr. Corelli, it's come to our attention that you are illegally employed in the United States. Under the terms of your student visa, you have no right to take paid employment. Furthermore, your visa has expired, and you no longer have right of residence in this country. You may, if you wish, return to Italy on the next available flight and avoid all penalties. Otherwise, under the terms of the Immigration and Naturalization Act of 1990, I am authorized to detain you until a hearing can be arranged in an appropriate federal court." Agent Dennis recited his piece in a singsong monotone. Drawing breath, he continued almost without pause, "You may, of course, request release from custody while awaiting your hearing, and your application will be processed through the appropriate channels." With clear and ominous intent, Dennis put his hand over a pair of handcuffs hanging from his belt. "Now, Mr. Corelli, you're a sensible man, and I'm sure you understand all the reasons why you need to come with me. Your efforts to avoid us have gone on quite long enough."

"But, Officer, I cannot come with you now! Trust me, you're making a terrible mistake."

"That's what they all say." Agent Dennis sounded weary.

"Look, be reasonable." Stefano kept his voice carefully controlled, but Laura could see the involuntary flick of a muscle in his jaw. "Let me call the university lawyers," he said. "We'll arrange a meeting in your office first thing on Monday morning. It's simply a case of clerical error, I promise you."

"You can call for your lawyer after we get downtown, Mr. Corelli."

"But you can't put Stefano in jail!" Laura exclaimed. "For heaven's sake, he's done nothing wrong."

Agent Dennis frowned at her. "I'm not taking him to jail," he said. "Contrary to popular opinion, the INS isn't staffed by sadists. We're simply overworked, understaffed and trying our best to do our duty. I'm taking Mr. Corelli downtown to our offices in response to a complaint filed by a U.S. citizen. Once he's downtown, Mr. Corelli can call his lawyer and make a legal deposition concerning—"

"Wait!" Laura had a great deal of experience dealing with government officials, and Dennis was obviously one of those people who followed department rules to the letter. Stefano was seconds away from being marched downtown, and once he was locked up in an INS office, Laura hated to think what would happen to Aunt Bette.

She suddenly remembered that she and Stefano had gone through a wedding ceremony yesterday precisely to take care of his problems with the INS. She took Stefano's hand, holding it up to display their wedding rings.

"Look, Officer, you can see there's been a mistake," she said, flashing him one of her best and friendliest smiles. Agent Dennis looked thoroughly unimpressed. Laura let go of the smile, drew herself up to her full five foot six and switched to cool and dignified. "I'm a U.S. citizen," she said. "Born and bred, third generation. How come my husband has no right to live with me?"

"Your husband?" Agent Dennis blinked, then jerked his thumb toward their clasped hands. "You tellin' me this man's married to you? Since when, I'd like to know."

"Since yesterday," Laura said. She found her purse and scrabbled with feverish haste through its once-orderly contents. "Here!" she exclaimed triumphantly. "Here's our wedding certificate, signed and sealed by Judge Sol Waterman. You know the immigration judge will give Stefano permission to stay in this country now that he's married, so couldn't you wait until Monday to have him fill out the paperwork?''

Agent Dennis looked momentarily taken aback, but he soon recovered. He directed a withering glare at Laura. "I hope you know, Miss . . . er, ma'am, that it's a federal offense to aid and abet a foreigner to obtain legal residence status in the United States by entering into a false contract of marriage—"

"Officer, how could you even suspect us of such a thing?" Stefano asked, hugging Laura and smiling at her with sickly sweetness. "This is not a false contract of marriage. Can you not see that we are in love? Passionately in love."

"Surely it's not part of your duty to break up a happily married couple," Laura said, resisting the strong urge to tell Agent Dennis to go to hell and let them get out of here while her aunt was still alive.

"How long have you known each other?" the agent asked.

"A very long time," Stefano said.

"Not too long," Laura said simultaneously.

Stefano managed a chuckle. "Well, I guess the wait seemed longer to me than it did to Laura. I have been wishing to call her my wife from the first moment we met."

"And when was that?" Agent Dennis asked. He held up the handcuffs. They rocked gently back and forth, the stainless steel glinting in the morning sunlight. Laura gulped and wiped her sweating palms against the sides of her jeans.

"At a party," Stefano said.

"At my aunt's house," Laura said simultaneously.

They exchanged wan smiles. "At a party at my aunt's house," Laura amended, sick to her stomach as she heard a clock chime in the distance. Seven-thirty. The minutes were ticking away inexorably toward eight o'clock. She pleaded with Agent Dennis. "Officer, now that you know we're married, couldn't you let us go? We have to leave right now—it's really very important. Someone's life might be at stake."

Dennis snorted. "Right," he said dourly. "Like I said before, it always is. But I'm a nice guy. Since you're claiming to be married and your papers look to be in order, I'm willing to promise that Mr. Corelli will get a prompt hearing. You can come downtown with me to the office and we'll take depositions from both of you—"

"Now!" For once, Stefano and Laura said the same thing at the same time. "Both of us?"

"Of course *now*. Of course both of you. You're married, aren't you? You should do this together."

Good Lord, mentioning the wedding had only made things worse, Laura thought. Now neither of them would be able to meet up with the kidnapper. Despairingly she turned to Stefano. "What are we going to do?" she murmured, not caring if Dennis overheard. "Can we tell him the truth?"

"I think he would not believe us," Stefano said quietly. "We have waited too long to mention Bette and now he would think we are making one more excuse." He appealed again to Dennis. "Officer, we do not have time to confer with you right at this moment. As my wife promised, we will come to the INS office first thing on Monday morning, I swear to you. But we have an appointment that cannot be broken."

He might as well have spoken to a block of concrete. Agent Dennis didn't yawn in their faces, but his bored expression suggested that he had heard every impassioned plea imaginable, several times over, and no longer allowed himself to be swayed by the trivia of everyday life. He opened the handcuffs and dangled them from his fingers. "Mr. Corelli, we can make this easy or we can make it nasty. You can come willingly, which I'd sure like, or I can take you out of here cuffed. The choice is yours."

"Yes," Stefano muttered, "I can see that it is." He smiled brightly. "Then I make my choice and face the consequences, no? I hope you approve." His hand shot out, landing a solid punch square on Dennis's jaw, followed by a blow that smashed into the agent's stomach. Dennis's eyes crossed, rolled upward and swiftly closed. He collapsed neatly into Stefano's waiting arms.

"Oh, my God!" Laura stared at the agent's limp body.

"Get the disks!" Stefano said, arranging Dennis on the hall carpet and stuffing a cushion under his head. "We must get out of here."

Too shocked to do anything other than obey, Laura jumped over Dennis and grabbed the disks and car keys from the counter. Her heart pounded and her mouth felt dryer than cotton fluff, but she was aware of a surge of relief, along with the shock and the anxiety. At least they could now keep their appointment with the kidnapper.

"Where in the world did you learn to hit like that?" she asked, handing the keys to Stefano.

"On the street corners of Milan during a notably misspent youth." Stefano took her hand and ran toward the stairs. "Come on. Let's get out of here before he wakes up. We have only a few minutes."

"Maybe you should hit him again."

"How unexpectedly bloodthirsty you are, *cara*. But there is no need to compound the crime. We will be on our way before he recovers, and he will have no idea where we have gone."

"True." Laura ran down the stairs behind Stefano, adrenaline pumping into her system. She was in the car when the enormity of what she had just done suddenly occurred to her. "My God! I've aided and abetted a brutal physical assault on a representative of the U.S. government. I've committed a major crime! I could go to jail!''

Stefano didn't seem to take her worries with the seriousness they deserved. In fact, he laughed. He raised her hand to his lips and kissed the tips of her fingers. "If you go to jail, then I will certainly be condemned, also. I will write you love letters from my cell, *cara.*"

The man should have that damn smile of his registered as a lethal weapon, Laura thought. "Great," she muttered, ignoring an illogical flutter in the region of her heart. "That certainly makes it all worthwhile."

To LAURA'S RELIEF, the traffic was light, and Stefano obviously knew where he was going. He drove aggressively but within the speed limit, so that they ran no risk of attracting attention from a skulking traffic cop. Laura spent the journey on pins and needles, but they arrived at the café parking lot with a couple of minutes to spare.

The café was undergoing renovations, its windows and entrance sealed by heavy-duty sheets of plastic tacked onto wooden frames, and the parking lot itself was cluttered with construction debris. There were no other cars in the lot, although the parking area across the street contained a small Chevy pickup, three bikes locked to a rack and a couple of cars. Of Aunt Bette and her kidnapper there seemed no sign.

Stefano stopped the Buick in the middle of the lot, where it was instantly visible from all sides. He left the engine running and the windows rolled up. Ready for a quick getaway, Laura realized, not sure whether to be impressed by his forethought or worried by his expertise in dealing with criminals.

The car's air-conditioning was on full blast, but the sun was already hot, and Laura's T-shirt was beginning to stick to her back. She felt hot, disheveled and scared. She drew a deep breath. "What do we do now?"

"We wait."

His cool self-control irritated her raw nerves. "How can you be do damned relaxed?"

"Because it is necessary. For Bette's sake."

"Maybe the phone call was a hoax. Maybe Bette's at home, tucked up in bed."

"Could be. Thanks to our friend Dennis, we did not have time to drive by her house and check. But if the call was a hoax, we have lost nothing save nervous energy by coming here as he instructed."

Laura was about to mention that they were looking at life in jail for punching an INS agent in the nose when she heard the faint ring of a phone. Stefano had the car in gear before she could say anything. He drove quickly to the side of the parking lot where a public phone box stood in the shade of a scraggy hedge. Lowering the car window, he picked up the phone without getting out of the car.

"Hello."

Laura leaned across the seat, straining to hear the kidnapper's reply.

"You haven't come alone, Doctor. That wasn't smart of you."

If the kidnapper knew Stefano wasn't alone, then he had to be calling from somewhere nearby, where he had a clear view of the car. Laura glanced around, squinting against the bright sun, but she couldn't detect any sign of the caller or of Bette. That didn't mean much. The parking lot was ringed on two sides by office buildings, and the kidnapper would be able to see their car from any number of windows.

"Laura is Bette's niece and my wife," Stefano said. "She was with me when you phoned this morning. Would you have preferred her to stay at home and report your call to the police?"

"Don't try to get smart, Corelli. You're not in any position to get smart. Do you have the disks?"

"All six of them. I trust that you have Bette."

"If you have the disks, we're ready to do a deal. Here are your instructions, Corelli. Get out of the car *real* slow. Keep your hands away from your body and hold the disks in your left hand. Go into the café and turn to your right. You'll find an open door. We'll be waiting inside. Understood?"

"Understood."

"And, Dr. Corelli?"

"Yes?"

"Make sure the broad stays in the car." The kidnapper disconnected the phone with a gentle click.

Laura thrust the box of disks into Stefano's hands, allowing herself to feel hope for the first time. Impulsively she reached up, pulled his face down and kissed him hard on the mouth. "Take care," she said. "Don't get yourself hurt."

He paused in the act of exiting the car. "You sound as if you really care." His voice held none of its usual teasing undertone.

"Well, of course I care." Under his steady gaze, she blushed, then tried to make light of her feelings. "I don't want to be left alone to face charges of assaulting Dennis the Menace."

Stefano touched his fingers to her lips. "I will not fail you," he said. "That is my promise."

He got out of the car before she could reply. Laura watched him cross the parking lot to the café. She saw a man with an athletic build, his thick hair gleaming blue-black in the sun, walking with his hands held carefully away from his body. *Her husband.* She let the words rattle around inside her head, but they no longer sounded quite as incredible as they had yesterday. Which, Laura decided, probably had something to do with the fact that she'd spent most of the previous night making love with *her husband* to mutually mind-blowing effect.

Stefano disappeared into the café and Laura unclenched her hands, willing herself to wait patiently as instructed. The hum of distant traffic drifted in through the open car window, punctuated by the barking of a dog and the thunk of tennis balls landing on a nearby court. The parking lot itself remained quiet, the uneven surface baking in the morning sun. However hard Laura strained her ears, she could hear nothing from inside the café.

Half a minute ticked by. Two minutes. What the heck was going on in there? How long could it take to swap a set of computer disks for Aunt Bette?

A sputter of sound drew her attention to the parking lot across the street. A gray Ford Taurus drew out from its half-concealed parking spot behind a dumpster. JMT 261. Laura strained to see the driver, but the sun was shining on his windshield, and she had no more than a blurred impression of a gray-haired man wearing dark glasses, before the car turned into the alley behind the café. She heard the engine cut, then nothing.

Laura considered her options for about a second and a half. Then she grabbed the keys, jumped out of the car and crept toward the café, keeping close to the perimeter of the parking lot, where the leafy branches of the hedge gave her at least the illusion of being protected from immediate discovery. She sneaked up to a window on the far side of the café and carefully lifted a loose corner of plastic so that she could see inside.

What she saw was Stefano, struggling in the midst of wood shavings and discarded paint cans to fight off the attacks of two masked men. He was a much stronger and more coordinated fighter then either of his attackers, but it was two against one, and they were smart enough to keep coming at him from opposing angles.

With a swift whirling turn, Stefano delivered a kick that knocked one of the men clear to the ground, but even as he swung back around to defend himself from behind, the second attacker, a giant wearing an oil-stained athletic shirt, grabbed a plywood board and brought it crashing down on Stefano's head. Stefano swayed for an instant, then fell to the floor, landing in a pile of wood shavings. Laura barely managed to smother a cry of outraged sympathy.

"Was that really necessary, Joe? You know how much I loathe violence." A stout gray-haired man stepped out from behind the ladder that had obscured him from Laura's sight. The man who'd been driving the Ford Taurus, she realized. He took off his sunglasses and she recognized him at once. She'd seen him just yesterday, lurking in the bushes outside the restaurant where they'd gone for their celebratory lunch.

Aunt Bette's kidnapper, Laura thought grimly, loathing the man's self-satisfied smirk. He might claim to hate violence, but apparently not enough to leave poor Bette safe in her own home.

Joe looked sulky at the reproach from his boss. He poked Stefano with his foot. "Damn dago wouldn't hand over the disks until he saw the old woman. He said if she ain't here, he ain't dealin'."

The man Stefano had knocked over got to his feet, brushing sawdust from his hands and wincing with pain. "The son of a bitch kicked me right in the crotch. Damn near castrated me."

The kidnapper-in-chief had no interest in the state of his underling's health. "I hope you didn't crush the disks when you fell," he said. "Give them to me and let's get out of here."

"We ain't got the disks yet."

"What?"

"I'm getting 'em now." The oil-stained giant rolled Stefano onto his back and gave a grunt of satisfaction. "Here they are." He aimed another kick at Stefano's rib cage. "Damn foreigners. I hate 'em all. Takin' jobs from honest Americans."

"And even from dishonest ones," the elderly man murmured. Smiling at the sight of the computer disks, he moved across the littered floor with a speed and agility that belied his girth. "I'll take care of those," he said, seizing the box of disks. He paused and stared at Stefano. "Dr. Corelli, are you awake?"

Silence.

"I hope you can hear me, Dr. Corelli, because I'm not planning to repeat myself. If these disks contain the promised information, Bette will be released later today. I will call your apartment at two o'clock and tell you where you may go to pick her up."

Either Stefano was unconscious or he chose not to reply. The kidnapper prodded him a couple of times, then shrugged. He waddled back to the rear door, the disks cradled protectively against his chest. "Let's move it, my friends. We need to print out the information on these to make sure he's not selling us a bill of goods."

Ducking below the level of the windows, Laura sped to the corner of the building. She waited just long enough to see the three men jump into the Taurus and take off in a northerly direction before dashing back into the café, no longer bothering to hide. Stefano was already hauling himself to his feet, using a carpenter's trestle to help lever himself upright.

"Can you walk?" she asked. "Did you hear what the fat guy said?"

"Yes to both questions." He spoke through gritted teeth. "Lend me your shoulders, will you?"

Laura grabbed his arm and draped it around her neck, torn between the need to get back to the car and give chase to the kidnappers and the equally urgent need to get Stefano some medical help. "How badly are you hurt?" she asked.

"I'll live." His mouth twisted in a parody of his familiar teasing grin. "Maybe."

His attempt at a smile produced in her the craziest impulse to burst into tears. She took his hand and held it briefly against her cheek. "Ready to go?" she asked.

"Yes." Stefano's face was white beneath the streaks of dirt and sawdust, but he was already moving at a fast clip, his spare arm wrapped around his waist, nursing his bruised ribs.

"I recognized one of the kidnappers," she panted. "He was the same man who was lurking in the flower bed outside the restaurant."

"Which means he is also the man who tried to break into Bette's house last month," Stefano said, reaching into his pocket for the car keys. "You drive."

She took the keys and turned on the ignition while Stefano eased into the front passenger seat in dogged silence. Neither of them made any comment about the sweat beading his forehead as she reversed out of the lot, or about the rigid line of his mouth as they bounced over the speed bump at the exit onto the street. "Do you think the kidnappers really will release Bette later?" she asked.

He hesitated. "I do not believe they will harm her. She is their only bargaining chip."

Laura drew what comfort she could from his reply. She calculated that the kidnappers had less than a two-minute head start. She knew in her heart of hearts that they might as well have had two hours. How in the world could they hope to pick up the trail of a gray Ford Taurus, the most popular car in America, even if she did know the license-plate number? Nevertheless, she headed north at high speed, praying for a glimpse of the kidnappers' car. Praying for a miracle.

Stefano leaned forward and opened the glove compartment, taking out a small device that looked like a cross between a fuzzbuster and an electronic game board. Frowning, he fiddled with the dials until the machine began to emit a thrumming intermittent beep. His face broke into a beatific smile. "We have them!" he said. "Turn right here. They are obviously heading for the interstate."

"How do we have them?" Laura asked, turning right as directed. "How can that...thing possibly tell you where the kidnappers are going?"

"I bugged the plastic container that holds the disks," Stefano said, looking extremely pleased with himself. "Provided the kidnappers do not get outside a ten-mile radius of our car, we can follow them on screen. With luck, they will lead us straight to Bette."

"You managed to make coffee, get dressed *and* bug a package of computer disks all while I was taking a thirty-second shower this morning?" Laura asked.

"Of course not. I had the package of disks already bugged. Just as a precaution."

Laura should have been delighted at Stefano's news, but she wasn't. What sort of man built an electronic homing device into a package of computer data just in case it got stolen? Her doubts must have shown on her face, because Stefano laid his hand on her knee. "Remind me never to gamble with you as my partner, *cara*. You have the most expressive pair of eyes I have ever seen."

"Do I? Then you must know that I'm wondering why you seem to have expected Aunt Bette to be kidnapped."

"If I had expected Bette to be kidnapped, I would never have left her alone," Stefano said coolly. "However, I did expect someone to make another attempt to steal the computer disks. Naturally I took precautions."

"*Another* attempt?"

"I told you about the burglar I surprised outside Bette's house a couple of weeks ago. Besides, to take precautions was entirely logical. Somehow, word has gotten out that your aunt has developed a process that will revolutionize cloth production. Naturally the sharks are circling. If those disks had truly contained details of Bette's new process, they would be worth at least a million dollars, even on the black market."

Laura's ears pricked up. "What do you mean, *if* those disks had truly contained details of the process?"

Stefano grinned. "I prepared them with a built-in self-destruct program. The moment anyone tries to print out the information on any of those disks or send it over a modem, the entire contents of the disk will automatically erase." He broke off. "Take the next exit. Quick, move into the right-hand lane! They're leaving the highway."

Laura looked into her rearview mirror as she prepared to shift lanes, and her stomach clenched with fright. "Oh, my God! Police! Lights flashing, sirens blaring, the whole works."

Stefano glanced over his shoulder. "Damn! They look as if they are coming after us."

"Dennis the Menace must have called in the license number of your car."

"Lose them," he said. "We don't have time for explanations."

Laura shot across two lanes of traffic, leaving a trail of blaring horns and infuriated drivers. What's happening to me? she wondered, not slowing the car. She'd left New York a law-abiding accountant, who had dated the same man for ten months without ever exchanging more than a chaste good-night kiss. Since arriving in Columbus, she'd married a man she barely knew; she'd spent the entire night making passionate love to him; and now she was being chased down the interstate highway by a cop who wanted to arrest her for assault and battery. Obviously she'd lost her mind in midair, somewhere between Manhattan and Columbus, Ohio. Obviously she had no choice but to pull over to the side of the road and apologize profusely. Perhaps the cops would accept a plea of temporary insanity. Perhaps they'd recommend a good psychiatrist.

"Double back once we've lost the cops!" Stefano yelled. "Get back on the highway if the lights aren't against you."

The lights were against her. Laura sped out of the exit lane, veering right so that she didn't have to brake for more than a second or two. She doubled the car back on itself, and when another set of traffic lights impeded her progress, she spun right again and sped down a deserted side street.

"Great driving. I am impressed." Stefano gave her knee an admiring pat.

"Have we lost them?" she demanded, staring anxiously into her mirror and executing another swift turn just to be on the safe side.

"We have lost the policemen, for sure," Stefano said.

"But?" she queried. "I hear a 'but' in your voice."

"Unfortunately, *cara*, I'm afraid we have also lost the kidnappers."

Chapter Six

THEY PARKED the Buick at the rear of a busy McDonald's, deciding they were as safe from discovery there as they would be anywhere. Once inside the restaurant, Stefano disappeared into the men's room and emerged wet-haired but free of dirt streaks and sawdust. They ordered french fries and orange juice so that they'd have an excuse to sit down and discuss what to do next.

"We should probably consider going to the police," Stefano said, not quite hiding a wince as he slid along the bench and his sore ribs hit the table.

"Good grief, we just spent ten minutes escaping from them!" Laura protested.

"And that's what changed the situation. Until the police chased us off the highway, we had a good chance of following the kidnappers and finding Bette quickly. Now that hope is gone, and so our options have narrowed."

"Going to the police might put Aunt Bette at greater risk," Laura said. "Remember, the kidnappers warned us not to tell the authorities anything."

"What else would you expect them to say?" Stefano slammed his fist into the palm of his other hand. "Damn, this is my fault! We need to be in my apartment to take the next phone call from the kidnappers, but we cannot return to my neighborhood without running the risk of being arrested for assaulting Dennis the Menace. *Dio mio,* I thought I was so smart, with my fancy electronic gadgets. I was sure I would be able to find Bette before the kidnappers realized the disks I had given them were programmed for self-destruct.''

He didn't need to point out that the kidnappers would be furious when they saw their stolen data unraveling into gobbledygook right in front of their eyes. Nor did he need to point out that angry kidnappers were almost guaranteed to take out their frustration in physical violence. Laura's imagination was working overtime, and she was sure his was, too.

Stefano pushed his french fries away untouched. "We really have no choice," he said. "We'd better find the nearest police station. I hope to God they believe our story and take quick action.''

Laura wasn't optimistic. She could visualize all too clearly the painful delays as the lumbering wheels of a police investigation rolled into operation. Her chest tightened with panic. She had a mental flash of Aunt Bette's cherubic face as she'd last seen it, eyes twinkling, laughter lines crinkling her cheeks, when she raised her champagne glass to toast the newlyweds. A picture of the kidnapper's smirking features superimposed itself on the happy memory, and Laura's entire body turned cold with dislike. Even when he'd been hiding in the bushes outside the restaurant, the kidnapper had worn an infuriating expression of smug self-satisfaction.

A nagging sense of familiarity tickled at the edges of Laura's anger. She'd seen those sneering features somewhere before, and recently, too. But where? She lived in Manhattan, and the kidnapper presumably lived in Columbus. So where in blazes could she have met him? Or even glimpsed him?

The answer came in a flash of subliminal memory. "In the photo on Aunt Bette's dressing table!" she exclaimed, grabbing Stefano's hands in her excitement. "Good grief, that's it! He's in Aunt Bette's wedding picture!"

Stefano looked understandably blank. "Who is in Bette's wedding picture? What are you talking about?"

"Aunt Bette's ex-husband." Laura jumped to her feet, unable to sit still any longer. "Except he wasn't her ex-husband then, of course. He was the bridegroom."

"Well, I daresay the bridegroom has every right to appear in his own wedding picture—"

"I'm talking about the kidnapper! *Bette's husband*—that's who kidnapped her. Or I should say her ex-husband, Walter what's-his-name! Come on, let's go find him!"

"You believe Walter Willis is behind this kidnapping?" Stefano rose to his feet, but he could hardly have looked more skeptical if she'd accused Mother Teresa. "But he is a most respectable man! He is a college professor."

"So are you," Laura pointed out. "That's no guarantee of virtue. You're being chased by half the Columbus police force."

"But that is a misunderstanding—"

"It all fits." Laura insisted, already halfway to the exit. "Walter is a chemical engineer. He and Bette met in college, and she dropped out in her junior year to marry him. Bette mentioned that they'd run into each other at a college reunion a few months ago, and I'll bet she couldn't resist telling him what she was working on. And who better than Walter to know that Bette is brilliant enough to have discovered something valuable?"

Panting but triumphant, Laura arrived back at the car. "Get in," she said, annoyed with Stefano's lack of excitement. "Let's go!"

"Go where?"

"To Walter's house!" Stefano was really being infuriatingly dense. Laura almost stamped her foot with impatience.

"Even if Walter Willis has taken Bette back to his house—and that's a big if—do you know where he lives? I don't."

Laura's mouth opened, then closed again. She collapsed against the side of the car, as deflated as yesterday's balloon. "Damn!" she exclaimed softly. "I haven't the faintest idea where Walter lives, except that it's probably somewhere in Columbus. My God, isn't there any way to track him down?"

"He might be listed in the phone book," Stefano suggested.

She brightened. "It's sure worth a try. Where can we find a directory?"

"There's a phone booth over there." Stefano pointed to the corner of the parking lot.

Unlike any public phone Laura had ever seen in New York City, this one actually had two current directories suspended from metal binders just as they were supposed to be. Midwestern living, she decided, had its advantages. They searched swiftly through the directories, but without success. No Walter Willis, no W. Willis, not even somebody Willis with W. as a middle initial, appeared anywhere in the area listings.

"I guess that's that," Laura said gloomily. "At least we know what we have to do next. We have no choice but to go to the police. Thank goodness we have a name to give them." She bit her lip, scowling anxiously. "I'm scared they'll throw us in jail for assaulting Dennis the Menace and ignore our story about Aunt Bette. Of course they won't keep us in jail for very long, but Bette's nowhere near as strong as she looks, and time isn't on our side. . . ."

Stefano was looking progressively more miserable as she spoke. "Unfortunately I'm afraid we may have a worse problem than you know."

"What's that?"

"Even if the police believe Bette is being held hostage, I'm sure they won't believe our claim that Walter Willis is responsible for the kidnapping."

"Why not? Ex-husbands are mean and vicious to ex-wives all the time. They're usually the prime suspects."

"True, but in this case, I'm afraid the police will think we are accusing Walter out of a desire for vengeance."

"Why would they think something so silly? We'd never even met Walter Willis until he pulled this dumb stunt."

Stefano grimaced. "I have been wondering for the past couple of weeks why the INS pursued me with such determination. After all, this country is swamped by illegal immigrants, and a college professor with a clerical error in his paperwork doesn't merit a full-time agent working on his case."

"It is strange," Laura agreed. "But you told me the INS must have decided to make an example of you."

"That's what I believed until this morning. But do you remember what Agent Dennis said when he waved that bundle of official papers at me? He said a complaint had been filed with his department 'by a U.S. citizen.' According to him, a U.S. citizen had sworn that I was involved in illegal activities, and because of that, the INS checked into my visa status and discovered it had expired."

"Yes, you're right, Dennis did say that, and it explains why the immigration people are pursuing you so actively." Laura frowned. "But I don't see . . ." She paused. "Good grief, are you suggesting that Walter reported you to the INS?"

"Do you not find it a most strange coincidence that very soon after I foiled Walter's attempt to break into Bette's basement, my problems with immigration began?"

Laura breathed in sharply. "Bette always said her ex-husband was a snake, but it never occurred to me that he was reptilian enough to swear a false complaint about you so that Aunt Bette would be left to market her new miracle fiber without your help and advice.''

"But that is what happened, I am almost sure of it. Walter had very good reasons to want me out of the picture, and so he set the INS on my tail.''

"It sounds horribly logical,'' she admitted.

Stefano's eyes darkened with foreboding. "Can you imagine how the police will react if we march into the local station and tell them that Walter Willis has kidnapped Bette?''

"They'll think you're trying to get back at Walter...."

"Or even that I have kidnapped Bette myself,'' Stefano said glumly. "If we mention her great discovery, they will think I wish to steal it. After all, what do they know about me except that a U.S. citizen has accused me of being a criminal—probably a member of the Mafia—and that I am in the country without the correct visa? Not to mention the fact that I brutally assaulted Agent Dennis.''

"What can we do?'' Laura asked, her voice cold and flat with fear. "If your theory's correct, we daren't risk going to the police, but we sure can't leave Bette in Walter's hands. The man's a monster.''

"Or a jealous scientist, which sometimes is close to the same thing.''

At that moment, a squad car cruised by on the opposite side of the road. Laura's stomach plummeted to her sneakers. Quick as a flash, she jumped into the Buick, and Stefano followed almost as fast. His attention caught by the blur of movement, the cop glanced across to the parking lot, but he didn't stop or turn around. Laura's stomach gradually eased back to its normal resting place, but her heart continued to pound at twice its normal rate.

"This is ridiculous," Stefano said. "We cannot carry on like this, ducking and hiding every time we catch a glimpse of a police car."

"If only we could get into Aunt Bette's house," Laura said. "We could check her address book and see if she has a listing for Walter Willis. They might have exchanged addresses when they met at their college reunion. When people have been divorced for as long as Bette and Walter, they forget all the reasons they split up and start to think they can be friends again."

"For what it's worth, we *can* get into Bette's house," Stefano said. "I have her house key."

Laura smiled delightedly. "You do?"

He nodded. "Right there on the same ring as the car keys."

Laura was so relieved she flung her arms around his neck and kissed him exuberantly. "Stefano Corelli, you are a wonderful magnificent man."

He slanted her a sideways look that was hard to interpret. "You almost sound as if you mean that, *cara*."

"Why shouldn't I mean it?"

His eyes gleamed. "When you arrived in Columbus, I am not sure you would have called me wonderful. Arrogant, perhaps, or more likely... a scoundrel."

"I didn't know you then," she said.

"We both had misconceptions." He looked at her, his dark melting gaze suddenly intense. "Getting to know you has been a great pleasure for me, *cara*. I hope for you, too."

"It's been... interesting," she said.

His gaze became quizzical, and she felt herself grow hot and flustered. "What are we going to do if we can't find Walter's address at Bette's house?"

Stefano accepted her change of subject without comment. "Call a priest or a psychic," he said. "Or maybe both.

If we don't soon find out where Walter lives, we are going to be in serious need of divine intervention."

THE MORNING'S EVENTS had not left Laura in an optimistic mood, so she was overjoyed when they discovered Walter Willis's address and phone number listed in Bette's Rolodex, not under *W*, but under *E*.

"How in the world did you know to start looking at the beginning of the alphabet?" Stefano asked, tugging the card free and shoving it into his pocket.

"She files my address under *N* for niece, so I didn't expect to find his under *W*." Laura hurried toward the back door, where they'd parked their car out of sight, they hoped, of passing policemen.

"But why under *E?*" Stefano asked.

She grinned. "I'm guessing *E* stands for ex-husband."

"You're right, of course." Stefano chuckled. "Just when I think I have finally fathomed the way Bette's mind works, she surprises me again."

Memories of Bette crowded in thick and fast, all of them warm and happy. Fighting back unexpected tears, Laura reached for the door handle. "God, I hope we find her soon."

"We will. Worthington isn't all that far from here and it's still barely lunchtime— Don't touch the door!" Stefano lunged for her hand, but he was a split second too late. A cacophony of howling sound broke out, blasting the quiet neighborhood.

Belatedly Laura remembered the fancy burglar-alarm system Stefano had installed. "I thought you disarmed the darn thing when we came in," she yelled over the blare.

"It has an automatic re-arming system, and it's keyed straight into the local police station," he yelled back. "Come on! Let's get out of here before we have the entire Columbus police force on our heels."

Given that they already had half the police force out looking for them, adding the other half seemed almost a minor problem to Laura. The noise of the alarm, however, was earsplitting, disrupting the entire neighborhood. "Can't you turn it off?" she asked.

Stefano was sprinting to the car, dragging her with him. He ignored the neighbors who were beginning to poke their heads out of various doors and windows. "Only from the master panel in the basement. No time. We must get out of here and rescue Bette."

Laura scooted behind the wheel of the Buick and slammed the door with one hand, simultaneously turning on the ignition with the other. She reversed out of the driveway at a speed that would have terrified her under normal conditions. One of Aunt Bette's rosebushes encountered a spinning car wheel and bit the dust. The tires burned rubber as she swung out onto the road and depressed the accelerator so hard the car fishtailed. She hung on to the steering wheel and fought to bring the car back under control without losing speed.

"See any cops?" she asked tersely as soon as the car was secure on the road.

"None. At least a dozen astonished neighbors, however."

"They'll get over it." The blare of the alarm finally faded into the distance. "Give me directions," she said. "Where am I going?"

"Right at the second light, then left lane onto the highway." He leaned across and locked her seat belt.

"Thank you." Laura drew a calming gulp of air and forced her fingers to relax their death grip on the steering wheel. "Maybe it's a good thing the burglar alarm went off," she said. "The cops are bound to investigate a signal, aren't they?"

"Sure to. Is that good news?"

"The cops will at least know Aunt Bette isn't at home and that someone tried to break into her house. Maybe they'll chase us right to Walter's lair."

"I'm beginning to suspect you like being chased by police cars."

"Of course I don't!" Her denial was instant and indignant. "Except...except today it might be convenient as long as they don't actually catch us."

Stefano laughed, the sound oddly tender. "Do you know something, Laura? You are a complete and utter fraud. A total impostor."

His words stung. She stared ahead, mouth held firm against an ominous tendency to quiver. "I'm sorry you feel that way. This is a difficult situation, and I've tried to—"

He put his hand over her knee and squeezed gently. "I did not make my meaning clear. I intended to pay you a compliment."

"I don't see how it's a compliment to call me a fraud."

"Then let me explain. You have spent so many years trying to make yourself look and sound like the woman you think you ought to be that you have forgotten the woman you really are."

She shook her head. "I'm very much aware of my own basic character."

He grinned. "On the contrary, my love, you are delightfully deluded. You would like to believe that you are dedicated to your career. You struggle to create the impression that you have all your feelings boxed into neat rational compartments. The truth is something quite otherwise."

Laura could feel herself blushing. "You're wrong," she said, her voice low and oddly husky. "I'm exactly the person I appear on the surface. I believe it's essential for people to conduct their lives in a logical manner, to base their decisions on reason, not on impulse and half-baked emotions—"

"Liar," he said softly. "You know very well that the most important decisions we make have little to do with reason. Quite often we must grope and feel our way to the truth. Sometimes we must risk a leap into the unknown, trusting only our gut instincts."

"Not me," Laura said firmly. She cleared her throat, trying to get rid of the thickness that refused to go away. "I *never* take chances. I base all the important decisions in my life on a careful analysis of the facts—"

Stefano burst out laughing. "Right," he said, still chuckling. "I have seen that prudent behavior pattern a lot over the past two days."

"What does that sarcastic remark mean?"

"Well, let me see." He ticked off on his fingers. "First, you came running from New York to Columbus just because Bette said she needed you. You didn't even bother to call first. Then you married me, a virtual stranger. You made love to me within twelve hours of our marriage—a wonderful glorious experience that I am burning to repeat. So far this morning, you have helped to vanquish Dennis the Menace, unmasked the identity of Bette's kidnapper, led the police on a high-speed chase, and now you are about to confront Walter Willis in his lair, all without batting the eyelash, I think you Americans say. And you wish to claim, *carissima,* that you are a woman who doesn't take chances?"

Laura gulped. "But I'm not really the way you make me sound," she protested. "I'm not irrational and . . . and undisciplined. Everything that's happened in the past two days is completely out of character for me."

"On the contrary," Stefano said. "I believe that in the past two days you have behaved as the woman you truly are. Impulsive, emotional, brave." She heard the smile enter his voice. "Passionate. Loyal. Sexy. Not to mention very beautiful. Shall I go on?"

He thought she was brave? And passionate? Not to mention beautiful. Laura blinked, telling herself to concentrate on the traffic and not allow herself to melt into a puddle of warm chocolate. Why did his assessment of her character leave her feeling so admired, so...cherished? In truth, she disapproved of people who acted impulsively. She was the member of the family who could be relied on to behave sensibly no matter what the provocation. Good grief, the last thing she wanted was for Stefano to start believing she was passionate and impulsive—the sort of woman who met the man of her dreams and fell instantly in love with him.

She drew her mouth into a tight line, trying to look stern. Making love to Stefano last night had obviously been a major mistake. In view of the wanton feverish way she'd behaved, he had every right to wonder if she was falling in love with him. And of course she wasn't even a tiny bit in love with Stefano. She couldn't be. Falling in love was a slow process that took months and months of careful consideration. She still hadn't managed to fall in love with Brett Hotchkiss after dating him for almost a year. How could she have fallen in love with Stefano after only two days? She knew nothing about him. Well, only a few unimportant things. Like the fact that he made her laugh, and that he was the most exciting lover she'd ever dreamed of, and that he was a unique source of strength in a crisis...

"You must be thinking very interesting thoughts, *cara*." Stefano's voice was husky. "Your eyes are full of dreams, and your cheeks have turned the most delightful shade of pink."

"I'm hot!" she snapped. "That's all." Good Lord, if she carried on like this, blushing and simpering every time he looked at her, he'd start to wonder if she wanted to turn their fake marriage into a real one. Which would be embarrassing, to say the least, because obviously a man like Stefano would never tie himself for life to a plain boring woman like her. Except he didn't consider her boring, she reminded herself, or even plain. He'd said she was passionate and beautiful. And sexy.

Laura's thoughts skittered to a confused halt, and she gave her throat another clearing rasp. "How much farther to Walter's house?" she asked. This time her voice emerged as a high-pitched squeak, instead of a throaty growl.

"The next exit." Thankfully, Stefano accepted the change of subject without comment. He glanced through the rear window. "This is the most subdued ride I have taken with you, *cara*. Not a police car in sight. Not even an eager INS agent pursuing us."

"That figures," Laura muttered, still trying to get a grip on her wayward feelings. "There's never a squad car around when you need one."

"I see your point," Stefano said. "If Bette really is being held captive at Walter's house, it would be quite helpful for us to turn up with a police escort." He read from the card they had taken from Bette's address file. "1762 Hillview Road. Make a left turn here, *cara*. It should be about halfway down the block."

Number 1762 turned out to be a slightly shabby bungalow in a row of well-maintained houses dating from the sixties. Its quiet exterior and lace-curtained windows gave no hint that it might contain a trio of kidnappers and their seventy-two-year-old victim. Laura drove past the house once, turned at the end of the road, then drove back and parked the Buick a couple of doors down on the same side. They both sat in silence for a second or two, considering their next move.

"As far as I can see, our only choice is to march up to the front door and ring the bell," Laura said.

Stefano gave her a faint smile. "I share your impatience, *cara*, but they are more likely to cut and run than to answer the door. It would seem wise if we could first check out the lay of the land a little."

"But we can't see anything from outside. There are blinds or curtains at every window."

"At the front that is true. But perhaps if we check in the back of the house, we shall find an uncurtained window and some sign of your aunt's presence."

Laura frowned, squinting against the midday sun. "Can we get to the back of the house without being seen by any people who are inside?"

"If we walk around by the garage, I believe we can reach the backyard without being observed."

"Then let's go." Laura was out of the car in an instant, compelled by a nagging sense of danger. "I have this horrible feeling that we don't have time to hang around out here twiddling our thumbs and hoping Aunt Bette's okay."

"You are right." He followed her out of the car and took the keys, unlocking the trunk. "If we have to do any breaking and entering, this tire iron might be useful," he said.

Laura swallowed hard, but she didn't protest when he tucked the lethal-looking weapon under his arm. Stefano brushed his knuckles lightly across her cheek. "Don't look so worried, my heart. We shall rescue your aunt, never fear."

My heart. Why did the wretched man choose the most ridiculous moments to say something that sent her pulses careering into overdrive and her lungs into a state of instant oxygen deprivation? Spine ramrod straight, Laura walked down the path at the side of Walter's house and rounded the corner into the backyard.

A screened porch, jutting out some eight feet or so, ran across most of the rear of the house, and a chestnut tree, thickly festooned with the bright green leaves of early summer, shielded the far corner. Fortuitously, they had ended up by the kitchen, the only part of the rear not blocked by the porch. From inside the house, wafting out through the porch, they heard the murmur of masculine voices, several of them seeming to talk at once.

The sounds were clear enough that it seemed likely that the doors leading from the house to the porch were open, but not quite clear enough to identify individual voices. Unfortunately, however hard she strained, Laura couldn't detect any trace of a female voice that might be Aunt Bette's.

Stefano cupped his hands together, then mimed to indicate that he would give Laura a leg up so that she could see in through the kitchen window.

She shook her head. "I'll hurt your ribs," she mouthed into his ear.

"No choice," he mouthed back. "You are light. I will survive."

Reluctantly Laura stepped into the cup of his hands, clutching the window ledge with her fingers and using as much of her own strength as she could to pull herself up high enough to peek inside. The kitchen window was uncurtained and the blind was rolled up. Despite his battered ribs, Stefano was very strong, and within seconds her nose was resting on the sill, and she had a clear view of the interior.

There was nobody in the kitchen, although a couple of glasses in the sink still had ice in them and an open box on the counter contained a slice of fresh-looking pizza. Someone had obviously eaten lunch, but there was nothing in the kitchen to indicate if that someone was Bette or her captors or some totally innocent householder. Laura wriggled her foot free of Stefano's supporting hands and jumped quietly to the ground.

"I saw pizza and ice water," she said softly. "No people. The house looks as if it has a standard suburban-home layout. The family room leads off to the side of the kitchen, and I think that's where everyone is, but I couldn't see in."

Stefano's gaze became speculative. "I could get a clear view of the family room through the roof," he said. "Look, there is a skylight right in the center."

"But how would you get up there?"

"That chestnut tree is better than a ladder."

Just as he spoke, a howl of mingled dismay and fury exploded through the porch screens. "What the hell is happening to this program?" yelled a voice.

This time the question was so loud Stefano and Laura had no difficulty in hearing it. They exchanged glances. "Walter Willis?" she murmured.

"Sounds like him, no?"

"God awmighty!" A stream of profanity wafted out into the backyard. "What the bloody hell is going on?"

"Exit the freakin' program!" Another voice, shrill with panic, shouted the instruction.

"I can't! It's not responding to any cues."

"My God, we're losing the whole data base!"

"Shut the friggin' system down! The main drive is going to crash!"

Stefano grinned. "I do believe our friends have discovered the special feature of my disks," he whispered.

Laura swallowed the urge to laugh. Stefano spoke into her ear. "Don't move. Stay out of sight. I'll signal if I see Bette."

Before she could respond, he had swung himself up into the chestnut tree and was lost in its leafy branches. A couple of seconds later she saw the top of the tree sway and heard a soft thud. Stefano had landed on the roof of the porch and was scrambling toward the skylight, tire iron grasped firmly in his right hand.

He moved with amazing speed and agility. Even so, Laura was sure his presence would have been detected if the kidnappers hadn't been too busy yelling, cursing and hurling accusations at each other to hear anything beyond the sound of their own voices. Stefano reached his goal and crouched down, staring into the room beneath the skylight. Then he turned, standing up just far enough to give Laura a thumbs-up. She felt a flash of jubilation. Bette was here! And presumably Stefano wouldn't look so cheerful unless she seemed in reasonably good condition.

Laura returned his signal, following it up with an enthusiastic wave. Stefano didn't get off the roof. Instead, he hunched once again over the skylight, slipping the tire iron under the frame and levering with all his strength. Laura's momentary good cheer vanished. Surely this crazy man wasn't planning to drop down from the roof into the family room below! Who did he think he was? Superman? Batman? The Italian Terminator?

Above the noisy thumping of her heart and the sporadic shouts of the kidnappers, Laura became aware of another sound—the unmistakable wail of a police siren. Within a few seconds, the kidnappers would hear it, too. Laura didn't know whether to cheer for the arrival of the cavalry or panic at the thought of how the kidnappers might react. Joe, the oil-stained giant, had not seemed the sort of man likely to hold out his hands and wait politely for a policeman to snap on a pair of cuffs.

Stefano obviously heard the same mournful wail and must have decided Bette was at risk. He abandoned any attempt to work silently and brought the tire iron crashing down on the skylight, smashing a hole in the glass and then levering the broken twisted remains to the side of the roof. They fell onto the path with a resounding crash, spraying splinters of wood and glass in all directions. Simultaneously Stefano swung himself into the hole left by the empty skylight and disappeared from view.

Laura had absolutely no intention of cowering in the safety of the backyard while Stefano and Bette faced the brunt of the kidnappers' anger. She ran across the yard and grabbed a hunk of wooden frame from the wrecked skylight. The wailing of the police siren reached a crescendo, cutting off all sounds from inside the house. Spinning around, poised on the brink of making a dash for the porch door, she automatically jumped back behind the chestnut tree as Aunt Bette stumbled into sight.

Her hands were bound, her mouth was taped, and ropes dangled from her ankles where she had presumably been tied to a chair. But her blue eyes flashed fire, and her hair stood up in a frizz of outraged gray curls that seemed to epitomize Bette's indomitable spirit. Laura's split second of joy quickly turned to horror when she saw that Aunt Bette hadn't escaped, but was being forced out into the backyard at the point of Walter Willis's gun.

Laura's hands tensed around the hunk of wood that was her only weapon. What in blazes was she supposed to do now? Even if she managed to get behind Walter and bring the piece of skylight frame crashing down on his skull, she might do more harm than good. What if she caused Walter to give a reflexive jerk on the trigger and fire the gun?

The police were already here, Laura reasoned. Stefano was inside, presumably playing superhero and taking care of Joe and the other thug. Walter was a scientist, a man dedicated to rational assessment of the facts. He would have to accept that the game was over and that he'd lost. Right now, all that mattered was saving Aunt Bette before Walter stumbled over a tree root or a rabbit hole and caused a terrible fatal accident.

Drawing a deep breath, Laura stepped out from behind the chestnut tree. "Aunt Bette!" she called. "Professor Willis! I'm over here!"

As she had hoped, Walter and Bette spun around. Quick as a flash, Bette assessed the situation, realized that Walter's gun was no longer pointed at her and dodged back into the house. Hallelujah! Laura's plan had worked. She would have raised a hearty cheer—except for the unfortunate fact that Walter's gun was now aimed at a point somewhere between her second and third ribs.

"Well, well, well," Walter said, looking at her with acute loathing. "If it isn't the interfering niece from New York. You're a chip off the old block if ever I saw one."

Laura tried to keep her voice calm. "Listen," she said. "The police are at the front door. Put the gun away, Walter. You're not going anywhere and neither am I."

"Want to bet?" Walter's breath was coming in puffs and pants. Sweat poured from his forehead, dripping down his cheeks and along his nose. Worst of all, his eyes were wild and his movements uncoordinated. Rationally, he must know he had nothing to gain and much to lose by continuing to threaten Laura. With a surge of fear strong enough to set her entire body shaking, Laura realized that Walter was long past the point of being rational.

Walter started to walk across the grass toward her. Laura tried to move behind the chestnut tree when, horrifyingly, she heard the thunderous sound of a gun being fired. She froze in place, clutching the tree trunk and half expecting to feel the searing pain of a bullet exploding in her gut.

Instead, she saw blood spurt from Walter's arm in a gush of bright scarlet. He stared down at his hand, and the gun he was holding dropped to the ground. "I've been shot!"

he moaned. "My God, I'm dying!" He swayed, eyes rolling upward, and fell in a crumpled heap on the grass.

Laura had no time to think or even to react. Within the space of a heartbeat, Stefano was at her side. He pulled her into his arms, smothering her with kisses. "Are you all right?" he demanded, his voice rough with fear. "He did not hurt you?"

"You shot Walter," she said, her voice blank with shock.

Stefano held her tight. "Only in the arm," he said. "Trust me, *cara*, he will recover in plenty of time to stand trial."

Aunt Bette trotted into the backyard, still trailing rope from her ankles and wrists, but with no trace of a gag. She was followed by a young policeman, who was trying hard to look as if he knew what he was doing and not succeeding very well.

"Darlings!" Aunt Bette rushed over to Stefano and Laura and wrapped them in an all-purpose hug. "You rescued me! I knew you would." She beamed at them both, then gestured to the policeman who was kneeling beside Walter Willis and looking more bewildered by the second. "This is Officer Paderewski. He came to arrest Stefano, but I explained to him that he should arrest my kidnappers, instead."

"Right now, I'm calling for the paramedics and reporting the situation to my superiors," the policeman said.

"Wonderful." Bette smiled at him as if he'd made an astonishingly wise suggestion. She placed an arm around Stefano and Laura. "My niece and her husband are on their honeymoon."

"Congratulations," Officer Paderewski said sourly. He eased the collar of his shirt and swallowed hard, clearly aware that the situation was slipping out of his control.

"Where are the other two kidnappers?" Laura asked.

"They're handcuffed to the dining room table," Bette said with obvious relish. "You should have seen Stefano when he jumped down from the ceiling! My dear, your husband was simply magnificent! He had the two of them stretched out unconscious within seconds of touching the ground."

Laura avoided Stefano's eyes. "Just what I've always wanted in a husband," she muttered. "A man who can swing from the ceiling and knock kidnappers unconscious."

Stefano took her hands and pulled her gently into his arms. "I have other qualifications," he said, "although none quite as splendid as that one, of course." His voice was warm with laughter, but his gaze was entirely serious.

Laura felt the inevitable breathlessness that always seemed to afflict her whenever Stefano took her into his arms. "What other qualifications do you have?" she asked.

"Well, let me see. I can drive almost as fast as you," he said. "I am sure not many men could make such a claim." He kissed her lightly on the nose. "I make better spaghetti sauce than you—"

"You do not!"

He silenced her protests by the simple method of kissing her senseless. "I am a most expert deliverer of kisses," he said softly.

"Why you arrogant, macho—"

He kissed her again. "And then, of course, there is the minor fact that I have fallen hopelessly, totally and crazily in love with you."

Laura was afraid to let herself feel the joy that was waiting to burst inside her. "You can't be in love with me," she said. "We haven't known each other nearly long enough."

He took her hands and carried them to his lips. "My heart, falling in love has nothing to do with how long we have known each other. I love you, and I believe you love me. Now all we need to do is make the commitment to share our lives, so that our love can become deeper. Will you do that, Laura? Will you share my life? Grow old with me? Have my babies?"

She let down the barriers and happiness flooded her. "Yes," she said softly. "Yes, yes, yes. I love you so much, Stefano."

Bette watched her niece and her nephew-in-law melt into each other's arms. She turned to Officer Paderewski, her face alight with smiles. "Look what I did!" she said. "And I didn't even need to blow up my garage."

A Note from Jasmine Cresswell

When I was seventeen, my parents took me to Italy as a high school graduation present. I was living in London at the time, and we went by train, setting off in the dampness of an English summer morning, and chugging our way across cloudy northern Europe. We finally crossed the Alps at dawn the next day, just as the sun was rising behind the mountains, turning the waters of Italy's Lago Maggiore (Great Lake) into a shimmering sheet of golden satin.

As you can imagine, I have never forgotten that wonderful first glimpse of Italy—or the charming young Italian who bought me a cup of espresso coffee as we stood in the corridor admiring the view. He didn't speak English and I didn't speak Italian, so we could only smile at each other and stare out the window in silent appreciation of the beautiful sight.

My parents and I spent six weeks on the Adriatic coast, in a small village that in those days still retained much of the rustic charm of earlier generations. The Mediterranean wasn't polluted, and we swam in clear blue waters, waiting for the fishermen to arrive and sell us their catch in time for lunch.

I fell in love that summer with Italy's warm sunshine and its even warmer people—and, yes, with an Italian university student staying in the villa next door, who had *far* more than his fair share of Italian charisma!

When Harlequin asked me to write a story about a marriage of convenience that included a dash of intrigue, it seemed entirely natural for my hero to be Italian. I wanted my heroine, Laura, to have the very best, and I hope you'll agree that Stefano Corelli is the perfect match for her.

DON'T TELL GRANDFATHER
Glenda Sanders

Chapter One

WAS THE BABY *ever* going to cry? J. Havelock Dean III
wondered, while his friend and attorney Alan Hamlin ex-
pounded on the potential pitfalls of extended cohabitation
outside of a traditional marriage situation.

The women he'd assembled for this little charade, all unmarried employees of Dean Industries between the ages of
twenty-two and twenty-eight, were listening with various
degrees of polite attentiveness. Two had indicated by a show
of hands that they were currently living with a man. Lock
had immediately ruled them out. That left seven. Lock
surveyed them curiously as Alan discussed the complications inherent in obtaining a home mortgage with a non-
spousal co-owner.

There were two blondes, one of whom was too flashy for
Lock's taste. The raven-haired sophisticate was beautiful
but aloof. Lock would be genuinely surprised if she rushed
to the aid of a squalling infant. The brunettes were crisp,
suited, all career.

His gaze lingered awhile on an auburn-haired woman with
peaches-and-cream skin. Scarlett Blake. He'd met her before, he was sure of it. Blake—oh, yes! Memory dawned
suddenly. How could he possibly have forgotten? The disastrous gorilla-habitat unveiling two years ago. She'd been
in charge of the gorilla project from its hopeful beginning
to its humiliating end.

He hadn't remembered her being so . . . nubile. But then,
the gorillas had provided a distraction.

A whimper rose from the plastic contraption used for transporting infants. Alan tensed, then went on with his lecture. For the plan to work, the baby had to work herself into a healthy fit of crying, an eventuality Alan had assured Lock was inevitable at this time of day.

The unanswered whimper swelled to a demanding wail. Lock marveled at his friend's newly acquired fatherly instinct as he watched Alan cringe, then force himself to go on talking.

Full daddy mode, Lock thought in amusement. He could remember when women would ask Alan if he liked children, and Alan would quip that he loved children—barbecued.

The baby was crying in earnest now. Lock directed his attention to the women. Raven hair was scowling. The brunettes looked uncomfortable, as if they weren't quite sure what to do.

Alan apologized for the disruption and explained, "My wife's out of town and the baby-sitter called in sick."

The baby kept on crying.

"What's wrong with her?" the flashy blonde asked.

"She's probably hungry," Alan said, pulling out a bottle from the diaper bag in the chair near the infant. He uncapped the nipple and poked it into the child's mouth, then braced the bottle with a rolled-up blanket.

The blanket quickly shifted under the weight of the full bottle, and the nipple slid out of the baby's mouth. The baby howled furiously. Alan fussed with the blanket again. Again the bottle slid away, and the baby screamed furiously.

"Oh, for—" Peaches-and-cream rose and slipped off her suit jacket. "Give me that baby. I'll feed her."

For the next ten minutes, J. Havelock Dean III observed Scarlett Blake's interaction with Alan's child. He noted the confident way she nestled the baby in her arms and tilted the bottle to the proper angle. He saw her smile at the tiny face and tweak the tiny nose with her fingertip. He watched her toss the receiving blanket over her shoulder and efficiently burp the sated baby, then settle the child in her lap and take off her silver bangle bracelet and entertain the child with it.

So, he thought grimly, ignoring the unfamiliar and conflicting emotions warring within him at that moment, *the die is cast.*

THE NEXT MORNING Scarlett Blake stood in an elevator making its way to the executive suites of Dean Industries and wished she had worn her black suit, instead of her blue suit, and that she hadn't been summoned to the top floor on a bad hair day.

Scarlett didn't have many great hair days, but some days were less awful than others. On her best hair days, her thick, wavy, midcheek locks bordered on sleek. Today was not one of those days. Today the look was sleep tousled; the various layers kicked out at rebellious angles, and only the miracle of modern chemistry that had led to the development of firm-holding styling mousse spared her the humiliation of being invited to compete in an Alfalfa look-alike contest.

Inside, she felt as disheveled as her hair. She didn't have a clue what had prompted this audience with Dean Industries' second in command, but the scenarios that formed in her fertile imagination were not pretty.

The elevator jarred to a stop. Still wishing she'd worn her black suit, Scarlett stepped into what was popularly acknowledged to be one of the most elegant reception areas in downtown Indiannapolis. She was greeted by a warm smile from the gray-haired woman sitting sentinel behind a semicircular desk centered between two doors. "J. Havelock

Dean, President & CEO'' was engraved in the plaque on the door to the woman's left. "J. Havelock Dean III, Executive Vice President" was engraved in the plaque on the door to her right.

Grandfather and grandson, the two Mr. Deans were known throughout the building as the bear and the fox, J. Havelock Dean the elder being the bear, J. Havelock Dean the younger being the fox.

Despite the secretary's friendly demeanor, Scarlett experienced a sense of being evaluated by shrewd eyes as the woman—Margaret Thomas, according to the nameplate on her desk—said, "You must be Miss Blake. Mr. Dean III is expecting you. I'll tell him you're here." Scarlett thanked her, then made a conscious effort not to fidget as the older woman lifted the telephone, pressed a button and spoke softly into the receiver. She listened a few seconds, then hung up after a crisp, "I'll tell her."

She smiled at Scarlett again. "He'll be right out."

The door opened, and the fox appeared in the doorway, nodded an imperial greeting and gestured her inside. He was charming in a cool detached way, and as Scarlett took a seat in front of a desk the size of Rhode Island, she thought it would be easy to fall under the spell of his sleek good looks and gracious manners. If he weren't J. Havelock Dean III, vice president of Dean Industries, of course. And if his charm weren't so practiced.

She noted that every golden hair on his head was in perfect conformity with the fashionable cut. It didn't boost her confidence.

"Would you like something to drink?" he asked as he settled imperiously into his thronelike leather chair.

Scarlett wasn't about to risk spilling coffee down her blouse in front of the executive vice president. "No, thank you."

"You're probably wondering why I asked you here."

Scarlett's confident demeanor snapped, giving way to a nervous giggle. Mortified, she said, "I'm sorry, Mr. Dean. It just...it sounded like the line in an old drawing-room mystery."

"I guess it did, at that," J. Havelock Dean III said, with a smile so indulgent, so controlled and so condescending that Scarlett found herself entertaining fantasies of ways a person might spoil that sterile perfection of his. A bowl of spaghetti smeared over his pristine shirt and scrupulously immaculate tie, motor oil poured over that thick thatch of acquiescent golden hair—the possibilities were endless and delicious.

"May I call you Scarlett?" he asked. "My fifth-grade schoolteacher's name was Miss Blake."

Scarlett nodded. "Of course."

"Well, then... *Scarlett*, do you consider yourself discreet?"

"Discreet?" Scarlett repeated. *Was this...could it possibly be...a proposition?* She dismissed the idea at once. J. Havelock Dean III had too much ice water in his veins to summon a lowly public-relations representative to his office and proposition her.

"Can you keep a confidence?" he pressed.

"I think so. Yes."

J. Havelock Dean III took a deep breath, then exhaled it slowly. "Good. Because what we're about to discuss must never go outside this room. I must have your absolute assurance that it won't. Later..."

He took another deep breath, and for a moment his mouth compressed into a hard line. And for that fleeing moment, Scarlett thought she detected some real emotion in that hard set of jaw and deep in his golden brown eyes. It was gone, suppressed as quickly as it had flashed, when he continued, "Later we'll arrange a more binding agreement, but for now, I must rely on your word."

"My word is all you need," Scarlett said, bristling.

I hope so, Lock thought intensely. *I sincerely hope so.* He was not accustomed to making himself vulnerable to other people; relying on the word of a near stranger was nerve-racking, but then, there were times when a man had no choice. This was one of them.

They were staring at each other, gazes locked in subtle confrontation. He liked the fact that she was not afraid to look him in the eye, particularly when she was defending her integrity. She was an intriguing moppet, gamin and wholesome girl-next-door, but with an underlying suggestion of sensuality. If his plan worked out, its execution could prove interesting.

"I'll get straight to the point," he said after a prolonged silence.

Scarlett nodded. And waited.

"I would like to have a child as soon as possible."

Shock registered on her face. She didn't reply.

"That's not entirely true," he amended. "The truth is I *must* have a child as soon as possible."

"Why?"

"I'm not prepared to discuss the reason for my urgency, but I can assure you it is compelling. I must have a child, and for that I must have a woman to carry it."

"Mr. Dean—"

"I don't have the luxury of time to go through the standard courtship rituals, so I did a systematic search—"

"You're making me extremely uncomfortable, Mr. Dean. I don't know why you're telling me this, but I don't even know you, and what you're discussing is personal, so if you don't mind, I'd like to leave." She rose.

"Sit down, Scarlett."

She responded to the sheer authority in his voice and plopped back into the chair. But her gaze met his defiantly as she said, "I won't mention this . . . discussion to anyone, if that's what you're worried about, but there are laws about sexual harassment, and I don't have to—"

"I'm not harassing you, sexually or otherwise," Lock said coolly. "I'm asking you to marry me. Temporarily."

"Whoa!" Scarlett said, springing out of her chair again. "That's it. I'm out of here. This is too weird for me."

"Sit down!" Lock snarled.

Scarlett remained standing, glaring defiantly, until his expression softened. "Please," he said, "stay. I know this is a bit abrupt—"

"*Abrupt?* It's not abrupt, it's…bizarre. I don't know what you're up to, Mr. Dean, but whatever it is, count me out. I enjoy working for Dean Industries, but my job description doesn't include—"

"This has nothing to do with your job."

"The vice president and owner of the company I work for—whom, I might add, I've met all of twice, both times in a business situation—summons me to the executive suite and asks me to marry him because he has to have a child, and that has nothing to do with my job?"

"Indirectly perhaps," Lock said, "but only because you work at Dean Industries, and it was expeditious to look for a wife within the company."

Scarlett's eyes narrowed suspiciously. "Expeditious how?"

"The computerized personnel files gave me access to a large pool of potential choices and a quick way to identify them."

Scarlett was incredulous. "You used the personnel files to look for a wife?"

"A few keystrokes gave me a list of unmarried women with at least four years of college. After that it was a matter of reading files and eliminating obvious unsuitables."

"Is that legal?"

"Probably not," Lock conceded. "But I'm in a hurry, and it was the shortest means to my objective."

"Which is?"

"To find a suitable woman to bear my child."

Silence loomed as Scarlett considered that bit of information. "Why are you in such a hurry?"

Lock remained still for almost a full minute, and Scarlett wondered if he intended to answer her. Finally he said bluntly, "My grandfather is dying."

"Big Jake Dean?" Scarlet blurted.

Lock nodded. "You see why it can't become public information. Big Jake isn't a man who tolerates pity well."

Scarlett pictured the CEO of Dean Industries in her mind. Robust, energetic and charming, Big Jake Dean had always seemed larger than life. The thought of his dying was somehow incomprehensible.

"It seems incredible, doesn't it?" Lock asked, as though reading her mind. "Big Jake, dying. I always thought he was indestructible." He released a ragged sigh. "He doesn't know I know. I overheard a conversation he had with his doctor."

"This must be difficult for you. I'm sorry."

Lock ignored her sympathy. "His one regret is that I've never married and had children." He laughed, a brief mirthless chuckle. "He's afraid I'll be the last of the line."

Scarlett was racked by his inner turmoil as his eyes met hers and he said, "I want to give him a great-grandchild, or at least the knowledge that one is on the way. If it comforts him..." He released an anguished sigh. "It may be the only comfort I could possibly give him."

Scarlett was torn. He obviously loved his grandfather. He was sincere about wanting to comfort him. But was that a valid reason to bring a child into the world?

"Scarlett?"

She jerked to attention. "I'm sorry. I—"

"I would be interested in your reaction to what I've told you so far."

"I've got mixed feelings. Your wanting to ease your grandfather's mind is, well, honorable. And I think your intentions are good."

"But?" he urged, when she hesitated.

"Have you thought about what's going to happen to the baby after...later on? It's not going away, you know. A child is a lifelong commitment."

"That's why I chose a prospective mother so carefully."

Scarlett considered that a moment before asking, "Why me, Mr. Dean? I mean, of all the women in the company, why pick on me?"

"I'm not picking *on* you," he said. "I *picked* you. Very carefully. You come from a large family, you're the perfect age to bear a child, and you're good with children. You handled Alan's baby beautifully."

"It was a test!" Scarlett said as realization dawned. "Yesterday was a test. You were watching us, waiting to see which one of us picked up the baby."

"It was the most efficient way I could think of to find out who related to children. I know any number of women who'd marry me to get their social-climbing mitts on the Dean name and money. I wanted a woman who'd be a good mother for my child."

"A woman like me."

"You'd be an excellent mother."

She glared at him accusingly. "You want to turn my life upside down!"

"I'm prepared to compensate you generously and provide more than generously for you and the child. I took the liberty of having this contract drawn up—"

"That was quite a liberty!" Scarlett snapped.

Lock nodded as if to say, "Touché," and slid the contract across his desk in her direction. "If you take a look at it, you might think it could be worthwhile having your life turned upside down."

Scarlett wished she had the fortitude to fling the legal-sized blue-bound contract back at him—the fortitude or the integrity or whatever noble quality was required to just walk out and forget all about his dying grandfather and his insane plan. She wished she could get up, tell him he was manipulative and she was not going to be sucked into his crazy attempt to ease his grandfather's last days, then march out of his office and forget they'd ever had this conversation.

But curiosity compelled her to pick up the contract and scan it. What she read on the front page compelled her to keep reading. Finally, numb and trembling, she laid it on his desk as though it were made of fragile glass.

A long silence ensued before she said, "Did you mean to use all those zeroes?"

"I like to think I'm a fair man. What I'm looking for is important to me."

"And you'd really give me money every year?"

"I would want you to have the option of staying at home with the child if you chose to," he said. "That's your current annual salary at Dean Industries. I checked."

"No one gets ten-percent annual increases," Scarlett said miserably. She hated being confused. She hated issues that were fuzzy and gray, instead of black and white. She hated the temptation all those zeroes presented. And she resented J. Havelock Dean III for drawing her into a situation that was not of her making and forcing her to make a difficult decision. She despised him for being cool and smug and so damnably good-looking.

"You would, if we had a child," he said matter-of-factly.

"You're trying to buy me."

"Don't you want children?"

"Of course," Scarlett admitted. "But not without a husband."

"You'd have a husband."

"Until three months after the child was born or your grandfather died, whichever came later," she quoted from the contract.

"The marriage would be legal. The child would be legitimate."

"I want a home," she said. "And love."

"Love doesn't come with guarantees. My contract does."

"I can't think," Scarlett said desperately. "I have to think about this."

"I expected you would. Take the rest of the day off. I'll clear your absence with your supervisor. Take tomorrow morning, too. I have an important meeting that'll run through lunch. You can come in around two and let me know what you've decided."

"Tomorrow?" Scarlett protested. "That's not enough time."

"Time is the one indulgence I don't have the power to grant you," Lock said sadly. "If you accept my offer, then we don't have a single hour to lose in getting the plan into action. If you don't accept, I'll be forced to make alternative arrangements."

With another suitable woman, Scarlett thought bitterly. Oh, it was humiliating to know how interchangeable his candidates were. How could a man be so cold? "Thank goodness for word processors, eh, Mr. Dean? If you have to find another woman, it'll just be a matter of doing a search and replacing the names and figures on the contract. Or have you already printed out three versions with different names just in case?"

"This is the only contract," he said glibly.

"Printed out, maybe," Scarlett replied, then added sarcastically, "How wonderful it must be to have so much confidence."

Lock appeared genuinely disheartened. "I was hoping we could be friends."

"I've never started a friendship by being bought."

Lock laughed bitterly. "Then you're luckier than most people." He opened a folder on his desk and said without looking up, "Don't forget to take the contract with you. I'll see you tomorrow afternoon."

She was being dismissed, and dismissed quite efficiently. It made her furious. And it cut her to the quick. She rose, snatched the contract from the desk and eyed him defiantly. "Will you tell me one thing?"

He granted her an expectant look.

"Do you plan to feel anything for your child if you have one?"

"I assure you, Scarlett, I *will* be involved in the life of any child I sire." Pain flitted across his face before he was able to hide it, but he quickly recovered his facade of detachment. "I know what it's like to grow up without a father."

Chapter Two

THE NEXT THIRTY HOURS were the most difficult Scarlett had ever lived through. She read the contract. She reread the contract. She fretted. She paced. She fumed.

She called her mother and pretended nothing was wrong.

She talked to her four-year-old niece, who was staying with Grandma, and yearned for a child.

She remembered J. Havelock Dean III's arrogance, his obvious affection for his grandfather and that flash of pain on his face when he talked about knowing what it was like to grow up without a father. She remembered his smug confidence, his desperation, his determination. She remembered the way he'd ordered her to sit down and the gentle politeness with which he'd asked her to stay. She remembered the way his lips were shaped and the color of his eyes.

She thought about having a child. She imagined making a baby with J. Havelock Dean III. She speculated about what their child would look like. She thought about the marriage and love relationship she'd always dreamed about, and about J. Havelock Dean III's aloofness, and then she pondered the fact that she was twenty-six and hadn't dated anyone seriously in more than two years.

She thought about the financial terms of the contract—a hefty endowment upon their marriage, an even heftier endowment upon their eventual divorce, an annual endowment for the rest of her life if she carried a child of J. Havelock Dean III to term. She thought about never having to work again or having the freedom to set up her own public-relations firm and taking only accounts that appealed to her.

She thought about J. Havelock Dean—Big Jake, the dynamic CEO of Dean Industries—and about the fact that he was dying, and that he could die wondering if there would ever be another Dean child. She considered the possibility that she might be instrumental in giving him peace of mind in his final days, that she might be able to present him with a great-grandchild.

She could not sleep. She could not eat. She could only hold the contract in her hands and wonder what she should do.

She told herself that the Dean men were total strangers and no concern of hers. She told herself that a woman would have to have rocks in her head to marry a man who didn't even make a pretense of loving her. She told herself that even if she had legal custody of J. Havelock Dean III's child, as guaranteed clearly in the contract, J. Havelock Dean III would probably be a force to reckon with when it came to his child.

She told herself that there were more important things in life than financial security. She told herself that she still had years ahead of her in which she could have a baby and that the man of her dreams could be waiting just around the corner.

At noon the next day she dressed in her best black suit. At one-thirty she drove to the Dean Industries building, where she took the elevator to the top floor. And at two o'clock, she walked into J. Havelock Dean III's office and told him she would marry him with the express purpose of bearing his child.

He smiled radiantly, and she reflected it was perhaps the first genuine smile she'd ever seen on his remarkably handsome face. Her pleasure in the smile, however, lasted only until she realized he was pleased at having accomplished his goal, rather than pleased at her agreeing to become his wife.

It shouldn't be this way, she thought, suddenly in a panic. *This is not the way a woman is supposed to feel when she accepts a proposal of marriage.*

"Excellent," Lock said, relieved that everything was falling into place so nicely. "We can go over the basic agenda now and get this project kicked off."

Scarlett nodded her acquiescence, and he continued authoritatively, "The plan is quite simple. We are about to fall in love—so madly in love, in fact, that when we have the executive meeting in Reno week after next, you and I are going to be swept up in a wave of romantic fancy and elope."

"In Reno?" Scarlett asked, suppressing the urge to shove his agenda and his project and the rest of his executive-in-charge terminology straight down his throat. *What had made her agree to this insane plan?*

"This meeting has been scheduled for months. It works out beautifully for our needs, with the lenient marriage laws and the abundance of chapels. We'll start laying the groundwork immediately. As of this moment, you're taking over the coordination of the meeting."

"I am?"

"You've handled special-events planning for us in the past, so it won't be too far out of line when I assign you the job to give Margaret a break."

He took a breath and exhaled slowly. "Margaret's shrewd. If I break the news in just the right way, she may become suspicious and wonder if I'm getting sweet on you. She's too discreet to voice her speculation to the other employees, but she'll be able to lift her eyebrows and say, 'I knew it!' when the news of our elopement breaks. If she says as much to my grandfather, so much the better. It'll make our marriage all that more believable.''

His eyes narrowed as he gave her a look obviously designed to quell and intimidate subordinates. It was quite effective. Scarlett found herself tensing, steeling herself against it, determined not to cower. "My grandfather *must* be absolutely convinced that I've been knocked flat on my ass in love," he said. "If he suspects—"

"Flat on your ass in love," Scarlett said sarcastically. "Now there's a romantic turn of phrase."

"If I were going to fall flat on my ass in love, I'd have done so long before now," Lock responded. "Obviously that's not going to happen."

"Obviously not," Scarlett said, humiliation burning her cheeks.

Lock sensed an underlying hostility in Scarlett's attitude he hadn't anticipated. He couldn't figure what possible reason she had to be hostile. He'd dropped an offer of a lifetime in her lap—more money than she'd ever have made sitting at some public-relations desk, the prospect of a child and the social advantages of being Mrs. J. Havelock Dean III, which would inevitably open doors for her even after she became the ex-Mrs. J. Havelock Dean III.

"Just so Big Jake believes that it's happened," he said. "That's the point of this whole charade."

"I thought a child was the point of this charade."

"Big Jake is a traditionalist. He *must* believe that my marriage is real." Lock's eyes narrowed as he turned that intimidating look on her again. "And for all practical purposes, it will be. As long as you are legally my wife, you'll have every privilege that position brings, socially and financially. In return, I insist on absolute fidelity. You will live in the Dean mansion, spend the Dean money and wear my grandmother's heirloom jewelry, but you will not be unfaithful to me, no matter how discreet you think you could keep an affair.''

"If you knew me, you wouldn't insult me by implying that the possibility exists," Scarlett said testily.

"But I don't know you," he replied. "I just know *about* you. There's a difference. I just wanted to clarify up front—"

"And you?"

He stared at her incredulously. "Me?"

"What's good for the goose is good for the gander," Scarlett said. "Especially in this day and age. Obviously our...arrangement is going to necessitate..." She blushed becomingly. "Obviously we're going to have to..."

"Consummate the marriage?" he supplied drolly.

"Unless you're planning on my conceiving through artificial insemination."

He had the audacity to laugh aloud. "I think we can do it the old-fashioned way. It'll be nasty work, but we'll muddle—"

Her expression told him that she did not share his amusement. Lock stopped midsentence and exhaled wearily. "This doesn't have to be so awkward, Scarlett. After all, we're going to be married. But to respond to your concern, I assure you that—how did you phrase it?—what's good for the goose *will* be good for the gander. I haven't had time for women since I took over the vice presidency, so I certainly don't expect to have time to start chasing them when I have a wife waiting for me at home. A pregnant wife before too very long, I hope."

Scarlett stared down at her hands. She couldn't look at him when she was thinking about being pregnant with his child. About getting into bed with him and having sex in order to conceive his child.

"I embarrassed you," he said. "I'm sorry."

She laughed softly. "I'm developing an empathy for nineteenth-century virgins in arranged marriages."

"You're not a virgin, are you?" Lock hadn't considered *that* possibility, and he didn't find it comforting.

"No," she said hoarsely, shaking her head and still not looking at him. "But...I've never slept with a man I didn't know on a first-name basis."

She was just full of surprises, Lock mused. "I thought we covered that yesterday."

"I don't know what to call you. Jason, or Jake for short, like your grandfather?"

"There's only one Big Jake. My father was Jason, so when I was born, they took the second half of my middle name. Call me Lock."

"Havelock is an unusual name."

"It was my great-grandmother's maiden name. The family money—the old money—comes from the Havelock side. My great-grandfather established Dean Industries with a stake from the Havelock coffers."

"Lock," Scarlett said, trying out the sound of it. It conjured up images of hard steel, strength and integrity. "It suits you."

"How did you ever get a name like Scarlett?"

She shrugged. "How else? They rereleased *Gone with the Wind* when my mother and father were dating. It was *their* movie. The fourth time they went to see it, my father proposed to my mother during the scene where Rhett kissed Scarlett before leaving to join the war."

Lock's mouth hardened just enough to reveal a scorn for the romance of the story. "I suppose you have a brother named Rhett."

"No. But I have a sister named Ashley." She waited for a reaction. None. "Some people find that amusing," she said finally.

"But Ashley was a man."

"That's why it's amusing."

Dead silence. At last Lock asked, "Did you have any questions about the contract?"

"No. Everything was spelled out quite clearly."

"Good. As soon as you have an attorney read it over, we can sign it and get that out of the way."

"An attorney won't be necessary."

"An attorney will be *absolutely* necessary," Lock said. "The terms of this contract will affect you for the rest of your life. You should never sign anything with such far-reaching ramifications without advice of counsel. If you wish, I can have my attorney recommend someone."

Scarlett chuckled. "That's rich. You want me to have benefit of counsel and then offer to have your attorney find me an attorney."

"It's done all the time," Lock assured her.

"My brother has a college friend who settled here after law school. I'll call my brother and get his name."

"As soon as possible, please. The sooner we get everything settled, the better."

"I'll call him tonight."

Lock nodded. "Keep me posted so Alan can set up a meeting."

This time it was Scarlett's eyes that narrowed. "My people will call your people?"

Lock shrugged. "I guess so."

"Did it ever occur to you that people sometimes just . . . talk to one another? And trust one another?"

"Nothing is simple when there are large sums of money involved."

"And lives."

"I beg your pardon?"

"I said, 'And lives.' There's a lot more involved here than money. My life, your life, your grandfather's life and, most of all, our child's life."

"Which makes it all the more important for us to have a very clear understanding before a child is conceived. A solid agreement will protect everyone involved. We'll know exactly how to proceed and what to expect. I won't have anything mucked up with claims that you didn't understand what you were signing."

"Oh," Scarlett said. "Of course."

The words were packed with so much disillusionment that Lock stared at her for a long moment. "I'm detecting a pronounced lack of enthusiasm and a good measure of resentment from you, Scarlett."

She didn't reply, and after an awkward silence, he said, "Do you mind telling why you agreed to this arrangement if you find it so . . . distasteful?"

She hesitated before answering. "You want me to say that you made me an offer I couldn't refuse."

"I want you to tell me the truth."

"That *is* the truth. The money appeals to me. I've been in the work force long enough to know that I have what it takes to succeed, but I've been feeling fenced in creatively. The cash settlement will enable me to open my own firm, if and when I decide to go back to work. And there's your grandfather, and you—the way you want to ease his mind.

It's, uh, a little bit off-the-wall, and a little noble. But the real bottom line is, I want a child."

She forced a small smile. "I'm a pragmatist. My clock isn't exactly racing, but I don't have any assurances that I'll meet Mr. Right in the next couple of years. And even if I wanted to take the gamble and hold out for the whole package of love and marriage, it's not a great time to be pounding the pavement looking for work."

"Your job at Dean Industries wasn't in jeopardy if you'd turned me down."

Her smile turned smug. "I became a liability the moment you told me what you were planning. If I'd turned you down, you wouldn't have been comfortable with me in the building, knowing I knew what I knew, even if you'd found another woman to accept your offer. You'd have had to transfer me at the very least."

"I never meant for your job, or the fear of losing it, to become a lever," Lock said somberly. "Is that why you resent me so much?"

"I don't resent you," she replied. "Not really. It's just . . . so calculated. I'll get used to the idea eventually and it won't seem so . . . cold. Maybe, the way you said yesterday, if we become friends, this'll be easier."

The realities of the situation hung in the air like a miasmic cloud until Lock said, "I've told Margaret you may be taking over the Reno meeting. She'll brief you with the details, and then, if you're up to it, you can go back to work."

"I'm up to it," Scarlett said.

But Lock wasn't finished; he'd just switched into his executive-in-charge mode. "I'll be arranging for a credit card for you. It'll be in your name, but I'll take full responsibility for anything you buy from this point on, in case you want to do some shopping."

He could tell from Scarlett's expression that she wasn't pleased at the prospect. "It would be advantageous if people started speculating about the possibility of a brewing romance. I'll be calling you up here any time we have business to discuss. Someone's bound to notice."

She nodded, and he continued, "Other than vague references to working on the Reno meeting, I want you to be glib about the fact that you're coming up here so much. Nothing fuels gossip like a lack of solid information. Also, if you have friends in the company, you might hint that you've got a new man in your life, but insist on keeping his identity a secret. Eventually someone will put two and two together, especially if we give them something to think about."

"How would we do that?"

"We'll think of something. It doesn't take much." Lost in thought, he drummed his fingers on his desk blotter, then said abruptly, "Who's the number-one company gossip?"

"The company gossip?"

"Every company has one. The person who knows everything before anyone else. Who's the gossip in your little milieu down there?"

"You're not going to use this against her, are you?"

Lock liked the fact that Scarlett wasn't comfortable snitching on a co-worker. Loyalty was an admirable character trait, especially in a mother. He smiled reassuringly. "To the contrary, Scarlett. We're going to use her...special talent to our advantage."

"I guess it would be Theresa Nevins."

"Where does she work?"

"Accounts receivable. Seventh floor."

"She needs to catch us together somewhere. I'll give it some thought." He reached for the phone. "I'll call Margaret now and confirm that you're taking over Reno. I'll be expecting the name of your attorney tomorrow."

THE NEXT AFTERNOON, the phone on Scarlett's desk rang. She picked up the receiver. "Scarlett Blake."

"Not for long."

She recognized the voice instantly. Lock forged ahead in his usual manner. "I'm going to be talking to Alan. Do you have that name for me?"

"No. My brother wasn't home when I called. I'll try again tonight."

"Tonight? Don't you have his office number?"

"I can't call him at work. I wouldn't do that except in a dire emergency."

"This is a dire emergency."

"Yes, sir," she said, crisply respectful. "I'll be right up, Mr. Dean."

She slammed the phone into the cradle and marched to the elevator, then straight past Margaret to knock on his office door. He called for her to come in, and she stormed through the door, stopping in a hands-on-hip, feet-spread confrontational stance.

"Exactly *what* am I supposed to tell my brother when I call him at his office—that my lunatic multimillionaire boss has decided he wants an heir and so he's paying me to marry him and bear his child and I need an attorney to counsel me because he wants to be sure I understand all the fine print in the contract? That, as I understand the contract, would be a violation of the contract."

Lock gave her his best executive-in-charge look. "Are you finished?"

"Yes!" Scarlett snapped. "I mean, no! We might as well get this settled right now. If you want my signature on that contract, and my hand in marriage and your heir in my womb, then you're going to have to quit bullying me!"

Lock appeared genuinely surprised. "Bullying you? When did I ever bully you?"

"When have you bullied me?" Scarlett mocked. "When haven't you? You haven't stopped giving me orders since I told you I'd marry you. No. I take that back. Longer than that—since you asked me to marry you. Since you called me into your office."

"I never meant to bully you," he said with irritating calm.

Scarlett was too wound up to let a show of contrition slow her down. "I took it at first because, after all, you were J. Havelock Dean *the Third* and I was just a junior member of the public-relations staff. I was your employee when I walked into your office that day. But I can't enter into a marriage as a . . . a servant. Marriage, under any circumstances, must be a partnership. There must be equality, which means you're going to have to trust my judgment about some things, one of which is what I'm going to tell my family about our marriage, and *how* I'm going to tell my family. And if I tell you that I can't call my brother at work and then give him some cockamamy story about a friend needing an attorney and expect him to swallow it, then you're just going to have to live with it."

She glared at him. He stared at her in consternation. Finally he defused the charged silence by saying mildly, "All right."

Scarlett's jaw dropped. "All right? That's all you're going to say?"

"I could tell you that you're cute when you're angry, but I don't think that would do much for our budding friendship." *Even if it's true,* he thought. She *was* cute when she was all stirred up, with her eyes flashing and her cheeks flushed and her chest heaving. Cute *and* appealing. The V-neck of her blouse, though conservative, hinted promisingly of cleavage.

He hadn't expected her to respond to his rather outrageous compliment, and she didn't. She was still glaring at him, her breathing labored from the emotion of her outburst. "Why don't you sit down so we can talk about this calmly over a cup of coffee?" he suggested.

He waited until she was seated, then walked behind the small bar in the corner of his office and filled two cups. "Cream and sugar?"

"Sugar," Scarlett said. "Two packets." Embarrassment was slowly replacing the outrage that had brought her charging up to his office. She'd overreacted, of course. But a woman had a right to be a little edgy when she found herself secretly engaged to a man she hardly knew. Her overreaction didn't make him any less bossy, and dealing with two older brothers had taught her that you had to stand firm against bossy males or submit to their petty tyranny.

He handed her a steaming mug on his way back to his chair. Glad to have something active to do, Scarlett sipped the hot coffee and waited for Lock to resume their conversation.

He took a swallow of coffee, then finally said, "If I seemed abrupt with you, I'm sorry. I'm not a patient man under the most ordinary circumstances, and since I found out about my grandfather..."

He studied the surface of the dark liquid as if searching for a way to change the fact that his grandfather was dying. "Naturally I'm anxious to get all the loose ends tied up."

"My brother had a business dinner last night. He should be at home tonight, but if for some reason I don't reach him there, I'll call his office tomorrow and tell him that my friend who needs legal advice is really in a hurry," she said.

Lock nodded thoughtfully, then took another swallow of coffee. Idly cradling the mug in his hands, he studied Scarlett's face. Until she'd stormed into his office, her family—and to a great extent Scarlett herself—had been abstracts. The fact that she was one of four siblings of a very traditional family in America's heartland had made her attractive as a prospective mother, but he hadn't really thought about her accountability to such a close family, and the impact a sudden marriage might have on her relationship with its members.

"What are you going to tell your family about getting married?" he asked curiously.

Scarlett pondered the question a moment before replying, "The same thing you're going to tell your grandfather—that we fell so madly in love that we succumbed to the passion and romance of the moment. Hopefully my mother will be enchanted enough by the romantic angle to forgive me for eloping."

"She's going to be upset?"

"That's putting it mildly."

"Would you like to invite her to the ceremony? We could fly your parents to Reno."

"No," Scarlett said, shaking her head somberly. "I may be able to pull off this madly-in-love business over the phone, but if they were there, they'd know something wasn't right. Besides, my sister's due around that time, and they wouldn't want to be away. I'm hoping the impending blessed event will provide a distraction."

"Your sister's pregnant?"

"Uh-huh. We're a prolific clan. Mother used to tell her friends that all she had to do to get pregnant was share my father's drinking glass."

"That's reassuring. However, I don't think we ought to count too heavily on that drinking-glass bit."

"No," Scarlett murmured, averting her eyes. She was well aware that she soon would be sharing more than a drinking glass with the man sitting opposite her. And while their eventual coupling seemed to be the only subject about which he'd displayed a sense of humor, it was the one aspect of this entire scheme she approached with absolute seriousness.

Not that the prospect of consummating her marriage to J. Havelock Dean III was unpalatable. She was, after all, as healthy as the next woman, with all the standard urges and needs, and he was, after all, a stunning-looking man. In fact, physically, he was just her type—tall and lean. The first time she'd seen him—at that disastrous gorilla-house opening—she'd fantasized about what it would be like to have him make love to her.

The fantasy had been delicious and exciting because she'd known J. Havelock Dean III was unattainable. He was the god on the mountain, the lord of the manor, and she was the lowliest of commoners, the hired help. The sweetest part of the fantasy had been that none of that mattered and that he adored her.

Of course, Scarlett had been rudely snatched from the fantasy of the moment when the curtains had been pulled back to show the world the new gorilla habitat—the one that had been built at Dean Industries' expense.

Up to that moment, the project had been a foolproof public-relations project. How could it fail? A struggling Midwestern zoo trying to save an endangered species. Koko and Miko, the zoo's gorillas who'd been reluctant to mate in captivity. And Dean Industries, a company with a heart, underwriting the costs of a new natural habitat where zoo officials and animal experts and the public were hopeful that the pair would feel comfortable enough to mate.

The eyes of the public had long been on Koko and Miko, and the opening of the exhibit had drawn news crews from across the state hungry for a story rife with environmentalism, hope and an underlying theme of sexuality.

Then, as Scarlett, coordinator of the gorilla project for Dean Industries, had stood there fantasizing about J. Havelock Dean III, the curtains had opened. And there, for all the world to see, had been Koko and Miko, engaged in the act of procreation with all the pent-up sexual energy and enthusiasm of gorillas who'd been celibate for six years and suddenly remembered what sex was.

Scarlett's fantasies were lost in her rush to salvage the situation amid the flurry of flashing strobes, clicking camera shutters and film crews jockeying for position. Everyone, it seemed, wanted film of the X-rated spectacle being acted out in front of them—right under the sign identifying Dean Industries as sponsor of the exhibit. Now, a scarce two years later, Scarlett sat across from the object of her fantasies, and knowing that within weeks she would be in his bed for the express purpose of conceiving his child made her self-conscious in his presence.

In Reno fantasy would become reality, but with all the harshness and cruelty of reality. Oh, the job for which she'd been selected was a real plum; she should feel honored to have been chosen to bear J. Havelock Dean's child. But when he took her into his bed and spilled his seed into her, it would not be an act of love, but of duty. He would still be lord of the manor, and she would still be the hired help.

She could command his respect perhaps, but love could not be legislated. They would join their bodies with a shared objective, but not with shared affection. He would be performing with the woman he'd hired. She would be fulfilling their contractual agreement. They would both benefit. But there would be no bond between them beyond the contract that bound them and their involvement with their child.

"You needn't be embarrassed," he said, breaking into her reverie. "We'll be lawfully wed."

She forced herself to look at him, to smile, to nod.

"There's no reason it shouldn't be a pleasurable experience for both of us," he continued, in a matter-of-fact tone. "I'm rather looking forward to it myself."

Scarlett blinked back threatening tears. She couldn't, she wouldn't, she absolutely refused, to fall apart. She was a sophisticated woman of the nineties, not a shrinking-violet Victorian virgin. She'd made an agreement and she'd see it through. She'd be pragmatic and count herself fortunate that she was going to end up with a baby and financial independence out of the deal.

She sucked in a deep breath, which escaped as a weary sigh. She would get through that wedding night. It would be awkward perhaps, but weren't most first times with any partner? She'd close her eyes and abandon herself to the physical feelings of the moment, and eventually natural urges would prevail. How bad could it be with a man like J. Havelock Dean III?

"I've never had any complaints," he said drolly, as if reading her mind.

"Neither have I!" Scarlett snapped defensively.

His gaze settled on her face, paused briefly, then moved with an evaluating, predatory air to the V of her blouse, where it lingered appreciatively. Finally his eyes lifted to meet hers again, and he cocked an eyebrow in a purely sexy gesture. "I'll just bet you haven't."

Chapter Three

LOCK'S PRIVATE LINE rang at nine-forty-five the next morning.

"I have an appointment with the attorney at three o'clock Tuesday."

"Tuesday?" Lock said. "That's impossible. We need to get this settled this week."

"It was his earliest opening."

"Give me his name," Lock said, sounding disgruntled. "I'll have Alan give him a call."

Minutes later the phone on Scarlett's desk rang. "You're scheduled with your attorney at eleven tomorrow. I'll meet you for lunch at noon, and Alan will join us at your attorney's office at one-thirty to sign the contracts."

"But... how?"

"Alan gave him a call."

"But he was booked up. If he'd had any time, he'd have scheduled me when I called."

"He may have gone to school with your brother, but he belongs to the same golf club as Alan."

"I see."

"You're going to find that wealth and the right golf club open a lot of doors," he said.

"More than friendship, obviously."

Lock thought about that remark and the disillusionment in her voice for the rest of the day. Maybe he'd made a mistake bringing a woman like Scarlett Blake into his bizarre scheme to give his grandfather a great-grandchild. There were a number of women who would have jumped at the chance to bear the Dean heir, women with backgrounds compatible with his, whose lives and familial relationships wouldn't be disrupted by a mutually compatible arrangement.

A woman just like your mother, nettled an inner voice, and Lock tensed. He hadn't wanted a woman like his mother. For his child, he'd wanted a woman like Scarlett Blake, a woman who'd take off her coat and roll up her sleeves and feed a baby in the middle of a business meeting. A woman grounded in family. A woman who would consider a child a central part of her life. A woman who would be there to hug a child on its birthday, instead of sending cards and exotic novelties from the site of her latest archaeological dig.

In short, a woman as unlike his mother as a woman could get.

Nothing about Scarlett Blake had dissuaded or disappointed him so far. He'd been more than fair to the child he hoped to have; he could only hope that he wasn't being unfair to the mother he'd selected.

In the attorney's office the next afternoon, Lock decided he didn't have to worry about Scarlett Blake; Scarlett Blake proved, once again, that she was more than capable of taking care of herself.

"My client had one minor concern about the contract," her attorney, Mac McGonigle, said.

So she's going to gouge me for money, Lock thought, surprised at the way his stomach knotted in disappointment.

"She's pointed out a possible inequity," McGonigle continued, "and frankly, her point is well taken."

"Inequity?" Lock said. He'd thought the contract more than fair.

"It's the clause dealing with medical proof of her fertility," McGonigle said. "She feels it's superfluous, since she was assured three months ago by her gynecologist that she has a pelvic region adequate to deliver a baby up to twelve pounds."

"Is a—" Lock looked from Alan, to McGonigle and finally to Scarlett "—an adequate pelvic region indicative of fertility?"

McGonigle deferred to Scarlett. "You can speak with more knowledge of this than I can."

Scarlett, blushing, replied, "It doesn't have anything to do with fertility per se. It just means that if I should become pregnant, I could probably carry anything smaller than an elephant without complications."

"That's somewhat reassuring," Lock said, then turned back to her attorney. "However, I'd prefer some proof of fertility. If she should prove infertile, then this whole thing would be futile and, frankly, I can't afford an exercise in futility."

McGonigle nodded, and Scarlett avoided his gaze. Lock sensed the impending landing of a bombshell.

It was not long in coming. "In that case," McGonigle said, "my client agrees to submit to the appropriate tests, but requests that you submit to equivalent tests to certify your fertility."

Lock flew from his chair and directed scathing glances at McGonigle and Scarlett in turn. "My fertility is not in question! I don't have any problems in that department."

"With all due respect," McGonigle said, struggling to maintain a dignified demeanor, "my client has pointed out to me that because of fundamental differences between the sexes, a woman is far more likely to know if she has fertility problems than a man. She has had no indications of problems. On the other hand, a man with an inadequate sperm count usually has no indicators of that problem."

"My sperm count is perfectly fine."

"Oh, so you've had a test?" McGonigle said.

"No. But—"

"Then, as my client pointed out, you're asking her to take a bigger gamble on your fertility than you would be taking on hers." McGonigle looked at Scarlett. "How was it you put that? Oh, yes."

He turned to Lock, this time unable to suppress a grin. "She's afraid you might be shooting blanks, Mr. Dean. As she pointed out, what's good for the goose—"

"—is good for the gander," Lock said through clenched teeth. With fury flashing in his face, he turned to Alan for counsel. He was even more infuriated to discover that his attorney—his friend—was also unable to suppress a grin.

"She has a point, Lock," Alan said. "And as your attorney I feel compelled to point out that in the event you should prove infertile, you would have saved yourself a great deal of money by acquiring that knowledge before entering into a situation destined for failure."

Lock harrumphed exasperatedly. "I am *not* going to go popping off into a cup while reading a skin magazine in order to prove anything to anybody."

"At least you'd have privacy," Scarlett said. "The tests they do on women are spectator events, not to mention humiliating and uncomfortable."

"In light of the fact that my client is in good general health and has no history of reproductive problems, she asks that the clause requiring her to submit to fertility tests be stricken," McGonigle said.

Lock considered it a moment, then looked at Alan, who shrugged and said, "You're the client. It's your decision."

"Strike the damned clause," Lock directed McGonigle, then turned a pointed glare at Scarlett. "Is there anything else?"

"There's a noncontractual concern," McGonigle answered for her.

"Just something that occurred to me," Scarlett said meekly.

"Well, speak up, by all means," Lock said. "Don't be shy. We've already discussed my sperm count and your pelvic region. What could possibly be more embarrassing?"

"It's not embarrassing," Scarlett said.

"I can't tell you how happy I am to hear that."

"It's my cat."

"Your . . . Did you say cat?"

"Whiskers," Scarlett confirmed. "I've had her since my first apartment. She's like a member of my family. I wondered . . . You're not allergic to cats, are you?"

"I'm not allergic to cats," Lock said, rolling his eyes. "But I don't know how the labs would react to a cat."

"Labs?" Scarlett asked.

"Labrador retrievers."

"Those huge black dogs?"

"Napoleon and Josephine."

Scarlett's face registered total surprise, then she laughed delightedly. "You have a pair of Labrador retrievers?"

Her amusement nettled Lock. "They're handsome, well-behaved animals. I don't see what's so amusing—"

"Named Napoleon and Josephine?"

"Nap and Josie for short. And I still don't see what's so amusing."

With determined effort, Scarlett turned her laughter into a smile, and her gaze met Lock's evenly. "I think that's wonderful," she said. And then she burst into tears.

Lock shrugged helplessly at the attorneys. "Would you two give us a moment alone?"

McGonigle tossed Lock a box of tissue, and he and Alan fled the room with an air of making a narrow escape. Lock knelt beside Scarlett's chair and offered her a tissue.

She took it gratefully and, sniffing, blotted her eyes and nose. "I'm sorry," she said. "I'm not usually such a ninny. It's just a bit…overwhelming. I mean, I'm not one of those women who's been planning her wedding from the time she was a little girl playing with a bride doll, but I didn't think… I never thought…"

She gave in to another bout of tears before finishing, "I never thought I'd be sitting in a lawyer's office discussing my pelvic region in front of three strangers, one of whom is my fiancé."

"Look at it this way, Scarlett—after the last fifteen minutes, we're not strangers anymore."

She laughed and cried at the same time, then took a fresh tissue and blotted again.

"What was it about my dogs that set you off?" he asked.

"It's just so…you're so…you've always seemed so… remote and…detached. The fact that you have dogs that you're crazy about, well, it's just reassuring."

Lock sighed dismally. "I don't mean to be remote. I just…I don't relate to people very well, I guess. Big Jake raised me. He had me in boardrooms by the time I was old enough to sit still, but I was never around anyone my age except at school."

Smiling, Scarlett reached out and touched his hair, his golden perfect hair. It was softer than she expected, silky beneath her fingertips as she brushed it off his forehead and watched it spring back into place. "I think I could be friends with a man who calls his dogs Nap and Josie."

He slid the pad of his thumb over the crescent under her eye, as if wiping away the tears that had so recently spilled there. "It was always my hope that we could be friends."

Something changed between them, something elemental and irreversible. The touch of his thumb, so gentle and innocent, suddenly was provocative. Scarlett was aware of the pressure of his fingertips near her ear.

"Bring Whiskers," he murmured. "If Nap and Josie don't have her for lunch, we'll work something out."

Scarlett nodded. His fingers were in her hair now, cradling her scalp. Slowly he straightened to his full height, and Scarlett rose, too—rose into the comfort of his arms around her. Rose to the reassuring hardness of his male body against hers. Rose to the thrill of his eyes warm on her face and the first exciting brush of his lips against hers.

She closed her eyes and his proximity filled her senses: his warmth, the scent of his after-shave, the gentleness of his hands as they caressed her, the moisture of his mouth on hers as the kiss deepened. She softened under his touch, she parted her lips, she slid her arms around him and embraced the pleasure and the reassurance and the promise in their touching.

He released her slowly, breaking the kiss, then kissed her again briefly before pulling away entirely. When she opened her eyes, he was looking at her face and smiling with sweet intensity.

Scarlett gave in to the temptation to burrow her cheek against his broad chest and cling to his strength. He stroked her hair and kissed her forehead, and for a moment, she allowed herself to believe that what was between them was real enough to last beyond the three months after the birth of their child or the death of his grandfather—whichever came later.

"Well, I guess we've confirmed that we're compatible," he said.

She let her arms slide from around him, letting go of the man and the illusion at the same time. "Yes," she said, "I guess we proved that."

Chapter Four

SIGNING THE PAPERS that would influence the rest of her life was as simple as writing her name and watching Lock write his. As their gazes locked across the multiple copies of the contract lined up on McGonigle's conference table, Scarlett wondered if Lock felt any of the emotions she was feeling—the uncertainty, the confusion, the fear, the doubts, the emptiness. She knew he was apprehensive, impatient to get his plan into action, but beyond that, who could tell?

Once again she realized how little she actually knew about him, and the realization saddened her. As often as she told herself to be pragmatic and embrace their agreement as a serendipitous windfall, she couldn't still the inner voice telling her that this was not the way it was supposed to be between two people entering marriage and planning the conception of a child.

She walked out of Mac's office resolved not to fret about it anymore. The deal was struck and the signatures were on the contracts. So, being a perfectly normal woman with good instincts and the rest of the afternoon free, she decided to do what any woman would do in her position: she shopped.

If she didn't feel like a true bride, at least she could affect the look of a woman who could, credibly, turn the head of a man like J. Havelock Dean III—which was why she figured J. Havelock Dean III had provided her with a credit card in the first place.

She bought a week's worth of underwear, a suit for the Reno meeting, a gorgeous sweater to wear with her black knit pants, a dozen pairs of the silky sheer stockings that were usually a splurge item, a pair of leather sports shoes she'd been putting off buying until she could afford them, and a pair of dressy pumps that matched the new suit. She bought the perfume she preferred but usually couldn't afford, and a floor-length, lace-and-satin gown with a matching robe for her wedding night.

When she arrived at her apartment with her arms filled with packages and shopping bags, she still didn't feel like a bride, but she was confident that if she ever had an accident and had to be taken to the hospital where a roomful of emergency-care workers got a glimpse of her underwear, she wouldn't be embarrassed.

Her mother would have been proud of her, she thought.

At work, she visited Lock's office daily in accordance with his plan that her sudden frequent trips to the executive suite might start rumors flying. He was friendly and business-like, inquiring about preparations for the Reno meeting and inquiring after her health and welfare. He seemed pleased when she told him she'd been shopping for the trip, but expressed no particular curiosity about what she'd bought.

On the Monday before their Wednesday departure, he surprised her by stepping into the elevator with her as she left to return to her office. He pressed the button for the seventh floor.

"I'm on five," she said.

"I know," he said. "But Theresa Nevins is on seven. And with luck she's waiting for an elevator. Which means this could be an interesting ride."

She was in his arms before she realized what he intended. "Relax," he ordered, when her surprise registered as tension.

She relaxed as instructed, and his mouth claimed hers with deft efficiency. She parted her lips as his tongue brushed over them, and by the time the elevator door swooshed open and he jerked guiltily away from her, she couldn't have appeared—or felt—more kissed. Her face was flushed, her breathing labored, her lips swollen. Theresa was standing in the hallway, apparently waiting on an elevator.

Scarlett didn't have to fake her embarrassment at being caught making out with the boss in the elevator. The flush of arousal on her face easily became a blush, and she couldn't quite make her eyes meet Theresa's as she murmured a hello. Lock, totally unruffled, nodded a greeting as he might to any employee he chanced to encounter in the building. But the look on Theresa's face confirmed that she had seen enough to assure that the news of a brewing romance would be broadcast throughout the building by the end of the workday.

Theresa hesitated judiciously before barging into the elevator. "Going up?"

"Actually we were going down," Lock said, and grinned lasciviously at Scarlett. "We must have hit the wrong button."

"I'll wait for the next elevator," Theresa said.

Lock nodded and pressed the button for Scarlett's floor. But as soon as the door was closed, he also pressed the button for the intervening floor, and when the car stopped, he pressed the "door close" button and turned the power off in the elevator. Then he grabbed Scarlett by the shoulders and gave her a loud smack of a kiss on the cheek. "You were fantastic! If she had any doubts about what she'd seen, your reaction put them to rest."

"It was nothing," Scarlett said quite sincerely.

Lock rubbed his hands together in satisfaction. "It's all going according to plan."

"How did you know she'd be there?"

"I had Margaret send something for Theresa to the tenth-floor receptionist with a note that Theresa would pick it up at two o'clock. Then Margaret called Theresa and told her there was a memo for her that had been misdirected to the tenth floor and that she should pick it up at two. Luck was on our side—she was precisely on time."

"You're a very resourceful man," Scarlett observed.

"I just start with the result I want and work backward to make it happen. And you were great! If you're that convincing in Reno, we're home free."

"I didn't do anything," Scarlett said. "If I was great, it was because I wasn't acting. I just . . . reacted."

"You were sensational just the same. Just keep on reacting that way, and no one at the Reno meeting will be shocked to learn on Monday morning that we eloped on Friday night."

THE MEETING officially ran from the Wednesday-night dinner through midafternoon on Friday. Employees were given the option of staying on in Reno through the weekend at their own expense, but the majority of them, Big Jake and Lock included, were booked on the last flight home on Friday.

The fact that Scarlett was a bundle of raw nerve endings during the entire meeting had worked in her favor. She was every bit the blushing Cinderella totally overwhelmed by the attentions of Dean Industries' second in command. And Lock was convincing as the besotted suitor. If she hadn't known better, even she would have been convinced that his smoldering looks and sensuous suggestive smiles were actually those of a man who'd been, as he'd so aptly put it, knocked on his ass by love.

Lock waited until the meeting was adjourned to tell his grandfather he'd decided to stay on until Sunday night. A pointed look at Scarlett, who was busy collecting her things at the far end of the table, was all it took for Big Jake to divine the reason for his change in plans.

"She's a looker, our Miss Blake," Big Jake said with a sly smile.

"She's making life interesting at the moment," Lock confessed, then said, "You haven't had a vacation in ages. Why don't you stay on, too?"

"Oh, no," Big Jake said. "These meetings seem to wear me out lately. I'll get a better night's sleep at home in my own bed. Besides, I want to get these tapes to Margaret so she can transcribe them."

"Since you didn't let her make the trip, the least you can do is give the woman the weekend off," Lock said. "I don't know why you didn't just bring her along if you wanted meticulous notes."

"You know she keeps everything together when we're out of the office. She's more valuable to us there than here."

"At least buy her lunch when you drop off those tapes," Lock said.

Big Jake gave him an odd look. "I might just do that. It would beat eating alone since you're going to be... occupied here."

Occupied at the nearest wedding chapel, Lock thought.

"This one's special," Big Jake observed.

"Yes," Lock said, too distracted by Scarlett upon whom his gaze had unconsciously settled to revel in the fact that his grandfather was swallowing his ruse hook, line and sinker. "This one's special."

After the chapel, there would be the diverting task of impregnating his new wife.

It wasn't the most unpleasant prospect he'd ever faced on a Friday night.

THEY MET in the lobby. Lock wore a dark suit. Scarlett wore a white dress with a lace-trimmed collar. Background ambiance was provided by the dings and rings and buzzes of the slot machines in the lobby.

The bride thought the groom looked elegant and suave.

The groom thought the bride looked innocent and apprehensive. He took her hands in his and kissed her chastely on the cheek. "Ready?"

"As I'll ever be," she replied.

After standing in line for their license at the courthouse, they asked the taxi driver to take them to a nice chapel and wound up in a fake Victorian monstrosity where a ludicrous sound system was repeatedly shrilling a horrid organ arrangement of "I Love You Truly." A bored-looking woman with an abundance of orange hair greeted them tiredly, thrust a register at them and asked to see their marriage license.

"There's a couple ahead of you," she said, popping her gum and tilting her head to indicate the couple seated in the waiting area.

They signed the register and returned it to the attendant.

"Now the formalities, Mr.—" she consulted the register "—Dean. We're a full-service chapel. This book—" she handed him a binder "—describes our various wedding services. Will you be needing a ring or rings?"

"Do you have any plain gold bands?" Lock asked. *When they got home, he'd present Scarlett with his grandmother's wedding set—the set she would return upon their separation.*

"Page five," the woman said glibly. "Bouquets begin on page seven. We have a wide selection of cut flowers and artificial. The artificial bouquets can be rented for the ceremony if you're on a budget."

Book in hand, Lock and Scarlett sat down to select a wedding package. Curious, Scarlett stole a surreptitious glance at the other couple waiting to be married. The bride was dressed in a stretch-knit leopard-print jumpsuit with a plunging neckline. She was perhaps Scarlett's age; the groom was pushing seventy.

"I feel like Little Mary Sunshine," Scarlett whispered.

Lock smiled and whispered back, "You smell too sexy for Little Mary Sunshine."

"Glad you like the perfume. You'll be getting the bill at the end of the month."

Somehow, they got through it, the whole horrible travesty of a wedding, and they left though the back door of the chapel under a shower of glitter confetti, which would undoubtedly be swept up and recycled.

Lock sensed Scarlett's somber mood the moment they were in the taxi. She was quiet, ominously so.

"At least it was legal," he said.

"It was that," Scarlett said.

"Do you suppose we'll ever look back on it and laugh?"

"Not in this lifetime."

"Not everyone has wedding music by the Lawrence Welk orchestra. Or a room filled with flowers."

"When they said artificial, I thought they meant silk. I've never seen that much plastic in a single room."

"At least we have a commemorative portrait," Lock said drolly, looking down at the instant photo he'd been handed at the end of the ceremony.

Scarlett took the picture and studied it. "It doesn't show much of my face." She sighed, and gave the picture back to Lock. "That's probably best. When we have it copied and send it to my mother, she won't be able to tell—"

"Big Jake, either," Lock said. "Incidentally, he bought our act. I don't think he doubted for a minute that we would be spending the weekend together."

"Good," Scarlett said pensively. "I'm glad." Then, "Your grandfather is very charming. I think I'm going to like him."

"Everyone likes Big Jake," Lock said. He became lost in deep thought, then recalled dismally, "He mentioned that these meetings wear him out. I've never heard Big Jake say anything wore him out."

"He's not a young man."

"No. But he's always been indefatigable," Lock said. "The fatigue must have something to do with his illness."

"Does his . . . illness have a name?"

"I wish I knew. My grandfather has chosen to protect me from the fact that he's dying." His voice carried a tinge of bittersweet irony. His grandfather's withholding something so essential hurt him almost as much as knowing Big Jake was dying. "He wouldn't do that if it wasn't completely hopeless. I know Big Jake. He's a fighter. If there was any chance at all, he'd be fighting for his life."

Scarlett heard all the pent-up pain behind his words and glimpsed the depth of his devotion to the older man. Instinctively she reached for his hand and wove her fingers through his. He seemed to appreciate the comfort as he curved his fingers around her hand and exhaled a morose sigh.

Such a lonely man, she reflected, wondering if he'd shared his pain over his grandfather's impending death with anyone; if, in fact, he had anyone with whom he could share it.

"I arranged for dinner in my suite," he said as they reentered their hotel. The vulnerable lonely man from the taxi had disappeared, to be replaced by the competent, crisp executive-in-charge.

In charge of my life until three months after our child is born or his grandfather dies, whichever comes later, Scarlett thought frantically. Oh, God, what was she doing walking through a casino with this stranger, wearing a white dress and carrying a nosegay of daisies and baby's breath? What had possessed her to agree to marry him and carry his child when she was nothing more to him than a computer readout?

The casino was getting crowded, and the lights of the slot machines and the keno board seemed brighter and more garish than ever.

Lawrence Welk, plastic flowers and slot machines! Scarlett felt like running screaming from the room, but where would she run to? And what purpose would it serve? She wouldn't even raise eyebrows; everyone would simply assume she'd won or lost a jackpot.

Lock cupped her elbow solicitously as they stepped into the elevator with a woman herding a little girl. Scarlett thought of another elevator ride, the way Lock had kissed her, the way she'd responded. Then she recalled how unaffected he'd been, how he'd greeted Theresa, the company gossip, as though nothing had happened between them, and then complimented her on acting embarrassed.

"Are you a bride?" the child asked, awed.

Scarlett looked down at the little girl, a cherub-cheeked cutie with long straight blond hair and bangs. She formed her lips to reply, but discovered that her mouth had gone dry. "Yes," was all she could manage.

"Would you like to see our wedding picture?" Lock asked.

The little girl nodded enthusiastically and Lock knelt on one knee and showed her the photo. "See—here's Scarlett, and here I am, and here's the notary who married us."

Obviously the child did not see tacky plastic flowers and hazy focus and poor composure. She saw a bride and a groom and romance. With a languid sigh, she said, "When I get growed up, I'm going to be a bride. I'm going to have a long dress and one of those white things over my face and lots and lots of flowers."

"This is our floor," her mother said, taking the little girl's hand.

"'Bye," the child said as her mother guided her toward the opening doors.

"Wait!" Scarlett said. She plucked a daisy from her bouquet and handed it to the child with a gentle smile. "Here you go—a real wedding flower."

The girl smiled from ear to ear as she accepted the daisy, then, at her mother's prompting, added, "Thank you very much."

"You're very welcome," Scarlett said. For a moment her gaze locked with the child's, and the innocent hope and awe glowing in the little girl's eyes made her want to cry. She felt deceptive and dishonest, as though she'd given the child a fraudulent gift. The daisy was from a wedding bouquet. That much was true. But it had not been the bouquet of a starry-eyed bride speaking vows of love.

The door closed, and the elevator continued its upward climb.

"Sweet kid," Lock said.

"Yes," Scarlett agreed.

"Are all little girls fascinated by weddings?"

"A lot of them are."

Were you? Lock wanted to ask. *Have I forced you into a situation that shattered all your little girl dreams?* But he had neither the courage nor the opportunity to ask before the elevator glided to a stop at their floor.

As they walked toward the suite, he hoped that room service had done a good job of setting everything up and that Scarlett would be pleased when she saw the surprise he'd arranged. "Should I carry you across the threshold?" he asked at the door.

"No!" Scarlett snapped, then explained weakly, "It's supposed to be the threshold of your home, not a hotel."

"At the house, then," Lock said.

He flung the door open with a flourish and stepped back so Scarlett could precede him into the suite. She took a few steps, then froze.

In the center of the room, a table had been set for two. The napkins were folded into hearts. Three candles in long-stemmed holders of varying heights provided a centerpiece. Next to the table was a cart holding a bottle of champagne cooling in a crystal ice bucket.

Surrounding the table were flowers, hundreds of them—bouquets in vases, sprays on easels, roses and mums and tropical exotics, brilliantly colored blossoms tucked between pristine white blooms.

"At least they're not plastic," Lock said when Scarlett was too still for too long.

She spun to face him. "You did all this?"

"I wanted tonight to be memorable," he said. He stepped behind her, close enough for her to feel the heat of his body, and capped the tops of her shoulders with his hands.

"Our...*partnership* might be a bit unconventional, but that doesn't have to diminish the significance of what we're attempting to do. There's no reason we shouldn't enjoy this—shall we call it a joint-venture project?"

A joint-venture project, Scarlett thought. *They were making a child, creating a new and unique individual human being, and he called it a joint-venture project!*

"There's a bathroom off the bedroom if you'd like to freshen up before dinner," he said tactfully. "I'm going to see if the champagne's chilled yet."

So gracious. So courteous. Scarlett felt as though her heart had been ripped out, leaving a horrid hollow where it should be. Everything he did, everything he said, reminded her of the gap between what should have been and what actually was.

She nodded an acknowledgment of his suggestion and found the bathroom, welcoming the sanctuary of the small room. The mirror reflected the face of a woman whose eyes held apprehension and regret, a white dress that only parodied a wedding gown.

Scarlett clung to the vanity as though she might crumple to the floor without its support and closed her eyes against the mocking image in the mirror. Another image invaded her mind unbidden: the face of J. Havelock Dean III.

It was a nice face. She could not deny that she found it attractive. Nor could she fault his manners. He could not have been more charming or solicitous. But they were married. He was her husband, she his wife, but everything between them was off center. Where there should have been familiarity, there was formality; where there should have been personal consideration, there was politeness.

He had filled the room with flowers not with the romantic impulse of a groom, but with the deliberate purpose of a man with a well-defined goal. The uniting of his sperm and her egg in an environment receptive to conception was his real objective, the flowers and candlelight mere props to achieve that end as expeditiously as possible.

Scarlett didn't have any problems with uniting the egg and sperm. She wanted a child. It was what they had to *do* to get those little guys together that had her tied up in knots.

It wasn't that she had anything against sex. She liked sex as much as the next woman. She'd just never had sex with a stranger before. And J. Havelock Dean III, though handsome and charming, was a stranger.

A stranger to whom you've been legally wed, she told herself sternly. She sucked in a deep breath and released it slowly to calm her nerves. *You can do this*, she told herself. *You... can... do... this.*

In the living room of the suite, Lock tipped the bellman who'd delivered their dinner and wondered what was taking Scarlett so long. His nervous bride was hiding in the bathroom—the situation was almost amusing in a high camp sort of way. Nevertheless, the fact that the bathroom didn't have any windows through which she might escape was reassuring.

At last he heard the creak of the door opening in the adjoining room. He greeted Scarlett's return with his most reassuring smile and bent to drop a swift kiss on her lips. She ducked nervously, so that the kiss ricocheted to a point somewhere near her ear.

Her skittishness annoyed him. She had said she felt like a nineteenth-century virgin in an arranged marriage, and now she was beginning to act like one. Which meant he was going to have to be the soul of patience and do everything he could to put her at ease. Which was going to be like using gasoline to put out a fire.

"You're back just in time," he said, indicating the cart laden with food. He pulled out her chair for her.

Scarlett smiled lamely as he took the seat opposite her. The candles were lit, the room lights lowered. The scene had been conspicuously choreographed for seduction, every prop carefully selected. Though she was fully clothed, Scarlett felt exposed.

She wondered if he'd played this scene before, without the wedding beforehand or the expectation of making a baby as the climax of the evening's entertainment. How many women had he wooed with wine and candlelight? With flowers and finger food? She was neither unsophisticated nor naive. She'd seen movies. She'd read romantic novels. Doubtless he planned to feed her the jumbo shrimp nestled on the bed of shaved ice or kiss the liqueur from the dark-chocolate truffles from her lips.

It would have been wildly romantic if he thought of her as an alluring woman, instead of an incubator. If they had come together out of attraction, instead of pragmatism. If their wedding had truly been a celebration of love, instead of a business arrangement. If their impending sexual encounter could be fueled by passion, instead of deliberate purpose.

The champagne cork yielded to Lock's ministrations with a healthy pop, and he filled their flutes, then held his up in a salute to her. The reflected flame of the candle gave the pale amber liquid the look of liquid fire.

"To the promise of success," he said.

It was all Scarlett could do to swallow the bubbly liquid after clinking her glass against his. She forced down half a shrimp before giving up on eating altogether and slowly sipping her champagne.

At length Lock noticed she wasn't eating. "If you don't care for shrimp, we could order something else."

Scarlett shook her head, not quite meeting his eyes. "I'm not hungry. I, uh, ate too much at lunch."

He didn't call her on the blatant lie. Instead, he picked up the champagne bottle and refilled the flute she'd almost emptied.

"We'll stick everything in the refrigerator. We might get hungry . . . later." His inflection gave the comment a suggestive connotation, and he punctuated it with a warm smile.

"Please," she said. "Finish yours."

He smiled again as he pushed his plate aside. "My mind's not on food, either—unless you'd like one of those chocolate things."

She had to try to cooperate. Scarlett knew she had to try. "Maybe a chocolate."

It was a major mistake. As predicted he reached across the small table to feed it to her, letting her bite off the edge, then tilting the shell so that the liqueur inside drizzled over her tongue and burned its way down her throat. It was a very strong liqueur; it didn't sit well with champagne on an empty nervous stomach. The truth was, she hadn't really eaten too much at lunch. She hadn't eaten two bites of her lunch. She began to feel nauseated about the time his lips reached hers, but forced herself not to move as he kissed her.

"You're tense," he said softly, as he drew away and settled back in his chair.

"Would you excuse me just for a moment," Scarlett said, not waiting for a reply as she dashed toward the bathroom.

She rinsed the taste of the liqueur from her mouth and then gooed toothpaste over her teeth with her forefinger—another mistake, since mint and fluoride didn't settle any better than the liqueur had. She downed two glasses of tap water, hoping at least to dilute the alcohol.

Feeling a bit better, she returned to the living room. Lock had cleared away the perishables and moved their glasses and the ice bucket to the table in front of the sofa. The radio provided soft music. The candles on the table were still burning.

Lock had removed his tie, opened the top two buttons of his shirt and rolled up his sleeves to reveal beautifully muscled forearms.

Tennis? Scarlett wondered. *Golf? Boxing in a gym? Weights?* How little she knew about this man whose child she hoped to conceive!

"Are you comfortable?" he asked. "Feel free to kick off your shoes or whatever."

Scarlett self-consciously slipped off her heels and wiggled her stockinged toes against the carpet.

"Better?" he asked, and she nodded grinning.

"Sit down," he said, indicating the sofa, and suddenly, they were side by side: Mr. and Mrs. J. Havelock Dean III. Strangers, with very little in common beyond a shared desire to have a child.

If only she wasn't so tense! Lock thought. She was so uptight he was afraid if he touched her she'd spring straight off the couch and up to the ceiling. Maybe a little more champagne...

He lifted his glass. "To you, Mrs. Dean."

Forcing a smile, Scarlett touched her glass to his and sipped. When she replaced it on the coffee table, Lock picked up the bottle. "I'll freshen this for you."

"Look," Scarlett said, "I know what you're going after here, but I'm not much of a drinker, and if I swill any more of that champagne, I'm either going to pass out or become intimately acquainted with your john.''

Frowning, Lock put the bottle back into the bucket. ''I suppose a certain amount of awkwardness is inevitable.''

''A certain amount,'' Scarlett agreed sarcastically.

''Maybe if we . . . touched a little,'' he suggested.

''Touched?'' She said it as though she'd never heard of the concept.

''Would you like to dance?''

''Dance?''

''It's a simple procedure,'' he replied drolly. ''We stand up, I put my arms around you, and we move around in time to the music.''

''Okay.''

''You're hell on a man's ego,'' he grumbled as they rose. He regretted the wisecrack instantly when her face clouded. His guts knotted with the fear that she might cry.

''I'm trying,'' she said.

''I know,'' he said sadly. His touch was more soothing than sexual as he slid his arms around her. ''So am I.''

''You're going to get a crick in your neck holding it back like that,'' he said a moment later. ''You could put your head on my shoulder, you know. Teenagers do that much at eighth-grade dances.''

She allowed her cheek to rest against his chest with a sigh. Lock's warmth, his strength, the gentleness of his touch were alluring as they moved to the slow song. Scarlett closed her eyes and tried to imagine that she was at the prom with a boy she was crazy about.

''Whatever I'm going to pay for that perfume, it's worth it,'' Lock murmured.

It was the first time he'd ever known a woman to stiffen at a compliment, instead of warm to it. Still, her cheek was on his shoulder, and her temple was near enough to kiss. He kissed—gentle, nibbling kisses—and hoped that it wasn't his imagination that her pulse rate was going up.

Gradually he eased his mouth lower, trailing butterfly kisses across her cheek until finally he reached her lips and tested their fullness with the tip of his tongue, tasting champagne, before sealing her mouth with his for a more persistent exploration.

He pulled her more tightly against him, hoping she could feel his response to her through the fullness of her gathered skirt. He brushed the knuckles of his left hand back and forth across her cheek, then let his hand slide down, over her jaw, along her neck to her chest. Heartened by her lack of resistance and the growing malleability of her soft body, he cupped her breast, covering it with his palm.

The effect was electric, but not in the way he'd hoped. She stiffened from head to toe and jerked away from him. "I can't do this!"

He reached for her. "Take it easy," he said. "We have all weekend. We'll take it a little slower."

If she heard him, she didn't acknowledge it. "I never should have agreed to this."

"You're overwrought," he said. "We'll work through this. Sit down and—"

"You're always telling me to sit down!" she cried. "I don't want to sit down. I want to get far away from here as fast as I can go. I must have been as nuts as you are to ever think I could do what you hired me to do."

"I didn't hire you!"

"Didn't you?" Tears were streaming down her cheeks, but she paid them no heed.

"We struck a mutually advantageous deal," he said. "That's not the same thing as hiring."

"Pardon me for not appreciating that distinction right now. Right now I feel like a hired woman." Groaning miserably, she sank onto the sofa and covered her face with her hands. "You don't even see me. I'm not a person to you. I'm a . . . a computer spit-out."

"That's not true," he said.

"The only thing you like about me is the perfume you're going to pay for, and that comes out of a bottle."

"That's entirely untrue," he protested. "You're a beautiful compassionate woman. When you were holding Alan's baby—"

"You were shopping for a mother, not a . . . companion." She lifted her head and glowered at him through tear-reddened eyes. "You didn't feel anything in the elevator."

"The elevator?" His mind flitted back to the child who'd asked if Scarlett was a bride. He'd thought the child was cute. He'd thought Scarlett was gracious. What more was he supposed to have felt?

"You had your arms around me," she said accusingly. "You . . . you *kissed* me, but you weren't involved. Not emotionally. It was just a show for Theresa."

That elevator. His mind spun back to that afternoon, to that kiss.

"I was a prop. Just a prop for your plan."

"You're wrong," Lock said.

"Oh-h-h," she cried miserably, "you're right. I'm wrong. I was wrong to have signed that contract. I'm not the kind of woman who . . . signs contracts. I'm the old-fashioned, mortgages-and-meatballs type. I don't want a check every month for services rendered. I want a man who loves me and a baby who's a baby, and not an . . . an *heir*."

A prolonged silence trailed her outburst. Lock slumped miserably on his end of the couch. Scarlett sagged miserably on hers.

The silence stretched longer. It became an entity in the room, an uncomfortable, mocking third presence. Scarlett would have done anything to defeat or escape it, but neither her mind nor her voice seemed to be working.

Finally Lock said, "Do you want out?"

Chapter Five

SCARLETT STARED at him blankly. "Out?"

"Contracts are easily torn up. An annulment should be a simple matter, considering that the marriage was never consummated. The, uh, termination settlement would be out of the question, but I imagine some sort of compensation..."

The return of the executive-in-charge! Scarlett thought, still on the edge of hysteria. But when she looked at him, Lock didn't look confident or in control; he appeared desperate and defeated. And terribly sad.

"What about your grandfather?" she asked.

"What about him?"

"I thought you wanted..."

"I did. But my plan doesn't seem to be working out."

"I'm sorry." She was sorry for everything—for his grandfather's illness, for saying yes, instead of telling him to find someone else more suitable while there was still time, for disappointing him, for disappointing herself.

He shrugged miserably. "It was probably a flawed plan from the very first."

"No! It's not as though it was an ego thing with you. It was... sweet of you to want to do that for your grandfather. And it wasn't a bad plan. It was extremely generous. It's just... you just... you picked the wrong person."

He grinned sadly at that. "I hadn't thought so."

She cocked her head interestedly. "Really?"

"I thought I had chosen exactly the right person." He pinned her with a harsh look. "And if you think I wasn't involved in that kiss in the elevator, you're sadly mistaken, Miss Blake."

"Mrs. Dean," she corrected.

"Not for long it would seem."

She put her hand atop his. "Did you mean what you said about the kiss?"

He frowned. "Let's just say it left me with the impression that our honeymoon might be...interesting."

This time, it was Scarlett who breached the awkward silence between them. "I'm not a welsher."

Lock gave her blank look. "I beg your pardon?"

"I'm not a welsher. I don't make deals and then chicken out at the critical moment."

"You want to try again?" he asked dryly.

Because she had seen his vulnerability, Scarlett was able to steel herself against his sarcasm. She searched his eyes and found remnants of that vulnerability still lingering in their depths. "Yes. I'd like to try."

"I thought you were into mortgages and meatballs and true love."

"In a perfect world I would be. It's not a perfect world."

"I'm not going to force a woman into my bed."

Scarlett smiled softly. "Like you said, we have all weekend. Why don't we just focus on getting better acquainted and see what happens by Sunday night."

Maybe it was because giving up without a fight went against her grain. Or maybe it was because she knew how desperately he wanted to give his dying grandfather the gift of progeny. Whatever the reason, Scarlett found herself holding her breath as she waited for his decision.

He rose abruptly and looked down at her. "Is that dress comfortable? And those shoes?"

"Not particularly," she admitted.

"Then change into something that is. We're getting out of this room for a while."

It was strange opening her suitcase and seeing the lacy edges of her underthings peeping out here and there, in Lock's bedroom. Stranger still to peel off her clothes and stand in the middle of that room in nothing but her bra and panties. She put on a pair of black jeans and the new over-size sweater and instantly felt better about life in general. After panty hose and heels all day, it was heaven to put on soft cotton socks and her new sport shoes. Pausing briefly in front of the mirror, she fluffed her hair whimsically and saluted her reflection.

Lock was staring out the window when she reentered the living room. He snapped instantly to alertness. "Ready?"

She nodded.

"Then let's go," he said, grabbing her hand and leading her out of the room and into the corridor.

"So where are we going?" Scarlett asked, scurrying to keep pace with his longer stride. He seemed to have a definite destination in mind.

"We're going to do something guaranteed to jump start a woman's libido," he answered acerbically. "The mall is open. We are going to spend money."

Spend money? Scarlett had nothing against spending money, but she'd never thought of it as foreplay. She tried to sound cooperative and enthusiastic, instead of just curious. "Are we shopping for anything in particular?"

Lock considered the question only for a moment before making an executive decision. "It's our wedding day," he said. "We'll buy each other wedding presents."

The mall was filled with avant-garde specialty stores, many of them themed either toward gambling or Nevada's Western orientation.

Lock led her into a pricey jewelry boutique. While Scarlett admired a key chain with a silver coyote charm, Lock had the saleslady take a tray of rings out of the glass display case. He insisted Scarlett pick her favorite, then he slid the silver ring with pearls set into a swirling, ocean-wave design onto the third finger of her right hand. Nodding gallantly, he kissed her finger just beneath the ring and said, "To commemorate our friendship."

Their next stop was a lingerie shop. Scarlett fidgeted self-consciously while Lock made a methodical survey of the lace, satin and chiffon sleepwear. He took a gown of silver gray chiffon from the rack and held it under her chin, sizing it.

"Lock," she said through gritted teeth.

His naughty-boy grin almost won her forgiveness—until he teased, "Embarrassed, Mrs. Dean?"

"We're in public," she rasped.

"And you have a wedding band on your left hand—or had you forgotten we're honeymooning?"

Scarlett sniffed in exasperation, which added a twinkle to his eyes as his naughty-boy grin widened.

"Now we know where the term 'blushing bride' came from. Your face is bright red."

Her hands flew to her burning cheeks, and he laughed aloud. "You're cute when you're embarrassed." He kissed her cheek flamboyantly. "I believe this one's you. These roses are scarlet, not true red."

She looked down at the front of the gown, where satin roses had been worked into the cutwork lace panel on the bodice—the lace panel that would reveal almost everything above the waist.

"You don't have to— It's too expen— I've already bought a gown. You'll be getting—"

"The bill," he finished for her. "Trust me, Scarlett. I can afford to buy you two."

"But . . ."

He grinned again. "Bet the other one doesn't have scarlet roses on it."

A woman could get used to that grin, Scarlett thought. *To that amused twinkle in his eyes. To the sensual gleam.* She looked at the gown he was holding. The roses *were* scarlet, not true red; few men would have made the distinction.

"Speechless?" he teased. "I take it that means you like it."

As they waited for the clerk to ring up the purchase he slid his arms around her waist and whispered in her ear, "I can hardly wait to see you in it."

"Lock," she said, tilting her head toward the clerk.

Lock laughed and nipped her earlobe. "We're honeymooners, remember?"

The suggestion in the comment slivered titillatingly over her nerve endings, and as Lock stood so near her, touching her, whispering sexy entreaties in her ear, Scarlett was aware of everything that was male about him—his size, his hardness, his strength, his heat. His after-shave was subtle but potent. His eyes were expressive. His lips were nicely bowed and sensuous. His fingers were long and beautifully tapered.

And he noticed the difference between scarlet and true red.

The clerk folded the gown in tissue and tucked it into a bag. Lock reached for it, then hesitated, eyeing the lilac-printed bag dubiously.

Laughing merrily, Scarlett stood on tiptoe and kissed his cheek. "You can buy a see-through nightie, but you can't carry a flowery bag through the mall!"

He snatched it from the counter and jammed it under his left arm. Scarlett looped her arm around his right arm and reached for the bag. "Give it here. If you carry it like that, the heat from your body will wrinkle it."

He placed it carefully in her hand and captured her gaze. "We wouldn't want it wrinkled when you model it for me."

They window-shopped their way to a sporting-goods store. "This brings back memories," Scarlett said, pausing at the display of bats, gloves and mitts.

"You don't have a baseball player in your past, do you?" Lock asked.

"Dozens of them," Scarlett replied. "My father coached baseball before he became principal. I was always the un-official bat-and-water boy."

"That's a physical impossibility," Lock said, letting his gaze settle blatantly on the way her sweater draped over her breasts.

"Nevertheless, I did it until I was about fourteen," she said. "My dad was principal by then. Do you play?"

"Baseball?"

"Anything," she replied. "Baseball. Golf. Tennis. Bas-ketball."

"Big Jake had me on the tennis courts before he had me in the boardrooms."

"I don't suppose there's anything you need desperately in the tennis section."

Lock shrugged. "Big Jake orders balls by the case, and I have a new racquet."

"You're not pining after a purple satin warm-up jacket, are you?"

"Sorry."

Scarlett sighed. "I haven't bought you anything yet."

"You don't have to buy me anything."

"Of course I do. You've done all the spending so far." She stepped back and studied him critically. "There must be something . . ."

Inspiration hit when she spied a Western-wear shop on the opposite side of the mall. Smiling smugly, she asked, "If I picked out something for you, would you wear it?"

"As long as it's not made of purple satin."

"This way, then," she said, grabbing his hand.

"You can't be serious," he said a few minutes later.

"It's not purple satin."

"It's a cowboy hat."

"It'll go perfectly with your boots."

"What boots?"

"The boots you're going to try on as soon as you get into your jeans."

"Jeans? *Blue* jeans?"

"You'll love them once you get used to them," she assured him. "And while you're trying on jeans, I'll pick out a shirt for you."

"Not a Western shirt with braid and pearl snaps?" he asked, appalled.

"Well, if you insist on pearl snaps, sure. What's your sleeve length, cowboy?"

"Thirty-four," he replied. "But I do *not* want pearl snaps."

She gave him an exasperated scowl. "Trust me—my husband can afford pearl snaps. He's loaded."

Half an hour later the metamorphosis from executive to cowboy was complete. He stood before her, long and lean, in form-fitting, button-fly jeans, a chambray shirt, tooled leather belt with a silver-and-turquoise buckle, tan boots and the cowboy hat.

"Well?" he asked. He felt like a fool, but at least she hadn't made him wear pearl snaps.

"Just a tiny tilt," she murmured thoughtfully, adjusting his hat. She stepped back to admire her work. "Perfect. You can water your horse in my corral any time, cowboy."

They window-shopped their way back to the hotel lobby. "Now what?" Scarlett asked.

"We could always go for a drink," Lock said. "Or feed the one-armed bandits."

"Whatever you want," she replied with a marked lack of enthusiasm.

"Or we could see what the rental-car people sent over and take a moonlit drive around the lake." He laughed, gratified by her surprised expression. "I called for a car while you were changing clothes earlier. I thought you might enjoy seeing Tahoe at night."

They stopped at the suite to drop off their parcels and get jackets for when the night turned cold. For the first time, they actually entered the bedroom together. Lock tossed the bag with his clothes into the closet and pulled an all-weather jacket from a hanger. Scarlett dug her Windbreaker from the corner of her suitcase and would have deposited the lilac-printed bag from the lingerie shop safely out of sight if Lock hadn't shown up at her elbow just as she was getting ready to close the suitcase.

Deftly he retrieved the bag and grinned gloatingly. "We wouldn't want this wrinkled, now would we?"

She shook her head.

"Why don't we take it out of the bag?" he continued, reaching inside. He separated the tissue from the chiffon with infinite care and spread the garment on the bed, straightening the diaphanous skirt with great concentration and a certain awkwardness, as if unaccustomed to touching such frilly fare, but nonetheless determined to do the job.

Scarlett found greater reassurance in the slight awkwardness of his movements and his apparent self-consciousness than she would have if he had been cocksure and competent. She found the fact that he wasn't entirely comfortable fussing with a woman's nightgown endearing.

She was beginning to like J. Havelock Dean III.

"It'll be here waiting for you when we get back," he said with a bedroom smile, and suddenly the prospect of consummating their marriage did not seem so much intimidating as titillating.

She was beginning to like J. Havelock Dean III. *A lot.*

Chapter Six

"IT'S A CONVERTIBLE!" Scarlett exclaimed delightedly a few minutes later, when the valet handed the keys to Lock.

"The better to gaze at the stars, my dear," he replied.

Half an hour later they had left Reno and were on a twisting mountain road that wound round Lake Tahoe. The mountain darkness cloaking the scenic highway made the curves seem sharper, the rises and declines more dramatic. Above them the cloudless Nevada sky stretched into infinity, the stars twinkling like diamonds spilled onto indigo velvet.

It was cool, but neither minded the bite of the wind sweeping over the windshield; the sense of freedom provided by the open air more than compensated for the discomfort of a slight chill.

"Have you ever seen Lake Tahoe at night?" Lock asked.

"I've never seen Lake Tahoe, period."

"Ah," he said, smiling. "You're in for a treat."

A mile or so up the road, they stopped at an overlook, which offered a panoramic view of the lake. They were the only car there, which pleased Lock. They could use a little privacy with a romantic view. He switched off the ignition and turned to Scarlett. "What do you think?"

"It's stunning," she said, awed by the spectacle of the water far below, deep and dark and glistening with starlight and moonlight and the reflected lights from dots of civilization along the shore.

"That's Stateline, on the Nevada-California border," Lock said, referring to a cluster of bright lights. "There's a string of casinos on the Nevada side."

"Do you come here often?" she asked.

"I used to. I was into skiing for a while. My friends and I used to make Tahoe every year."

"Why'd you stop?"

"You know how it is—you get busy."

"Too busy for something you love to do?"

"Skiing's too time-consuming. The travel, being away a lot—it just wasn't practical anymore."

Scarlett thought about what he'd said as she studied the play of lights on the water. "Your job is very demanding, isn't it?"

"Yes."

"From the bottom of the corporate structure, it looks like you have it all. Second in command before you're thirty. But all that responsibility...Don't you ever feel like just chucking it all and running away?"

Lock cocked an eyebrow. "Running away to Tahoe to ski?"

"Just...running."

"Occasionally. For five minutes or so. Never long enough to act on the impulse. The truth is ..." His lips curled in a bittersweet smile. "The truth is, I'm too much Big Jake's grandson to run away. He loves the business. He thrives on it. And so do I. That's why..."

His voice trailed off and he got a faraway look in his eye. Scarlett reached for his hand, lifted it, stroked the top of it gently with her fingertips. "Why what?"

For a moment he didn't answer, but stared at his hand held in hers. She had a soft touch. It had been a long time since he'd known such gentleness from a woman. His gaze moved upward to her face, pale and translucent in the moonlight.

"That's why my grandfather was convinced that once I'd moved into the big office, the odds of my finding a wife and producing a new generation of Deans were nil. He knew the work would consume me, because it's always consumed him. He was already married to my grandmother and was raising my father when he took on the job."

"Is your grandmother...?"

"She died two years after my father was killed. My grandfather believes she died of a broken heart."

"How did your father—if I'm not intruding to ask...?"

He appeared genuinely surprised by the question. "Didn't you know? He was killed in Vietnam."

"I didn't. I'm— How old were you?"

"He held me once before he shipped out," Lock said. "So you see, I know him by reputation only."

"That's sad," Scarlett said. "What about your mother? You never mention her."

"My mother was working on her doctorate when my father was killed. She went on a three-week dig and met another archaeologist, very respected in the field. When he offered her a chance to participate in a project in South America, she leapt at it."

He frowned. "A small child would have been inconvenient on a primitive site, and she knew Big Jake would throw a fit if she tried to take me out of the country, so she left me with him. She married the archaeologist. They've done some major work in the field. She visits when she's between projects."

"How could a woman do that?"

"She was widowed so young, and her life just...changed direction. It's not as though she left me on a strange doorstep. I'd lived in my grandfather's house all my life, and she knew Big Jake would take care of me."

"But you must have missed having a mother."

He pulled his hand from hers to cradle her face between his palms. "If we have a child, you can be assured I'll be involved in his life." He stared intently into her eyes. "Will you give me a child, Scarlett?"

Scarlett's lips parted, but the only sound she made was the softest imaginable sigh. His lips settled on hers, lightly, exacting with gentleness what force could never have achieved. He trailed kisses across her cheek, then whispered sensuously in her ear, "Let's make a baby tonight, Mrs. Dean."

It was the most blatantly sexual thing any man had ever said to her, and reaction shivered through her as he claimed her mouth again in a plundering kiss. Her body heated to the touch of his restless questing hands, and as he deftly breached the bottom edge of her sweater and curved his right hand around her ribs, she wondered with her last shred of reason if he planned to take her there, on the front seat of a rented convertible.

She would never be sure, because a car turned off the highway onto the overlook, shocking them with a jarring blast of headlights. Lock lifted his head, breaking the kiss, and they stared at each other with the dazed stares of interrupted lovers.

The moment was gone, but not the intimacy that had developed between them, and not the promise of greater intimacy to come. Lock smiled, and Scarlett's heart swelled. He looked so different in casual clothes, with the cowboy hat tilted back at a ridiculous angle—so human and approachable and . . . real.

"I want to see you in that new gown, anyway," he said, his eyes catching the starlight.

Scarlett envisioned the nightgown spread over the bed in his suite and thought perplexedly that she should have been embarrassed; instead, she was exhilarated. Anticipation thrilled through her as she thought of being alone with him again, of wearing the gown he'd chosen and so self-consciously laid out for her, of making a child with this man next to her who no longer seemed like a stranger, but like a dear, dear friend.

Reluctantly he pulled his hand from under her sweater and moved back into position to drive. "Let's see if we can find a different vantage point down the road."

They parked at the next overlook even longer, enjoying the moonlight, smooching like teenagers and aching with pent-up need as their kisses grew hotter and their embraces bolder. Coyotes yipped and howled in the distance, calling for mates.

Scarlett explored Lock's broad shoulders through his shirt. Lock, his hands under her sweater, kneaded the small of her back. She slipped her fingers between the buttons of his shirt to caress his hard chest. He slid his hand down to splay his fingers over the roundness of her hip through the taut denim. Their bodies heated as they pressed closer, frustrated by the clothes they wore and the restricted space in the car.

Lock groaned as she stroked his thigh through his jeans. Scarlett gasped as he massaged her breasts with his palms through the thin fabric of her bra. They broke apart, heaving for breath, when a car turned off the highway.

"You've got me hotter than a two-dollar pistol, ma'am," Lock drawled.

"Just be sure you're packing plenty of firepower, cowboy," she said, touching the thatch of hair under the front brim of his hat. "We're going to give that baby-maker of yours a real workout."

As Lock brought the convertible's engine to life, he cast a silent entreaty heavenward that Scarlett wouldn't have any abrupt change of heart once they were back at the hotel. His "baby-maker" was stiff as a poker and ready to play—aching, literally, for the workout she promised. For a woman who'd been ready to tuck tail and call off their deal, she'd certainly warmed to the call of duty. If she turned skittish again, he was going to swear off women, take a vow of celibacy and move to a monastery in Tibet. Or get more stinking than a prairie polecat on firewater in the nearest saloon. His choice would depend on whether or not he was able to refrain from strangling her before he made his move.

"Are you champing at the bit to see the casino lights at Stateline?" he asked.

"Not especially."

"Then what do you say, little lady? Want to head back to our corral and stake out a little piece of heaven?"

Scarlett giggled. "I'm with you, cowboy, but John Wayne is rolling in his grave."

She reached into the back seat for her Windbreaker.

"Are you cold?" Lock asked. "I could put the top up."

"And block out that sky? No way."

"Are you sure? It's getting chilly." He didn't want her cooling down too much.

"I'll keep warm," she said, wrapping her arm around his and cuddling her cheek against his upper arm.

After a while she snuggled closer, sighed and murmured sleepily, "I think I've already pinched off a little bit of heaven."

He couldn't disagree with her. It felt good to have a woman cuddling up against him and obviously enjoying it. He reminded himself that this was the same woman who'd been near hysterics just hours ago and fought the affection welling up inside him for her. *Carpe diem,* he cautioned himself. *Seize the moment. Enjoy it if it works out. Let it go if it doesn't.*

It was the only way he could work it. What you can't control, you do not allow to control you. If they consummated the marriage, if she conceived a child, if they could be friends, so be it. If not . . .

He had enough on his mind with Big Jake dying. He was doing everything—the only thing, really—that he could do for Big Jake. If it worked, it worked. If it didn't, it didn't.

And if Scarlett Blake Dean just happened to feel like a bit of heaven snuggling against him, and if she sighed like an angel and smelled like temptation itself . . . well, sometimes things worked out better than a man had a right to expect. He just hoped she turned out to be as fertile as she was desirable.

Except for an occasional sigh and some feline nestling, she was quiet on the drive back to the hotel. He thought perhaps she'd fallen asleep, but she lifted her head slowly as he turned into the hotel lot. She smiled up at him seductively while they waited for the valet. "Ready to make a baby, cowboy?"

"If I wasn't five seconds ago, I am now, ma'am. You just got my little ol' baby-maker standing at attention."

He'd never seen a woman blush quite as thoroughly. Even her earlobes turned red. But before he had a chance to repair the damage, the valet was at the door, grinning broadly and clearing his throat tactfully. "Good evening, sir."

Chapter Seven

"I'M NOT GOING to chicken out this time," Scarlett said with a determined thrust of chin as she stood in their hotel room.

All of Lock's philosophical resolve just to let things happen—or not happen—faded as he looked at her. She was beautiful. She was alluring.

And she was his wife. No matter what he was telling himself, something deep inside him, something elemental and instinctive, was reacting to that knowledge. Reaching for her hand, he said, "Damned straight you're not, Mrs. Dean."

Wrapping his hand around hers, he gave a yank, pulling her close. Their bodies touched in random places. He could smell her perfume. He remembered the arcs and curves of her body under his hands. "We've got unfinished business, Mrs. Dean. It's time we found that bit of heaven."

He found an outside edge of it as his arms slid around her waist and their bodies aligned full-length. She fit him the way a woman should, her breasts firm but pliant against his chest, her thighs solid and warm against his.

Heat flared between them the instant their lips touched, and as he deepened the kiss, he cupped her bottom and pressed her into his hardness, wanting her to feel the burn of his arousal, wanting the fire to consume her as it was consuming him.

Scarlett gasped at the intimacy of their embrace, but the gasp was swallowed by his kiss. Greedy, restless with need, she slid her arms over his shoulders and clung to him, pressing closer, while stroking her hands over his broad back.

His mouth left hers to savor the tenderness of her neck.

"The gown," Scarlett rasped, hanging on to her control by the thinnest of threads as his right hand splayed over the small of her back. How had he gotten past her sweater so deftly?

He froze for a moment, then growled, "Some other time. Right now . . ." He shoved the sweater up, bunching it under her arms, and his fingertips feasted on velvety skin. When he used his cheek to lever the sweater higher in front, his hat was knocked askew.

Scarlett grabbed it by the brim and tossed it across the room. Lock's chin, rough with several hours' growth of beard, scraped over her midsection with electric results. She combed her fingers into his hair and he groaned against her midriff, heating her skin with his breath. Her fingers convulsed, then opened gently, releasing him so she could grab the sweater and pull it over her head out of the way.

A feral growl escaped his throat as he covered her exposed skin with kisses, and an answering moan rose from within her as his temple brushed a taut nipple still imprisoned by her bra. Lock grasped the bra, searching for the clasp, driving her crazy as his knuckles kneaded her breast while he fought the tiny unfamiliar fastener.

Scarlett worked the buttons on his shirt more easily, and by the time he pushed her bra over her arms and crushed her against him, his shirt was open. They clung to each other in a wordless desperate embrace. Scarlett's breasts compressed against his muscular chest, and she felt the joining all the way to her womb. Coarse hair grated her aroused nipples with a friction so delicious it coaxed a rugged sigh from her throat.

"Let's make a baby," she said breathlessly.

He was the first man ever to sweep her into his arms and carry her to bed. The covers had been turned back, her gown arranged artfully on the pillow. Lock lowered her gently to the edge and dramatically tossed the gown across the room with a cavalier chuckle. She sat there, naked to the waist and still dazed from his kisses, and watched with rapt attention as he worked impatiently at the buttons on his jeans.

"Not used to button flies?" she taunted.

"Any civilized clothing manufacturer would use zippers."

"Well, you wouldn't be having nearly as much trouble if you weren't so..." She didn't see the need to finish the sentence, even if she'd had the nerve.

"Oh, and just who do you think is responsible for that? I didn't get this way by looking in the mirror." He groaned. "God, you have incredible breasts."

Part of his problem all along, Scarlett thought, was that he'd been staring at her, instead of the buttons he was trying to unbutton.

"Let me help you," she offered sensuously. He stood stoically while she worked the buttons through the stiff denim, but if the sounds issuing from his throat and heat emanating from behind the fly were any indication, he was suffering the same sweet torture she had endured with the bra. Or worse.

Worse, Lock would have told her. Her breasts were incredible, but her hands—her hands were pure magic. Could this sweet tormentor of swollen male flesh really be the woman who'd almost run from the suite in hysterics? The same woman who'd blushed to her roots when he'd told her about his arousal in the car? She was full of contradictions—and utterly fascinating.

And she was his wife. When he'd cooked up this baby idea, he hadn't expected to feel quite so involved. Of course, it would be difficult not to be involved with a half-naked woman who was unbuttoning his pants, even if he weren't legally married to her. Or even if her breasts weren't so incredibly beautiful.

"There," she said, patting the front of his briefs through the gaping fly. "All done."

He gave her a look hot enough to singe the soles of her feet. "I assure you, Mrs. Dean, we are not anywhere *near* done."

"Obviously," she said, unabashedly eyeing the bulge outlined by his cotton briefs. Smiling wickedly, she grasped the side seams of his jeans and yanked them down over his knees. "How about some action, cowboy?"

Lock shook the jeans the rest of the way down his legs and then growled an obscenity when they caught on his boots. Dropping onto the edge of the bed, he bent his left leg at the knee and, wresting with the stiff denim, propped his ankle on his right knee and tugged at the boot. To no avail.

Scarlett took off her shoes. Lock was still struggling with the boot, grunting with the effort. "Now we know why the Old West died out," she said drolly.

"They're new," he said defensively. "The leather's stiff."

"The leather's not the only thing that's stiff," she teased, focusing her gaze interestedly on his lap.

"How can anyone so damned sexy be so damned perverse?" Scowling, he stretched out his leg in front of him. "Why don't you quit tormenting me and make yourself useful?"

Scarlett grinned. "All right," she said, standing up and grabbing his boot at the heel and toe, "but I'm not straddling your leg, and you are *not* going to put your foot on my behind and push.''

"You're no fun at all,'' he grumbled.

"I'm not the one who can't get my footwear off,'' she said, looking down at her socked feet. She tugged and the boot came off, sending her stumbling backward.

She quickly regained her balance, and Lock frowned. "For one delicious moment there, I thought you were going to land flat on your behind.'' Ignoring her answering scowl, he nonchalantly extended his other leg. Scarlett feigned an exaggerated sigh and took his boot in hand. "The things a woman has to do to get pregnant!''

Once the boot was removed, Lock stood up, kicking off his jeans when they bunched at his ankles. The look he gave her as he shrugged out of his shirt and let it glide to the floor could have come out of a bottle labeled ''sin.''

He took a step toward her.

Scarlett took a step back.

His expression turned gentle, and a smile softened his features as he extended his hand, palm up. "Mrs. Dean.''

Scarlett placed her hand in his and returned his smile. "Mr. Dean.''

He lifted her hand to his face and slid his cheek back and forth against it. Then, his eyes locked with Scarlett's, he kissed it—the top, her palm, each finger.

Scarlett closed her eyes and sighed, savoring the sweet sensations, amazed at how the simple brush of his lips over her knuckles could make her tingle in so many places.

Groaning, Lock covered her breast with his hand. Scarlett trembled as the nipple peaked against his palm. Lock raised his hand to cradle her head and pull it against his chest. "Let's make a baby, Mrs. Dean.''

Scarlett nodded and got into bed with him. Perhaps the knowledge that they were married and this was their wedding night had some psychological effect that even the lack of romance in their marriage could not defeat. Perhaps the knowledge that they hoped to create life with their lovemaking gave it a dimension she had never before known with a man. She was making love to him with the hope of making life; perhaps it was the primitive instinct to procreate that made their coming together feel so right.

She seemed to have no shame with him. She explored him greedily, rejoicing in the textures of his body. She was both appreciative and demanding, responsive and aggressive.

For Lock, it was as though he'd fallen onto the bed and into a world where none of the usual restrictions applied. Her quivering reaction to his every touch inflamed him. Her restless stroking of his body drove him to peaks of pleasure he had never visited with any other woman. The urgent primal sounds she made danced over his nerve endings like dancing points of fire. With every in-drawn breath he was tantalized by her scent.

Her flesh was pliant, firm, round, curved; smooth where he touched her, where muscle pressed muscle, where his tongue swept across her. He grew hot and hard and throbbed with the need of her.

She wrapped her leg around his thigh and thrust upward, inviting him inside her, and when he probed her depths, she was soft and warm and tight around him. She moved with him, she moved in opposition. They shared a singular desperate yearning for fulfillment and the gripping terror that when they found it, it might be too intense or too consuming or, somehow, too dangerous to endure.

He was one with her in a way he'd never been with any other woman, attuned to her needs, mystified by the affinity that linked them. He felt the tension building in her, felt her desperate physical questing for release as she strained and thrashed beneath him. Her very need, raw and primitive, set him afire. Her vulnerability gave him strength and forced him to be gentle.

Crying out, she clung to him and thrust against him as, inside her, her body convulsed around him. Slick with her essence, he spilled his own essence into her as he reached his own fulfillment.

Long moments afterward they lay together, spent, heaving and exhausted, unable to speak but feeling no need for words.

Seconds grew into minutes. Their hearts slowed to normal, their breathing became even. Lock felt her wiggle beneath him and lifted his head to look at her face. "Are you . . . ?"

"Pregnant?"

His eyes narrowed. "You couldn't tell yet, could you?"

Scarlett chuckled. "Not quite yet."

He shifted to his side, taking his weight from her. "Are you all right?"

She smiled, then, sighing languidly, reached up to brush his hair from his forehead. "Yippee-eye-cay-yo, cowboy."

A few seconds later he asked, "Do you think it's possible . . . ?"

"Cowboy, those sperm from your little ol' baby-maker are swimming upstream faster than a posse after a pack of cattle rustlers."

Lock laughed. For the first time in longer than he could remember, he just cut loose and laughed because he felt like laughing.

"Hey," Scarlett said. "It wasn't *that* funny."

"I know," he wheezed, still chuckling. "It's just—" he pushed up on one elbow and looked down at her "—no one ever told me being married felt this good."

"You'll have to remember to give the computer a raise," she said, and suddenly Lock didn't feel like laughing anymore.

Chapter Eight

"WHAT'D BIG JAKE SAY?" Scarlett asked.

Upon their return home Big Jake had appeared to take the news of their marriage well, breaking out a bottle of champagne and toasting their happiness and charmingly claiming a kiss from the bride. Then he'd asked if he could talk to Lock privately.

Lock had suggested she go on to their room so she could rest up from their long flight. So she'd soaked half an hour in a sunken bathtub big enough for a hippopotamus, wondering what J. Havelock Dean was saying to J. Havelock Dean III in the downstairs study. Then she'd put on the gown Lock had bought her in Reno and crawled between the sheets of his bed to wait for a full report.

It was odd being alone, odder still that she should miss Lock's company when, two days before, she'd thought of him as a stranger. But, oh, what a difference two days made!

It wasn't difficult to play the role of a blushing love-struck bride after a weekend of lovemaking, picnicking on the floor of their suite in the middle of the night and parking on the scenic overlook, smooching and listening to coyotes yip. She'd lost count of the times he'd whipped out his little ol' baby-maker on the theory that the odds of her conceiving a child went up every time he sent the posse out after the cattle rustlers.

She was sore and exhilarated. She might already be pregnant. And as she held her breath at the sound of the doorknob twisting, knowing Lock was returning to her, she'd felt dangerously like a woman who was madly in love.

Lock looked at his wife, thinking how odd it was that, although he'd never had a woman in this room, she looked perfectly natural in his bed, propped against the pillows. Dwarfed by the king-size mattress, she appeared tiny and isolated.

The better to keep you company, my dear, he thought, feeling himself stiffen at the sight of her in the sheer gown with the scarlet roses.

Scarlet roses. And Scarlett Blake Dean.

"Lock?" she prompted.

"Hmm?" He'd forgotten she'd even asked him a question.

"What did Big Jake say?"

He walked to the bed and sat down on the edge next to her and announced jubilantly, "He bought it. The whole package! He thinks you're wonderful, he hopes we'll be very happy, he hopes we'll want to live here, although he'd understand if we want to find a place of our own."

She'd bathed in the bath oil of the same fragrance as the perfume that drove him crazy. Her face was squeaky clean, her hair bed-rumpled. It was going to be odd making love to her here, where he'd grown up, knowing Big Jake was down the hall. But she was his wife, and one of the benefits of marriage was being able to make love in your own room, in your own bed, even when your grandfather was right down the hall.

He reached for her hand. "I assured him we wanted to live here. He seemed relieved."

"Good."

"It's been an all-male household for a while. He says you should feel free to redecorate if you'd like."

"Redecorate?" she said with a smile. "You've got fine art on the walls and antiques all over the place. I wouldn't know where to begin."

"It might be a good idea if you made a few changes—frilly touches. Maybe some pillows, or new draperies. Anything that makes it appear you're nesting."

She nodded. "Frilly touches." *To appear as though she was nesting.* "Is there anything else?"

"As a matter of fact, there is," he said, his voice turning into a sensual drawl as he traced a scarlet rose with his forefinger.

"Well?" she prompted when he left the conversation dangling.

With a throaty chuckle, he leaned close enough for his lips to graze her ear as he whispered, "My baby-maker's lonely. Why don't you invite him inside to play?"

THE NEXT THREE WEEKS were idyllic. If she hadn't kept reminding herself she was only playing a role for Big Jake's benefit, Scarlett could easily have believed she was a bride in every traditional sense. She settled into life at the Dean mansion without any major crises. Whiskers and Napoleon and Josephine staked out their separate territories without too much fur flying, her furniture went into storage, she converted the bedroom next to Lock's into a sitting room and moved in her personal belongings. She bought a new bedspread for Lock's bed and ordered matching curtains.

She opened wedding presents and wrote thank-you notes to people she'd never met and to people who'd known her all her life. As she wrote she wondered how they would feel when they learned of her divorce—following the birth of her child or the death of Big Jake, whichever came later.

She went to the kitchen to get an apple and ended up with a plate of apples and strawberries precisely sliced and artfully arranged by the cook and delivered to her sitting room by the day maid. After staring at the plate for five minutes, she laughed aloud at the absurdity of it.

Then she burst into tears and sobbed until her body was sore.

When she'd regained her composure, she called her gynecologist to make an appointment for a pregnancy test.

"He wants you to come with me," she told Lock. "Can you get away from the office on Friday? I know that's the worst possible day, what with Big Jake's party that night, but it was his first available appointment."

"Of course," Lock said. "I was planning on leaving at noon on Friday, anyway." He smiled wickedly. "So the baby-maker got the job done."

"All the signs are right," she said.

"The timing couldn't be more perfect," he said Thursday night as they lay in bed. "If the doctor confirms you're pregnant, we'll be able to make an announcement at dinner."

They were hosting a dinner party to celebrate Big Jake's seventy-fifth birthday, and Lock had been increasingly apprehensive about the evening. Although he seldom talked about it, Scarlett knew he feared it would be Big Jake's last birthday party. He was also under pressure because he knew that Big Jake would be announcing his retirement as CEO of Dean Industries.

He drew Scarlett close, hugging her fiercely as they lay in bed. "This is his way of breaking the news gently. He's always said he'd die before he'd retire. He's got to know I'll question his sudden decision to step down."

He released a ragged anguished sigh. "It's almost going to be a relief to have it out in the open."

Almost, Scarlet thought, thinking that the need for pretense would be replaced by the harsher crueler need to face the reality of Big Jake's impending death.

His hand was splayed possessively over her stomach, above her womb, as though he was protecting the child growing inside her. *Did he even realize it was there?* she wondered, and hoped that the promise of a child would be a solace to him, as well as to his grandfather.

The doctor's visit was both joyful and sobering. The tests and internal examination confirmed that she was indeed carrying Lock's child. The doctor called Lock into the conference room with Scarlett so he could give them the news together.

"Whenever possible," he said, "I like to talk to the father and the mother together because, ideally, carrying a child and raising a child is a team effort, just as making the child was."

He assured them that Scarlett was as healthy as a plow horse and should have no problem carrying or delivering a healthy baby, then stressed to Lock that pregnancy generated psychological, as well as physical changes, and challenged him to be supportive in all ways.

"Women are strong. They can survive very well on their own if they have to, but this woman is your wife," the doctor said. "She's your partner in life, and the child she's carrying is as much yours as hers. Take care of her. Pamper her. Remind her to take her vitamins and eat plenty of vegetables. Tolerate her moods and let her know she's beautiful, even when she can't see her feet."

He gave them a packet of information, which included schedules of childbirth-preparation classes. "Go with

Scarlett," he told Lock. "Learn what she'll be going through as she gives birth to your baby. Coach her. Hold her hand. And hold your baby when it's still slick and wet from the birth process. You may be apprehensive at first, but you'll never be sorry that you were involved in this part of your child's life."

On the way home in the car, Scarlett was unnaturally silent, which Lock had come to recognize as a sign of trouble. "That was some lecture, huh?" he said.

She nodded.

"We've, uh, never discussed childbirth classes or childbirth."

"No. We never have."

"I'll go to the classes," he said, then tacked on, "If you want me to, of course."

She nodded silently.

"I just wanted you to know that I'm in for the whole thing."

"Until three months after the child is born or Big Jake dies, whichever comes later," she said.

"Scarlett—"

"I don't feel like talking right now," she said, curling up in the seat and tucking her cheek against the seat back. "It's been a long afternoon, and I still have several details to tend to for Big Jake's party, so I'd just like to rest, if you don't mind."

"Of course. And when we get back to the house, you can tell me what needs to be done for the party and I'll take care of it while you have a quick nap."

It was everything Scarlett could do to hold back the sob ripping through her chest. He'd taken the lecture to heart. He was being *nice* to her. He was pampering her. He was going to do everything the doctor ordered—*until three months after the birth of their child or Big Jake's death, whichever came later.*

LOCK ANNOUNCED Scarlett's pregnancy immediately following the standard toasts to Big Jake's health and welfare.

Visibly moved, tears brightening his eyes, Big Jake gave Scarlett a bear hug and said, "You've given me the best birthday present imaginable."

He led a toast to his great-grandchild, then, with the presence that had given him control over many a board meeting, he commanded the attention of the friends and family assembled to celebrate his birthday.

"I feel a speech coming on!" his close friend and physician joked.

Big Jake laughed. "When you turn seventy-five next month, we'll indulge you, Gil. Tonight is my night, and I have an announcement of my own—two announcements, in fact."

As she watched Lock brace himself for Big Jake's retirement bombshell, Scarlett cursed the conventions of civilization that had put her across the table from her husband, instead of next to him. She wished desperately that she was close enough to hold his hand and lend him her support.

"Those of you who know me have heard me say that I'd rather die than retire," Big Jake said. "But I'm living proof as I stand before you that an old dog can learn new tricks. You heard it here first, folks. Monday morning I'll be officially announcing my retirement, effective at the next board meeting, where I'll be turning over control of Dean Industries to my grandson."

He raised his glass. "To the new CEO of Dean Industries—may the man and the corporation prosper."

All eyes went to Lock as glasses were raised.

"I'm honored, sir," Lock said.

"For the second half of my announcement, I'd like for Margaret to come stand by my side."

Margaret—his quiet, efficient, dignified, discreet administrative assistant—rose and walked to the head of the table. Big Jake welcomed her with a kiss on the cheek and stretched his arm across her shoulders. "It's very rare for a man to enjoy the love of not one, but two wonderful women in a single lifetime. Frankly I never expected to fall victim to Cupid's nonsense in the fall of my seventy-fifth year."

He turned to Lock. "You've made this much easier for me. I wasn't sure you'd understand what it was like to fall flat on your ass in love, but since you've taken the plunge yourself and brought the lovely Scarlett into our house and our lives, I'm much reassured that you'll feel happiness for me when I tell you, and everyone here, that Margaret and I plan to marry the day after my retirement becomes effective."

Lock's chin dropped in incredulity. The emotions that slid across his face in rapid progression were meaningful to Scarlett, who knew so well his fears and concerns. Their eyes met with unanswered questions, and she could only shrug helplessly. She had no answers for him.

"I can see you're speechless," Big Jake said graciously. "Margaret and I made the decision to keep our relationship private to avoid the inevitable gossip and possible repercussions within the company."

He gazed at Margaret with love in his eyes, and Scarlett noted that he looked a decade younger than he had at the beginning of the evening.

"Margaret came to work for us after losing her husband to a long progressive illness. She's given Dean Industries five years of excellent service, and I've given it a lifetime.

Now we'd like to be selfish and take some time for ourselves. My grandson may be satisfied with a weekend in Reno, but Margaret and I have mapped out a two-year itinerary that will take us around the world in cruise ships and airplanes and trains. While we hope to avoid it, there's even a remote possibility that we might be riding camels at one point. I hope now that you'll join us in celebrating our engagement."

Scarlett held her breath as Lock rose and made the requisite toast. Everyone kissed Margaret on the cheek and shook Big Jake's hand, and Scarlett bawled like a baby as she hugged Big Jake. Though embarrassing, the emotional outburst paved the way for her to plead fatigue and excuse herself from the party as soon as Big Jake had opened his presents.

She bathed and curled up in the bed, but exhaustion refused to yield to sleep. She was still wide awake when Lock stole into the room.

Again their eyes met with unanswered questions as he loosened the knot of his tie and begun unbuttoning his shirt. She'd never seen him so disconcerted. "Big Jake isn't dying," he said at last. "I misunderstood the whole conversation. He doesn't have two years left to live. He's going to be honeymooning for two years!"

"Are you sure?"

Frowning, he nodded. "This time I did what I should have done in the first place. I cornered Gil and demanded the truth. Gil has known about the romance all along."

He laughed bitterly. "The kicker is, Big Jake was afraid to tell me. He didn't think I would understand because I don't have a romantic bone in my body!"

He dropped into an overstuffed chair and kicked off his shoes.

"How do you feel?" Scarlett asked softly.

He stared at her a moment before answering. A rugged sigh tore from his throat. "Relieved, of course. Thrilled for him and Margaret." His gaze locked with hers. "Foolish. Confused."

Groaning, he leaned forward and buried his face in his hands. "I've made quite a mess, haven't I?"

" 'Oh, what a tangled web we weave...' " she quoted blithely, then sighed.

He sat up, meeting her eyes. "Scarlett, I'm sorry. I never meant to bring you into some harebrained windmill-tilting scheme."

"We'll have a child," she said. "I want this baby. You said you wanted a child. No one knows about the contract except us. We can just wait until the baby's born and..."

Her voice trailed off and she rolled over, burying her face in the pillow and damning the hormonal fluctuation that turned her into a slobbering mass of jelly twice a day. She refused to admit, even to herself, that the tears were real: That they were for Lock, and for her, and for the child she carried, and for the desperate longing to spend the rest of her life with Lock, raising their children and growing old together.

Falling in love hadn't been part of the agreement, and she wasn't going to burden him with one more brick of guilt. He might have been tilting at windmills, but he'd been sincere. And she loved him almost more than life itself—certainly enough to protect him from knowing she'd been foolish enough to fall in love with him.

She could hide her tears, but not the quivering of her shoulders as she cried into the pillow. Lock would have submitted himself to an hour on the rack if he could have taken back everything he'd done to disrupt her life.

Gingerly he sat down on the bed beside her and stroked her back. "There's so much I need to say to you, Scarlett. I wanted to talk to you this afternoon, but you were tired, and now, in light of what's happened tonight, it's all going to sound . . . convenient. But it's not. I . . ."

She stopped sobbing and pushed up on one elbow, regarding him with red-rimmed eyes. He touched her cheek with his fingertips. "I never expected this to happen."

"I know," she said, swallowing.

"No, you don't," he said. "I'm not talking about Big Jake now. I'm talking about me. Big Jake was right. I don't have a romantic bone in my body. I thought . . . I wanted it all without having to go through all that nonsense of falling in love, and acting like a fool, and taking emotional risks. It all seemed so simple and civilized—a contract, a friendship, everything all worked out ahead of time without any emotionality."

She lifted her hand to brush his hair from his forehead. "It was a good plan," she said. "Sometimes things just don't work out the way you think they will. But it's okay. I understand."

Unable to look him in the eye, she stared down at the lace edge of the sheet.

"You *don't* understand," he said. "It wasn't a good plan. It didn't work. Not from the moment you charged into my office and told me off about wanting you to call your brother about the attorney. I couldn't admit it until this afternoon, when the doctor was lecturing me about being a part of our child's life and taking care of you, and I realized then that I don't ever want to stop taking care of you. I need you, Scarlett. Not just to carry my child, but to love me and take care of me, too."

She was looking at him with eyes filled with love. It gave him the strength to admit, "I'm flat on my ass in love, Mrs. Dean. I think I must have known it the minute I let you put that ridiculous cowboy hat on my head. I don't want a divorce. I want you."

"Oh," she said. "Oh-h-h." She threw her arms around him.

"I'm not very romantic," he warned, "but I love you, and that has to count for something."

Scarlett nodded against his shoulder. If Lock wanted to believe he wasn't romantic, she wasn't going to be the one to disillusion him.

"What would you think of a double wedding with Big Jake and Margaret?" Lock asked. "I ran it past them, and they think it's a great idea. We could fly your family in."

"You ran it past Big Jake and Margaret?"

"I know it was presumptuous, but I hoped maybe you felt the same way I did, and I know you'd like to have a proper wedding dress, and—"

"You're right," she said, snuggling her cheek against his shoulder. "It *was* presumptuous." It was also wildly romantic, but she didn't think it prudent to mention that at the moment.

"Say something," he said when she remained silent too long.

Scarlett was so filled with love for him, that for a moment all she could do was cling to him, savoring the hardness of his chest against her cheek, the scent of his after-shave. She could have stayed right where she was for the rest of her life and been perfectly content.

"I guess," she said with a sigh, "that it wasn't too presumptuous for a man who's willing to admit that he's flat on his ass in love with his wife."

A Note from Glenda Sanders

Two strangers agree to get married because he wants an heir. A deal is struck; a contract is signed. Without the usual emotional entanglements attached to the institution of marriage—the romance, the love, the commitment of hearts—it's all so simple.

Whoa! As the characters in "Don't Tell Grandfather" find out, marriage, even when reduced to its most pragmatic, is seldom simple. This point was driven home to me as I wrote "Don't Tell Grandfather," because while I was describing the world's tackiest wedding on paper, I was, in my nonwriting time, mired in preparations for my daughter's real-life wedding.

The similarities were few.

Unlike Scarlett and Lock, Kathy and Tim were surrounded by loving family members who had traveled from Texas, Minnesota and North Carolina to watch them exchange their vows. The groom's uncle Bob officiated at the ceremony, and attendants included brothers, cousins, a nephew, dear friends and the bride's dog.

The bride was beautiful in the dress she'd picked out on a chaotic shopping trip that involved a crisis with a cat. (Ask us about the anecdote!) The groom was late (only slightly) due to a mix-up in closing times at the tuxedo rental store, but he looked dashing despite that. All in all, the real-life wedding of Kathy and Tim was fairly typical— beautiful, full of love and laughter and an occasional tear.

The biggest difference between the fictional wedding of Scarlett and Lock and the real wedding of Kathy and Tim can be summed up in two words: love and romance. The real-life bride and groom were starry-eyed, excited, nervous, impatient and jubilant as they faced the event that would mark the beginning of their lives as husband and wife.

A romance novelist could ask for no better reminder of what she's supposed to be capturing in her stories. So "Don't Tell Grandfather" is dedicated to Kathy and Tim, with gratitude for their inspiration and heartfelt wishes for a happy future together.

They'll be off soon—to Tim's home state of Minnesota. The mother in me wants to caution him that she's going to need some help dressing for the harsh winters. After all, she's a child of the South and knows nothing of ice and snow beyond the words to "Frosty the Snowman." But then, the romance writer in me doesn't think staying warm will be a problem for either of them!

THE ENCHANTED BRIDE
Margaret Chittenden

Chapter One

THE ACCIDENT HAPPENED on her wedding day.

Rowan Pengelly was slowly, reluctantly, driving her old Austin Mini from Mousehole, where she owned a sweet little cottage and a large herb garden, to her fiancé's dairy farm near Lamorna.

On either side of the narrow winding road, the rolling incredibly green fields of Cornwall, England, girded by hedges and low stone walls, spread into infinity, like a patchwork quilt. Usually this was a sight that lifted Rowan's heart, but today she was so busy complaining to God, she paid no heed to the magnificent scenery. Rowan complained to God quite frequently when she was less than happy. And on this particular day she was verging on miserable.

"It's like this, God," she said, then paused to glance up at the high afternoon sky, which was so clear she ought to have been able to see right through to whatever was beyond.

"I think I've made a bit of a mistake here, saying I'd marry Hal Hotchkins. He's a nice enough lad—it's just that he talks too much about uninteresting things. Like cows. And let's face facts, he's none too bright. Then there's this—I don't love him. And I think he doesn't love me. We were just lonely and of an age to marry, and we were handy to each other."

She sighed, decreasing the pressure of her foot on the accelerator so that the car slowed even more. "If you could

think of a way to get me out of marrying Hal without hurt-
ing his feelings," she added, "I'd be forever grateful."

AFTERWARD SHE KNEW absolutely that she had not pressed
her foot down on the accelerator. There was no reason for
the car to speed up so suddenly, or for the steering wheel to
pull sharply to the right. There was no reason for the car to
meet head-on with a tall stone that had stood in that spot
since the early Bronze Age and had no intention of giving
way.

Up and over went the little car, landing on its back at the
side of the road like a dead turtle, its wheels spinning. Lights
were spinning, too, inside Rowan's brain, spinning faster
and faster, their colors flashing streaks of diamond fire—
green, gold, white, indigo.

And then the colors all faded and the lights died away and
inside Rowan's brain there was only a darkness that was like
the middle of a long and silent moonless night.

Time passed.

"Well," she muttered as she came to. "There's a surprise. I thought I was dead. Which would have been a trag-
edy, considering I'm only twenty-three. But it seems I'm
alive, after all."

She'd been thrown out of the car and was lying in a gap
in the hedge that surrounded a familiar field. Her tan leather
carry-on bag that had been on the passenger seat had been
thrown out with her. But somehow she had lost her shoes.

Getting gingerly to her feet, she looked down at herself.
Her long white Empire-style gown wasn't stained or even
creased. That was surprising. And fortunate. The herbal
garland she'd made for a headdress was still in place. No part
of her was in pain. She wasn't sure her wits were function-
ing too well, though; there was a definite feeling of fluctu-

ation, as if whatever energy normally illuminated her brain was switching on and off. But that was to be expected, she supposed.

"You didn't have to take me so literally, God," she grumbled. "You might have offered the suggestion first, to see what I'd make of it. Given me a chance to turn it down. As it is, I don't see what good it's done, except to put paid to my poor old car."

Weaving a little, she bent down and picked up the carry-on bag. It had all her important papers in it—birth certificate, driver's license, passport. Hal had impressed on her that she must not forget her passport. Over her stated objections, he had insisted they spend their honeymoon in America's Disney World. They were to fly out of Heathrow tomorrow.

Shaking her head, not for the first time, over what she thought was a rather childish choice for a grown-up honeymoon, she started into the field, in the middle of which was a circle of nineteen upright standing stones called the Merry Maidens. They were of the same Bronze Age vintage as the stone she'd crashed her car into.

If she cut across the field to the opening on the other side, she could take the footpath to Hal's farm. She had no idea how long she'd been unconscious, but it felt as if she was already late for her wedding. Hal would be upset. One of the many sayings he was forever quoting was "Time and Tide wait for no man." Which was a fairly obvious comment if ever she'd heard one.

Abruptly she stopped walking. Something didn't feel right. What was it?

The sun was still high in the unmoving blue sky. The thick grass under her feet glinted with droplets of water. There had been a heavy shower earlier in the day. Yet she could not feel the dampness of the grass on her bare feet. Nor could she feel the warmth of the sun on her head.

As well, she seemed unusually light. She was small and slender, but as a rule she was at least aware of her body. Now it seemed weightless, as though she was just now rising from a sick bed after a long wasting illness.

She walked on a little way, then stopped again. She had seemed to glide over the grass, rather than walk. Looking back, she could see no imprint of her feet on the wet grass.

Another oddity—she could smell the clean and salt-scrubbed breeze, hear it rattling the dense leaves of the hedgerows, but it wasn't lifting her long dark hair. Also, and this was the oddest thing of all, there was a strange sort of silence inside her.

She stood still, listening, and after a minute or two realized she could not hear her heart beating. Could she normally? Perhaps not, but this was hardly a normal situation. She'd had a terrible shock. It seemed to her that she should at least be able to *sense* her heart beating. Prodding her wrist with two fingers, she tried to find her pulse.

She couldn't feel a thing.

There was no pulse in her neck, either.

How very peculiar.

Puzzled, but not yet afraid, she continued to the end of the field where there was another gap in the hedge. But just as she reached it, she walked straight into an invisible wall. She didn't hurt herself. She just bounced backward. Putting out one hand, she felt the barrier. It was as solid and smooth as a sheet of glass, yet she'd rebounded from it as if it was made of rubber. She tried pushing it, she tried kicking it. She even picked up a fair-size rock and attacked the barrier with that. It held firm.

Flattening her right hand against the invisible wall, she started walking around the perimeter of the field. The barrier was all around—a huge invisible cage. She couldn't even get out of the field the way she'd been thrown in, though her car was only inches away.

Obviously she'd suffered a concussion. All of this was a hallucination and she was probably still inside the car. In a little while she'd wake up completely, or someone would drive by and see her in the car and ring up an ambulance.

If she was still in her car, shouldn't she be able to see herself there?

She felt light-headed again. As a matter of fact, she felt light all over. Looking down, she saw that she was fading away, vaporizing into a mist. Rowan held one hand in front of her face, then stared and squinted, but couldn't see it. She concentrated hard, trying to make it become visible again, but the effort wearied her. Stumbling over to the hedge, she sat down in the grass to rest, feeling as if her legs would no longer hold her upright. She was going to faint, she felt certain.

Someone would come along and find her, she assured herself. Hal would come. But what if someone else came first? What if she did faint and someone saw her sitting there and stole her bag while she didn't have the strength to hold on to it? It had money in it, too, her share of the honeymoon money, which she had insisted on paying.

Most of Cornwall's hedges had grown up over ancient stone walls. With the last of her failing strength, Rowan pushed with her invisible hands through the hedge until she felt the wall. Wonder of wonders, there was a fair-size niche between the ancient stones, and she was able to fit the bag right into it and let the branches fall back into place.

A LONG FLOATING TIME later, she heard a vehicle stop nearby. Doors slammed. Male voices exclaimed. Pushing herself eagerly to her feet—apparently she still had feet even if she couldn't see them—Rowan ran to the opening in the hedge.

Hal Hotchkins, looking quite handsome in his neat dark suit and white shirt and dark tie, was crouched on his heels, peering in through the side of her upside-down car. His brother, Leonard, was walking along the other side of the road with his head bent down. "Here's her shoes!" he exclaimed, picking them out of the bottom of the hedgerow.

Hal straightened and looked at the shoes, then looked all around. "Well, where's Rowan then?" he asked.

Rowan could see Hal clearly, such a long drink of water he was. He'd combed his brown hair straight back, the way she kept telling him not to. She could see Leonard, the car, her white satin-covered shoes. But the clear-as-glass barrier was still firmly in place. She couldn't get through it to join the two men. "Hal," she called, "I'm over here! I need a hand getting out of this field."

He didn't hear her. How could he not hear her when her voice echoed so?

Why did it echo?

Because it was thrown back at her by the invisible wall.

Beating on the barrier, she yelled again and again while Hal and Leonard walked through the neighboring field. But they couldn't hear her, not even when, without encountering any obstruction, they entered the field she was in. Nor could they see her, any more than she could see herself. Following them as they hunted under the hedgerow—for her body, she supposed—she tried to touch them, but there seemed to be yet another barrier between herself and them. Still, she kept calling out to them to no avail. At last the two men left the field. They climbed into Hal's milk lorry and drove slowly along the road, both of them looking carefully from side to side. A minute later, the lorry turned onto the road to Lamorna.

Soon after, several white cars, each with a blue stripe along its body and a blue light on top, came along. The Devon and Cornwall constabulary. One policeman took pictures of Rowan's car inside and out, then it was towed away. Other police officers examined the fields all around, including the field of the Merry Maidens. Inside her invisible body Rowan sobbed and screamed and raged until she was so hoarse and tired she couldn't shout anymore.

Chapter Two

Five years later

IT SEEMED to Nate he must finally be homing in on the turnoff to Lamorna. He'd take a quick look at the cove, he decided, shoot a little tape on the camcorder, then hightail it back to the Chy-Trewin Bed and Breakfast Inn at Mousehole. His landlady had said the old smuggling village and its beautiful cove were worth a look on his way back from Land's End, but he'd lingered too long at the wonderful Minack Outdoor Theatre and then managed to miss the road to Lamorna after two attempts.

This was going to be his last try. It had been a while since lunch and his stomach was rumbling. Besides which, he was a nervous wreck from driving the narrow Cornish lanes. This particular road couldn't be more than eight feet wide, and if the white line down the middle of it was anything to go by, it was meant to be two-way. There was no shoulder, either. Just a hedge on each side, right on the edge of the road.

No sooner had he thought this than a bus appeared dead ahead, coming toward him. He pulled over sharply, too sharply, and cursed loudly when he heard a scraping sound followed by a sharp clatter just as the bus eased by. Evidently the hedge concealed a stone wall. Dammit, the guy at the car-rental place had warned him about that. Why hadn't he rented him a car skinny enough to slide past a bus?

Pulling into a small space at the side of the road—an opening into a field—he stopped the car, got out and walked around to the left. The front hubcap was missing and the rear one was dented in two places.

The missing hubcap had rolled into the hedge on the other side of the road. Nate picked it up and tossed it into the trunk, along with another choice word or two. Dusting off his hands on the seat of his blue jeans, he comforted himself with the thought that at least he was going to get his money's worth out of the incredibly high insurance he'd paid on the Peugeot. About to get back into the car, he hesitated as something caught his eye.

Standing stones. A whole circle of them in the middle of the field. He'd read about such things in one of the brochures he'd picked up at the information center in Land's End. He couldn't remember what they signified, but they were interesting enough to warrant taking out the camcorder, he thought, and reached into the car for it.

Entering the circle, he panned slowly, turning carefully, keeping the video camera steady. He was probably halfway around when he saw the woman.

Hands clasped at her waist, she was dancing gracefully, solemnly and quite unselfconsciously, in and out between the three-foot-high stones, her bare feet hardly seeming to touch the rough grass. The late-afternoon light seemed brighter around her. She was young, petite and slender, dressed in a long white gown that clung to the contours of her small firm breasts, then to her slim waist and hips, flaring out a little at the back. Her long waving hair, which was as black as his own, was crowned with what he first took to be a circlet of braided grass. But as he zoomed in he saw it was more likely a wreath of herbs.

She was beautiful, her eyes as dark as her hair, her skin pale but luminous. More than beautiful. Enchanting. Breathtaking.

Lowering the camera, Nate watched her dance a little longer before he spoke. "I hope you didn't mind me taping you," he said after a while.

She jumped, obviously startled. Had she been so engrossed in her dancing that she hadn't noticed him?

"I'm sorry," he said. "I thought you knew I was here. I thought you must surely see me taping you."

She came toward him across the grass, her bare feet skimming lightly over the coarse blades. Her skin seemed even paler, her eyes dark and huge. "I saw you, all right," she said, stopping a couple of feet away. "I just didn't think you could see me."

He laughed. "I could hardly miss you." He looked around, wondering if anyone had accompanied her. "Are you part of some kind of ceremony?"

"Why would you think that?" she asked.

He gestured at her dress, the garland on her head, the circle of standing stones.

"I look like this all the time," she said, touching the garland. "I used to make these from herbs I grew in my garden. I made door wreaths and swags and bouquets, too."

After a brief pause, she added, "I don't have a herb garden anymore." She shook her head, then smiled brightly. "You know, in olden times when young women married, the bridegroom's parents would make the bride a bouquet of herbs for luck. So in my small way, I brought one of the old customs alive again."

She couldn't seem to stop staring at him. "This is really amazing. It's been a while since anyone—" She broke off. "It must be meant," she murmured, then looked him over with an admiring and very speculative glint in her dark eyes. "You're an American, aren't you?"

He nodded. "I'm from Seattle, Washington. I spent a few days in London, rented a car and drove south a couple of days ago. I'm here for a month."

"Just passing through Cornwall, do you mean?"

"No, I'm not the kind of tourist who wants to do seven countries in seven days. I like to concentrate on one area. It's more restful that way."

"You don't seem so old as to be in need of rest," she said with a lift of a bird-wing eyebrow.

He laughed shortly. "I'm thirty-four. So age is hardly a problem. But I do have a high-stress, high-tech job, and I have to fight Seattle traffic twice a day. I just happened to recognize the need for a change of scene at the same time as I read an article about Cornwall in a Seattle paper. It must have been a very well-written article, because it lured me here right away."

Now why was he babbling like this? Because she was such a sympathetic listener probably.

She was shaking her head now. "Fighting traffic sounds exciting to me," she said. With a sigh she added, "I lead a very quiet . . . life."

"You're lucky," he told her.

She seemed inclined to argue, but changed her mind, saying instead, "Does your wife not mind you going off alone like this, then?"

The coy note in her voice gave him pause. A woman who would fish for that kind of information made him nervous. "I'm not married," he said flatly.

"You don't like women?"

"I like women a lot. I'm just not the marrying kind."

Before she could comment on that, he gestured at the standing stones. "Can you tell me what these are all about?"

"They're the Merry Maidens," she said, her pale brow still creased in the frown that had come upon her. "Nineteen of them, there are. They danced on the Sabbath, it's said, and so were struck into stone for punishment. The two taller stones in the other field over there are the pipers who played for them. They've all been here since the Bronze Age."

"Did people celebrate the Sabbath during the Bronze Age?" he queried. "It's a cute story, but I think it more likely that the circle was originally the site of some pagan ritual."

Her mouth, which he'd just noted was particularly fine, tightened. "It's not very nice to come to a country and start rewriting its legends when you've no idea what you're talking about," she said sternly.

She had a point there. "I'm sorry," he said, offering what he hoped was a sufficiently contrite smile. "I'm an electrical engineer. I work on flight-control systems at Boeing. I tend to be practical, rather than whimsical. It's a major flaw in my character."

Her mouth became luscious once more and her dark eyes glinted with something that again looked suspiciously like mischief. "It's not too wise of you to scoff about Cornwall, Mr. . . . ?"

"Edwards. Nate Edwards." Switching the camcorder to his left hand, he held out his right. She hesitated, then gave him her hand. It was a slim hand, but warm and firm in its clasp. Her skin was as velvety as the surface of a peach.

She looked at her hand thoughtfully as she withdrew it, turning it this way and that as though admiring it herself. Then she smiled. It was a quick smile that went all over her face and made her eyes glow. The glint of mischief had returned.

"How's this for an idea?" he said. "I have half a Cornish pasty left over from my picnic lunch in Land's End. I gave up on eating when the sea gulls started diving in formation. Why don't I split it with you? I think there's a soda, too." Without waiting for a reply, he headed for his car and brought back the sack and the bottle.

She'd sat herself down at the base of the stone, her knees bent sideways, her bare feet tucked under her white dress. He squatted cross-legged beside her, hung the camcorder around his neck by its strap and offered her a share of his pasty. She shook her head and gave him another smile—a regretful one this time.

"The reason you should watch what you say about whimsy while you're here, Mr. Edwards," she said as he started eating, "is that Cornwall is a magical place, a mysterious place. I know for a fact there are piskies and knackers. Some of them may be listening."

"And what might piskies and knackers be?" he asked. Something flashed in her dark, dark eyes, and he thought she was going to object to his indulgent tone, but instead, she just laughed softly and leaned back against the standing stone.

Nate wondered that the stone didn't feel cold to her. Sitting still, he felt a little chilled himself, in spite of the sweater he wore with his jeans. There was a definite feeling of fall in the air, but she seemed not to notice it.

"A pisky is the Cornish version of a pixie," the young woman said, shaking her head again when he offered the Coke. "He or she is a ragged merry little person who has an abiding interest in human affairs, often threshing the farmer's corn for him at night or doing housework, and maybe pinching a woman or two who leaves the house dirty at bedtime. There was a pisky used to sit by my fireside when I was—"

She broke off, and he wondered what sadness had come to her mind to make her eyes lose all their light like that. A moment later the cheerful glint was back and she continued. "It was once the custom in parts of Cornwall to leave holes in the walls by which these little beings could enter. But nowadays people put more faith in winning at bingo than in piskies bringing them luck."

"And the knackers?" Nate asked to keep her talking. Her voice was very attractive, he thought. It didn't have the strangled sound common to some of the ultrarefined English voices he'd heard in London—it was musical and countrified, with a soft buzz to every *s*.

"Knackers are mine fairies," she said. "There's not much tin mining nowadays, but it was of great importance in Cornwall since before the Roman occupation of Britain. The working conditions of the early miners were intolerable, but they improved in the eighteenth and nineteenth centuries with the technical advances that came about. But then, you see, at the same time, cheaper production methods in other countries gradually forced the Cornish mines out of business."

She gave a sheepish little smile. "I sound like a travel guide, don't I? I meant to be telling you about the knackers. Tradition has it the knackers haunted only the richest mines during the boom years. Miners would hear them knocking and singing underground and the sound would lead them to lodes of the best ore. Knackers can be ugly, mind you. And if you don't treat them in a friendly way they can be vindictive."

"I'll be careful not to offend any I meet," Nate promised solemnly.

She narrowed her eyes at him. "You're still scoffing, Mr. Edwards." Raising her eyebrows, she asked, "What is your feeling on ghosts, might I ask?"

He grinned. "Right up there with my thoughts on piskies and knackers."

"We've an old prayer in Cornwall," she said softly. "From ghoulies and ghosties and long-leggety beasties and things that go bump in the night, good Lord deliver us." Her forehead puckered above her nice straight nose. "People don't seem to like ghosts all that much."

"I'm not sure *I* do," Nate admitted.

She gave him a somewhat irritated glance, then shrugged. "I didn't believe in ghosts either until I saw one," she confided, leaning forward slightly. "When I was seventeen, in a place not too far from here, I saw the ghost of a huntsman on horseback followed by his dogs and galloping across a field, the dogs in full cry. While I watched, they all leapt a wall and disappeared in midair." She sighed. "I wish it had been this field they inhabited." She inclined her head. "Though they'd be tedious company after a while, I suppose."

He frowned, but decided not to pursue this talk of ghosts any further. She was obviously a fanciful young woman, as well as a lovely one. And a young one. No more than twenty-four or so, he thought. At least ten years younger than he was.

"I'm staying in Mousehole," he told her in an effort to change the subject.

She gave him an approving smile, for pronouncing the name of the town correctly, he supposed. Mow-zil. His landlady had made him repeat it until he got it right. "I used to live there myself," she said. "One of the cottages on the bluff overlooking the bay."

"Where do you live now?" he asked.

"Nearby." She ducked her head. "I miss watching the sea," she said sadly. Then she looked flirtatiously up at him through her dark lashes and smiled, her eyes glinting again. "I'm glad you came to my field, Nate."

"Me, too," he said, feeling a little awkward. He had finished his pasty and Coke, but his appetite was not appeased. He should be going. But he didn't want to. He had the strangest desire to sit right here on this rough grass beside this beautiful young woman for as long as she would let him. He looked around vaguely. He didn't remember seeing a house in the area. But she'd called it *her* field.

She'd also said she dressed this way all the time. Which seemed a little strange. Unless it was to advertise her herb garden. No, she'd said she *used* to have a herb garden.

Maybe she was one of those country women who were just a little...simple? She did seem ingenuous. After all, he could be a mad rapist. Yet she'd very trustingly squatted down with him in this otherwise deserted field.

To give himself time to decide what he wanted to say or do next, he held the camcorder up, rewound the tape, then viewed what he'd done since leaving the Minack Theatre. As usual he'd gone back a little too far; he had to fast-forward through some footage of the Porthcurno beach before he got to the Merry Maidens.

That was odd. He rewound the tape again and started over. Beside him he heard the young woman say, "Oh, damn and blast!" but he was too involved in figuring out what had happened to his tape to look at her.

He had the Merry Maidens on tape, all right. All nineteen of them, with nice contrasting shadows. But the young woman wasn't there and he knew for a fact he'd taped her dancing—he'd even zoomed in for a closer look at her face. And if he'd been able to see her through the viewfinder, she should be there on the tape.

"Do you suppose you could redo your little dance for me?" he asked as he switched off and lowered the camcorder.

She was gone.

Now, how had she taken off so fast without his even noticing any movement? Standing up, he turned to look toward the gap in the hedge and saw a young man with a dog looking back at him. "Did 'ee say something?" the man asked.

Nate shook his head. "I was talking to—" He stopped abruptly. The young woman's sudden disappearance was really strange and he didn't relish looking stupid. "Talking to myself," he finished as he walked briskly toward the man. "That's a fine dog you have there. A collie?"

"That she is, sir. A tricolor. Champion Shadow's Lady is her name. Five best-in-shows, fourteen group firsts, seven best-of-breeds. Dam of nine champions, all sired by my brother Leonard's stud—Champion Shadow's Playboy. Man's best friend, a dog is," he added with an air of importance, as though he'd coined the phrase himself.

He held out his hand and Nate shook it. "Shadow's the name of my farm," he explained. "Used to belong to my mother's people. Shadows, they were."

For just a second Nate could have sworn he heard a giggle, but there was no one in sight, so it must have been a bird twittering in the hedge or the wind teasing sounds from holes in the ancient stones.

"Hal Hotchkins is my name, sir," the young man went on. He was over six feet—close to Nate's height, but skinnier, lanky rather than lean. He had a fresh complexion, brown hair combed straight back from his forehead, good teeth, but rather small brown eyes.

Nate introduced himself.

"You'll be a Yank, I'm thinking," Hal said.

"Seattle, Washington."

"Does 'ee have a dog?"

"Unfortunately, no. You breed dogs, I take it?"

"That's a hobby, that is. I'm a dairy farmer. Down the road." He frowned. "Don't know how much longer I'll have the farm, though, I'm tellin' 'ee." Gazing off into the middle distance, he started droning on about some kind of milk quotas and the difficulties of keeping up with them, and then segued into a story about a friend of his who had gone to America and been "bravun well treated," and then switched from that to talk about his three daughters and what a joy they were except that they weren't boys.

When Hotchkins finally paused for breath, Nate managed to make a getaway without appearing too rude, he hoped.

Driving on to Mousehole, having given up on Lamorna for today, he thought again about the oddly endearing young woman he'd met in the field of the Merry Maidens. She really was enchanting. He wished he had asked her name. Why hadn't she mentioned it when they shook hands?

He caught himself sighing, which surprised him. Normally he wasn't the kind of man who sighed. He had an idea the young woman in the long white dress would linger in his mind for some time to come. He felt pleasantly sad that he'd never see her again.

Chapter Three

THE CHY-TREWIN Bed and Breakfast Inn was a handsome villa perched high on a cliff. Beyond its casement windows was a spectacular view of Mousehole's harbor with its immense and ancient stone quay and breakwater, colorful fishing boats bobbing serenely at anchor.

There were six other guests beside Nate—married couples, all of them Londoners. After a wonderful dinner of sole cooked with whole peppercorns and a masterpiece of an apple pie, they all lingered in the dining room's comfortable chintz-cushioned chairs drinking excellent coffee, while Ivor Trewin, their landlady's brother, entertained them with stories. Most of the tales dealt with the smuggling of tobacco, tea, brandy, rum, silk and salt that had once been, according to Ivor, a logical extension of the Cornish fishing trade.

"Cornwall was so conveniently near the European continent, you see," he explained. "And it was no trouble at all to create secret landing places with tunnels leading up to the villages."

Ivor was a minister who lived down the hill in a small house adjoining his chapel. He'd admitted cheerfully that when his wife had a garden-club meeting, as she had this evening, he usually managed to wander up to his sister's kitchen about dinnertime.

He was altogether a cheerful sort of man, probably in his early fifties, with a round face and sturdy body, graying reddish brown hair and calm gray eyes that frequently dis-

played a twinkle. He quoted Kipling to conclude his final
story about the smugglers, who had been known locally as
"fair traders" and were basically honorable men, if Ivor was
to be believed.

His voice was low, humming theatrically with menace:

If you wake at midnight, and hear a horse's feet,
Don't go drawing back the blind, or looking in the street,
Them that asks no questions isn't told a lie.
Watch the wall, my darling, while the gentlemen go by.

Ivor shook his head, smiling. "Those were wild days in
Cornwall's history."

"Much of which has been wildly exaggerated," Miss
Bertha Trewin contributed. She was her brother's twin,
even to the twinkle.

Ivor nodded agreement. "Cornishmen—and women—are
great ones for telling tall tales," he allowed. "And we believe them ourselves. When we speak of King Arthur and
his knights of the Round Table up at Tintagel, we're talking of people who existed, never mind that the history books
call them legends. We know that Guinevere and Lancelot
and Sir Galahad were all real. Why, they're probably distant relations of mine."

Nate laughed along with the others. "I heard a couple of
tall tales today," he said. "I met a strange young woman in
a long white dress in the field where the Merry Maidens are,
and she told me about piskies and knackers. She even had
a ghost story for me."

Ivor and his sister exchanged startled glances. "Well now,
piskies and knackers could consume a whole other evening," Ivor said with a briskness that apparently signaled
an end to the conversation.

The Londoners began murmuring among themselves. Before Nate could decide if he'd been squashed deliberately, Ivor leaned toward him with a genial smile. "Would you care to join me in a postprandial excursion to the pub, Mr. Edwards?" he asked.

Nate's pulse accelerated slightly as he went to get his windbreaker, though he wasn't quite sure why.

The steep alleys Ivor led him through were so narrow the two men had to walk single file. Ivor set a good pace, though dusk was gathering and their way was illuminated only by the door lights on the old granite houses that huddled against the hillside. "This young woman in the long white dress," Ivor said over his shoulder after a minute or two. "You say she was strange?"

His voice sounded casual, too casual. Nate was convinced Ivor had brought him out here to talk specifically about the young woman in the Merry Maidens' field.

"She looked like the original flower child," Nate said. "Long white dress with long tight sleeves, some kind of herbal wreath around her forehead, no shoes."

"Cornish-looking, was she?" Ivor asked. "Black hair, dark eyes, on the small side?"

"That's her," Nate agreed. "She's very beautiful," he added. "Maybe twenty-three, twenty-four. Amazingly luminous skin."

"'Twas Rowan Pengelly," Ivor said in a hushed voice. "No doubt about it."

"You know her? Oh, that's right, she told me she used to live in Mousehole. She had a cottage and a herb garden here."

"This one," Ivor said.

Without Nate's noticing, they had turned onto a street of cottages that overlooked the bay. A narrow road ran in front of the row of small houses. On the other side, at the edge of the bluff, was a row of small walled gardens, each with its own wooden or iron gate and with its own individuality. Nate could just make out in the fading light that one of them featured some of the tropical plants he'd been surprised to see in Cornwall, even including a couple of short palm trees. Another was set out like a miniature park, with tiny walkways and a small fountain. Rosebushes filled the still evening air with their perfume. The manicured green lawns were surrounded by the same kind of flowers that grew in Washington State, though it seemed late in the year to be seeing sweet peas, nasturtiums, impatiens and poppies. The southwest coast's climate was so mild the area was known as the Cornish Riviera, he recalled reading.

The garden Ivor had indicated had obviously been neglected for some time. "Evidently the present tenant is no gardener," Ivor said. "That's too bad. 'Twas lovely in its prime. Rowan Pengelly kept Penzance restaurants and the local housewives supplied with rosemary, basil, thyme and all the rest. Not to mention the lovely garlands and bouquets she made. People came from miles around to buy them."

A gray-and-white cat had approached while he talked, and Ivor picked it up and petted it absentmindedly as he gazed at the wretched-looking garden. "No, to answer your question, I never did know Rowan well when she lived . . . here. But I knew her to say hello to, and I knew her enough to be sure 'twould have been a mistake for her to marry Hal Hotchkins."

"I met him, too!" Nate exclaimed. "As a matter of fact, it was just as he came along that the young woman disappeared. You say she was going to marry him and changed her mind? That would explain why she took off in such a hurry, then. I was looking in my camcorder and I heard her say, 'Damn and blast.' Next thing I knew, she was gone and he was there. She must have seen him coming."

Ivor laughed softly. "It doesn't sound as if young Rowan has changed much," he said. "She was always one to speak her mind."

Nate frowned. "Hotchkins seemed pretty stodgy. Was that why Rowan decided not to marry him?"

They had to leap up on one of the cottage doorsteps as a car came along. As soon as it passed, Ivor set the cat down gently and indicated they should continue their walk.

After they turned the corner, they were able to walk comfortably side by side. Ivor waved a hand. "I hear tell of Rowan being seen every once in a while," he said. "I even caught a glimpse of her once myself, just at twilight. I'd gone into the field, hoping to see her, and there she was, just as you described her."

He sighed. "I was a coward, I'm afraid, I ducked back out of the field before she could speak to me."

Nate frowned again. "I'm not sure I understand what you're telling me here."

"Of course you don't," Ivor said. He stopped walking and gave Nate a sheepish grin. "I always did go five times round the gatepost before going into the yard. What I'm trying to lead up to in my subtle yet notably clumsy manner is the fact that Rowan Pengelly is a ghost."

Nate laughed. Ivor gazed at him solemnly. Somewhere nearby a seabird made a mewling sound. In the distance another bird answered, mournfully.

"Are you serious?" Nate said. "You can't be serious."

Ivor moved his head gently but firmly up and down.

"I shook her hand," Nate said. "She asked my name and I introduced myself and shook her hand. It was warm and pink and slender—soft as . . ." He laughed again, but nervously. The intensity of Ivor's silence was unsettling. "Come on," he said. "You've pulled my leg long enough."

Ivor resumed walking. "Five years ago," he said, peering up at the darkening sky as if for inspiration, "Rowan Pengelly drove her car into a tall stone near the entrance to the field of Dawns Myin—the Merry Maidens. She was on her way to be married to Hal Hotchkins at his dairy farm. Hal had asked me to perform the wedding ceremony. I'd agreed. So we waited. Rowan was often late, so Hal said, but when time went by and she still hadn't turned up, he and his brother went looking for her."

He paused dramatically. "They found her car overturned. They found her white satin shoes. They found no trace of Rowan. And no trace of her remains has been discovered to this day. 'Twas thought she might have wandered off in a daze and drowned in the sea, or else lost herself in some woods somewhere. But she continues to haunt the field of the Merry Maidens. For a time people came from miles around hoping to see her. Most of them didn't. It seems she's visible to only a chosen few, all of them men."

He glanced thougthfully at Nate. "I haven't heard of a sighting in over a year. Until now."

He hesitated as if expecting Nate to comment.

"You said only men could see her?" Nate managed. There was no way he was going to believe this wild story, but he was curious to see how far Ivor would go in the telling of it.

"Several men have seen her over the past five years," Ivor answered. "Word gets around. A couple of times there were stories in the local paper. The men not only saw her, they talked to her. And she talked to them, just as you say she did to you. One lad—" He broke off, frowning, then went on. "Thomas Oates, his name was. Out of Penzance. A good-looking lad, well set up. Played guitar in a rock band, worked in a bank in the daytime. Came to see me at the chapel after meeting Rowan. Said they'd talked for a long time. Wouldn't say what about."

Nate looked in vain for the twinkle he expected to see in Ivor's eyes. "Did he see her more than once?" he asked.

Ivor shook his head. "Frightened almost witless, he was. Said she was quite put out when he left the field. Wanted him to stay. He said he'd never go near that field again." Ivor allowed himself a small smile, but it was in no way a mocking one. "The Cornish people, Nate, are a superstitious lot. We have a long history of belief in magic and fairies and giants and hauntings of all kinds. Thomas told me I should exorcise that field. I told him 'twas a little outside my job description, and in any case exorcism would surely only be necessary if the spirit was evil. All I've ever heard of Rowan seems to indicate she was a good person when she was alive. I've not heard of anyone turning evil *after* death."

"She didn't show up on my videotape," Nate said slowly. He attempted a smile that felt very weak. "It's a great story, Ivor, but I'm not buying it. If the young woman I met is Rowan Pengelly, then she was—is—as alive as you and I. Maybe more so."

Ivor raised skeptical eyebrows. "She disappeared quite abruptly, I believe you said?"

"I was reviewing the videotape, running it back to check on it. I thought I'd caught her doing this little dance in and out of the standing stones, but she hadn't appeared on the tape at all. I couldn't figure it out."

"Interesting," Ivor said.

"Yes. Well, anyway, while I was checking the tape she disappeared. When I looked up, she was gone and Hal Hotchkins was there. I thought I heard her giggle when he said something about his family being Shadows."

Ivor laughed. "That's not surprising. The members of the Shadow family are mostly built like tanks, Hal and Leonard being the sole exceptions."

"The point is," Nate said, "Rowan was still there. Obviously she was hiding behind the hedge—which is why I couldn't see her."

"If that's what you want to believe, I don't suppose I can change your mind," the minister said. "Time I saw her, she was sort of drifting across the field, walking slowly, but hardly seeming to touch the ground. The minute I stepped back out of the field, she vanished, right in front of my eyes. I'd heard similar tales. 'Twould seem to me that she somehow inhabits a different dimension inside that field." He chuckled. "Perhaps the people who can see her have the right vibrations. One of my wife's nieces puts a lot of faith in vibrations—chooses her boyfriends by them."

They had reached the pub. Ivor stopped to let Nate precede him through the door. "You don't really believe that young woman's a ghost," Nate said, staring at him.

Ivor's gray eyes met his, unblinking. "Indeed I do," he answered, and he refused to change his mind, although Nate argued with him the rest of the evening.

Chapter Four

NATE HAD INTENDED driving to Penzance the next day. But the road signs seemed to beckon him toward Lamorna instead. Curiosity was a powerful impetus, he told himself as he parked the Peugeot outside the field of the Merry Maidens. He sat for a minute admiring the surrounding countryside. Each patchwork section of land was a subtly different but equally vibrant shade of green.

He saw her as soon as he entered the field. She was sitting on the grass at the foot of one of the standing stones, her head tilted back as if she was studying the fluffy white clouds scudding across the blue sky. Perhaps she was seeing them as animal shapes the way children do.

"Hi!" he called, feeling a ridiculous rush of pleasure.

Pushing nimbly to her feet, she ran toward him, light as air, her quick smile illuminating her face. "You came back," she said happily.

"I had to," he said. "I heard stories about you that you wouldn't believe. I also had to make sure I hadn't dreamed you. The way you disappeared yesterday—"

"I saw Hal coming," she interrupted. "I was afraid you'd say something to him about me. He's a perfectly nice man, even if unimaginative and . . ."

She paused, tilting her head to one side, her long black hair delicately brushing her shoulder. "Well, we must face facts. Hal's a bit boring. But he did marry someone else and have children by her, I understand, so I don't want him upset. He may have heard that I'm still round and about, but as long as he can't see me, he doesn't have to believe it's true."

"What do you mean, Hal can't see you?" Nate demanded.

"What stories have you been told about me?" she countered.

He laughed. "That you've been dead for five years. That you're a . . . ghost."

Her forehead creased in a frown. "You think that's funny? Believe me, there's nothing funny about being a ghost." She gave him a reproving glance. "What else have you heard?"

He eyed her skeptically. "I was told you died in a car accident on the way to your wedding, though your body was never found. That you haunt this field, but only a few people have seen you. That those few were all men. And you terrified at least one of them."

"Thomas Oates," she said with a wistful expression. "He wasn't much of a man, but as Hal would say, beggars can't be choosers. Did he tell anyone what he was terrified of exactly?"

Nate shook his head, feeling a sudden spurt of annoyance. "Rowan, surely you don't think you can make me believe—"

"You found out my name, did you?" A slightly arch look accompanied the question.

Nate nodded. "It's a lovely name. Rowan Pengelly." He hesitated. "Much more tuneful than Rowan Hotchkins would have been."

She made a face, then sat down on the grass and drew her knees to her chin, putting her arms around them. He could smell the freshness of the herbs in the garland she wore around her head. She looked so fragile, so lovely, so child-like, his annoyance melted away. "You're very flexible for a ghost," he teased, sitting down cross-legged next to her.

Her dark eyes held not even the suggestion of a smile. A vast silence seemed to descend on the field and Nate was suddenly aware of the sound of his own pulse beating in his ears. There was such sadness in Rowan's eyes, a sadness so deep there was no end to it. Caught in her gaze as though mesmerized, he felt her drawing him into her mind. There was loneliness there—unending, hopeless and fierce. Coupled with despair. He was moved to an overwhelming pity.

"I'll not have you feeling sorry for me, Nate Edwards," she said sharply, surprising him out of his near trance.

"You can read minds?" he asked.

"I can read faces. I'll not have you pitying me. I want you to be my friend."

He took in a deep breath and let it out. "Friendship can only be based on trust," he said. "Unless you're willing to tell me the truth, instead of this fanciful story..."

"I am telling you the truth, Nate," she interrupted, her eyes solemn, her mouth soft.

"Rowan, you can't expect me to—"

"Another doubting Thomas," she said with a laugh that held more despair than amusement. "Listen now, Nate Edwards from the United States of America. No one can ever be sure of what is real and what isn't. The sea looks blue or gray or green, depending on circumstances. But if you take a cup of it, the water has no color. You're an electrical engineer, you told me, which means you must believe in electricity. Have you ever seen it with your own eyes?"

"I've frequently seen the results of it," he said flatly.

Mischief dimpled one corner of her mouth. "It's results you want, is it?" Still smiling, she shuffled herself onto her knees in front of him. "Watch then, doubting Nate. This is where I went yesterday when I saw Hal Hotchkins coming up the road.''

Taking hold of both his hands, she closed her eyes, frowning in obvious concentration. He could feel the vibrancy of her being pulsing from her hands to his, feel her breath sweet on his face, see the bloom of health and beauty on his wonderfully clear skin.

And then she faded away and he was left holding nothing.

Nate swallowed, suddenly out of oxygen. Nothing in his thirty-four years of life had prepared him for such an unbelievable experience.

A moment later he felt fingers touch his shoulders, comb through his hair, felt them wander down over his sweater, pressing lightly. An invisible hand moved up under his sweater, removed his billfold from his shirt pocket and put it into his hand.

He heard Rowan giggle, then felt her hands cup his face. Her lips brushed his cheek, his eyelids, his nose, his mouth. And lingered, soft as a whisper. Gradually the air in front of him became translucent, then opaque, finally filling with the color and form of a living, breathing woman.

Surrendering, he put his arms around her, thrilling to her slender shape, her softness. As he responded to her kiss, he heard her breath catch, and at the same moment felt his own breath rushing out of him. Never in his life had he been so conscious of his own being. He could feel the blood racing through his veins, feeding his heart, carrying oxygen to his brain. He could feel that same heart beating strongly against his ribs, feel the warmth of Rowan's mouth on his, taking all the air out of him and giving it back.

It was a kiss like no other he had ever experienced. A sweetness seemed to fill his mouth and spread through every part of his body like liquid honey. He couldn't get enough of her sweet mouth. He wanted never ever to let go of her. He wanted to make love to her, he wanted . . .

She slipped out of his arms. Bereft, breathing heavily, he opened his eyes and stared at her.

Rowan, fully restored, smiled sympathetically at him. "It's a shock, isn't it? I quite understand, you know—I was really taken aback when I saw that ghostly huntsman I told you about. And *he* didn't speak to me or even slow down." Mischief lit her eyes once more. "He certainly didn't kiss me," she added.

Nate was unable to speak. He was, quite literally, paralyzed.

"You have to believe I'm a ghost," she said. "It's very important that you do. Once you believe, I can tell you the rest."

He could hear her, see her. He had watched her disappear. He had watched her come back. He was a rational human being. He was not crazy. Ergo: she had to be what she said she was. A ghost.

Blood flowed again in his veins.

"Who told you I was a ghost?" she asked.

"Ivor Trewin, the minister. I'm staying at his sister's bed-and-breakfast place."

"Ivor." She nodded. "He saw me once himself, didn't he? But he ran away."

"He was afraid."

"Are you afraid, Nate?"

For a moment, Nate busied himself putting his billfold back in his shirt pocket, smoothing his sweater over it. "No. Yes. No." He laughed shortly. "I don't know what I am."

"But you do believe."

He took a deep shaky breath, then let it out. "I believe."

She gazed at him in grateful silence for a while. He was a lovely-looking man, Nate Edwards, tall and slender and marvelously well put together in his gray cashmere sweater and form-fitting blue jeans. She liked his lean face with its well-defined cheekbones and generous mouth, she liked his thick springy hair that was as black as hers, as black as anthracite coal, and she liked his eyes that were the profound blue of a summer sky.

But it wasn't just his looks that appealed to her.

It was an established fact that after the age of thirty the human face mirrored the underlying character. Honesty and truth showed in Nate's direct gaze, strength of purpose in the firmness of his jaw. The patterns formed by the lines at the corners of his eyes and mouth told her that his basic nature was kind and compassionate and his disposition even. But the best thing about him was that he'd come back. No one else she'd appeared to and spoken to had ever come back. He *had* to have been chosen—there was no doubt in her mind.

"You did it right this time, God," she murmured, too quietly for Nate to understand her words. "Help me reel him in, will you?"

Nate looked at her questioningly. "I have this habit of talking to God," she told him. "It's what got me into trouble in the first place. I told Him I needed an excuse not to marry Hal Hotchkins and He slammed my car against that stone over there."

Nate shook his head abruptly, obviously having a crisis of belief again. Better keep talking, Rowan decided. "Soon after I...died, I became sort of...transparent. Yet my body was still there—I could feel it. You'll have heard perhaps of people who've had a limb amputated but can still sense it? I suppose it's something like that. I found I could make my body appear or disappear whenever I wanted. I stay materialized most of the time. It seems less lonely."

He gazed at her in silence for a minute, and she couldn't tell whether he accepted what she was saying or not. "You've lived . . . you've been in this field for five years?" he asked finally.

Maybe she *should* play on his pity. Did it really matter what kind of emotion she aroused in him as long it worked in her favor? Though she did wish it might be a *different* emotion, like the one she'd aroused in herself as she'd teased him with kisses. She hadn't even known that the ability to feel passion had survived her death. She'd always be grateful to him for that knowledge, even if he didn't agree to help her.

"Five years," she repeated heavily. "Five years, all alone." All of a sudden she couldn't stand herself. "Aargh!" she exclaimed, throwing up her hands. "It's no use. I cannot abide people who wallow in self-pity."

Letting out an explosive breath to cleanse herself, she smiled wryly. "It's not always that bad, Nate. Certainly I'm a lot better off than Jan Tregeagle, the Cornish Bluebeard."

Nate looked blank.

"Jan Tregeagle made the mistake of selling his soul to the Devil," she said. "He was sentenced to empty Dozmary Pool with a leaky limpet shell. Dozmary Pool, you may not be aware, is the place where King Arthur's sword, Excalibur, was thrown after his death. A ghostly hand came up to catch it."

Nate looked a little overwhelmed. She'd best go easy on the legends. "Sometimes I go into a kind of hibernation where time goes by quickly without troubling me," she told him. "And then there are times when I have lots of company. People come from all over to see the standing stones. Usually they can't see me or hear me, though sometimes they've heard *about* me. They take photographs, laugh, talk. I walk around with them, listening to them, pretending I'm part of their families. When they leave, I try to go with them. But there's some kind of physical barrier round the field that affects only me. I've tried to break through it but I can't." She sighed. "However, as Ivor told you, occasionally there's someone who *can* see me. Someone like you."

"A man."

She nodded. "The worst thing is when the man who sees me has heard about me and he's too afraid to talk to me. Or else he'll talk until he decides it's time to leave and off he'll go, without even giving me a chance to tell him what he could have done for me."

"What he could have done?"

A slip of the tongue, that. Was it still too soon? He was so perfect, the most exciting man she'd ever seen, even when she was alive. She had to draw a fine line here—to keep him long enough to tell him what she wanted, *needed* from him, without frightening him away as she had Thomas Oates and a few other men whose names she couldn't remember. It was significant that Thomas apparently hadn't told anyone what she'd asked. Which showed how frightening the idea had been to him.

"Thomas Oates could have kept me company a while longer," she offered lamely. "I asked him to come back to see me—just to talk, maybe catch me up on what was happening in the world. I like to hear what's going on, so I don't feel so cut off. Once in a while visitors leave their car radio running while they look at the Merry Maidens. Sometimes a teenager will carry a portable radio round with him. But people are more likely to play music than the news, so there are still large gaps in my knowledge of world affairs. For example, I'm not even sure if the prime minister..."

This wouldn't do at all. She had to bind Nate closer to her, make him putty in her hands, not dazzle him with her intellect. She needed to flirt with him, enslave him, enchant him.

An idea occurred to her. "I've noticed lately there's more country-and-western music playing on the radios," she said. "I particularly like Garth Brooks. Have you heard of him in Seattle, Washington?"

He grinned, relieved at the change of subject. "I don't think you could find anyone in the U.S. who hasn't. Yes, I do like country and western and I even own some Garth Brooks CDs. Though for regular listening, I prefer the great composers—Bach, Mozart, Beethoven."

"I like the classics myself," she said eagerly, "though I'm fondest of the Romantics like Tchaikovsky and Chopin." She tilted her head again in the endearing way she had. "You like to dance, do you, Nate?"

He nodded, and at once she was on her feet, reaching for his hand, pulling him up. He marveled at how clean her flowing white dress stayed, how pink and sweet her toes were, peeking out from under the hem.

Illusion. Molecules of matter assembled to fool the eye. Yet he could *feel* her...

He shook his head. "No, you don't, Rowan. I'm still reeling from the shock of finding out you're not really...here. There's no way I'm going to dance with you."

"But I haven't danced with anyone in over five years," she said pleadingly. "Dancing alone isn't near the fun." A reminiscent expression flitted over her face. "I watched an American honeymoon couple this summer, right here in the field in the moonlight, dancing a little bit of something they called the ten-step in and out between the standing stones. It looked pretty, but they stopped before I could work out what they were doing."

He shook his head again, but he was smiling. "You know how to do it!" she exclaimed. Quickly she twisted herself around and held up her hands so he could take hold of them from behind. "What do I do first?" she asked.

"Left foot forward," he said with an exaggerated sigh, assuming his proper position. "No, don't point your toe. Put your heel down, toes up. Now bring your foot back alongside the other one and put your right foot back—that's it."

If anyone was to come to this field, they would see him dancing alone with his arms in the air, Nate realized. They'd probably call the police or the guardians of whatever establishment England kept its moonstruck individuals in.

Somehow he couldn't bring himself to care. Rowan was a quick study, and her joy in the lesson, her lissome grace as she executed the steps and discovered the rhythm of them, was an unqualified delight. A cold breeze was blowing, but the sun shone, the air was crystal pure and fragrant with the scent of the sea, and he was with a beautiful woman who was having an absolutely wonderful time. He couldn't think when he'd enjoyed a dance more.

He'd tell any busybody bystanders who happened to show up that he was a serious researcher of the Bronze Age. The dance he was performing was a pagan ritual that preceded the sacrifice of some virginal maid to the gods. That would be a hell of a lot more believable than the truth—that he was teaching a country-and-western dance to a woman who'd been dead for five years.

He stopped abruptly.

"Don't stop, Nate," Rowan protested. "I'm just now getting the hang of it."

"I think I should be going," he said shortly.

Her eyes were suddenly desolate. He couldn't bear to look at them. "Going," she repeated dully. "But I thought—it seemed like such fun—I thought you were enjoying yourself."

"I was," he said gently. "But I can't spend my whole vacation gamboling around some field like a crazed colt."

"Just a little more time, then," she said softly. Taking his hand, she led him over to the hedge and drew him down beside her on the grass. "We don't have to dance. We could talk a little while longer. Please. There's something I want to—*have* to tell you."

How could he refuse her? Was it even possible to refuse a ghost? A *ghost!* For one moment disbelief raced through him again and he was tempted to hightail it to the gap in the hedge, jump in his car and drive off and, like Thomas Oates, never ever come back. But he just couldn't bring himself to leave her like that.

He needed to put this relationship on a more clinical basis. "I have a couple of questions," he said briskly.

"Fire at will," she said. He wished she wouldn't gaze at his mouth so soulfully.

He swallowed. "I'm not clear on this business of when you can be seen and when you can't. Is this something *you* decide?"

"Not altogether. As I told you, I can appear or disappear whenever I want to, but I can't control whether or not someone sees me while I'm in my body, so to speak. The reason I was so surprised when you saw me was that it's been over a year since anyone has."

"Why do you suppose those who do see you are all men?"

She looked up at him through her long dark lashes, then averted her eyes and began tugging at little clumps of grass. "I'm not sure you're ready to know that."

"You do know the answer then?"

"I think so." She hesitated. "You'll remember I told you I have this habit of complaining to God?"

He was unable to keep himself from smiling. She smiled back across the highly charged force field that was fast developing between them again. "Well, naturally," she said slowly, "when I was first . . . in this condition, I did a lot of complaining. I found that God answered me in a way. When I demanded to know where my body had gone, I started being able to materialize, which seemed to indicate to me that the shell of my body was all right, but it was missing a few interior parts that made the difference between being alive and being dead."

She didn't shirk the word. That took courage, he thought. "If I was a computer," she continued thoughtfully, "you might say a few of my files have been deleted. What I'm looking for is the key that operates the 'restore' function."

"Haven't you asked God about that?"

She nodded solemnly, apparently not noticing the edge of amusement in his voice. "I noticed this pattern of being seen only by men almost straight away. They were never boys, nor old men, either. Just men between the ages of, oh, perhaps twenty-five and fifty. I asked was there some purpose to this. And gradually I perceived an answer."

A frown creased her forehead. He wanted to smooth it out with his fingers but decided that wouldn't be clinical. Or wise. "There's a knowing in all of us," Rowan went on after a moment. "We know when we've done wrong, we know when something is right. We know when our bodies are well, and when they are sick. If we concentrate and practice, we even know what time of day it is without looking at a clock. So I concentrated on knowing the answers to my questions."

She was still tugging up little clumps of grass. It was possible for her to feel nervous apparently. "It came to me that I was meant to fulfill my destiny," she said slowly.

"Which is?"

She glanced at him, then away. "It seems to me that when I was killed it was as if I got off a train at the wrong station— at a stop before my intended destination. So what I need is something that will make it possible for me to hop back on that train and go on with my life's journey as if there'd never been an interruption."

He frowned, trying to comprehend.

"The men who've been able to see me have all been of an age to be married," she said gently. "But they *weren't* married, they were single. Why would only *single* men see me? I asked myself. Could it be they were chosen *because* they were single? And if so wouldn't that mean I was being given a chance to marry one of them?"

"Ivor saw you and he's not single," Nate pointed out, resisting her argument, afraid he was beginning to understand where it was leading.

"Ivor might be an exception to the rule," she returned. "He may have another part to play. He didn't stay long enough for me to find out."

A thought struck him. "Did you tell all this to Thomas Oates?"

She wouldn't look at him at all now. "I did."

"That's what frightened him?"

She leaned back on her hands and looked up at the sky, watching the clouds again. Then she sat forward and looked at the Merry Maidens, standing in their everlasting circle.

"He wasn't really frightened until I proposed to him," she said.

That was exactly the conclusion Nate had been trying to resist coming to. "You proposed to him," he echoed. "What did you expect to happen if he married you?"

Her eyes were clear, candid, her expression solemn. "I expected to fulfill my destiny," she said. "I expected to get back on that train and to travel to my real destination." She paused. "I expected I'd come back to life."

Chapter Five

HER WHOLE HEART, if she had a heart, was there in her eyes for him to see. By now, of course, he knew exactly what she wanted, had wanted all along. Still, he had to ask, to be sure. "Were you planning to propose to me?"

"I was hoping you might consider marrying me, yes."

He shook his head with some violence. "Forget it, Rowan."

"But Nate—"

"No." He got to his feet and looked down at her. "I don't have any intention of getting married to anyone," he said. "I grew up with parents who stayed together long after they hated each other—for my sake, they kept saying. So I lived with these silent angry unhappy people all my young life. They made themselves miserable and they made me miserable." He shook his head again. "Marriage isn't for me, Rowan. I decided that years ago. And if I don't want to marry a live woman, why on earth would I want to marry a dead one, a ghost? Even if such a thing was possible. Which it isn't."

"Yes, it is," she said sharply.

Standing up, she put her hands on her hips and leaned her head back so she could look him directly in the eye. "I've had plenty of time to think about this, Nate. And I *know* it's possible. Ivor Trewin could perform the ceremony. I think that might be why he was allowed to see me—he's part of the overall plan."

She inclined her head in the way he'd found so enchanting earlier, but now found irritating, because it made him soften toward her. He couldn't afford to do that for a moment. "You told me you like women," she reminded him, sounding hopeful.

He ran a hand through his hair, trying to force the cobwebs out of his brain. "Yes, I like women. I love women. I date women. Frequently. I just don't want to marry one. I'm a busy man, a happy man. I have a comfortable home, a job I love, friends, a good life. Why should I ruin that with marriage?"

For one more minute she stared at him, then she put her hands over her face and began to sob.

"Ah, no," Nate exclaimed. "Don't do this to me, Rowan. I can't stand to see anyone cry." He put one hand on her quivering shoulder. With the other hand he gently eased her fingers away from her face.

"There's not a single tear in your eyes," he said accusingly.

"I can't make tears," she said. "That doesn't mean my grief isn't real." Her eyes pleaded with him. "Oh, Nate, I want so badly to get back on that train. To live again."

"It's no good, Rowan," he said softly, resisting the urge to put his arms around her. "You've managed to convince me you are a ghost. But there's no way on earth you'll make me believe that marrying you would bring you back to life. Such a thing is beyond belief. It's just not possible."

"It's not that long ago you didn't think it possible for me to be a ghost," she argued. Sorrow enfolded her like a heavy cloak. "Would you believe that I have no pulse?" she asked.

Startled, he let her take his hand and press his fingers against the spot where her carotid artery ought to be. He could feel the silky smoothness of her skin. Nothing else.

"Some parts I have, some parts I'm missing," she said, still holding his fingers against her throat. He could feel her voice, as well as hear it. "As you may have noticed yesterday, when I refused your kind offer of a part of your pasty, I have no need to eat or drink. So I suppose I must not have a digestive system. I don't feel heat or cold or physical pain. On the other hand, I can taste the salt in the air, smell the freshness of the breeze and the perfume of the wildflowers that grow in the hedge. I could even smell your pasty. Wonderful it was. I can hear the wind in the trees, see everything that is before me, feel the touch of your hand on my neck. When you kissed me I felt excitement. I felt joy."

Letting go of his fingers, she continued to look directly into his eyes, her own eyes shining with intensity. "I have a brain, Nate. I can think and reason. All my emotions seem to be intact. What would be the point of leaving me like this if I wasn't meant to come back to life someday? If I'm not meant to live again I might as well have been turned to stone—like them."

Dramatically she flung an arm in the direction of the standing stones. "The part of me that is really *me* is still alive," she continued. "Somehow I got trapped in the wrong dimension. All I'm asking for is a chance to assemble the rest of me. I know I'm right about this. I know I am."

Moved by her passion, he put his arms around her and pulled her close. Her trembling body felt so light against his he could probably lift her easily in his arms. He could lay her down on the grass by the hedge there, and he could lie down beside her and touch the soft yet firm breasts that were pressing against his chest at this very moment. He could kiss her as he had before, but deeper, longer. He could touch her and learn her secret places and make them part of his own. All he had to do was give in to the demands that were spreading urgently through his body, making it impossible to resist this lovely woman who enchanted him so.

Suddenly horrified by the images clamoring in his brain, half-afraid he was indeed enchanted—hadn't Rowan said that Cornwall was a mystical magical place—he released her. "I'm sorry, Rowan," he said.

She looked at him mournfully. "Must you make up your mind so fast? Did anyone ask you to decide this instant? It wouldn't be a *real* marriage, you must see that. We could have it annulled immediately. Just as soon as I'm myself again, just as soon as the rest of me is restored. It would be a marriage of convenience only."

How reasonable her argument sounded. For one mad minute, Nate stared at her, tempted beyond reason to agree.

Sanity prevailed. Shaking his head to clear it, he backed away from her, trying to devise an argument that would convince her the thing she'd proposed was too outrageous to be considered. Somehow he had to talk her out of this impossible scheme, make her truly understand how hopeless it was. She must have gone through the humiliation of being rejected before, and he couldn't bear the thought of her going through it again and again.

"Look," he said, "let's be practical about this. Getting married isn't just a matter of standing up and saying a few traditional words. You have to have a license, witnesses, a certificate afterward. There are certain requirements—paperwork, birth certificates . . ."

Her forehead creased. "You don't have your birth certificate with you?"

"I was thinking of yours," he said dryly.

Her quick darting smile filled her eyes with radiance. Turning away, she ran to the hedge and flung herself down on her knees. Poking inside the hedge, she came up with an extremely shabby-looking tan leather tote bag.

"I hid this in the wall the day of the accident," she explained, her eyes sparkling as she danced back to him. "I was a little muddled, you might say. I had this idea someone might come along and rob me. I didn't yet know I was dead."

She was fairly simmering with excitement. "I check on it every once in a while. It's a good-quality leather and it was well protected from the elements. Everything inside it is fine. My birth certificate, my passport—we were going to America, Hal and I—he wanted to go to Disney World... Well, that's another story, though I did hear afterward that he and his brother, Leonard, went so as not to waste the tickets. Would you believe anyone could be so callous as to do that?"

She sighed hugely, then went on, "The important thing is that if you wanted to take me to America before getting our marriage annulled, I've even got the passport to do it." Her face took on a worried expression. "Or if you wanted to just walk away after the wedding, that would be all right, too, and I wouldn't need the passport at all. Except I think I should go away from here so as not to disturb anyone. My parents died long since, when I was still in my teens, but—"

She stopped, her eyes showing sadness. "My father was a fisherman, but after a while there weren't so many fish in these parts, and then he and my mother had this scheme of taking tourists out to fish for mackerel at Port Isaac. One day a storm blew up unexpectedly after they'd dropped the tourists off on shore and were heading back out to try to catch a few more fish to sell. Anyway, they were lost at sea."

She sighed again. "But at least I haven't had a need to worry about them hearing I was haunting the field of the Merry Maidens, which would have been a load on my mind. And I wouldn't have to worry about shocking them into heart attacks if I came back to life. But other people who knew me, well, they're probably all getting along fine without me, so it would most likely be best to go somewhere else and..."

She thrust the bag at him so forcefully he had no choice but to take it. "Rowan," he said gently. "None of this will make a difference. All someone has to do is come up with a death certificate and—"

"They never found my body!" she said triumphantly. "How could they declare me dead?"

"Presumptive death?" Nate muttered, more to himself than to her. "No, maybe this situation wouldn't qualify. I think the general rule is that the presumption of death cannot be made until seven years from the time the person was last known to be living."

"Seven years," Rowan repeated. Her face lit up. "I might still be legally alive? That's wonderful!"

Unwittingly he'd handed her another tool to use to persuade him. "I may be wrong about the law," he said hastily. "I'm no lawyer." He shook his head. "It won't work, Rowan. Surely you can see that."

She was very pale. She seemed insubstantial somehow, heartbreakingly fragile, as though she might be on the verge of fading away again. Beseeching him with her eyes, she put her hands on his upper arms—he was still clutching her leather bag. When she spoke, her voice was scarcely above a whisper. "But what if it did work, Nate? Just think about that. What if it did?"

For an instant her intensity forced him to see the wonder of such an outcome, especially from her point of view. His head swam with the possibilities. He had to get away from her so he could think coherently.

"Look, Rowan," he said softly, "I need some time to sort this out. But I promise you this—I'll at least ask Ivor to check on this matter of whether or not you've been declared dead. And see if he thinks it's possible for you to marry someone in your current . . . condition."

He decided not to mention that there was no one to ask about the chances of a marriage ceremony resurrecting someone from the dead.

Her eyes shone like twin stars in a midnight sky. Her hands clutched his arms tighter. "You'll do it. Oh Nate, you'll really marry me?"

He couldn't let her think that. "I can't, Rowan."

She backed up a step, letting her hands drop to her sides. "You mean you won't."

"I won't," he had to agree. He tried, through his look, through his tone, to show all the sympathy he felt for her.

She closed her eyes momentarily, then opened them. When she spoke again her voice was leaden. "You promise you'll come back and tell me if it's legally possible?"

He met her gaze directly. This much he could certainly guarantee. "I promise."

She let him go then, though she still looked as desolate as though the end of the world, the end of *her* world, had arrived.

After he went through the break in the hedge, he glanced back. She was nowhere to be seen.

What on earth had he been thinking, to make such promises to her? Now he was committed to telling Ivor Trewin the whole story. The minister might have readily accepted the notion of Rowan as ghost, but that didn't mean he could stretch his mind to encompass Rowan as a bride. He was going to think Nate was completely, utterly mad.

"THE SCHEME HAS a certain merit to it," Ivor said.

They were standing in the back garden of Ivor's small house next to his chapel, the minister leaning on his hoe.

"Rowan does have this perfectly recognizable body," he went on in a ruminative way. "And, as she says, the few who've been allowed to see her have all been eligible men. She may have hit on the right interpretation. Persuade one of the men to marry her, and her missing faculties just might be fully restored." He rubbed his smooth round chin thoughtfully. "'Tis an idea that has a certain internal logic."

He gave an elfin grin. A pisky grin. "It also has a cosmic humor that appeals to me," he concluded.

Nate stared at him. "You're out of your mind," he said.

Ivor looked at him solemnly, the twinkle absent from his eyes for once. "You won't consider doing that poor lost soul this service? If the legal end of it seems possible, I see no moral reason I couldn't proceed. It might take a little time, but you're here for a month, I believe?"

"I'm not even going to discuss it," Nate said. "I promised Rowan I'd ask you to find out where she stands legally. That's all I promised."

Ivor sighed. "If I were single I'd do it myself, I would. Just to satisfy my curiosity if nothing else. I don't see what I'd have to lose by it."

Nate decided to ignore his heavy-handed hint. "How long do you think it'll take you to work this out?" he asked.

"A few days perhaps. No more than a week."

Nate nodded.

Ivor was still looking at him alertly, as though watching for a sign that his attitude might soften. "I'll see you later, then," Nate said, and took himself off.

IT WAS FOUR DAYS before Ivor toiled up the hill to Chy-Trewin to tell Nate he was ready to talk. Four days in which Nate assiduously stayed away from the field of the Merry Maidens. Four days in which he drove and hiked over much of the southwest corner of England, sightseeing like one possessed, almost convincing himself that nothing in the world interested him as vitally as old castles and abandoned tin mines, granite seawalls and fishing boats, lonely moors and thatched cottages.

"Would you care to join me in a postprandial excursion to the pub?" Ivor asked, poking his head around the dining-room doorjamb, his round face beaming in obvious delight at the repetition of his earlier invitation.

"I'd be delighted," Nate said, though if the truth be told he was more than a little fearful.

This time Ivor didn't say anything meaningful until they arrived at the pub, though as they hiked down the hill he kept up a monologue about the weather. First he expressed his hope that a warmer spell might be due before autumn began to slide into winter, then he backed up his optimism with a long list of signs and portents that were universally, at least in Cornwall, agreed to be reliable.

There were only a few people in the pub—a group of rowdy young men playing cards at a table in the corner, a man and woman throwing darts with expert precision, a bewhiskered old codger nodding over a glass of beer.

Ivor offered to fetch the drinks—a couple of pints of half-and-half, which was a mixture of mild and bitter draught beers and which, Nate decided, resulted in one of the truly great drinks of all time.

"Rowan's not been declared dead," Ivor said after a long swallow and a satisfied sigh. "No body was found, you see. It's theoretically possible that she might just have wandered away from the wreck, lost her memory. Not that anyone believes it after the reports of her haunting the field, but still there's no absolute proof that she's dead." He hesitated before going on. "I checked on her bank account. 'Tis intact, with considerable interest added. I spoke with Kenneth Hawkey, the bank manager. If our project is successful, he'll be willing to let Rowan draw out her funds discreetly."

"He actually accepted the possibility that Rowan might come back to life?" Nate asked, astonished.

"He's a Cornishman," Ivor said as if that explained everything, as perhaps it did.

"After her... accident Rowan's belongings were moved out of her rented cottage," Ivor continued. "They're stored in a garden shed at her friend Kate Manley's house in Penzance. 'Tis a good sturdy shed—Kate uses part of it as a studio for her painting. Rowan's clothing, pots and pans, they're all there. Kate couldn't bear to part with anything. She's very excited," he added.

"You told her, too?" Nate said with a groan.

"She won't tell anyone. We're agreed this must not get out to the television or newspaper people." He took another long swallow of beer, then said with an air of great satisfaction, "'Twill all be as if Rowan had just gone away on a trip. Though she's right in what she said to you—'twould be best if she left here at once."

He shrugged. "'Twould be just the ticket if you were to be the bridegroom, Mr. Edwards. Nate. The two of you could stay with my sister until arrangements are made for you to take her to America. I've found out it would be much easier if you're married. She wouldn't have to wait for an immigration quota—" He held up a hand as Nate began to protest. "I know, I know, you've got your mind set against it. 'Tis all right. I've been thinking I may be able to come up with a likely candidate."

About to take a swig of his beer, Nate halted the mug in midair and stared at the older man. "A candidate?"

Ivor nodded, his eyes twinkling. "'Tis not really necessary, as I see it, for the man to be able to actually see Rowan in the flesh, so to speak, though 'twould certainly be an advantage if he could. A judicious offer of a few pounds to the right person, a bottle of the good stuff to stiffen his spine..."

Nate set his beer down on the scarred table. "You'd *pay* some drunk to marry her?"

One of the card players turned his head abruptly, his eyebrows shooting up. Nudging one of his friends, he jerked his head toward Nate and Ivor, and said something that made the others laugh. Nate lowered his voice. "Rowan would be humiliated by such a suggestion," he said in a fierce whisper.

Unperturbed, Ivor shook his head. "I think not. If she's as desperate as you've told me she'll take anyone willing to stand up and say the words."

He was probably right. With life as the prize, who wouldn't be willing to grab such a chance? Nate took a deep breath and sat back in his chair. "I don't know why I'm getting so steamed up about it. It's not going to work, anyway."

"Perhaps yes, perhaps no," Ivor said agreeably. "But it seems a shame not to give it a go. What's to lose, after all?"

The phrase seemed to echo in Nate's mind as Ivor went on to explain just how he would iron out all possible difficulties.

NATE COULDN'T SLEEP that night. An hour or so after midnight he went to look out his bedroom window. The moon was in its last quarter, a half circle of brightness riding behind a wispy veil of cloud. Wearing only the boxer shorts he usually slept in, Nate stood gazing at the moon. He imagined it shining down on the field of the Merry Maidens, causing mysterious shadows to reach out from the bases of the standing stones. He could almost see Rowan stepping in and out between the stones, her white dress flaring around her slim legs, her bare feet hardly touching the ground as she performed her solitary dance.

Solitary.

Abruptly he closed the window, pulling the blue-flowered curtains across to shut out the moon. Then he climbed into bed, turned on the lamp and looked blankly around the room. It was a little too frilly for his taste, with its flowered duvet and its chintz-covered chairs, but clean and neat and very comfortable. He allowed his mind to play with the possibility Ivor had suggested. A candidate. Someone brought in to stand beside Rowan for the ceremony. What a mockery that would be. The minister might as well rig up a cardboard cutout of a man.

Why should it matter to him? he asked himself toward morning.

And answered himself in the next breath.

It just did. It mattered a lot.

Chapter Six

IVOR'S WIFE, a bustling little dumpling of a woman in a yellow-flowered apron, welcomed Nate with a dimpled smile, even though it was barely past seven in the morning. Gladys even offered him a full English breakfast of bacon and sausage and tomato and egg, but he was far too agitated to eat.

Ivor looked up from his plate and smiled at him, his gray eyes as calm as ever. "You didn't sleep at all?" he asked.

Nate gave an impatient shake of his head. "I'm going to do it," he blurted out.

"I thought you might," Ivor said complacently.

Gesturing Nate to a chair, he poured him a cup of coffee, then took a slice of toast out of a metal rack, buttered it and spread it thickly with marmalade. "I've already set the special licensing procedure in motion," he said after chewing thoughtfully for a while. "We'll need to send for your birth certificate."

Nate smiled wryly. "I called a neighbor in Seattle this morning," he admitted. "He's taking care of my plants and so he has a key to my house. He's going to express the certificate to me today."

Ivor raised slightly grizzled eyebrows. "Will you be going to tell Rowan?" he asked.

"I think it's better not to see her until we're sure there aren't any obstacles," Nate said. "If anything went wrong she'd be devastated."

And if he went to the field of the Merry Maidens and faced the folly of the thing he'd agreed to do he'd be liable to race off to the appropriate authorities and get himself committed.

"How long will it take?" Nate asked.

"I expect we can get it done directly," Ivor said. Then he chuckled. "There are three things to be learned when you visit this part of the world, Nate my lad. You must learn to drive more slowly and think more slowly, and you must learn what is meant by directly—or dreckly—as we say it here. If a tradesman says he'll be sure to do something dreckly, he might do it today or he might do it tomorrow. Then again, he might not ever do it."

"But you will do it?"

"Dreckly," Ivor said with a twinkle.

Five days passed. Nate traveled over parts of Cornwall he hadn't yet seen, hiking, boating, driving. He climbed the ancient steps to St. Michael's Mount, which was supposedly built by a black-bearded giant who used to wade ashore regularly in order to capture sheep and cattle that belonged to the local folk. Until he was finished off by a boy named Jack.

At Zennor, he photographed the Quoit, a very different grouping of ancient stones from the Merry Maidens. He noted thankfully that there wasn't a ghost in sight. In the same district he learned of a mermaid who had been attracted by the singing of Matthew Trewhella in his church choir and had enticed him to come live with her beneath the waves.

Nate supposed wryly that he was lucky; he'd only been asked to marry a ghost, not to walk into the sea.

Feeling it was time to take a break from legend and fantasy, he ventured into Devon, to Plymouth, seeking out the stone that marked the spot where the Pilgrims set sail for America on the *Mayflower* on September 6, 1620.

Looking at models of that fabled ship, he wondered that it had survived such a journey, and thought it would be easy to believe the *Mayflower* story was a legend, too, rather than fact.

But at least all this feverish activity kept him from taking the road to Lamorna. Every night he told himself he'd been crazy to allow his pity for Rowan Pengelly to persuade him to agree to this marriage of convenience that was convenient only to Rowan. Every night he assured himself it didn't matter, anyway, because Ivor wouldn't be able to collect all the necessary paperwork or get the necessary license.

Not that Ivor seemed to be meeting with any difficulty. He reported every step as he accomplished it, occasionally asking Nate to sign a form or two. Nate complied, feeling that the whole situation was out of his hands and in those of the Fates. "I've been out to the Merry Maidens field," Ivor reported one evening. "I needed Rowan's signature on a couple of the documents."

"You saw her?" Nate asked.

"I did indeed. And she's still every bit as charming as she was when she was alive. Why I was so fearful before I don't know. 'Tis not like me to be so timid."

"She was able to sign the documents?" Nate asked, once more feeling a sense of utter disbelief in this whole undertaking.

"I lent her a pen," Ivor assured him as though that had anything to do with Nate's question.

"You told her I'd agreed to go along?"

Ivor shook his head. "Like you, I didn't want to build up premature hopes. I told her only that I needed the documents signed so I could look further into the possibilities of the thing." He hesitated. "She did ask if you were still here. I told her you were. I hope that was all right."

"Sure," Nate said. "Did she say anything? I mean, when you told her I was still here?"

Ivor shook his head. "Not a word." The twinkle showed up in his eyes. "She did look pleased, though. And hopeful."

On the sixth day Ivor told Nate he was ready to perform the ceremony. Nate's stomach did a complete somersault, then settled down. He had said he'd do it, and do it he would. Besides, there was no way he could back out now. What he needed was to cultivate a sort of scientific detachment so that he wouldn't be affected whatever the outcome. He was simply doing a favor for an extremely eccentric friend. That was all.

The warm weather Ivor had wished for had arrived with a vengeance. The sun was high and hot when he and Nate headed for the Lamorna road in the middle of the afternoon. They were accompanied by Ivor's wife and sister, who had agreed to be witnesses even though they probably wouldn't be able to see Rowan.

They were all crazy, Nate thought, when Miss Bertha Trewin quite nonchalantly told him this. Himself included. Did England still have any dungeons around? he wondered. The whole bunch of them were likely to be locked away in one if today's proceedings ever came to light!

ROWAN KNEW what Nate had decided the minute she saw the four of them entering the field. Nate had evidently dressed in the best he had with him—a loose black lightweight jacket over a shirt and tie, tan pants. His dark hair was neatly brushed, his shoes polished. He looked tall, lean, magnificent. His right hand straight down at his side, he was carrying a small bouquet of wildflowers and herbs, obviously a gift for her.

What a kind and thoughtful man he was! The despair of the past five years, which had increased a hundredfold during the past several days and nights, fell away from her spirit, and joy washed over her like a wave. Followed by gratitude.

And then fear.

Trembling, she shook hands with Ivor Trewin, who apologized one more time for running off the first time he saw her. "It's all right," she assured him. "I might have done the same if I'd seen your ghost."

Through Ivor, she thanked Miss and Mrs. Trewin for helping with the ceremony even though they couldn't see one of the main participants. "Tell them I'll thank them properly afterward," she said. "They'll be able to see me and hear me then."

As Ivor passed on this confident message she looked at Nate again. What a fine figure of a man he was! His hair so black and his eyes so blue, like the cornflowers that grew in cottage gardens. Not to mention his smile that was so kind. And sexy.

He held the bouquet toward her. "I'm not sure if this wedding is a good idea or not," he said. "But it seemed to me you ought to have flowers." He pointed to a slightly wilted bit of greenery. "This is basil from your own garden. Most of it has gone to seed, but there was a small clump in a shady corner."

She was touched all over again.

He looked at her worriedly. "The only thing is, will the flowers... Will you able to hold on to the flowers even though..."

"You think it might unnerve the ladies, seeing a bouquet float around in the air by itself?" she finished for him. "You don't need to worry, Nate. Things I pick up seem to be pulled into my invisible shield. The ladies won't see anything."

He seemed unsure if that was a good thing or not.

Rowan held out her right hand. "I don't know how to thank you," she said awkwardly.

He gripped her hand between both of his. There was an immediate warmth between them, a glowing encircling warmth, the kind you feel when you come in out of the cold and the wet to a fire in the hearth and a cup of hot tea. If marriage to this man could not bring her back to life, nothing ever would, Rowan thought.

"There's no need for thanks," Nate said. "I just hope—" He broke off.

He sounded very nervous, she thought. Almost as nervous as she felt. "May I speak to you a moment in private?" she asked.

Nate nodded, glancing at Ivor. "No hurry, lad," Ivor said. "Whenever you and Rowan are ready, we'll commence."

Nate walked with her to the nearest Merry Maiden. She turned to face him, gripping the flowers tightly in both hands. "I'm frightened," she whispered.

"I'm apprehensive myself," he admitted. "I'm not sure what we're doing is at all legal, or even sane."

"Oh, I'm not worried about the sanity or the legality of it," Rowan said. "Mostly I'm afraid there might be some price to pay for my freedom. Like in *Dorian Gray,* for example."

He seemed puzzled, which wasn't too surprising.

"The *Picture* of Dorian Gray," she said to clarify.

He was still frowning. "The Oscar Wilde story that was made into a movie?" he asked. "I've heard about it, but I don't think I ever saw—"

"In the story, the portrait that was painted of Dorian Gray kept getting older, but *he* never did," she explained. "Not until the end, when it all overtook him at once and he was suddenly an old, old man."

Nate's expression was blank, uncomprehending.

"I've been out here in this field for five years," she reminded him. "I've been exposed to all kinds of weather, even though I couldn't feel it—the sun beating down, the rain, some hail, wind with dust in it, even a little snow one time. Yet I look the same as I did the day I—the day of the accident. I've seen myself in puddles of water. What if when I come back to myself all that ill treatment shows up? I died at twenty-three and I seem to still look twenty-three, but I'm really almost twenty-nine, you know, going on thirty. I might suddenly turn into an old hag."

For a minute she thought he was going to laugh, and she was quite prepared to kick his shins if he did. But then his face straightened and he said very solemnly, "I doubt very much that the weather could have been affecting your body while it's . . . lacking a completely material form."

"You think it'll be all right, then?"

"I think—" He stopped, then began again. "I don't think you have to worry about wrinkles," he said.

He didn't believe for one minute that she was going to be restored, she realized. Was it necessary that he believe? She hoped not. She didn't see why it would make any difference. All she could do was believe enough for both of them.

In any case she felt as if a load had been taken off her. What he'd said about her body lacking material form seemed a very sensible way of viewing the situation. Not that she'd complain too bitterly to God if she *did* end up with weathered skin and dull hair. Actually she didn't plan on complaining to God ever again. But if it was all the same to Him, she'd prefer to go on looking young for a while longer.

She was grateful to Nate for his reassurance, though perhaps the relief she felt was due only to his *wanting* to reassure her. Because it seemed to show he cared....

She drew herself up straight. There must be no thinking along those lines. Nate Edwards had agreed to marry her only out of pity, only to help her out. He wouldn't want anything further to do with her once the ceremony was over. Making up foolish fantasies about Nate wanting to stay married to her was asking for heartbreak. She was in danger of getting too greedy. The gift of life would be enough. She could not presume to ask for love, also. Even though her poor lonely heart ached with wanting it.

Biting hard on her suddenly trembling lower lip, she closed her eyes briefly, then opened them again and managed a smile. "I suppose we should get started."

Turning, Nate crooked his left arm and she put her hand there. She marveled at the solid masculine feel of him; her other hand holding fast to the bouquet he'd brought her. Together they walked slowly toward the trio of people who stood waiting together.

Ivor smiled broadly at them. He seemed perfectly comfortable about standing in the middle of a field in his smart suit. His wife and sister looked slightly ill at ease in their flower-trimmed hats and Sunday-best clothes. Their eyes kept darting sideways in a furtive sort of way, as though they wanted to avoid any chance of seeing her head on.

But how sweet they were to dress up, Rowan thought when she and Nate took their places in front of Ivor. She would buy them each a present, just as soon as she possibly could.

"Dearly beloved," Ivor said solemnly. "We are gathered together here in the sight of God, and in the face of this company, to join together this man and this woman in holy matrimony, which is an honorable estate."

Ivor had a wonderful voice for these traditional words, Nate thought. Deep and rich and mellow, it made them sound like poetry.

The amazing thing was that the minister conducted himself the whole time as if this was a normal occasion. He didn't even rush through the part that read, "If any person can show just cause why they may not lawfully be joined together, let him now speak . . ."

Nate had forgotten a wedding ceremony could take so long. He kept wondering what would happen if someone came into the field and caught the four of them going through a wedding service with an invisible bride.

But then it was time for him to repeat the vows, and as he did so, he realized fully for the first time in his life exactly what those vows were. *To have and to hold from this day forward, for better, for worse, for richer, for poorer, in sickness and in health, to love and to cherish till death us do part.* Pretty serious stuff.

Nate had bought a ring of plain gold, guessing at the size of Rowan's finger. It fitted perfectly. A good omen? Judging by the brilliance of Rowan's smile as she gazed down at it, she definitely thought so.

The clincher came a short time later as Ivor proclaimed in rounded sonorous tones, "Those whom God hath joined together let no man put asunder." Even he looked a little taken aback as he said that. Then he smiled, shook his head slightly and said to Nate, "You may kiss the bride."

Nate wasn't sure that was such a tremendously great idea, considering the turmoil that had engulfed his body the last time he'd kissed Rowan. And he wasn't at all sure how it would appear to the ladies. Would it look as if he was kissing empty air? Or would part of his face disappear as he entered Rowan's aura?

Rowan's lips brushed lightly as rose petals against his mouth while he was still pondering the problem. Every hormone he possessed paid immediate attention. He wanted more of a kiss than that, he wanted ...

He became aware that Rowan was trembling uncontrollably. "It's okay," he said soothingly. "It's all over."

"But nothing happened," Rowan pointed out. "I'm still as much of a ghost as I ever was."

Chapter Seven

NATE STARED AT HER. He'd been so caught up in worrying that people might see them, as well as noting the awe-inspiring significance of the wedding vows, he'd almost forgotten about the hoped-for result of this charade.

"Perhaps 'twill take a little time for you to become fully...integrated," Ivor suggested, squinting at Rowan. "Can you not feel any change taking place at all?"

"Not the least little bit."

Ivor glanced questioningly at his sister and his wife. They looked back at him in silence and shook their heads.

"We'll give it some time," Ivor said. But somehow the minister's voice didn't sound as sure of itself as usual, and the smile on his round face had a tentative look to it. "Well now," Ivor said awkwardly after a few more minutes of silence. "I'm not sure I can do much more to help here."

"Why don't you all go on home," Nate suggested. "I'll stay here with Rowan to see if, well, until—" His voice faded.

"How will you get back then?" Ivor asked. "You rode here with us, so..." He gave an awkward little laugh. "What am I thinking? Gladys and I will simply drive back here, with her driving my car and me driving yours. How will that be?"

"Thank you," Nate said. "Thank you for everything."

Ivor hesitated as if he wanted to say something more, but at last he shook hands with Nate, then with Rowan, and squired his two ladies from the field.

Nate watched them go, then turned back to Rowan. She was standing very still, her head bent, her eyelids lowered, both hands still clutching her bouquet. She looked very small, very young, very fragile. Sadness radiated out from her like a mist.

"I was so sure it would work," she said, her voice shaking. "I was so sure I had only to fulfill my destiny and God would relent and give me back my life."

"Maybe I was the wrong man."

Her eyes flashed as she darted a glance at his face. "You were the best to ever come into this field. The best I ever saw—even before I died."

His pleasure in this statement was out of all proportion. Which only proved what an ass he was. And now he had no idea how to comfort her. What could he possibly say? *Look, kid, we gave it a good shot and it didn't work, so it seems you'll just be dead for the rest of your life.*

He felt deeply disappointed himself, he realized, even though he had never truly believed the wedding ceremony would provide the necessary magic.

He felt responsible for Rowan, that was the problem. A direct result of making those vows. *For better, for worse.* From Rowan's point of view this was definitely worse.

"Maybe Ivor's right. Maybe it'll just take some time," he said. "Why don't we sit down and talk for a while and see what happens?"

She shook her head in a way that spoke of her deep despair, but she allowed him to propel her toward the hedge and sank down beside him in the grass.

"You make a lovely bride," he offered, after searching his mind for words of comfort. "It's astonishing how fresh and new your dress seems."

Rowan sniffled. Her head was still bent and her shoulders were shaking a little. Looking at her woebegone face, he felt his heart constrict with pity. Obviously he wasn't helping a whole lot here. Maybe he should just talk generally while she tried to get over her disappointment.

"It was nice that the sun shone," he said, taking refuge in talking about the weather, just as the English did when they didn't know what else to say.

Rowan nodded.

"It must rain a lot here, to keep the fields as green as they are. I haven't seen fields as green as these in my life."

Rowan nodded again.

"Washington fields are green, of course," he went on desperately. "We get a lot of rain, too, though not as much as some people think. But the green isn't quite this vivid."

She lifted her head and looked at him, her dark, dark eyes filled with shadows. But at least she'd lifted her head. He plunged on, talking about how the magazines had selected Seattle, with its water, its mountains, its arts community, its major symphony, opera and ballet companies and its friendliness, as the most livable city in the United States.

"It's even been called the best city for global business," he went on. "It's becoming known as the espresso capital, too—there's a *latte* stand on almost every corner."

Latte stands. What the hell was he doing talking about *latte* stands?

"It sounds wonderful," Rowan murmured, but he could tell she hadn't really been listening.

After a lengthy silence Rowan stood up and walked slowly to the center of the field. He wanted to go with her—she looked so lonely—but his instincts told him she wanted to be by herself. For a while she just stood there staring up at the sky, slim and lovely in her long white dress, her hands still clutching the bouquet. He thought he could see her lips moving. He wondered if she was complaining to God again and felt his mouth twitch into a smile.

A little later she began walking in and out between the standing stones, gradually working into the graceful little dance steps she had performed when he'd first come upon her. Watching her, he was charmed all over again. He might have wandered back into some prehistoric time to watch one of the Merry Maidens dance, except there was no merriment in her, rather a kind of funereal solemnity. "Don't turn into stone, Rowan," he murmured, and was suddenly conscious of an aching sensation in his heart.

How long he sat there he didn't know. After a while he loosened his tie, rolled it up and put it in his jacket pocket, then unbuttoned the top button of his shirt. He removed his jacket and rolled it into a cushion to lean against.

The afternoon wore on. He heard Ivor drive up, heard the sound of car doors closing. But no one came into the field. Craning his neck, he saw his car parked alongside the gap in the hedge. He could leave whenever he wanted to. If he ever wanted to.

Rowan danced on. Sometimes she appeared insubstantial and he was afraid she was going to fade away. At times she seemed no more than a flicker of light moving across the grass. It seemed that all he could do was keep watch over her while she came to terms with her disappointment, her grief. He began to feel weary, which was hardly surprising after the unusual stresses of the day.

Eventually he dozed off. When he awakened the light was rapidly disappearing. Rowan sat cross-legged beside his prone body. It was still very warm, even though the sun had gone down. Strangely, though he hadn't eaten for hours, he felt no hunger. Rowan's sadness, his own disappointment on her behalf, had driven out such physical needs.

Sitting up, he felt his heart contract as he looked at her unhappy face. "I'm sorry, Rowan," he said softly.

"You think I should give up hoping."

It was more a statement than a question.

"It doesn't look as if it's going to..." He let his voice trail away.

"I can't give up hope, Nate. I can't. Without hope I have nothing. I've always hoped, always. Next week, I'd say to myself—and if not next week, then next month—someone will come who will be able to see me and he'll agree to marry me and I'll be able to get on with my life."

Burying her face in her hands, she began sobbing again, that dry sobbing that sounded so incredibly painful.

He put an arm around her shoulders and held her close, letting her cry herself out, feeling as if any minute he might start crying himself. Probably he shouldn't have agreed to marry her. He'd wanted to help. He'd felt sorry for her. If he hadn't married her, at least she'd still have some hope left.

Holding her, he found it next to impossible to believe she wasn't alive. The warm weight of her felt so wonderfully pleasant next to his body. The clean and fragrant smell of her hair was emphasized by the crisp scent of the herbs in her garland.

His hand caressed the firm roundness of her upper arm, felt its warmth and softness under the tight silk sleeve, then slipped under it to gently cover her breast.

A moment, and her sobs quieted. After sniffing a couple of times, she raised her head and looked at him with wide dark eyes. Tension suddenly crackled between them with as much potency as an electrical charge.

"I wonder," he said, and hesitated. His voice had sounded husky. "We were able to kiss," he said.

She nodded. Then understanding came into her eyes and a faint flush of pink spread over her cheeks.

How was that possible? To blush you had to have blood circulating.

Illusion. It was all illusion.

But she looked real. She felt real.

"I wonder," he said again. "Do you suppose it would help at all if..."

He hesitated again and shook his head. She was going to think he was taking advantage, exploiting the situation. Maybe he was. The only thing he knew for sure was that he suddenly felt on fire, wanting her more desperately than he ever remembered wanting a woman.

She tilted her head in the way that never failed to enchant him. "You mean we might have to consummate our marriage before it can be recognized?"

The awakened hope that blazed in her eyes shamed him. "I'm not sure I believe that, Rowan. My motives aren't all that pure, I'm afraid."

"You want me?" she asked artlessly, her gaze meeting his. He swallowed. "Yes."

She smiled, then moved her upper body slightly, sensuously, under his hand. His senses exploded. "Rowan," he muttered thickly.

And then he pulled her down across him and rolled with her until he was leaning over her, gazing down into her eyes. "Are you sure?" he asked.

For answer she raised her arms to hold him. Her hands moved over his neck into his hair, her fingers exerting pressure, pulling him close.

He moved toward her willingly, his lips finding hers. Her response was so immediate, so passionate, his whole body came alive with primal male vitality. Gone were his concerns about her ability to make love. Gone was his pity. Gone was his so-called clinical detachment. Easing himself out of his clothing, he kept one hand on her, half-afraid that if he broke the connection between them she would disappear. When he pulled her against him again her dress had apparently dissolved and there was no impediment between his flesh and hers.

Ghost or no ghost, she was all woman. His mouth hungry on hers, he surrendered all thought, all anxiety and gave himself up to her compelling magic.

She would at least have this, Rowan thought at some point during that long warm magical night. The silent darkness enfolded them like a velvet blanket. Stars shone like fairy lights in the vaulted sky, but there was no moon tonight to expose the two of them to view.

It was good that it was so dark, she thought. Though she couldn't see Nate except in vague outlines, the acuteness of her other senses seemed to have increased in direct proportion to her lack of sight. She could smell the wonderful masculine scent of him, feel the crispness of his hair against her fingers, hear his breathing and feel the warmth of it on her skin. The grass-covered ground felt as comfortable to her as a feather bed.

Never had she expected to find a man so attuned to her every need. It was as though they moved to music that had been choreographed especially for them, touching, holding, kissing. Hands, lips, bodies moved in perfect unison. She could feel his heart beating against her—beating, beating. But only *his* heartbeat. Not hers. Never hers. During a quiet moment she touched her lips to his throat, tasting him lightly with the tip of her tongue. He tasted wonderful, warm and slightly salty. She could feel the heat still coming from his body, smell the sweetness of his breath. "So this is how a wedding night was meant to be," she said huskily.

Nate laughed, his arms tightening around her. "I guess every couple who ever got together thought they invented sex, but obviously they were wrong. The discovery was ours."

Sex, her mind echoed. She wished he'd said love, instead. Foolish woman, a small voice whispered at the back of her mind. Closing her eyes, she willed the warning voice away and pressed closer to Nate.

Amazingly, she realized, he was ready for her again. Her own readiness was never in doubt for a second. As she moved against him, his mouth, hard again in its demand, covered hers, and she opened to him willingly with a demand of her own, feeling liquid heat course through her entire body.

Such wanting, she thought, tangling her fingers in his thick dark hair. Such hunger, such need. Surely, now, surely, this must be the answer.

Pressure built inside her, spiraling upward, holding her motionless for long moments, her body as tightly strung as an archer's bow. And then the stars above reeled across the sky and her body let go of its tension and exploded against Nate's just as he cried out her name and found his own release.

Thank you, God, she said silently as Nate held her close and his body relaxed into sleep. *Thank you for giving me this night, these memories.*

Chapter Eight

A BIRD SANG SWEETLY in a nearby tree. Somewhere in the distance a dog barked. Sunlight touched Nate's closed eyelids. It was a moment before he remembered where he was.

His eyes flew open. Rowan was sitting cross-legged beside him, fully dressed, her feet hidden under her long white skirt. Afraid to ask, he questioned her with his eyes.

"Nothing's changed," she said softly.

He closed his eyes again. "You mustn't feel bad," she said, her voice firm now. "Last night was the most wonderful I've ever experienced. I will cherish the memory of it forever."

He sat up and reached for her, but she pulled back from him, her body stiff. "No, Nate," she said. "No more. It's not that I don't want you, but now that I know there's no future for me, I just can't bear..." She turned her head to one side and he saw her swallow. "No more," she whispered.

He sat silent for a full minute, feeling an emptiness inside him that was like nothing he had ever felt before. It was as though he had suddenly become a hollow shell of a man. "I'm so sorry, Rowan," he said. "Maybe—"

"No," she said sharply, getting to her feet. "No more maybes, either. It's time for me to face facts."

Running to the middle of the field, she flung her arms out and threw her head back and shouted, "Would it have been so bad to let me live again? Would it have hurt anybody? In this world or the next? If you weren't going to do it, why did you let me go on and on thinking, believing, hoping? Can't you see it's the thinking that hurts, the thinking and the wanting of what might have been . . ."

Her voice broke and she sank to her knees, her hands over her face.

Hurriedly Nate pulled on all his clothing except his jacket, then went to Rowan and squatted down next to her. "Is there anything I can do?"

She lowered her hands and looked at him. The despair was back in her eyes. "I've been sitting there next to you for hours," she said. "I kept thinking and thinking, and I've reached the conclusion that I've been fooling myself all along. I couldn't stand the thought of living what was not even a half life, so my mind very ingeniously invented the whole idea of bringing myself back to life through marriage. Obviously it was nothing more than a pipe dream. It wasn't meant to happen."

She gestured around her at the field, the hedge, the Merry Maidens standing so still. "*This* is my destiny. This is all there is for me."

He stood up and held out a hand to her. "Rowan—"

"No." She got to her feet and backed away from him, her own hands behind her as if to prevent him from touching them. "I want you to go away, Nate. It isn't fair to you, or to me, to prolong this when we know nothing can come of it."

"I can stay a while longer at least. We can be together until I have to leave." His stomach rumbled and he grimaced. "Okay, I guess I'll have to go eat. But I'll come back just as quickly as—"

"No."

He stared at her. She was standing very straight now, drawn up as tall as she could manage. Her eyes met his directly and he saw that she meant what she was saying. "You don't want me to come back?"

She drew a deep shaky breath. "It hurts too much, Nate. Can't you see that?" She averted her eyes. "Just go. Please."

Pain seared through him, as real as if it were physical. Hers or his? He didn't know. Nor did he know what to do. Ivor, he thought. Ivor could advise him.

"May I at least kiss you goodbye?" he asked.

Her face closed up so tightly it had the look of something carved out of ivory. "No," she said.

He had known the whole time that she'd really believed it would happen. She had truly believed marriage to him would restore her to life. But it hadn't occurred to him that when it didn't happen the disappointment might be more than she could bear.

"I probably shouldn't have stayed," he said tentatively. "I thought it would help, but I guess—"

She put her hands over her ears. "No more," she repeated. And then she closed her eyes and he saw her brow furrow in concentration. He suddenly realized what she was doing.

"Rowan!" he cried as she began to fade. "Please don't go. I can't just walk away."

The last little bit of color was gone and there was only silence in the field. The breeze lifted the leaves in the hedgerow and played lightly in Nate's hair. There was a chill suddenly and he shivered. Walking back to the hedge, he reached down for his creased jacket and put it on. He felt no warmer.

"Rowan?" he called tentatively, his voice forlorn.

There was no answer.

"AND THAT WAS IT?" Ivor asked. "You didn't see her again?"

Nate had tracked him down in his chapel office where he'd been preparing Sunday's sermon. After one look at him, Ivor had taken him by the elbow and walked him outside and down the road to a café, where he'd ordered the huge sausages called bangers and bacon and eggs and grilled tomatoes and mushrooms and what looked like half a loaf of bread, toasted, along with a pot of strong scalding coffee.

After watching Nate eat he'd sat back and listened as the words poured out of him. Fortunately it was past the usual breakfast hour and they had the café to themselves.

"She just disappeared?" Ivor asked now.

Nate nodded stiffly. A tight knot had formed in his chest when he'd realized Rowan wasn't going to appear again. The food and coffee had eased the congestion a little, but he was almost afraid to move in case something inside him broke.

"I called her name, but she wouldn't answer me. After a while I realized she was right. It wasn't going to do any good to put off the parting. It would only get harder to leave."

He sighed deeply. "She was stronger than I was," he said. "When she saw it wasn't going to happen she had the strength to just go. I kept babbling on about coming back, spending time with her, and finally she just stepped in and... ended it."

"You look terrible, you do," Ivor said.

Nate rubbed a hand over his cheek and chin, wincing at the raspy sound. His eyes felt bloodshot; his clothes looked as though they'd been stuffed in a laundry bag for a week. "I *feel* terrible," he admitted.

"You really cared about her, didn't you?" Ivor said gently.

Nate let out a long breath. "I obviously cared enough to want to do what I could for her. I wanted to help her. I feel so terribly sorry for her."

"'Tis pity you feel for her, then?"

Nate frowned. It had to be pity. What else could it be? "Who wouldn't feel pity?" he asked. "Didn't you feel sorry for her?"

"I did indeed," Ivor said.

"I suggested maybe I was the wrong man," Nate said heavily. "Maybe you should come up with your candidate and try again."

"I could put it to Rowan, I suppose. But it would seem to me that if she was meant to return to life—it would have happened yesterday."

"I don't know what to do now," Nate admitted. "I feel sort of let down, I guess. It's quite an anticlimax."

"Perhaps you should leave Cornwall, go on with your holiday somewhere else." Ivor's wise gray eyes seemed to be studying his face quite intently. "Rowan's not your problem, after all. You did what you could to help, more than anyone else ever tried to do for her. Time for you to move on, I'd say. Why not drive up to London? There'd be more to occupy you there. 'Tis a busy place, London."

Nate stared at him for a minute, feeling slightly offended. Ivor seemed far too ready to dismiss Rowan and her problem. He was the one, after all, who had been mainly responsible for Nate's even attempting to help her. All the same Nate felt he should consider the older man's suggestion. But it wasn't long before he shook his head. "I don't think I want to do that. Maybe I'll just take a few more trips from here. Like to St. Ives. I didn't get to St. Ives yet."

"As I was going to St. Ives, I met a man with seven wives," Ivor recited. "Every wife had seven sacks, each sack had seven cats, each cat had seven kits. Kits, cats, sacks, and wives, how many were there going to St. Ives?"

Nate looked at him blankly.

"One," Ivor said. "The narrator of the verse *met* them, you see, so they were all going the other way. Only the narrator was going to St. Ives."

Nate realized he had no idea what the other man was talking about or why he was even bothering him with a children's riddle.

"You're in a bad way, Nate my boy," Ivor said, evidently aware of his bewilderment. "I'm only trying to cheer you up, help you to forget. Perhaps you would be better off leaving England altogether."

"No," Nate said abruptly. He didn't want to forget her so quickly. It would be insulting to Rowan. Why didn't Ivor see that? He couldn't possibly leave the country yet. Nor could he contemplate leaving Cornwall. It would be like closing and locking a door behind him, and he wasn't ready to do that. He might not see Rowan again, but as long as he was in the same county he could get used to the idea of parting from her. Gradually. Gently. At that moment he caught a look on Ivor's face, a look of sympathy. He realized then that the minister had been using some kind of reverse psychology to help him clarify his thoughts and feelings. "Will you go see her?" he asked the older man. "I hate to think of her being so lonely all the time."

"I'll visit her every day," Ivor said with the air of a man making a holy promise.

THE WEATHER HAD TURNED cold and gray, which suited Nate's mood. A shower and shave had helped his physical self feel better, although mentally he was still a wreck. But he'd made the right decision, he thought as he headed for

St. Ives on the A-30 motorway, which just happened to be in the opposite direction from Lamorna. He had to keep moving, stay occupied. Most of all, he had to suppress all thought of Rowan Pengelly.

When he parked the car he pulled on his leather bomber jacket over his sweater. The air felt almost wintry here on the West Coast. Maybe that was why nothing seemed to please him as he walked around. The harbor was gorgeous, yes, and the beaches were scenic enough. They'd even been awarded two Euro blue flags for quality and safety. But who wanted to explore beaches on a cold day like this?

Ivor had told him there was a large artists' colony here, and there were certainly a great many paintings, prints, pots and woven items for sale in the small shops lining the streets. Yet somehow it all seemed too commercial—which was a ridiculous reaction. Normally Nate had no patience with tourists who decried the commercialization of attractive vacation spots. Everyone needed to make a living. In Cornwall the tin mines had closed, and the fishing was depleted. What were the people supposed to live on? Besides, it was tourists like him who had created a demand for the goods in the first place.

He ate lunch in an attractive café on the waterfront. A pretty black waitress with wild curly hair and a strong cockney accent served him plaice and chips, brown bread and butter, a pot of tea. It all smelled wonderful, but tasted like sawdust in his present gloomy mood. Halfway through his meal, he noticed that fog was rolling in off the Atlantic, wrapping itself around the beaches and town like a thick winter blanket.

Finally recognizing about midafternoon that his mood was too sour to let him enjoy anything today, he gave up trying and sat himself down in a pub to nurse a pint of half-and-half. After a while he allowed himself to think about Rowan.

He must have been sitting there thinking about her for a good thirty minutes when the "knowing" Rowan had talked about came to him. It was just a vague thought at first, a sort of sighing acknowledgment that this was a strange situation for a man who didn't believe in whimsy. He'd certainly been acting out of character for the past several days. He had given a ghost a lesson in country-and-western dancing. He had kissed a ghost, *married* a ghost, made love to a ghost. Then again, maybe, just maybe, Nate Edwards had changed into a man who *did* believe in whimsy. Which meant there was no reason to doubt he could believe in something else he'd been denying ever since the previous day.

He was astonished by this thought at first and inclined to disbelieve it, sure the beer must be affecting him. But the more he tried to deny the very idea, the more his inner self shouted at him that it was true, dammit, and it would be true for the rest of his potentially long and lonely life.

It was at that point that he realized he couldn't possibly end this interminable day without seeing Rowan one more time.

The admission had no sooner entered his mind than he was on his feet and out the door, and heading at a trot for the parking lot where he'd left the Peugeot.

He moved out of the fog as soon as he cleared the outskirts of St. Ives. Was that a good omen? he wondered. Since when had he believed in omens, anyway? Since becoming this changed person. Omen or not, the sun was certainly shining. The green fields gleamed as though they'd been sprinkled with emerald dust. Woolly sheep dotted the distant pastures, and cows gazed at him over ancient stone walls.

Entering Rowan's field was like walking onto a stage set after all the actors had gone home; the grass and the stones and hedgerows had been set up and colored in with just the right brushwork, but there wasn't a single vestige of life. The Merry Maidens stood silent guard. Rowan was nowhere in sight.

"Rowan!" Nate called.

There was no answer.

But she couldn't possibly have left. She'd mentioned some kind of invisible barrier around the field and she couldn't get out. She had to be here.

"Rowan!" he called again. "I have to see you. There's something I have to tell you. It's important. I can't leave England without telling you."

Nothing moved. But he suddenly felt a sort of presence behind him—as if someone was watching. He turned quickly.

She was there, looking at him with that same terrible sadness in her eyes, straight and slender as ever in her lovely white dress. "Did you come to see about the annulment?" she asked. "Is it really necessary, do you think, considering the circumstances? Couldn't Ivor just forget to register the whole thing?"

"I'm not worried about an annulment," he told her. "I came because I had to see you one more time."

"Oh, why did you come back?" she cried. "I was just telling myself that the worst day I ever knew would soon be over and it would get easier as time passed. And here you are. I'll need to part from you all over again."

She brought her left hand up and looked at it. "The ring? Did you come back for the ring? I should have given it to you. I didn't think, I was so distraught. I'm better now."

She began tugging at the ring, but he stopped her by taking hold of both her hands.

"I didn't come back for the ring," he assured her. "The ring is yours. I only came to tell you something." He tightened his hold on her hands slowly, carefully, afraid she'd fade on him if he startled her in any way. "Please say you'll hear me out, Rowan. Please don't disappear until I tell you what I came here to say."

After a moment or two she nodded, and he supposed he'd have to accept that as a promise.

How warm her hands felt, he thought. If only it was possible to somehow transfuse life from his hands into hers. "It took me a while to realize it," he told her, watching her face, imprinting it on his memory for all time. "I felt so bad about leaving you, and I thought it was because I felt sorry for you, but it wasn't that at all. You hadn't come to life the way you wanted to, but you *had* walked alive into my mind and heart."

He took a deep breath and stared down into her eyes, trying to open his soul to her, trying to let all his feelings show. "I love you, Rowan Pengelly. That's what I came back here to say. I love you. And if it was possible, I'd marry you all over again and take you back with me to Seattle and live with you and love you and make you happy for the rest of your life."

Her smile started at the corners of her mouth and spread upward to make a glory of her dark eyes. "Now there's a surprise," she said. Then she laughed. "I love you, Nate Edwards," she said. She had spoken as formally as he had, but her voice was music.

But then all of a sudden her face crumpled and she tried to pull her hands free. "You must go now, this minute," she said. "It hurts even more to know..."

He nodded, his own pain making it impossible for him to speak for a moment. "You'd rather I hadn't told you?" he asked when he could.

She looked at him, tenderness shining in her eyes. "No, don't think that. Don't ever think that."

Ducking his head, he kissed her softly, gently, on the lips. Then, releasing her hands, he turned quickly and strode away as fast as he could. Just once before he left the field he glanced back and saw her still standing where he'd left her. She raised a hand in farewell. She was trying to smile but not succeeding.

Swallowing against the lump that was fast forming in his throat, he got into the car and started the engine, not looking back anymore because it would do no good now that he was outside the field, and he didn't want to see or feel the emptiness.

Her attempt at a smile frozen on her face, Rowan watched Nate close the car door and adjust his seat belt. The sound of the engine starting made her jump slightly. He had given her such a wonderful gift, one she would treasure always, but he really was going this time. He would never return, and she wouldn't want him to as long as there was no hope . . . no hope . . . no hope . . .

Quite suddenly there was a stillness inside her mind. Something was happening to her face. It felt *damp*. Putting up a hand, she felt her cheeks.

She was crying. Really crying. Well, she thought, it was hardly surprising that such a great sadness as this should break that barrier and produce real tears.

But wait a minute. If that barrier had broken who was to say others hadn't broken, as well?

Nate was just now easing the Peugeot out into the road, looking carefully to see if anyone was coming. Almost paralyzed for a moment, Rowan started to run. Perhaps if she ran fast enough she could run right through the clear-as-glass barrier and out the other side.

The tears were still rolling down her face as she ran, but they were tears of wonder now, tears of hope. Her feet pounded on the hard ground. *Pounded*. They didn't skim the grass, or float on the grass, they *pounded*. And inside her body there was another pounding—the throbbing pulse of a heart at work.

There was, in the end, nothing dramatic about it, no tearing sound, no feeling of breaking through, breaking out. It just happened that she was all of a sudden running down the road, beyond the hedge, outside the field, running and running and shouting, feeling sharp little stones jabbing at her bare feet and reveling in the pain of it. She was running and running and waving both hands and calling after Nate, who couldn't possibly keep driving away from her. He *must* see her, he must.

And he did.

The car came to an abrupt halt and he climbed out and stood beside it for a moment, looking back at her. Even from a distance she could see his disbelief give way to joy.

And then he was running toward her and she was laughing and stumbling and crying all at the same time. Catching her in his arms, he picked her up and swung her around, then set her down as gently as if she were made of spun sugar. He lifted the herb garland from her head and held it for her to see.

"It's real again," she said with a sigh. Taking it from him, she tossed it aside into the hedgerow. "I don't need it. There'll be no more weddings for Rowan Pengelly."

His hands cupped her face, his thumbs lightly brushing away the last traces of her tears.

"My feet are cold," she told him solemnly. "And I really think, yes, it's true, I'm hungry. But I want you to understand now that this is just to let you know how much feeling I'm having and enjoying—it's not to be interpreted in any way as a complaint."

Such a smile there was on his face!

He kissed her and kissed her again. And she gave back to him every bit of passion that was in her, a considerable amount that seemed to be growing as fast as she used it up.

"It was love that was needed," she said softly after a while. "All the time that was what was missing."

"It's not missing now," he said. He was still smiling.

A sudden thought occurred to her. "Am I an old hag?"

He laughed. "You are beautiful, Rowan Pengelly Edwards." He bent to kiss her again. She thought she would never get tired of his kisses as long as she lived.

As long as she lived.

"I love you," Nate said.

She let out her breath on a long sigh and leaned her head against him for a moment. "I love you," she replied.

Hand in hand, they walked along the road to the car and got into it. Then they drove away and never looked back.

A Note from Margaret Chittenden

I have a theory that stories are waiting for me in many wonderful places in the world—all I have to do is go and find them. In search of stories, my husband, Jim, and I have visited Japan, Bermuda, England, Scotland, Paris, Hawaii, Mexico and several places in the United States and Canada. Jim does the driving and reads the maps and records everything on his video camera. I talk to local people and policemen and reporters and bed-and-breakfast managers and shopkeepers and anyone else I can find, and take copious notes.

Not long ago, Jim and I spent two weeks driving the magnificent coast of Cornwall, England. The streets were narrow and winding. Fear of a passing bus made us wobble into an ancient stone wall. While Jim assessed the damage to the car's tires, I walked across the road to a gap in the hedge and saw nineteen ancient stones standing in a perfect circle. Quite by accident, we had discovered the field of the Merry Maidens, the setting for "The Enchanted Bride."

I didn't know it was going to be a story at that moment, of course, but I did know it interested me and I wanted Jim to get it on tape.

The marriage of convenience theme has been a favorite with many readers since romance stories began. The idea of people planning to marry for practical reasons that have nothing to do with love, then falling in love almost in spite of themselves, appeals to the romantic in all of us. So when Harlequin asked me to write such a story, I was delighted to say yes. I was even more delighted when I was asked to make it a paranormal story. Several of my novels have had a paranormal streak—reincarnation, a psychic child, a ghost. I'd always wanted to write a romance in which a ghost was one of the main characters; it's such a challenge to come up with an ending in which hero and heroine could live happily ever after.

In all my novels, most of the incidents, all of the settings and legends and foods, are based on things I have seen and done and eaten during my travels. "The Enchanted Bride" is no exception. The legend of the Merry Maidens is true, we did crash into the wall, the field does exist, Jim and I did eat Cornish pasties. Rowan and Nate exist only in my imagination, however. I hope they also found a place in yours!

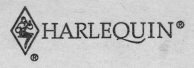

Fifty red-blooded, white-hot, true-blue hunks
from every State in the Union!

Look for MEN MADE IN AMERICA! Written by some
of our most popular authors, these stories feature fifty
of the strongest, sexiest men, each from a different state
in the union!

Two titles available every other month at your favorite
retail outlet.

In April, look for:

LOVE BY PROXY by Diana Palmer (Illinois)
POSSIBLES by Lass Small (Indiana)

In May, look for:

KISS YESTERDAY GOODBYE by Leigh Michaels (Iowa)
A TIME TO KEEP by Curtiss Ann Matlock (Kansas)

You won't be able to resist MEN MADE IN AMERICA!

Relive the romance....
Harlequin is proud to bring you

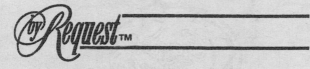

A new collection of three complete novels every month. By the most requested authors, featuring the most requested themes.

Available in May:

Three handsome, successful, unmarried men are about to get the surprise of their lives.... Well, better late than never!

Three complete novels in one special collection:

DESIRE'S CHILD by Candace Schuler
INTO THE LIGHT by Judith Duncan
A SUMMER KIND OF LOVE by Shannon Waverly

Available at your retail outlet from

Where do you find hot Texas nights, smooth Texas charm and dangerously sexy cowboys?

Crystal Creek reverberates with the exciting rhythm of Texas. Each story features the rugged individuals who live and love in the Lone Star State.

Don't miss the next book in this exciting series. Look for
RHINESTONE COWBOY by **BETHANY CAMPBELL**

Available in May wherever Harlequin books are sold.